TRANSGALACTIC

TRANSGALACTIC

by
A. E. van Vogt

Edited by
Eric Flint
and
David Drake

BAEN

A Baen Books Original

Baen Publishing Enterprises
P.O. Box 1403
Riverdale, NY 10471
www.baen.com

ISBN 10: 1-4165-2089-9
ISBN 13: 978-1-4165-2089-4

Cover art by Bob Eggleton

First Baen printing, October 2006

Library of Congress Cataloging-in-Publication Data

Van Vogt, A. E. (Alfred Elton), 1912-2000.
Transgalactic / by A.E. Van Vogt ; edited by Eric Flint and David Drake.
      p. cm.
    "A Baen Books orignal"--T.p. verso.
    ISBN 1-4165-2089-9 (pbk.)
    1. Science fiction, American. I. Flint, Eric. II. Drake, David. III. Title.

PS3543.A6546T73 2006
813'.54--dc22
                              2006015048

Distributed by Simon & Schuster
1230 Avenue of the Americas
New York, NY 10020

Printed in the United States of America

10 9 8 7 6 5 4 3 2 1

A note on the edition:

The text of the stories included in this volume is that of the original magazine editions first published in *Astounding Science Fiction*, not the later versions which A. E. van Vogt reworked for various novelizations.

The editors

TABLE OF CONTENTS

ACKNOWLEDGMENTS

"A Son is Born" was first published in *Astounding Science Fiction* in May, 1946.

"Child of the Gods" was first published in *Astounding Science Fiction* in August, 1946.

"Hand of the Gods" was first published in *Astounding Science Fiction* in December, 1946.

"Home of the Gods" was first published in *Astounding Science Fiction* in April, 1947.

"The Barbarian" was first published in *Astounding Science Fiction* in December, 1947.

"The Wizard of Linn" was first published in *Astounding Science Fiction* in a three-part serial, April-June, 1950.

"Co-Operate—Or Else!" was first published in *Astounding Science Fiction* in April, 1942.

"The Second Solution" was first published in *Astounding Science Fiction* in October, 1942.

"Concealment" was first published in *Astounding Science Fiction* in September, 1943.

"The Storm" was first published in *Astounding Science Fiction* in October, 1943.

"The Mixed Men" was first published in *Astounding Science Fiction* in January, 1945.

PREFACE

The Golden Age of SF is universally dated from the July 1939, issue of *Astounding* because that's when "Black Destroyer," A. E. van Vogt's first SF story, appeared. Isaac Asimov's first story also appeared in the same month but nobody—as Asimov himself admits—noticed it.

People noticed "Black Destroyer," though, and they continued to notice the many other stories that van Vogt wrote over the following decade. With the encouragement and occasionally the direction of John W. Campbell, Heinlein, deCamp, Hubbard, Asimov, and van Vogt together created the Golden Age of SF.

Each of those great writers was unique. What as much as anything set van Vogt off from other SF writers (of his day and later) was the ability to suggest vastness beyond comprehension. He worked with not only in space and time, but with the mind.

Van Vogt knew that to describe the indescribable would have been to make it ludicrous, and that at best description turns the inconceivable into the pedestrian. More than any other SF writer, van Vogt succeeded in creating a sense of wonder in his readers by hinting at the shadowed immensities beyond the walls of human perception. What we've tried to do in our selections for *Transgalactic* is show some of van Vogt's skill and range; but we too can only hint at the wonders of the unglimpsed whole.

Eric Flint and Dave Drake
2005

CLANE OF LINN

Part I:
Empire of the Atom

A Son is Born

Junior scientists stood at the bell ropes all day, ready to sound forth the tidings of an important birth. By night time, they were exchanging coarse jests as to the possible reason for the delay. They took care, however, not to be overheard by seniors or initiates.

The expected child had actually been born a few hours after dawn. He was a weak and sickly fellow, and he showed certain characteristics that brought immediate dismay to the Leader household. His mother, Lady Tania, when she wakened, listened for a while to his piteous crying, then commented acidly:

"Who frightened the little wretch? He seems already afraid of life."

Scientist Joquin, in charge of the delivery, considered her words an ill-omen. He had not intended to let her see the monstrosity until the following day, but now it seemed to him that he must act swiftly to avert calamity. He hurriedly sent a dozen slave women to wheel in the carriage, ordering them to group around it in close formation to ward off any malignant radiation that might be in the bedroom.

Lady Tania was lying, her slim body propped up in bed, when the astonishing procession started to squeeze through the door. She watched it with a frown of amazement and then the beginning of alarm. She had patiently borne her husband three other children, and so she knew that what she was seeing was not part of any normal observance. She was not a soft spoken creature, and even the presence of a Scientist in the room did not restrain her. She said violently:

"What is going on here, Joquin?"

Joquin fluttered his head at her in distress. Did she not realize that every ill-tempered word spoken at this period only doomed the handicapped child to further disasters? He noted, startled, that she was parting her lips to speak again—and, with a silent prayer to the atom gods, he took his life in his hands.

Three swift strides he made towards the bed, and clapped his palm over her mouth. As he had expected, the woman was too astounded by the action to utter a sound. By the time she recovered, and began to struggle weakly, the carriage was being tilted. And over his arm, she had her first glimpse of the baby.

The gathering storm faded from her blue eyes. After a moment, Joquin gently removed his hand from her mouth, and slowly retreated beyond the carriage. He stood there, quailing with the thought of what he had done, but gradually as no verbal lightning struck at him from the bed, his sense of righteousness reasserted. He began to glow inwardly and ever afterwards claimed that what he had done saved the situation as far as it could be saved. In the warmth of that self-congratulatory feeling, he almost forgot the child.

He was recalled by the Lady Tania saying in a dangerously quiet tone:

"How did it happen?"

Joquin nearly made the mistake of shrugging. He caught himself in time, but before he could say anything, the woman said, more sharply:

"Of course, I know it's due to the atom gods. But *when* do you think it happened?"

❖ ❖ ❖

Joquin was cautious. The scientists of the temples had had much experience with atomic mutation, enough to know that the controlling gods were erratic and not easily pinned down by dates. Nevertheless, mutation did not occur after an embryo baby was past the fish stage, and therefore a time limit could be estimated. Not after January, 470 A.B., and not before— He paused, recalling the approximate birth date of the Lady Tania's third child. He completed his figuring aloud— "Not before 467 A.B."

The woman was looking at the child now, more intently. What she saw made her swallow visibly. Joquin, watching her, thought he knew what she was thinking. She had made the mistake a few days before her confinement of boasting in a small company that four children would give her an advantage over her sister, Chrosone, who only had two children, and over her stepbrother, Lord Tews, whose acid-tongued wife had borne him three children. Now, the advantage would be theirs, for, obviously, she could have no more normal children, and they could overtake or surpass her at their leisure.

There would also be many witty exchanges at her expense. The potentialities for personal embarrassment were actually almost endless.

All that, Joquin read in her face, as she stared with hardening eyes at the child. He said hurriedly:

"This is the worst stage, Lady. Frequently, the result after a few months or years is reasonably—satisfactory."

He had almost said "human." He was aware of her gaze swinging towards him. He waited uneasily, but all she said finally was:

"Has the Lord Leader, the child's grandfather, been in?"

Joquin inclined his head. "The Lord Leader saw the baby a few minutes after it was born. His only comment was to the effect that I should ascertain from you, if possible, when you were affected."

She did not reply immediately, but her eyes narrowed even more. Her thin face grew hard, then harsh. She looked up at the scientist at last.

"I suppose you know," she said, "that only negligence at one of the temples could be responsible."

Joquin had already thought of that, but now he looked at her uneasily. Nothing had ever been done about previous "children of the gods," but it had been growing on him that the Linns at least regarded this as a special case. He said slowly:

"The atom gods are inscrutable."

The woman seemed not to hear. Her cold voice went on:

"The child will have to be destroyed, I suppose. But you may be sure that, within a month, there will be a compensatory stretching of scientific necks such as the world has not seen in a generation."

She was not a pleasant person when roused, the Lady Tania Linn, daughter-in-law of the Lord Leader.

❖ ❖ ❖

It proved easy to trace the source of the mutation. The previous summer, Tania, tiring of a holiday on one of the family's west coast estates, returned to the capital before she was expected. Her husband,

General of the Realm, Creg Linn, was having extensive alterations made to the Hill Palace. No invitation was forthcoming from her sister at the other end of the city, or from her stepmother-in-law, the wife of the Lord Leader. Tania, perforce, moved into an apartment in the Town Palace.

This assortment of buildings, though still maintained by the state, had not been used as a residence for several years. The city had grown immense since it was built, and long since the commercial houses had crowded around it. Due to a lack of foresight, by an earlier generation, title had not been taken to the lands surrounding the palace, and it had always been deemed unwise to seize them by force.

There was one particularly annoying aspect of the failure to realize the profitable potentialities of the area. This was the scientists' temple that towered in the shelter of one wing of the palace. It had caused the Lady Tania no end of heartache the previous summer. On taking up residence, she discovered that the only habitable apartment was on the temple side, and that the three most gorgeous windows faced directly onto the blank lead walls of the temple.

The scientist who had built the temple was a member of the Raheinl group, hostile to the Linns. It had titillated the whole city when the site was made known. The fact that three acres of ground were available made the affront obvious.

It still rankled.

The agents of the Lord Leader discovered at the first investigation that one small area of the lead wall of the temple was radioactive. They were unable to determine the reason for the activity, because the wall at that point was of the required thickness. But the fact was what they reported to their master. Before midnight of the second day after the child was born, the decision was in the making.

Shortly before twelve, Scientist Joquin was called in, and told the trend of events. Once more he took his life in his hands.

"Leader," he said, addressing the great man direct, "this is a grave error into which your natural irritation is directing you. The scientists are a group, who, having full control of atomic energy dispensation, have developed an independent attitude of mind, which will not take kindly to punishments for accidental crimes. My advice is, leave the boy alive, and consult with the Scientists' Council. I will advise them to remove the temple of their own volition, and I feel sure they will agree."

Having spoken, Joquin glanced at the faces before him. And realized that he had made a mistake in his initial assumption. There were two men and three women in the room. The men were the grave, lean Lord Leader and the plumpish Lord Tews, who was the Lady Leader's eldest son by her first marriage. Lord Tews was acting General of the Realm in the absence of Lord Creg, Tania's husband, who was away fighting the Venusians on Venus.

The women present were the Lady Leader Linn, wife of the Lord Leader, and stepmother-in-law to the two other women, Chrosone, Tania's sister and Lady Tania, still in bed. The Lady Tania and her sister were not on speaking terms, for a reason that need not be gone into here.

Joquin assumed that these five had called him for consultation, as they had on past occasions. Now, looking at them, realization came that their interest in him was psychological rather than logical. They listened intently to his words, but what he said apparently merely confirmed their previously held opinion.

Lord Tews looked at his mother, a faint smile on his plumpish face. She half lowered her eyelids. The two sisters remained frozen faced, staring at Joquin. The Lord Leader ended the tension by nodding a dismissal to the scientist.

Joquin went out, quivering. The wild idea came, to send a warning to the endangered temple scientists. But he quickly abandoned that as hopeless. No message from him would be allowed out of the palace.

He retired finally, but he was unable to sleep. In the morning, the fearful rescript that he had visualized all through the night was posted on the military board, for all to read. Joquin blinked at it palely. It was simple and without qualification.

It commanded that every scientist of the Raheinl temple was to be hanged before dusk. The property was ordered seized, and the buildings razed to the ground. The three acres of temple land were to be converted into a park.

It did not say that the park was to be added to the Town Palace of the Linns, though this later turned out to be the fact.

The rescript was signed in the firm hand of the Lord Leader himself.

Reading it, Joquin recognized that a declaration of war had been made against the power of the temple scientists.

❖ ❖ ❖

The Scientist Alden was not a man who had premonitions. And certainly he had none as he walked slowly along towards the Raheinl temple.

The morning glowed around him. The sun was out. A gentle breeze blew along the avenue of palms which stalked in stately fashion past his new home. In his mind was the usual cozy kaleidoscope of happy reminiscences, and a quiet joy that a simple country scientist had in only ten years become the chief scientist of the Raheinl temple.

There was but one tiny flaw in that memory, and that was the real reason for his swift promotion. More than eleven years ago, he had remarked to another junior that, since the gods of the atom had yielded certain secrets of mechanical power to human beings, it might be worthwhile to cajole them by experimental methods into revealing others. And that, after all, there might be a grain of truth in the vague legends about cities and planets ablaze with atomic power and light.

Alden shuddered involuntarily at the brief remembrance. It was only gradually that he realized the extent of his blasphemy. And when the other junior coolly informed him the following day that he had told the chief scientist—that had seemed like the end of all his hopes.

Surprisingly, it turned out to be the beginning of a new phase in his career. Within a month he was called for his first private conversation with a visiting scientist, Joquin, who lived in the palace of the Linns.

"It is our policy," Joquin said, "to encourage young men whose thoughts do not move entirely in a groove. We know that radical ideas are common to young people, and that, as a man grows older, he attains a balance between his inward self and the requirements of the world.

"In other words," the scientist finished, smiling at the junior, "have your thoughts but keep them to yourself."

It was shortly after this that Alden was posted to the east coast. From there, a year later, he went to the capital. As he grew older, and gained power, he discovered that radicalism among the young men was much rarer than Joquin had implied.

The years of ascendancy brought awareness of the foolishness of what he had said. At the same time, he felt a certain pride in the words, a feeling that they made him "different" from, and so superior to, the other scientists.

As chief he discovered that radicalism was the sole yardstick by which his superiors judged a candidate for promotion. Only those recommendations which included an account of unusual thinking on the part of the aspirant, however slight the variance from the norm, were ever acted upon. The limitation had one happy effect. In the beginning, his wife, anxious to be the power behind the power at the temple, declared herself the sole arbiter as to who would be urged for promotion. The young temple poets visited her when Alden was not around, and read their songs to her privately.

And then they discovered that her promises meant nothing. Their visits ceased. Alden had peace in his home, and a wife suddenly become considerably more affectionate.

His reverie ended. There was a crowd ahead, and cries. He saw that people were swarming around the Raheinl temple. Alden thought blankly, "An accident?"

He hurried forward pushing through the outer fringes of the throng. Anger came at the way individuals resisted his advance. Didn't they realize that he was a chief scientist? He saw mounted palace guardsmen urging their horses along the edge of the crowd a few score feet away, and he had his mouth open to call on them to assist him, when he saw something that stopped his words in his throat.

His attention had been on the temple proper. In his endeavor to move, his gaze flicked over the surrounding park.

Five of Rosamind's young poets were hanging from a tree limb at the edge of the temple grounds farthest from the temple. From a stouter tree nearby, six juniors and three scientists were still kicking spasmodically.

As Alden stood paralyzed, a dreadful screaming came from four initiates whose necks were just being fitted with rope halters.

The screaming ended, as the wagon on which they were standing was pulled from under them.

❖❖❖

The Lord Leader walked the streets of Linn. The downtown markets were crowded with traders from the hills and from across the lake, and there was the usual pack of wide-eyed primitives from the other planets. It was no effort at all to start a conversation.

He talked only to people who showed no sign of recognizing the unshaven man in the uniform of a private soldier as their ruler. It didn't take long to realize that the thousand persuasive men he had sent out to argue his side of the hangings were doing yeoman service. No less than three of them approached him during the course of the afternoon, and made skillful propaganda remarks. And the five farmers, three merchants and two laborers, to whom he talked, all answered his rough criticism of the Lord Leader with pro-government catchphrases they could only have heard from his own men.

It was gratifying, he told himself, that the first crisis he had forced was turning out so well.

The Linnan empire was only a generation out of the protracted civil war that had brought the Linn family to the leadership. His tax collectors were still finding the returns lean. And trade, though it was reviving swiftly in Linn itself, was making a much slower recovery in other cities, which were not favored by special exemptions.

Several wars of conquest were under way, three of them on Venus against the Venusian tribes. Ostensibly, these wars were being fought to punish the tribes for their raids against Earth. But the Lord Leader knew of at least two more important reasons. First, there was not enough money at home to pay the soldiers who, his generals reported, were still in a dangerously revolutionary mood. And second, he hoped to replenish the treasury with loot from conquered cities.

The Lord Leader paused mentally and physically before the open air shop of a dealer in ceramics. The man had the Linnan cast of feature and was obviously a citizen, or he wouldn't be in business. Only the opinions of citizens mattered. This one was in the throes of making a sale.

While he waited, the Lord Leader thought of the temples. It

seemed clear that the scientists had never recovered the prestige they had lost during the civil war. With a few exceptions they had supported Raheinl until the very day that he was captured and killed. (He was chopped into pieces by soldiers wielding meat axes.) The scientists promptly and collectively offered an oath of allegiance to the new regime, and he was not firmly enough entrenched in power to refuse.

He never forgot, however, that their virtual monopoly of atomic energy had nearly re-established the corrupt republic. And that, if they had succeeded, it was he who would have been executed.

The merchant's sale fell through. He walked over grumpily, but at that moment the Lord Leader noticed a passerby had paused, and was staring at him with half recognition.

The Lord Leader without a word to the merchant turned hastily, and hurried along the street into the gathering dusk.

The members of the Scientists Council were waiting for him when, satisfied that his position was inassailable, he returned finally to the palace.

❖❖❖

It was not an easygoing gathering. Only six of the seven members of the council of scientists were present. The seventh, the poet and historian, Kourain, was ill, so Joquin reported, with fever. Actually, he had suffered an attack of acute caution on hearing of the hangings that morning, and had hastily set out on a tour of distant temples.

Of the six, at least three showed by their expressions that they did not expect to emerge alive from the palace. The remaining three were Mempis, recorder of wars, a bold, white-haired old man of nearly eighty; Teear, the logician, the wizard of numbers, who, it was said, had received some of his information about complicated numbers from the gods themselves; and, finally, there was Joquin, the persuader, who, for years, had acted as liaison between the temples and the government.

The Lord Leader surveyed his audience with a jaundiced eye. The years of success had given him a sardonic mien, that even sculptors could not eradicate from his statues without threatening the resemblance between the referent and the reality. He was about fifty years old at this time, and in remarkably good health. He began with a cold, considered and devastating attack on the Raheinl temple. He finished that phase of his speech with:

"Tomorrow, I go before the Patronate to justify my action against the temple. I am assuming that they will accept my explanation."

For the first time, then, he smiled bleakly. No one knew better than he or his audience that the slavish Patronate dared not even blink in a political sense without his permission.

"I am assuming it," he went on, "because it is my intention simultaneously to present a spontaneous petition from the temples for a reorganization."

The hitherto silent spectators stirred. The three death-expecting members looked up with a vague hope on their faces. One of the three, middle-aged Horo, said eagerly:

"Your excellency can count upon us for—"

He stopped because Mempis was glaring at him, his slate-blue eyes raging. He subsided, but gradually his courage returned. He had made his point. The Lord Leader must know that *he* was willing.

He experienced the tremendous inner easing of a man who had managed to save his own skin.

Joquin was saying suavely, "As Horo was about to state, we shall be happy to give your words a respectful hearing."

The Lord Leader smiled grimly. But now he had reached the crucial part of his speech, and he reverted to legalistic preciseness.

The government—he said—was prepared at last to split the temples into four separate groups as had been so long desired by the scientists. (This was the first they had heard of the plan, but no one said anything.) As the scientists had long urged, the Lord Leader went on, it was ridiculous that the four atom gods, Uranium, Plutonium, Radium and Ecks should be worshiped in the same temples. Accordingly, the scientists would divide themselves into four separate organizations splitting the available temples evenly among the four groups.

Each group would give itself to the worship of only one god and his attributes, though naturally they would continue to perform their practical functions of supplying transmitted god-power to all who sought to purchase it under the government regulations.

Each would be headed, not by a council of equals as was the

temple system at present, but by a leader for whom an appropriate title must be selected. The four separate temple leaders would be appointed for life by a joint committee of government and temple delegates.

There was more, but they were details. The council had its ultimatum. And Joquin at least cherished no illusions. Four temple groups, each ruled by a willful scientist, responsible to no one except perhaps the Lord Leader, would end forever any hopes the more enlightened scientists entertained.

He rose hastily, lest one of the fearful councilors should speak first. He said gravely:

"The council will be very happy to consider your offer, and feels itself privileged to have in the government a lord who devotes his obviously valuable time to thoughts about the welfare of the temples. Nothing could—"

He had not really expected to manage a postponement. And he didn't. He was cut off. The Lord Leader said with finality:

"Since I am personally making the announcement in the Patronate chamber tomorrow, the Scientists Council is cordially invited to remain in the palace to discuss details of reorganization. I have assumed this will require anywhere from a week to a month or even longer, and I have had apartments assigned for your use."

He clapped his hands. Doors opened. Palace guards came in. The Lord Leader said:

"Show these honored gentlemen to their quarters."

Thus was the council imprisoned.

❖❖❖

Scientist Alden tottered through the crowd before the Raheinl temple on legs that seemed made of dough. He bumped into people, and staggered like a drunken man, but he was only dimly aware of his gyrations.

If he had been the only person in the group reacting, he would have been marked instantly, and dragged off to the gibbet. But the executions caught the throng by surprise. Each new spectator casually approaching to see what was going on suffered his own variation of tremendous shock. Women fainted. Several men vomited, and others stood with glazed eyes.

As he approached one trailing end of the crowd, Alden's brain began to trickle back into his head. He saw an open gate; and he had darted through it, and was floating—that was the new sensation in his legs—through the underbrush, when it struck him that he was inside the grounds of the Town palace of Lord and Lady Creg Linn.

That brought the most terrible moment of the morning. Trapped, and of his own doing. He collapsed in the shelter of an ornamental shrub, and lay in a half faint of fright. Slowly, he grew aware that there was a long, low outhouse ahead, and that trees would shelter him most of the way. He recognized that he could not safely hope to return the way he had come, nor dared he remain where he was. He rose shakily to his feet, and the gods were with him. He found himself shortly crouching in the long, narrow, hay storeroom adjoining the stables.

It was not a good hiding place. Its width was prohibitively confining, and only by making a tunnel in the hay near the door farthest from the stables did he manage to conceal himself.

He had barely settled down when one of the stable doors a dozen feet to his right opened. A four-pronged fork flashed in a leisurely fashion, and withdrew transporting a bundle of hay.

With a casual kick, the stable hand slammed the door shut, and there was the sound of retreating footsteps. Alden lay, scarcely breathing. He was just beginning to emerge from his funk a few minutes later, when, *bang!* another door opened, and another fork gathered its hay, and departed.

That was his morning, and yet, despite the repeated nervous shocks, by noon his mind had almost resumed normal functioning. He had his first theory as to why he had escaped the round-up that had caught the others. Only two weeks before he had moved to his new residence on the Avenue of Palms. The soldiers must have proceeded to his old address, and then had to cross the city to his new home, with the result that he had left the house by the time they arrived.

Of such tenuous fabrics the patterns of his escape were woven. Alden shivered, and then, slowly, anger built up inside him, the deadly, gathering anger of a man wrongly persecuted. It was a fury that braced him for eventualities, and he was able at last to think with a clear-cut logic of what he must do.

Obviously, he could not remain within the grounds of the Town palace. Odd little memories came to his aid, things he had observed in earlier days without being aware that he did so. He recalled that every few nights hay ricks turned into the palace gates. Judging by the emptiness around him, a new supply must be almost due.

He must leave before the afternoon was out.

He began to struggle along the line of hay to the right. There was a gate on that side, and he remembered having once glimpsed the stables through it while taking a walk.

By sneaking out of the end door and around to the side of the stable, and then through *that* gate— If only he could find another set of clothes— Surely, there would be work clothes hanging up in the stables, preferably in view of the long hair that scientists affected, a woman's overdress—

He found what he wanted in the right end of the stable, which was devoted to milk cows. The animals and he were quite alone while the arrayed himself in the raiment that the milkmaids pulled over their pretty dresses when they did their chores.

The Town palace, after its brief flurry the year before as a Linn residence, had reverted swiftly to its role of agricultural, industrial and clerical center. There were guards within sight of the gate, but they did not bother to question a rather stocky woman slave, who went out with a decisive manner as if she had been sent on an errand by a superior.

It was late afternoon when Alden presented himself at the Covis temple. He was admitted immediately by the astonished junior to whom he revealed his identity.

❖ ❖ ❖

On the fourth day, the baby was still alive. The main reason was that Tania could not make up her mind.

"I've had the turmoil of birth," she said savagely, "and no woman in her right senses nullifies that casually. Besides—"

She stopped there. The truth was that, in spite of innumerable disadvantages, she could imagine certain uses for a son whom the gods had molded in their peculiar fashion. And in this regard, the

urgings of Joquin were not without their effect. Joquin spent most of
the fourth morning on the subject.

"It is a mistake," he said, "to assume that all the children of the
gods are idiots. That is an idle tale of the witless mob, which pursues
these poor creatures along the street. They are not given an opportunity for education, and they are constantly under pressure so great
that it is little wonder few of them ever attain the dignity and sense
of mature development."

His arguments took on a more personal flavor. "After all," he
said softly, "he is a Linn. At worst, you can make of him a trustworthy aide, who will not have the same tendency to wander off to live
his own life as will your normal children. By keeping him discreetly
in the background, you might acquire that best of all possible slaves,
a devoted son."

Joquin knew when to stop pushing. The moment he noticed from
the thoughtful narrowing of the woman's eyes that his arguments were
weighing with her, he decided to leave her to resolve the doubts that
still remained. He withdrew smoothly, and attended the morning
court of the Lord Leader—and there once more urged his suit.

The great man's eyes were watching as Joquin talked. Gradually, his
satiric countenance grew puzzled. The Lord Leader interrupted at last:

"Old man," he said curtly, "what is your purpose in thus defending the right to life of a freak?"

Joquin had several reasons, one of them almost purely personal,
and another because he believed that the continued existence of the
baby might, however slightly, be an advantage to the temples. The
logic of that was simple. The baby's birth had precipitated a crisis. Its
death would merely affirm that crisis. Conversely, if it remained
alive, the reason for the ferocious reaction of the Linns would be
negated to some small degree.

He had no intention of stating that particular reason, and he did
not immediately mention his personal hope about the baby. He said
instead:

"Never before has a child of the gods been deliberately put to
death. It was always assumed the gods had their own obscure purpose in creating monsters in human form. Do we dare test at this
time that such is or is not the situation?"

It was an argument that made the other man stare in astonishment. The wars the Lord Leader had fought had thrown him into contact with advanced thinkers and skeptics on several planets, and he had come to regard the gods as a means for keeping his rebellious subjects under control. He did not absolutely disbelieve in them, but he had never in his practical life taken their possible supernatural powers into account.

But he respected this scientist. He climbed to his feet, and walking down the steps, drew Joquin aside.

"Do you actually," he asked, "believe what you are saying?"

The question was an uncomfortable one. There was a time in Joquin's life when he had believed nothing. Slowly, however, certain things he had observed had brought a half conviction that the mighty invisible force given forth by the tiniest radioactive substance could have no other explanation. He said carefully:

"In my travels as a young man, I saw primitive tribes that worshiped rain gods, river gods, tree gods and various animal gods. And I saw more advanced races, some of them here on Earth, whose deity was an invisible omnipotent being who lives somewhere in space in a place called heaven. All these things I observed, and in a similar fashion I listened to each group's particular account of the beginning of the Universe. One story has it that we all came from the mouth of a snake. I have seen no such snake. Another story is that a great flood deluged the planets, though how this could have been done with the available water, I do not know. A third story is that man was created from clay and woman from man."

He looked at his hearer. The Lord Leader nodded. "Continue."

"I have seen people who worshiped fire, and I have seen people who worshiped water. And then, as have so many others before me, I finally visited the valleys where our own gods are said to dwell. I discovered their residences on every planet, vast, desolate areas miles deep and miles long and wide. And in these areas, I saw from a safe distance behind lead embankments the incredible bright fires that still burn with unending fury in those fantastic deeps of Earth.

"'Truly,' I thought to myself, 'the gods, Uranium, Radium, Plutonium and Ecks are the most powerful gods in the Universe.

Surely,' I decided, 'no one in his right senses would do anything to offend them.'"

The Lord Leader, who had also examined some of the homes of the gods in the course of his peregrinations, said, "Hm-m-m!"

He had no time then for further comment. From somewhere—it seemed terribly near—there was a sharp sound louder than the loudest thunder that had ever bellowed from the skies. It was followed half a minute later by a roar so loud, so furious, that the palace floor trembled.

There was a pregnant pause, not silent. From all directions came the sound of windows shattering with a thousand tinkling overtones. And then, that disturbance was overwhelmed by a third explosion, followed almost instantly by a fourth.

This last was so vast a sound that it was clear to everybody that the end of the world was imminent.

❖ ❖ ❖

When Alden entered the great Covis temple on the afternoon of the third day after the birth of the Linn baby, he was a tired, hungry man. But he was also a hunted man with the special thoughts of the fugitive.

He sank into the chair that was offered by the junior. And, while the young man was still in process of realizing the situation, Alden ordered him to inform no one of his presence except Horo, chief scientist of the Covis temple.

"But Horo is not here," the junior protested. "He has but just now departed for the palace of the Leader."

Alden began briskly to remove his female disguise. His weariness flowed from him. Not here, he was thinking gleefully. That meant *he* was the senior scientist in the temple until Horo returned. For a man who had had as many thoughts as he had during the afternoon, that was like a reprieve. He ordered that food be brought him. He took possession of Horo's office. And he asked questions.

For the first time, he learned the only reason so far made public, for the executions at the Raheinl temple. Alden pondered the reason throughout the early evening, and the more he thought the angrier he grew. His thinking at this time must already have been on a very radical plane, and yet, paradoxically, he felt mortified that the gods had been so profoundly insulted in their temples.

Somehow, with a crystalline certainty—that, yet, had in it no disbelief—he knew that they would not show their displeasure of their own volition. The thoughts of a fugitive tended automatically towards such practical convictions. Before the evening was half through, he was examining the possibilities.

Certain processes the gods had favored from time immemorial. Naval captains and other legal owners of spaceships brought ingots of iron to the temples. The ceremonial and money preliminaries being completed, the iron was then placed in close proximity to the uncovered god-stuff for one day exactly. After four days, one for each god, the power of the god-stuff was transmitted to the ingot. It was then removed by the officer to his ship where, with simple ceremonials, it was placed in metal chambers—which any metal worker could make—and by the use of what was known as a pholectric cell— a device also known from the earliest times, like fire and sword and spear and bow—an orderly series of explosions could be started or stopped at will.

When enough of these metal chambers were used, the largest ships that could be constructed by man were lifted as easily as if they were made of nothingness.

From the beginning of things, the god-stuff in all temples had been kept in four separate rooms. And the oldest saying in history was that when the gods were brought too close together, they became very angry indeed.

Alden carefully weighed out a grain of each supply of god-stuff. Then he had four juniors carry a metal chamber from the testing cavern into the garden at the rear of the temple. At this point it struck him that other temples should participate in the protest. He had learned that six of the seven members of the Scientists Council were still at the palace, and he had a rather strong suspicion as to their predicament.

Writing from Horo's ornate office, he *ordered* the acting chiefs of the temples of the absent councilors to do exactly what he was doing. He described his plan in detail, and finished:

"High noon shall be the hour of protest."

Each letter he sent by junior messenger.

He had no doubts. By noon the following day he had inserted his grains of uranium, radium, plutonium and ecks into the pholectric relay system. From what he decided was a safe distance, he pressed the button that clicked over the relays in order. As the wonderful and potent ecks, the last grain, joined the "pile," there was an explosion of considerable proportions.

It was followed swiftly by three more explosions. Only two of the temples disregarded the commands of the fugitive. They were the fortunate ones. The first explosion blew half the Covis temple into dust, and left the remnant a tottering shambles of dislodged masonry and stone.

No human being was found alive in any of the four temples. Of Alden there was not even a piece of flesh or a drop of blood.

❖ ❖ ❖

By two o'clock mobs were surging around the foot of the palace hill. The palace guard, loyal to a man, held them off grimly, but retreated finally inside the gates, and the household of the Leader prepared for a siege.

When the pandemonium was at its height half an hour later, Joquin, who had been down in the city, returned by a tunnel that ran through the hill itself, and asked permission to speak to the mob.

Long and searchingly, the Lord Leader looked at him. Then finally he nodded.

The mob rushed at the gates when they opened, but spearmen held them back. Joquin pressed his way out. His was a piercing rather than a deep voice, but the rostrum that jutted out from the hill was skillfully constructed to enable a speaker to address vast throngs through a series of megaphones.

His first act was to take the ribbons out of his hair, and let it down around his shoulders. The crowd began to shout:

"Scientist. It's a scientist."

Joquin raised his hand. And the silence he received was evidence to him at least that the riots were about to end. The crowd was controllable.

On his own part, he had no illusions as to the importance of this mob attacking the palace. He knew that carrier pigeons had been dispatched to the three legions camped outside the walls of the city. Soon, a disciplined force would be marching through the streets, paced by cavalry units made up of provincial troops, whose god was a giant mythical bird called Erplen.

It was important that the crowd be dispersed before those trained killers arrived on the scene. Joquin began:

"People of Linn, you have today witnessed a telling proof of the power of the gods."

Cries and groans echoed his words. Then again, silence. Joquin continued:

"But you have misread the meaning of the signs given us today."

Silence only this time greeted his words. He had his audience.

"If the gods," he said, "disapproved of the Lord Leader, they could just as easily have destroyed his palace at they actually did destroy four of their own temples.

"It is not the Lord Leader and his actions to which the gods objected. It is that certain temple scientists have lately tried to split up the temples into four separate groups, each group to worship one of the four gods only.

"That and that alone is the reason for the protest which the gods have made today."

There were cries of, "But your temple was among those destroyed."

Joquin hesitated. He did not fancy being a martyr. He had seen two of the letters Alden had written—to the two temples which had not obeyed the instructions—and he had personally destroyed both letters. He was not sure how he ought to rationalize the fact that a purely mechanical union of the god-stuff had produced the explosions. But one thing at least was certain. The gods had not objected to their status of being worshiped four in one temple. And since that status was the only one that made it possible for the scientists to remain strong, then what had happened *could be* the gods' ways of showing that it was their purpose, too.

Joquin recognized uneasily that his reasoning was a form of sophistry. But this was no time to lose faith. He bowed his head before the shouting, then looked up.

"Friends," he said soberly, "I confess I was among those who urged separate worship. It seemed to me that the gods would welcome an opportunity to be worshiped each in his own temple. I was mistaken."

He half-turned to face the palace, where far more important ears were listening than any in the crowd below. He said:

"I know that every person who, like myself, believed the separatist heresy is now as convinced as I am that neither the four gods or their people would ever stand for such blasphemy.

"And now, before there is any more trouble, go home, all of you."

He retreated rather hastily back into the palace grounds.

The Lord Leader was a man who accepted necessities. "There remains one undetermined question," he said later. "What is your real reason for keeping my daughter-in-law's baby alive?"

Joquin said simply, "I have long wanted to see what will happen if a child of the gods is given a normal education and upbringing."

That was all he said. It was enough. The Lord Leader sat with eyes closed, considering the possibilities. At last, slowly, he nodded his head.

I was to be allowed to live.

Child of the Gods

By the time the boy was four, the scientist Joquin realized that drastic action was necessary if his mind was to be saved. Somewhere between three and four, Clane had realized that he was different. Enormously, calamitously different. Between four and six, his sanity suffered collapse after collapse, each time to be slowly built back again by the aging scientist.

"It's the other children," Joquin, white with fury, told the Lord Leader one day. "They torment him. They're ashamed of him. They defeat everything I do."

The Linn of Linn gazed curiously at the temple man. "Well, so am I ashamed of him, ashamed of the very idea of having such a grandson." He added, "I'm afraid, Joquin, your experiment is going to be a failure."

It was Joquin, now, who stared curiously at the other. In the six years that followed the crisis of the temples of the atom gods, he had come to have a new and more favorable regard for the Lord Leader. During those years, for the first time, it had struck him that here was the greatest civil administrator since legendary times. Something, too, of the man's basic purpose—unification of the empire—had shown occasionally through the bleak exterior with which he confronted the world.

Here was a man, moreover, who had become almost completely objective in his outlook on life. That was important right now. If Clane was to be saved, the cooperation of the ruler of Linn was essential. The Lord Leader must have realized that Joquin's visit had a specific objective. He smiled grimly.

27

"What do you want me to do? Send him to the country where he can be brought up in isolation by slaves."

"That," said Joquin, "would be fatal. Do not forget, normal slaves despise the mutations as much as do freedmen, knights and patrons." He finished, "The fight for his sanity must be made right here in the city."

The other looked impatient. "Well, take him away to the temples where you can work on him to your heart's content."

"The temples," said Joquin, "are full of rowdy initiates and juniors."

The Lord Leader glowered. He was being temporized with, which meant that Joquin's request was going to be a difficult one to grant. The whole affair was becoming highly distasteful. Six years before, a mutation had been born to the Lord Leader's daughter-in-law, the Lady Tania. The mutation resulted from carelessness in the handling of the radioactive god-metals in one of the temples. And, while similar mutations occurred from time to time, Clane was the first ever to appear in an important family. Or, at least, if a mutation had ever before been born to a nobleman's wife, there was no record of it.

At the time of the birth, the Lord Leader allowed himself to be persuaded to let the child live. Joquin, the persuader, desired then—and apparently still—to prove that mutations had basically normal minds, needing only normal handling to become mature beings.

That theory was yet to be proved.

❖ ❖ ❖

"I'm afraid, old one," said the Lord Leader gravely, "you are not being very sensible about this matter. The boy is like a hothouse plant. You cannot raise the children of men that way. They must be able to withstand the rough and tumble of existence with their fellows even when they are young."

"And what," flashed Joquin, "are these palaces of yours but hothouses where all your youngsters grow up sheltered from the rough and tumble of life out there?"

The old scientist waved his hand towards the window that opened out overlooking the capital city of the world. The Leader smiled his acceptance of the aptness of the comparison. But his next words were pointed.

"Tell me what you want. I'll tell you if it can be done."

Joquin did not hesitate. He had stated his objections, and, having eliminated the main alternatives, he recognized that it was time to explain exactly what he wanted. He did so. Clane had to have a refuge on the palace grounds, a sanctuary where no other children could follow him under penalty of punishment.

"You are," said Joquin, "bringing up all your male grandchildren on your grounds here. In addition, several dozen other children—the sons of hostages, allied chiefs and patrons—are being raised here. Against that crowd of normal, brilliant boys, cruel and unfeeling as only boys can be, Clane is defenseless. Since they all sleep in the same dormitory, he has not even the refuge of a room of his own. Now, I am in favor of him continuing to eat and sleep with the others, but he must have some place where none can pursue him."

Joquin paused, breathless, for his voice was not what it had been. And, besides, he was aware of the tremendousness of the request. He was asking that restrictions be put upon the arrogant, proud little minds and bodies of the future great men of Linn—patrons, generals, chieftains, even Lord Leaders of twenty, thirty, forty years hence. Asking all that, and for what? So that a poor wretch of a mutation might have the chance to prove whether or not he had a brain.

He saw that the Lord Leader was scowling. His heart sank. But he was mistaken as to the cause of the expression. Actually, he could not have made his request at a better time. The day before, the Lord Leader, walking in the grounds, had found himself being followed by a disrespectful, snickering group of young boys. It was not the first time, and the memory brought the frown to his face. He looked up decisively. He said:

"Those young rascals need discipline. A little frustration will do them good. Build your refuge, Joquin. I'll back it up for a while."

❖❖❖

The palace of the Leader was located on Capitoline Hill. The hill was skillfully landscaped. Its grounds were terraced and built up, begardened and be-shrubbed until the original hill was almost unrecognizable to old-timers like Joquin.

There was a towering rock on a natural peak at the west end of the grounds. To reach it one followed a narrow path up a steep slope, and then climbed the steps that had been cut into the solid rock to the top of the rock itself.

The rock was bare until Joquin took it over. Swiftly, under his direction, slaves carried up soil, and slave gardeners planted shrubs, grass and flowers, so that there might be protection from the hot sun, a comfortable green on which to stretch out and an environment that was beautiful and colorful. He built an iron fence to guard the approaches to the pathway, and at the gate stationed a freedman who was six feet six inches tall and broad in proportion. This man had a further very special qualification in that a child of the gods had also been born to his wife some four years before. The big man was a genial, friendly individual, who prevented the more rowdy boys from following Clane by the simple act of wedging his great body into the narrow gate.

For weeks after the aerie was ready, and the restriction imposed, the other children railed and shrieked their frustration. They stood for hours around the gate tormenting the guard, and yelling threats up to the rock. It was the imperviousness of the always friendly guard that baffled them in the end. And at long last the shivering boy on the aerie had time to become calm, to lose that sense of imminent violence, and even to acquire the first feeling of security. From that time on, he was ignored. No one played with him, and, while their indifference had its own quality of cruelness, at least it was a negative and passive attitude. He could live his private life.

His mind, that wounded, frightened and delicate structure, came slowly out of the darkness into which it had fled. Joquin lured it forth with a thousand cunnings. He taught it to remember simple poetry. He told the boy stories of great deeds, great battles, and many of the fairy tales currently extant. He gave him at first carefully doctored but ever more accurate interpretations of the political atmosphere of the palace. And again and again, ever more positively, he insisted that being born a mutation was something different and special and important. Anybody could be born ordinary human, but few were chosen by the gods of the atoms.

There was danger, Joquin knew, in building up the ego of a Linn to feel superior even to the human members of his own family.

"But," as he explained one day to the Lord Leader, "he'll learn his limitations fast enough as he grows older. The important thing now is that his mind at the age of eight has become strong enough to withstand the most vulgar and sustained taunting from other boys. He still stammers and stutters like an idiot when he tries to talk back, and it's pitiful what happens to him when he is brought into contact with a new adult, but unless surprised, he has learned to control himself by remaining silent.

"I wish," Joquin finished, "that you would let him accustom himself to occasional visits from you."

It was an oft repeated request, always refused. The refusals worried Joquin, who was nearly eighty years old. He had many anxious moments as to what would happen to the boy after his own death. And in order to insure that the blow would not be disastrous, he set about enlisting the support of famous scholars, poets and historians. These he first partially persuaded by argument, then introduced one by one as paid tutors to the boy. He watched each man with an alertness that swiftly eliminated those who showed in any way that they did not appreciate the importance of what was being attempted.

The boy's education turned out to be an expensive generosity, as neither the allowances of the Lord Leader, his grandfather, or of Lord Creg, his father, were sufficient to cover the fees of the many famous men Joquin employed. Indeed, when Joquin died, just before Clane's eleventh birthday, the liquid assets of the estate barely sufficed to pay the minor bequests after death taxes were deducted.

He left ten million sesterces to be divided among juniors, initiates and seniors of various temples. Five million sesterces he bequeathed to personal friends. Two million more went to certain historians and poets in order that they might complete books which they had begun, and finally there were five great grandnephews who each received a million sesterces.

That disposed almost entirely of the available cash. A bare five hundred thousand sesterces remained to keep the vast farms and buildings of the estate in operation until the next crop was harvested. Since these were left in their entirety, along with upward of a thousand slaves, to Clane, there was a short period when the new owner, all unknown to himself, was on the verge of bankruptcy.

The situation was reported to the Lord Leader, and he advanced a loan from his private purse to tide over the estate. He also took other steps. He learned that Joquin's slaves were disgruntled at the idea of belonging to a mutation. He sent spies among them to find out who were the ringleaders, and then hanged the four chief troublemakers as examples. It also came to his ears that Joquin's great grandnephews, who had expected the estate, were making dark threats about what they would do to the "usurper." The Lord Leader promptly confiscated their share of the inheritance, and sent all five of them to join Lord Creg's army which was on the point of launching a major invasion against Mars.

Having done so much, the old ruler proceeded to forget all about his grandson. And it was not until some two years later, when, seeing the boy one morning pass beneath the window of his study, he grew curious. That very afternoon he set out for the rock aerie to have a look at the strangest youth who had ever been born into the Linn family.

❖❖❖

At this time, the Martian war was two years old, and it was already proving itself to be the most costly campaign ever launched. From the very beginning, when it was still in the planning stages, it had aroused men to bitter passions. To fight it or not to fight it— three years before that had been the question that split the inner government group into two violently opposing camps. Lord Creg Linn, father of Clane, son of the Lord Leader, and general in chief of the expedition, was from the first completely and without qualification opposed to the war.

He had arrived at the city from Venus some three years before in his personal space yacht, and accompanied by most of his staff. He spent months, then, arguing with his family and with various powerful patrons.

"The time has come," he told his hearers, "for the empire to stand firm on all its frontiers. From a single city state we have grown until we now dominate all Earth with the exception of a few mountainous territories. Four of the eleven island continents of Venus are allied to us. And on the three habitable moons of Jupiter, our allies are the strong powers. The Martians of Mars, it is true, continue to rule that planet in their brutal fashion, but it would be wise to leave them alone. The tribes they have conquered are constantly rebelling against them, and will keep them busy for a measurable time. Accordingly, they are no danger to us, and that must be our sole consideration for all future wars."

If reports were true, many patrons and knights were convinced by this reasoning. But when they saw that the Lord Leader favored the war, they quickly changed their tune, at least publicly.

Lydia, the Lord Leader's wife, and Lord Tews—Lydia's son by a previous marriage—were particularly in favor of the invasion. Their argument, and it eventually became the Lord Leader's, was that the Martians had condemned themselves to war by their complete refusal to have commercial and other intercourse with the rest of the Solar System. Who knew what plans were being made, what armies were under secret training, or how many spaceships were abuilding on a planet that for more than a dozen years had admitted no visitors.

It was a telling argument. Lord Creg's dry suggestion that perhaps the method used by the empire to invade the Venusian island of Cimbri was responsible, did not confound the supporters of the war. The method had been simple and deadly. The Cimbri, a suspicious tribe, agreed finally to permit visitors. They were uneasy when over a period of several months some thirty thousand stalwart young male visitors arrived singly and in groups. Their uneasiness was justified. One night the visitors assembled in the three major Cimbrin cities, and attacked all centers of control. By morning a hundred thousand inhabitants had been slain, and the island was conquered.

The commanding general of that expedition was Lord Tews. At his mother's insistence, an ashamed patronate voted him a triumph.

It was natural that the Lydia-Tews group should regard Creg's remark as a product of envy. The suggestion was made that his words were unworthy of so illustrious a man. More slyly, it was pointed out that his own wars had been drawn out, and that this indicated a cautious nature. Some even went so far as to say that he did not trust the fighting abilities of Linnan armies, and they immediately added the comment that this was a base reflection on the military, and that the only real conclusion to be drawn was that he was personally a coward.

To Lord Creg, doggedly holding to his opinions, the greatest shock came when he discovered that his own wife, Tania, supported the opposition. He was so angry that he promptly sent her a bill of divorcement. The Lady Tania, whose only purpose in supporting the war was that it would enhance her husband's career, and accordingly improve her position, promptly suffered a nervous breakdown.

A week later she was partially recovered, but her state of mind was clearly shown by the fact that she took a gig to her husband's headquarters in the camp outside the city. And, during the dinner hour, before hundreds of high officials, she crept to him on her hands and knees, and begged him to take her back. The astounded Creg led her quickly through a nearby door, and they were reconciled.

From this time dated the change in the Lady Tania. Her arrogance was gone. She withdrew to a considerable extent from social activities, and began to devote herself to her home. Her proud, almost dazzling beauty deteriorated to a stately good looks.

It was an anxious wife who kissed her husband good-by one early spring day, and watched his spear-nosed yacht streak off to join the vast fleet of spaceships mobilizing on the other side of Earth for the take-off to Mars.

Spaceships, like all the instruments, weapons and engines of transport and war known since legendary times, had their limitations. They were the fastest thing possessed by man, but just how fast no one had ever been able to decide. At the time of the invasion of Mars, the prevailing belief was that spaceships attained the tremendous speed of a thousand miles an hour in airless space. Since the voyage to Mars required from forty to a hundred days— depending upon the respective positions of the two planets—the distance of Mars at its nearest was estimated at the astounding total of one million miles.

It was felt by thousands of intelligent people that this figure must be wrong. Because, if it was correct, then some of the remoter stars would be hundreds of millions of miles away. This was so obviously ridiculous that it was frankly stated by many that the whole uncertainty reflected on the ability and learning of the temple scientists.

A spaceship one hundred and fifty feet long could carry two hundred men and no more on a trip to Mars lasting sixty days. It had room for many more, but the air supply created an insurmountable limitation. The air could be purified by certain chemicals for so long, then it gave out.

Two hundred men per ship—that was the number carried by each space transport of the first fleet to leave Earth. Altogether there were five hundred ships. Their destination was the great desert known as Mare Cimmererium. A mild-wide canal cut through the edge of this desert, and for a hundred miles on either side of the canal the desert was forced back by a green vegetation that fed on the thousands of tiny tributary canals. Oslin, one of the five important cities of the Martians, was located in a great valley at a point where the canal curved like a winding river.

In a sense the canals were rivers. During spring, the water in them flowed steadily from north to south, gradually slowing until, by midsummer, there was no movement.

Oslin had a population which was reported to be well over a million. Its capture would simultaneously constitute a devastating blow to the Martians and an unmatched prize for the conquerors.

The fleet reached Mars on schedule, all except one ship turning up at the rendezvous within the prescribed forty-eight hours. At midnight on the second day, the vessels proceeded ten abreast towards the canal and the city. A site some five miles from the city's outskirts had been selected, and, one after another, the lines of ships settled among the brush and on the open fields. They began immediately to discharge their cargoes—all the soldiers, most of the horses and enough equipment and food for a considerable period.

It was a dangerous six hours. Spaceships unloading were notoriously vulnerable to certain types of attack ships fitted with long metal rams, capable of piercing the thin metal plates of which the outer walls were constructed. For an attack ship to catch a transport in the air meant almost certain death for everyone aboard.

The attacker, approaching from the side, transfixed an upper plate, and forced the transport over on its back. Since there were no drive tubes on the topside to hold the ship in the air, it usually fell like a stone. Periodic attempts to install drive tubes in the top as well as the bottom caused radioactive burns to crew and passengers, and no amount of interposed lead seemed to stop the interflow between the tubes.

❖❖❖

The six hours passed without an attack. About two hours after dawn, the army began to move along the canal towards the city. When they had marched about an hour, the advance guards topped a hill overlooking a great valley beyond which was glittering Oslin. They stopped, rearing their horses. Then they began to mill around.

Swiftly, a messenger raced back to Lord Creg, reporting an incredible fact. A Martian army was encamped in the valley, an army so vast that its tents and buildings merged into the haze of distance.

The general galloped forward to have a look. Those about him reported that he was never calmer as he gazed out over the valley. But his hopes for a quick, easy victory must have ended at that moment.

The army ahead was the main Martian force, comprising some six hundred thousand men. It was under the personal command of King Winatgin, and present was the king's famous brother, Sashernay.

Lord Creg had already made up his mind to attack at once, when a small fleet of enemy attack ships whisked over the hill, and discharged a shower of arrows at the group on the hill, wounding nearly four dozen soldiers. The commander in chief was unhurt, but the escape was too narrow for comfort. Swiftly, he gave the necessary orders.

His purpose was simple. King Winatgin and his staff undoubtedly knew now that an attack was coming. But it was one thing for him to have the information, and quite another to transmit it to an encamped and spread-out army.

That was the only reason why the battle was ever in doubt. The attackers were outnumbered six to one. The defense was stolid and uncertain at first, then it grew heavy from sheer weight of numbers. It was later learned that a hundred thousand Martians were killed or wounded, but the small Linnan army lost thirty thousand men, killed, prisoner and missing. And when it had still made no headway by late afternoon Lord Creg ordered a fighting retreat.

His troubles were far from over. As his troops fell back alongside the greenish red waters of the canal, a force of five thousand cavalry, which had been out on distant maneuvers, fell upon their rear, cutting them off from their camp, and turning their retreat away from the canal, towards the desert.

The coming of darkness saved the army from complete destruction. They marched until after midnight, before finally sinking down in a fatigued sleep. There was no immediate rest for Lord Creg. He flashed fire messages to his ships waiting out in space. A hundred of them nosed cautiously down and discharged more equipment and rations. It was expected that attack ships would make sneak attacks on them, but nothing happened, and they effected a successful withdrawal before dawn.

All too swiftly, the protecting darkness yielded to bright daylight.

❖ ❖ ❖

The new materiel saved them that day. The enemy pressed at them hour after hour, but it was clear to Lord Creg that King Winatgin was not using his forces to the best advantage. Their efforts were clumsy and heavy handed. They were easily outmaneuvered, and towards evening by leaving a cavalry screen to hold up the Martian army, he was able to break contact completely.

That night the Linnan army had a much needed rest, and Lord Creg's hopes came back. He realized that, if necessary, he could probably re-embark his forces and get off the planet without further losses. It was a tempting prospect. It fitted in with his private conviction that a war so ill begun had little chance of success.

But, reluctantly, he realized return to Linn was out of the question. The city would consider that he had disgraced himself as a general. After all, *he* had selected the point of attack, even though he had disapproved of the campaign as a whole.

And that was another thing. It might be assumed that he who had opposed the war, had deliberately lost the battle. No, definitely, he couldn't return to Linn. Besides, in any event he had to wait until the second fleet with another hundred thousand men aboard arrived about two weeks hence.

Two weeks? On the fourth day, the thin striplike ditches of canal water began to peter out. By evening the soldiers were fighting on sand that shifted under their feet. Ahead, as far as the eye could see was a uniformly flat red desert.

There was another canal out there somewhere about nineteen

days march due east, but Lord Creg had no intention of taking his army on such a dangerous journey. Seventy thousand men would need a lot of water.

It was the first time in Creg's military career that he had ever been cut off from a water supply. The problem grew tremendous when eleven out of a dozen spaceships sent for water exploded as they approached the camp, and deluged the desert and the unlucky men immediately below with boiling water. One ship got through, but the water aboard was beginning to boil, and the ship was saved only when those aboard operated the air lock mechanism, letting the steaming water pour out onto the sand.

The almost cooked commander emerged shakily from the control room, and reported to Lord Creg.

"We did as you ordered, sir. Got rid of all our equipment, and dunked the entire ship in the canal, using it as a tanker. It began to get hot immediately."

He cursed. "It's those blasted water gods that these Martians worship. They must have done it."

"Nonsense!" said Lord Creg. And ordered the man escorted back to his ship by four high officers.

❖❖❖

It was a futile precaution. Other soldiers had the same idea. The water and canal gods of the Martians had started the water boiling, and so the ships had exploded. Lord Creg in a rough and ready speech delivered to a number of legions pointed out that nothing happened to water brought in the ordinary water tanks of the ship.

A voice interrupted him, "Why don't you bring the water in them then?"

The men cheered the remark, and it was scarcely an acceptable explanation after that to answer that the main body of ships could not be risked in such an enterprise.

On the seventh day the army began to get thirsty. The realization came to Lord Creg that he could not afford to wait for the arrival of the second fleet. He accordingly decided on a plan, which had been in the back of his mind when he originally selected Oslin as the city which his forces would attack.

That night he called down two hundred ships, and packed his army into them, nearly three hundred and fifty men to the ship. He assumed that Martian spies had donned the uniforms of dead Linnans, and were circulating around his camp. And so he did not inform his staff of the destination until an hour before the ships were due.

His plan was based on an observation he had made when, as a young man, he had visited Mars. During the course of a journey down the Oslin Canal, he noticed a town named Magga. This town, set among the roughest and craggiest hills on Mars, was approachable by land through only four passes, all easily defendable.

It had had a garrison twenty years before. But Lord Creg assumed rightly that, unless it had been reinforced since then, his men could swamp it. There was another factor in his favor, though he did not know it at the time of his decision. King Winatgin, in spite of certain private information, could scarcely believe that the main Linnan invasion was already defeated. Hourly expecting vast forces to land, he kept his forces close to Oslin.

Magga was taken shortly after midnight. By morning the troops were ready for siege with a plentitude of canal water on one flank. When the second fleet arrived a week later, they too settled in Magga, and the expedition was saved.

The extent of this defensive victory was never fully appreciated in Linn, not even by Lord Creg's followers and apologists. All that the people could see was that the army was jammed into a small canal town, and seemed doomed, surrounded as it was by a force which outnumbered it more than six to one. Even the Lord Leader, who had taken many a seemingly impregnable position in his military days, secretly questioned his son's statement that they were safe.

Except for forays, the army remained all that summer and the following winter in Magga. It was besieged the whole of the next year, while Lord Creg doggedly demanded another two hundred thousand men from a patronate, which was reluctant to send more men into what they considered certain destruction. Finally, however, the Lord Leader realized that Creg was holding his own, and personally demanded the reinforcements.

Four new legions were on their way on the day that the Lord

Leader started up the pathway that led to the aerie-sanctuary of his mutation grandson.

❖❖❖

He was puffing by the time he reached the foot of the rock. That startled him. "By the four atom gods," he thought, "I'm getting old." He was sixty-three, within two months of sixty-four.

The shock grew. *Sixty-four.* He looked down at his long body. An old man's legs, he thought, not so old as some men of sixty-four, but there was no question any more that he was past his prime.

"Creg was right," he thought, aghast. "The time has come for me at least to retrench. No more wars after Mars except defensive ones. And I must name an heir, and make him co-Leader."

It was too big a subject for the moment. The thought, heir, reminded him where he was. One of his grandsons was up there with a tutor. He could hear the murmuring baritone of the man, the occasional remarks of the boy. It sounded very human and normal.

The Lord Leader frowned, thinking of the vastness of the world and the smallness of the Linn family. Standing there, he realized why he was come to this spot. Everyone of them would be needed to hold the government together. Even the lamebrains, even the mutations must be given duties consonant with their abilities.

It was a sad and terrible thing to realize that he was approaching the ever more lonely peak of his life, able to trust only those of his own blood. And even they clung together only because of the restless tide of ambition that surged on every side.

The old man smiled, a mixture of wry, grim smile. Something of the steely quality of him showed in the natural shape his jaws and chin assumed. It was the look of the man who had won the bloody battle of Attium that made Linn his, the smile of the man who had watched his soldiers hack Raheinl to pieces with battle-axes.

"There was a man," he thought, still amazed after nearly thirty years that the leader of the opposing group should have been so perverse. "What made him refuse all my offers? It was the first time in the history of civil war that such an attempt at conciliation was made. I was the compromiser. He wanted the world, and I who did not want it, at least not in that way, had to take it perforce to save my own life. Why must men have all or nothing?"

Surely, Raheinl, cold and calm, waiting for the first ax to strike, must have realized the vanity of his purposes. Must have known, too, that nothing could save him, that soldiers who had fought and bled and feared for their lives would stand for no mercy to be shown their main enemy.

In spite of the impossibility, Raheinl had received a measure of mercy. The Leader recalled with crystallike clarity his selection of the executioners. He had ordered that the very first blow be fatal. The crowd wanted a torture, a spectacle. They *seemed* to get it, but actually it was a dead man who was hacked to bits before their eyes.

Watching the great Raheinl being destroyed chilled forever the soul of the Lord Leader. He had never felt himself a participant of the murder. The crowd was the killer, the crowd and its mindless emotions, its strength of numbers that no man could ignore without the deadliest danger to himself and his family. The crowd and its simple bloodthirstiness frightened him even while he despised it, and influenced him even while he skillfully used it for his own ends. It was rather dreadful to think that not once in his entire life had he made a move that was not motivated by some consideration of the crowd.

He had been born into a world already devastated by two powerful opposing groups. Nor was it a question of which group one joined. When the opposition was in power they tried to kill, disgrace or exile all the members of every family of the other party. During such periods, the children of many noble families were dragged through the streets on the end of hooks and tossed into the river.

Later, if you were among those who survived, it was a question of striving to attain power and some control of your own group. For that, too, could not be left to chance and sympathy. There were groups within groups, assassinations to eliminate dangerous contenders for leadership, an enormous capacity on everybody's part for murder and treachery.

The survivors of that intricate battle of survival were—*tough.*

Tough survivor the Lord Leader Linn pulled his mind slowly out of its depth of memory, and began to climb the steps cut into the towering rock itself.

❖❖❖

The top of the rock had a length of twenty feet, and it was almost as wide. Joquin's slaves had deposited piles of fertile soil upon it, and from this soil flowering shrubs reared up gracefully, two of them to a height of nearly fifteen feet.

The mutation and the tutor sat in lawn chairs in the shade of the tallest shrub, and they were so seated that they were not immediately aware of the Lord Leader's presence.

"Very well, then," the scholar, Nellian, was saying, "we have agreed that the weakness of Mars is its water system. The various canals, which bring water down from the north pole, are the sole sources of water supply. It is no wonder that the Martians have set up temples in which they worship water as reverently as we worship the gods of the atoms.

"It is, of course, another matter," Nellian went on, "to know what use can be made of this weakness of Mars. The canals are so wide and so deep that they cannot, for instance, be poisoned even temporarily."

"Macrocosmically speaking," said the boy, "that is true. The molecular world offers few possibilities except the forces which man's own body can bring to bear."

The Lord Leader blinked. Had he heard correctly? Had he heard a boy of thirteen talk like *that*?

He had been about to step forward and reveal himself. Now, he waited, startled and interested. Clane went on:

"The trouble with my father is that he is too trusting. Why he should assume that it is bad luck which is frustrating his war, I don't know. If I were he I would examine the possibilities of treachery a little more carefully, and I'd look very close indeed at my inner circle of advisers."

Nellian smiled. "You speak with the positivity of youth. If you ever get onto a battlefield you will realize that no mental preconception can match the reality. Vague theories have a habit of collapsing in the face of showers of arrows and spears, and infighting with swords and axes."

The boy was imperturbable. "They failed to draw the proper conclusions from the way the spaceships carrying the water exploded. Joquin would have known what to think about that."

The talk, while still on a high grammatical level, was, it seemed to the Lord Leader, becoming a little childish. He stepped forward and cleared his throat.

At the sound, the scholar turned serenely, and then, as he saw who it was, he stood up with dignity. The mutation's reaction was actually faster, though there was not so much movement in it. At the first sound, he turned his head.

And that was all. For a long moment, he sat frozen in that position. At first his expression remained unchanged from the quiet calm that had been on it. The Lord Leader had time for a close look at a grandson whom he had not seen so near since the day Clane was born.

The boy's head was completely human. It had the distinctive and finely shaped Linn nose and the Linn blue eyes. But it had something more, too. His mother's delicate beauty was somehow interwoven into the face. Her mouth was there, her ears and her chin. The face and head were beautifully human, almost angelic in their structure.

It was not the only human part of him. But most of the rest was at very least subtly unhuman. The general shape was very, very man-like. The body, the torso, the legs and arms—they were all there, but wrong in an odd fashion.

The thought came to the Lord Leader that if the boy would wear a scholar's or scientist's gown, and keep his arms withdrawn into the folds—his hands were normal—no one would ever more than guess the truth. There was not even any reason why that face should not be put on one of the larger silver or gold coins, and circulated among certain remote and highly moral tribes. The angel qualities of Clane's face might very well warm many a barbarian heart.

"Thank the gods," thought the Lord Leader, not for the first time, "that he hasn't got four arms and four legs."

His mind reached that thought just as the paralysis left the boy. (It was only then that the Lord Leader realized that Clane had almost literally been frozen where he was.) Now, the transformation was an amazing spectacle. The perfect face began to change, to twist. The eyes grew fixed and staring, the mouth twitched and lost its shape. The whole countenance collapsed into a kind of idiocy that was terrible to see. Slowly, though it didn't take too long, the boy's body swung out of his chair, and he stood half crouching, facing his grandfather.

He began to whimper, then to gibber. Beside him, Nellian said sharply:

"Clane, control yourself."

The words were like a cue. With a low cry, the boy darted forward, and ducked past the Lord Leader. As he came to the steep, stone stairway, he flung himself down it at a reckless speed, almost sliding to the ground more than twenty feet below. Then he was gone down the pathway.

Silence settled.

Nellian said finally, quietly, "May I speak?"

The Lord Leader noted that the other did not address him by his titles, and a fleeting smile touched his lips. An anti-Imperialist. After a moment, he felt annoyed—these upright republicans—but he merely nodded an affirmative to the verbal request. Nellian went on:

"He was like that with me too, when Joquin first brought me up to be his tutor. It is a reversion to an emotional condition which he experienced as a very young child."

The Lord Leader said nothing. He was gazing out over the city. It was a misty day, and his left eye no longer had normal vision, so the haze of distance and the blur in one of his vision centers hid the farther suburbs. From this height, they seemed to melt into the haze—houses, buildings, land grown insubstantial. And yet, beyond, vaguely beyond, he could see the winding river, and the countryside partially hidden by the veils of mist. In the near distance were the circus pits, empty now that a great war was taxing the human resources of an earth which had attained the colossal population of sixty million inhabitants. In his own lifetime, the number of people had nearly doubled.

It was all rather tremendous and wonderful, as if the race was straining at some invisible leash, with its collective eyes on a dazzlingly bright future, the realities of which were still hidden beyond remote horizons.

The Lord Leader drew his mind and his eyes back to the rock. He did not look directly at Nellian. He said:

"What did he mean when he said that my son, Lord Creg, should watch out for treachery close to him?"

Nellian shrugged. "So you heard that? I need hardly tell you that he would be in grave danger if certain ears heard that he had made such remarks. Frankly, I don't know where he obtains all his information. I do know that he seems to have a very thorough grasp of palace intrigue and politics. He's very secretive."

The Lord Leader frowned. He could understand the secretiveness. People who found out too much about other people's plans had a habit of turning up dead. If the mutation really knew that treachery had dogged the Martian war, even the hint of such knowledge would mean his assassination. The Leader hesitated. Then:

"What did he mean about the spaceships with water blowing up just before they landed? What does he know about things like that?"

It was the other's turn to hesitate. Finally, slowly:

"He's mentioned that several times. In spite of his caution, the boy is so eager for companionship, and so anxious to impress, that he keeps letting out his thoughts to people like myself whom he trusts."

The scholar looked steadily at the Lord Leader.

"Naturally, I keep all such information to myself. I belong to no side politically."

The great man bowed ever so slightly. "I am grateful," he said with a sigh.

❖ ❖ ❖

Nellian said after an interval, "He has referred a number of times to the Raheinl temple incident which occurred at the time of his birth, when four temples exploded. I have gathered that Joquin told him something about that, and also that Joquin left secret papers at his estate, to which the boy has had access. You may recall that he has visited the main estate three times since Joquin's death."

The Lord Leader recalled vaguely that his permission had been asked by Nellian on several occasions. The man went on:

"I hope it is unnecessary for me to say that the boy's mentality, as distinct from his emotional nature, is very mature, at least that of an eighteen- or nineteen-year-old."

"Hm-m-m," said the Lord Leader. His manner grew decisive. "We must cure him of his weakness," he said. "There are several methods." He smiled reminiscently. "In war, when we want to end a man's fear, we subject him to repeated dangers in actual combat. He might be killed, of course, but if he survives he gradually acquires confidence and courage. Similarly, an orator must first be trained in voice control, then he must speak again to acquire poise and an easy address."

The Leader's lips tightened thoughtfully. "We can hardly initiate him into war. The soldiers unfortunately regard mutations as ill omens. Public speaking—that can best be done by putting him into a temple in one of the remoter temples. From the security of a scientist's robes, he can deliver the daily incantations, first to the atom gods in private, then in the presence of scientists, initiates and juniors, and finally before the public. I will make arrangements for that experience to begin tomorrow. He does not need to live at the temple.

"Finally, sometime next year, we will assign him a separate residence, and have a couple of attractive slave girls from his estate brought up. I want small, mild, meek girls, who will not try to boss him. I'll select them myself, and give them a good talking to."

He added matter-of-factly: "They can be sold later in remote regions, or put to death, depending on how discreet they are. After all, we can't have talkative fools giving detailed accounts of the physical defects of members of my family."

The Lord Leader paused, and looked keenly at Nellian. "What do you think of that as a beginning?"

The scholar nodded judicially. "Excellent, excellent. I am glad to see you taking a personal interest in the boy."

The Lord Leader was pleased. "Keep me in touch about"—he frowned—"once every three months."

He was turning away when his gaze lighted on something half hidden in the brush at one edge of the rock.

"What's that?" he asked.

Nellian looked embarrassed. "Why," he said, "why, uh, that's, uh, a device Joquin rigged up."

The scholar's self-consciousness amazed the Leader. He walked over and looked at the thing. It was a metal pipe that disappeared down the side of the rock. It was almost completely hidden by creeping vines, but little glints of it were visible here and there both against the rock and against the cliff farther down.

He drew back, and he was examining the open end of the pipe again, when it spoke huskily, a woman's voice:

"Kiss me, kiss me again."

The Lord Leader placed a tuft of grass over the pipe end, and climbed to his feet amused. "Well, I'll be a—" he said. "A listening device, straight down into one of the rendezvous of the palace grounds."

Nellian said, "There's another one on the other side."

The Lord Leader was about to turn away again, when he noticed the notebook beside the tube. He picked it up, and rippled through it. All the pages were blank, and that was puzzling until he saw the bottle of ink and the pen half hidden in the grass where the book had been.

He was genuinely interested now. He picked up the bottle, and pulled out the cork. First, he looked hard at the ink, then he smelled it. Finally, with a smile, he replaced the bottle in the grass.

As he descended the pathway, he was thinking, "Joquin was right. These mutations can be normal, even supernormal."

He was not greatly surprised two weeks later when Nellian handed him a message from Clane.

The letter read:

❖ ❖ ❖

To my grandfather,
Most Honorable Lord Leader:
I regret exceedingly that my emotions were so uncontrollable when you came to see me. Please let me say that I am proud of the honor you have done me, and that your visit has changed my mind about many things. Before you came to the aerie, I was not prepared to think of myself as having any obligations to the Linn family. Now, I have decided to live up to the name, which you have made illustrious. I salute you, honorable grandfather, the greatest man who ever lived.

Your admiring and humble grandson,
Clane

It was, in its way, a melodramatic note, and the Lord Leader quite seriously disagreed with the reference to himself as the greatest man of all time. He was not even second, though perhaps third.

"My boy," he thought, "you have forgotten *my* uncle, the general of generals, and his opponent the dazzlingly wonderful personality, who was given a triumph before he was twenty, and officially when he was still a young man voted the right to use the word "great" after his name. I knew them both, and I *know* where I stand."

Nevertheless, in spite of its wordy praise, the letter pleased the Lord Leader. But it puzzled him, too. There were overtones in it, as if a concrete decision had been made by somebody who had the power to do things.

He put the letter among his files of family correspondence, starting a new case labeled "CLANE." Then he forgot about it. It was recalled to his mind a week later when his wife showed him two missives, one a note addressed to herself, the second an unsealed letter to Lord Creg on Mars. Both the note and the letter were from Clane. The stately Lydia was amused.

"Here's something that will interest you," she said.

The Lord Leader read first the note addressed to her. It was quite a humble affair.

To my most gracious grandmother,
Honorable lady:
Rather than burden your husband, my grandfather, with my request, I ask you most sincerely to have the enclosed letter sent by the regular dispatch pouch to my father, Lord Creg. As you will see it is a prayer which I shall make at the temple next week for his victory over the Martians this summer. A metal capsule, touched by the god metals, Radium, Uranium, Plutonium and Ecks, will be dedicated at this ceremony, and sent to my father on the next mail transport.

Most respectfully yours,
Clane

"You know," said Lydia, "for a moment when I received that, I didn't even know who Clane was. I had some vague idea that he was dead. Instead he seems to be growing up."

"Yes," said the Lord Leader absently, "yes, he's growing."

He was examining the "prayer" which Clane had addressed to Lord Creg. He had an odd feeling that there was something here which he was not quite grasping. Why had this been sent through Lydia? Why not direct to himself?

"It's obvious," said Lady Linn, "that since there is to be a temple dedication, the letter must be sent."

That was exactly it, the Lord Leader realized. There was nothing here that was being left to chance. They *had* to send the letter. They *had* to send the metal dedicated to the gods.

But why was the information being conveyed through Lydia?

He reread the prayer, fascinated this time by its ordinariness. It was so trite, so unimportant, the kind of prayer that made old soldiers wonder what they were fighting for—morons? The lines were widely spaced, to an exaggerated extent, and it was that that suddenly made the Leader's eyes narrow ever so slightly.

"Well," he laughed, "I'll take this, and have it placed in the dispatch pouch."

As soon as he reached his apartment, he lit a candle, and held the letter over the flame. In two minutes, the invisible ink was beginning to show in the blank space between the lines, six lines of closely written words between each line of the prayer.

The Lord Leader read the long, precise instructions and explanations, his lips tight. It was a plan of attack for the armies on Mars, not so much military as magical. There were several oblique references to the blowing up of the temples many years before, and a very tremendous implication that something entirely different could be counted on from the gods.

At the end of the letter was a space for *him* to sign.

He did not sign immediately, but in the end he slashed his signature on to the sheet, put it into the envelope and affixed his great seal of state. Then he sat back, and once more the thought came:

But why Lydia?

Actually, it didn't take long to figure out the extent of the treachery that had baffled Lord Creg's sorely pressed legions for three years.

As close as that, the Lord Leader thought grayly. As close in the family as that.

Some of the plotting must have been done in one or other of the rendezvous some sixty feet below the rock aerie where a child of the gods lay with his ear pressed to a metal tube listening to conspiratorial words, and noting them down in invisible ink on the pages of an apparently blank notebook.

❖❖❖

The Lord Leader was not unaware that his wife intrigued endlessly behind his back. He had married her, so that the opposition would have a skillful spokesman in the government. She was the daughter of one of the noblest families in Linn, all the adult males of which had died fighting for Raheinl. Two of them were actually captured and executed.

At nineteen, when she was already married and with child—later born Lord Tews—the Lord Leader arranged with her husband for what was easily the most scandalous divorce and remarriage in the history of Linn.

The Lord Leader was unconcerned. He had already usurped the name of the city and empire of Linn for his family. The next step was to make a move to heal what everybody said was the unhealable wound left by the civil war. Marriage to Lydia was that move, and a wondrously wise one it had been.

She was the safety valve for all the pent-up explosive forces of the opposition. Through her maneuvers, he learned what they were after. And gave as much as would satisfy. By seeming to follow her advice, he brought hundreds of able administrators, soldiers and patrons from the other side into the government service to manage the unwieldy populations of Earth, and rule solar colonies.

In the previous ten years, more and more opposition patrons had supported his laws in the patronate without qualification. They laughed a little at the fact that he still read all his main speeches. They ridiculed his stock phrases: "Quicker than you can cook asparagus." "Words fail me, gentlemen." "Let us be satisfied with the cat we have." And others.

But again and again during the past decade, all party lines dissolved in the interests of the empire. And, when his agents reported conspiracies in the making, further investigation revealed that no powerful men or families were involved.

Not once had he blamed Lydia for the various things she had done. She could no more help being of the opposition than he, years before, had been able to prevent himself from being drawn, first as a youth, then as a man, into the vortex of the political ambitions of his own group. She would have been assassinated if it had ever seemed to the more hotheaded of the opposition that she was "betraying" them by being too neutral.

No, he didn't blame her for past actions. But this was different. Vast armies had been decimated by treachery, so that Lord Creg's qualities as a leader would show up poorly in comparison to Lord Tews'.

This was personal, and the Lord Leader recognized it immediately as a major crisis.

The important thing, he reasoned, was to save Creg, who was about to launch his campaign. But meanwhile great care must be taken not to alarm Lydia and the others. Undoubtedly, they must have some method of intercepting his private mail pouch to Creg.

Dare he stop that? It wouldn't be wise to do so. Everything must appear normal and ordinary, or their fright might cause some foolhardy individual to attempt an impromptu assassination of the Lord Leader.

As it was, so long as Lord Creg's armies were virtually intact, the group would make no radical move.

The pouch, with Clane's letter in it, would have to be allowed to fall into their hands, as other pouches must have done. If the letter was opened, an attempt would probably be made to murder Clane. Therefore—what?

The Lord Leader placed guards in every rendezvous of the palace grounds, including two each in the two areas at the foot of the aerie. His posted reason for setting the guards was on all the bulletin boards:

I am tired of running into couples engaged in licentious kissing. This is not only in bad taste, but it has become such a common practice as to require drastic action. The guards will be removed in a week or so. I am counting on the good sense of everyone, particularly of the women, to see to it that in future these spectacles are voluntarily restricted.

A week or so to protect Clane until the dedication at the temple.

It would be interesting to see just what the boy did do with the dedicated metal, but, of course, his own presence was impossible. It was the day after the dedication that the Lord Leader spoke to Nellian, casually:

"I think he should make a tour of Earth. Haphazard, without any particular route. And incognito. And start soon. Tomorrow."

So much for Clane. More personal, he made a friendly visit to the guards' camp outside the city. For the soldiers, it turned out to be an unexpectedly exciting day. He gave away a million sesterces in small but lavish amounts. Horse races, foot races and contests of every kind were conducted, with prizes for the winners, and even losers who had tried nobly were amazed and delighted to receive money awards.

All in all, it was a satisfactory day. When he left, he heard cheers until he reached the Martian gate. It would take several weeks at least, if not months, to cause disaffection among those troops.

The various precautions taken, the Lord Leader dispatched the mail pouch, and awaited events.

❖❖❖

The group had to work fast. A knight emptied the mail pouch. A knight and a patron scrutinized each letter, and separated them into two piles. One of these piles, the largest one by far, was returned to the pouch at once. The other pile was examined by Lord Tews, who extracted from it some score of letters, which he handed to his mother.

Lydia looked at them one by one, and handed those she wanted opened to one or the other of two slaves, who were skilled in the use of chemical. It was these slaves who actually removed the seals.

The seventh letter she picked up was the one from Clane. Lydia looked at the handwriting on the envelope, and at the name of the sender on one side, and there was a faint smile on her lips.

"Tell me," she said, "am I wrong, or does the army regard dwarfs, mutations and other human freaks as bad omens?"

"Very much so," said one of the knights. "To see one on the morning of battle spells disaster. To have any contact with one means a great setback."

The Lady Leader smiled. "My honorable husband is almost recalcitrantly uninterested in such psychological phenomena. We must accordingly see to it that Lord Creg's army is apprized that he has received a message from his mutation son."

She tossed the letter towards the pouch. "Put this in. I have already seen the contents."

Hardly more than three quarters of an hour later, the dispatch carrier was again on his way to the ship.

"Nothing important," Lydia said to her son. "Your stepfather seems to be primarily concerned these days with preserving the moral stature of the palace grounds."

Lord Tews said, "I'd like to know why he felt it necessary to bribe the guards' legion the other day."

Lord Creg read the letter from Clane with an amazed frown. He recognized that the boy's prayer had been used to convey a more important message, and the fact that such a ruse had been necessary startled him. It gave a weight to the document, which he would not ordinarily have attached to so wild a plan.

The important thing about it was that it required only slight changes in the disposition of his troops. His intention was to attack. It *assumed* that he would attack, and added a rather unbelievable psychological factor. Nevertheless, in its favor was the solid truth that eleven spaceships filled with water had exploded, a still unexplained phenomenon after two years.

Creg sat for a long time pondering the statement in the letter that the presence of King Winatgin's army at Oslin had not been accidental, but had been due to treachery hitherto unknown in Linn.

"I've been cooped up here for two years," he thought bitterly, "forced to fight a defensive war because my stepmother and her plumpish son craved unlimited power."

He pictured himself dead, and Tews succeeding to the Lord Leadership. After a moment, that seemed appalling. Abruptly, decisively, he called on a temple scientist attached to the army, a man noted for his knowledge of Mars.

"How fast do the Oslin canal waters move at this time of the year?"

"About five miles an hour," was the reply.

Creg considered that. One hundred and twenty miles a day. A

third of that should be sufficient, or even less. If the dedicated metal were dropped about twenty miles north of the city, the effect should be just about perfect.

The second battle of Oslin that was fought ten days later was never in doubt. On the morning of the battle, the inhabitants of the city awoke to find the mile wide canal and all its tributary waters a seething mass of boiling, steaming water. The steam poured over the city in dense clouds. It hid the spaceships that plunged down into the streets. It hid the soldiers who debouched from the ships.

By mid-morning King Winatgin's army was surrendering in such numbers that the royal family was unable to effect an escape. The monarch, sobbing in his dismay, flung himself at Creg's feet, and then, given mercy, but chained, stood on a hill beside his captor, and watched the collapse of the Martian military might.

In a week, all except one remote mountain stronghold had surrendered, and Mars was conquered. At the height of the triumph, about dusk one day, a poisoned arrow snapped out of the shadows of an Oslin building and pierced Lord Creg's throat.

He died an hour later in great pain, his murderer still unfound.

When the news of his death reached Linn three months later, both sides worked swiftly. Lydia had executed the two slave chemists and the dispatch carrier a few hours after she heard of Creg's victory. Now, she sent assassins to murder the two knights and the patron who had assisted in the opening of the mail. And, simultaneously, she ordered Tews to leave the city for one of his estates.

By the time the Lord Leader's guards arrived to arrest him, the alarmed young man was off in his private spaceship. It was that escape that took the first edge off the ruler's anger. He decided to postpone his visit to Lydia. Slowly, as that first day dragged by, a bleak admiration for his wife built up inside him, and the realization came that he could not afford to jeopardize his relations with her, not now when the great Creg was dead.

He decided that she had not actually ordered the assassination of Creg. Some frightened henchman on the scene, fearing for his own safety, had taken his own action; and Lydia, with a masterly understanding of the situation, had merely covered up for them all.

It might be fatal to the empire if he broke with her now. By the time she came with her retinue to offer him official condolences, his mind was made up. He took her hand in his with tears in his eyes.

"Lydia," he said, "this is a terrible moment for me. What do you suggest?"

She suggested a combination State funeral and triumph. She said, "Unfortunately, Tews is ill, and will not be able to attend. It looks like one of those illnesses that may keep him away for a long time."

The Lord Leader recognized that it was a surrender of her ambition for Tews, at least for the time being. It was in reality a tremendous offer, a concession not absolutely necessary in view of his own determination to keep the whole affair private.

He bent and kissed her hand. At the funeral, they marched together behind the coffin. And in all the great throng of mourners surely the least noticed was a boy wearing the robes of a scientist in the company of a scholar. It was even said afterwards that Clane Linn was not present.

But I was there.

Hand of the Gods

At twenty, Clane wrote his first book. It was a cautiously worded, thin volume about old legends. And what was important about it was not that it attempted to dispel superstitions about the vanished golden era which the atom gods had destroyed, but that for weeks it required him to go every day into the palace library, where, with the help of three secretary-slaves—two men and a woman—he did the necessary research work.

It was in the library that the Lady Lydia, his stepgrandmother, saw him one day.

She had almost forgotten that he existed. But she saw him now for the first time under conditions that were favorable to his appearance. He was modestly attired in the fatigue gown of a temple scientist, a costume which was effective for covering up his physical deformations. There were folds of cloth to conceal his mutated arms so skillfully that his normal human hands came out into the open as if they were the natural extensions of a healthy body. The cloak was drawn up into a narrow, not unattractive band around his neck, which served to hide the subtly mutated shoulders and the unhuman chest formation. Above the collar, Lord Clane's head reared with all the pride of a young lordling.

It was a head to make any woman look twice, delicately beautiful, with a remarkably clear skin. Lydia, who had never seen her husband's grandson, except at a distance—Clane had made sure of that—felt a constricting fear in her heart.

"By Uranium!" she thought. "Another great man. As if I didn't have enough trouble trying to get Tews back from exile."

It hardly seemed likely that death would be necessary for a mutation. But if she ever hoped to have Tews inherit the empire, then all the more direct heirs would have to be taken care of in some way. Standing there, she added this new relative to her list of the more dangerous kin of the ailing Lord Leader.

She saw that Clane was looking at her. His face had changed, stiffened, lost some of its good looks, and that brought a memory of things she had heard about him. That he was easily upset emotionally. The prospect interested her. She walked towards him, a thin smile on her long, handsome countenance.

Twice, as she stood tall before him, he tried to get up. And failed each time. All the color was gone from his cheeks, his face even more strained looking than it had been, ashen and unnatural, twisted, changed, the last shape of beauty gone from it. His lips worked with the effort at speech, but only a muted burst of unintelligible sounds issued forth.

Lydia grew aware that the young slave woman-secretary was almost as agitated as her master. The creature looked beseechingly at Lydia, finally gasped:

"May I speak, your excellency?"

That shocked. Slaves didn't speak except when spoken to. It was not just a rule or a regulation dependent upon the whim of the particular owner; it was the law of the land, and anybody could report breach as a misdemeanor, and collect half the fine which was subsequently levied from the slave's master. What dazed Lady Lydia was that *she* should have been the victim of such a degrading experience. She was so stunned that the young woman had time to gasp:

"You must forgive him. He is subject to fits of nervous paralysis, when he can neither move nor speak. The sight of his illustrious grandmother coming upon him by surprise—"

That was as far as she got. Lydia found her voice. She snapped:

"It is too bad that all slaves are not similarly afflicted. How dare you speak to me?"

She stopped, catching herself sharply. It was not often that she lost her temper, and she had no intention of letting the situation get out of hand. The slave girl was sagging away as if she had been struck with a violence beyond her power to resist. Lydia watched the process of disintegration curiously. There was only one possible explanation for a slave speaking up so boldly for her master. She must be one of his favorite mistresses. And the odd thing, in this case, was that the slave herself seemed to approve of the relationship, or she wouldn't have been so anxious for him.

It would appear, thought Lydia, *that this mutation relative of mine can make himself attractive in spite of his deformities, and that it isn't only a case of a slave girl compelled by her circumstances.*

It seemed to her that the moment had potentialities. "What," she said, "is your name?"

"Selk." The young woman spoke huskily.

"Oh, a Martian."

The Martian war, some years before, had produced some hundreds of thousands of husky, good-looking boy and girl Martians for the slave schools to train.

Lydia's plan grew clear. She would have the girl assassinated, and so put the first desperate fear into the mutation. That should hold him until she had succeeded in bringing Tews back from exile to supreme power. After all, he was not too important. It would be impossible for a despised mutation ever to become Lord Leader.

He had to be put out of the way in the long run, because the Linn party would otherwise try to make use of him against Tews and herself.

She paused for a last look down at Clane. He was sitting as rigid as a board, his eyes glazed, his face still colorless and unnatural. She made no effort to conceal her contempt as, with a flounce of her skirt, she turned and walked away, followed by her ladies and personal slaves.

❖ ❖ ❖

Slaves were sometimes trained to be assassins. The advantage of using them was that they could not be witnesses in court either for or against the accused. But Lydia had long discovered that, if anything went wrong, if a crisis arose as a result of the murder attempt, a slave assassin did not have the same determination to win over obstacles. Slaves took to their heels at the slightest provocation, and returned with fantastic accounts of the odds that had defeated them.

She used former knights and sons of knights, whose families had been degraded from their rank because they were penniless. Such men had a desperate will to acquire money, and when they failed she could usually count on a plausible reason.

She had a horror of not knowing the facts. For more than thirty of her fifty-five years her mind had been a nonsaturable sponge for details and ever more details.

It was accordingly of more than ordinary interest to her when the two knights she had hired to murder her stepgrandson's slave girl, Selk, reported that they had been unable to find the girl.

"There is no such person now attached to Lord Clane's city household."

Her informant, a slim youth named Meerl, spoke with that mixture of boldness and respect which the more devil-may-care assassins affected when talking to high personages.

"Lady," he went on with a bow and a smile, "I think you have been outwitted."

"I'll do the thinking," said Lydia with asperity. "You're a sword or a knife with a strong arm to wield. Nothing more."

"And a good brain to direct it," said Meerl.

Lydia scarcely heard. Her retort had been almost automatic. Because—could it be? Was it possible that Clane had realized what she would do?

What startled her was the decisiveness of it, the prompt action that had been taken on the basis of what would only have been a suspicion. The world was full of people who never did anything about their suspicions. The group that did was always in a special class. If Clane had consciously frustrated her, then he was even more dangerous than she had thought. She'd have to plan her next move with care.

She grew aware that the two men were still standing before her. She glared at them.

"Well, what are you waiting for? You know there is no money if you fail."

"Gracious lady," said Meerl, "we did not fail. You failed."

Lydia hesitated, impressed by the fairness of the thrust. She had a certain grudging respect for this particular assassin.

"Fifty percent," she said.

She tossed forward a pouch of money. It was skillfully caught. The men bowed quickly, stiffly, with a flash of white teeth and a clank of steel. They whirled and disappeared through thick portieres that concealed the door by which they had entered.

Lydia sat alone with her thoughts, but not for long. A knock came on another door, and one of her ladies in waiting entered, holding a sealed letter in her hand.

"This arrived, madam, while you were engaged."

Lydia's eyebrows went up a little when she saw that the letter was from Clane. She read it, tight-lipped:

To My Most Gracious Grandmother:

I offer my sincere apologies for the insult and distress which I caused your ladyship yesterday in the library. I can only plead that my nervous afflictions are well known in the family, and that, when I am assailed, it is beyond my power to control myself.

I also offer apologies for the action of my slave girl in speaking to you. It was my first intention to turn her over to you for punishment. But then it struck me that you were so tremendously busy at all times, and besides she scarcely merited your attention. Accordingly, I have had her sold in the country to a dealer in labor, and she will no doubt learn to regret her insolence.

> *With renewed humble apologies, I remain,*
> *Your obedient grandson,*
> *Clane*

Reluctantly, the Lady Linn was compelled to admire the letter. Now she would never know whether she had been outwitted or victorious.

I suppose, she thought acridly, *I could at great expense discover if he merely sent her to his country estate, there to wait until I have forgotten what she looks like. Or could I even do that?*

She paused to consider the difficulties. She would have to send as an investigator someone who had seen the girl. Who? She looked up.

"Dalat."

The woman who had brought the letter curtsied.

"Yes?"

"What did that slave girl in the library yesterday look like?"

Dalat was disconcerted. "W-why, I don't think I noticed, your ladyship. A blonde, I think."

"A blonde!" Explosively. "Why, you numbskull. That girl had the most fancy head of golden hair that I've seen in several years—and you didn't notice."

Dalat was herself again. "I am not accustomed to remembering slaves," she said.

"Get out of here," said Lydia. But she said it in a flat tone, without emotion.

Here was defeat.

She shrugged finally. After all, it was only an idea she had had. Her problem was to get Tews back to Linn. Lord Clane, the only mutation ever born into the family of the Lord Leader, could wait.

Nevertheless, the failure rankled.

The Lord Leader had over a period of years become an ailing old man, who could not make up his mind. At seventy-one, he was almost blind in his left eye, and only his voice remained strong. He had a thunderous baritone that still struck terror into the hearts of criminals when he sat on the chair of high judgment, a duty which, because of its sedentary nature, he cultivated more and more as the swift months of his declining years passed by.

He was greatly surprised one day to see Clane turn up in the palace court as a defense counsel for a knight. He stopped the presentation of the case to ask some questions.

"Have you experience in the lower courts?"

"Yes, Leader."

"Hm-m-m, why was I not told?"

The mutation had suddenly a strained look on his face, as if the pressure of being the center of attention was proving too much for him. The Lord Leader recalled the young man's affliction, and said hastily:

"Proceed with the case. I shall talk to you later."

The case was an unimportant one involving equity rights. It had obviously been taken by Clane because of its simple, just aspects. For a first case in the highest court it had been well selected. The old man was pleased, and gave the favorable verdict with satisfaction.

As usual, however, he had overestimated his strength. And so, he was finally forced to retire quickly, with but a word to Clane:

"I shall come to call on you one of these days. I have been wanting to see your home."

That night he made the mistake of sitting on the balcony too long without a blanket. He caught a cold, and spent the whole of the month that followed in bed. It was there, helpless on his back, acutely aware of his weak body, fully, clearly conscious at last that he had at most a few years to live, that the Lord Leader realized finally the necessity of selecting an heir. In spite of his personal dislike for Tews, he found himself listening, at first grudgingly, then more amenably, to his wife.

"Remember," she said, again and again, "your dream of bequeathing to the world a unified empire. Surely, you cannot become sentimental about it at the last minute. Lords Jerrin and Draid are still too young. Jerrin, of course, is the most brilliant young man of his generation. He is obviously a future Lord Leader, and should be named so in your will. But not yet. You cannot hand over the solar system to a youngster of twenty-four."

The Lord Leader stirred uneasily. He noticed that there was not a word in her argument about the reason for Tews' exile. And that she was too clever ever to allow into her voice the faintest suggestion that, behind her logic, was the emotional fact that Tews was her son.

"There are of course," Lydia went on, "the boy's uncles on their mother's side, both amiable administrators but lacking in will. And then there are your daughters and sons-in-law, and their children, and your nieces and nephews."

"Forget them." The Lord Leader, gaunt and intent on the pillow, moved a hand weakly in dismissal of the suggestion. He was not interested in the second-raters. "You have forgotten," he said finally, "Clane."

"A mutation!" said Lydia, surprised. "Are you serious?"

The lord of Linn was silent. He knew better, of course. Mutations were despised, hated, and, paradoxically, feared. No normal person would ever accept their domination. The suggestion was actually meaningless. But he knew why he had made it. Delay. He realized he was being pushed inexorably to choosing as his heir Lydia's plumpish son by her first husband.

"If you considered your own blood only," urged Lydia, "it would be just another case of imperial succession so common among our tributary monarchies and among the barbarians of Aiszh and Venus and Mars. Politically it would be meaningless. If, however, you strike across party lines, your action will speak for your supreme patriotism. In no other way could you so finally and unanswerably convince the world that you have only its interest at heart."

The old scoundrel, dimmed though his spirit and intellect were by illness and age, was not quite so simple as that. He knew what they were saying under the pillars, that Lydia was molding him like a piece of putty to her plans.

Not that such opinions disturbed him very much. The tireless propaganda of his enemies and of mischief makers and gossips had dinned into his ears for nearly fifty years, and he had become immune to the chatter.

In the end the decisive factor was only partly Lydia's arguments, only partly his own desperate realization that he had little choice. The unexpected factor was a visit to his bedside by the younger of his two daughters by his first marriage. She asked that he grant her a divorce from her present husband, and permit her to marry the exiled Tews.

"I have always," she said, "been in love with Tews, and only Tews, and I am willing to join him in exile."

The prospect was so dazzling that, for once, the old man was completely fooled. It did not even occur to him that Lydia had spent two days convincing the cautious Gudrun that here was her only chance of becoming first lady of Linn.

"Otherwise," Lydia had pointed out, "you'll be just another relative, dependent upon the whim of the reigning Lady Leader."

The Linn of Linn suspected absolutely nothing of that behind-the-scenes connivance. His daughter married to Lord Tews. The possibilities warmed his chilling blood. She was too old, of course, to have any more children, but she would serve Tews as Lydia had him, a perfect foil, a perfect representation of his own political group. *His* daughter!

I must, he thought, *go and see what Clane thinks. Meanwhile I can send for Tews on a tentative basis.*

He didn't say that out loud. No one in the family except himself realized the enormous extent of the knowledge that the long-dead temple scientist Joquin had bequeathed to Clane. The Lord Leader preferred to keep the information in his own mind. He knew Lydia's propensity for hiring assassins, and it wouldn't do to subject Clane to more than ordinary danger from that source.

He regarded the mutation as an unsuspected stabilizing force during the chaos that might follow his death. He wrote the letter inviting Tews to return to Linn, and, a week later, finally out of bed, had himself carried to Clane's residence in the west suburbs. He remained overnight, and, returning the next day, began to discharge a score of key men whom Lydia had slipped into administrative positions on occasions when he was too weary to know what the urgent business was for which he was signing papers.

Lydia said nothing, but she noted the sequence of events. A visit to Clane, then action against her men. She pondered that for some days, and then, the day before Tews was due, she paid her first visit to the modest looking home of Lord Clane Linn, taking care that she was not expected. She had heard vague accounts of the estate.

The reality surpassed anything she had ever imagined or heard.

❖ ❖ ❖

For seven years, Tews had lived in Awai in the Great Sea. He had a small property on the largest island of the group, and, after his disgrace, his mother had suggested that he retire there rather than to one of his more sumptuous mainland estates. A shrewd, careful man, he recognized the value of the advice. His role, if he hoped to remain alive, must be sackcloth and ashes.

At first it was purposeful cunning. In Linn, Lydia wracked her brains for explanations and finally came out with the statement that her son had wearied and sickened of politics, and retired to a life of meditation beyond the poisoned waters. For a long time, so plausible and convincing was her sighing, tired way of describing his feelings—as if she, too, longed for the surcease of rest from the duties of her position—that the story was actually believed. Patrons, governors and ambassadors, flying out in spaceships from Linn to the continents across the ocean, paused as a matter of course to pay their respects to the son of Lydia.

Gradually, they began to catch on that he was out of favor. Desperately, terribly dangerously out of favor. The stiff-faced silence of the Lord Leader when Tews was mentioned was reported finally among administrators and politicians everywhere. People were tremendously astute, once they realized. It was recalled that Tews had hastily departed from Linn at the time when the news of the death of General Lord Creg, son of the Lord Leader, was first brought from Mars. At the time his departure had scarcely been remarked. Now it was remembered and conclusions drawn. Great ships, carrying high government officials, ceased to stop, so that the officials could float down for lunch with Lord Tews. But that was the least important aspect. The deadly danger was that some zealous and ambitious individual knight might seek to gain the favor of Linn of Linn by murdering his stepson.

Lydia herself nipped several such plots in the bud. But each conspiracy was such a visible strain on her nervous system that the Lord Leader unfroze sufficiently to bestow on Tews a secondary military position on Awai. It was actually an insulting offer, but the panic-stricken Lydia persuaded Tews to accept it as a means of preserving his life until she could do more for him. The position, and the power that went with it, arrived just in time.

He had formed a habit of attending lectures at the University of Awai. One day, a term having expired, and a new one scheduled to begin, he made the customary application for renewal. The professor in charge took the opportunity during the first lecture of the first semester of the new term—the first lecture was free and open to the public—to inform him before the entire audience that, since the lists were full, his application was being rejected, and would have to be put over until the following year, when, of course, it would be considered again "on its merits."

It was the act of a neurotic fool. But Tews would have let it pass for the time being if the audience, recognizing a fallen giant, had not started catcalling and threatening. The uproar grew with the minutes, and, experienced leader of men that he was, Tews realized that a mob mood was building up, which must be smashed if he hoped to continue living in safety on the island. He climbed to his feet, and, since most of the audience was standing on seats and benches he managed to reach the outside before the yelling individuals who saw him were able to attract the attention of the yelling crowd that didn't.

Tews went straight to the outdoor restaurant where his new guard was waiting. It was a rowdy crew, but recently arrived from Linn, and with enough basic discipline to follow him back into the lecture room. There was a pause in the confusion when the glinting line of spears wedged towards the platform. In a minute, before an abruptly subdued audience, the startled professor was being stripped and tied to a chair. The twenty-five lashes that he received then ended for good the outburst of hatred against Tews.

He returned to his villa that afternoon, and made no further effort to participate in the activities of the community. The isolation affected him profoundly. He became tremendously observant. He noticed in amazement for the first time that the islanders swam at night in the ocean. Swam! In water that had been poisoned since legendary times by the atom gods. Was it possible the water was no longer deadly? He noted the point for possible future reference, and for the first time grew interested in the name the islanders had for the great ocean. Passfic. Continental people had moved inland to escape the fumes of the deadly seas, and they had forgotten the ancient names.

❖ ❖ ❖

During the long months of aloneness that followed his retreat to his villa, Tews' mind dwelt many times critically upon his life in Linn. He began to see the madness of it, and the endless skullduggery. He read with more and more amazement the letters of his mother, outlining what she was doing. It was a tale of endless cunnings, conspiracies and murders, written in a simple code that was effective because it was based on words the extra-original meanings of which were known only to his mother and himself.

His amazement became disgust, and disgust grew into the first comprehension of the greatness of his stepfather, the Lord Leader.

But he's wrong, Tews thought intently. *The way to a unified empire is not through a continuation of absolute power for one man. The old republic never had a chance, since the factions came up from the days of the two-king system. But now, after decades of virtual non-party patriotism under my honorable stepfather, it should be possible to restore the republic with the very good possibility that this time it will work. That must be my task if I can ever return to Linn.*

The messenger from the Lord Leader inviting his return arrived on the same ship as another letter from his mother. Hers sounded as if it had been written in breathless haste, but it contained an explanation of how his recall had been accomplished. The price shocked Tews.

What, he thought, *marry Gudrun!*

It took an hour for his nerves to calm sufficiently for him even to consider the proposition. His plan, it seemed to him finally, was too important to be allowed to fail because of his distaste for a woman whose interest in men ran not so much to quality as quantity. And it wasn't as if he was bound to another woman. His wife, seven years before, on discovering that his departure from Linn might be permanent, hastily persuaded her father to declare them divorced.

Yes, he was free to marry.

❖❖❖

Lydia, on the way to the home of her stepgrandson, pondered her situation. She was not satisfied. A dozen of her schemes were coming to a head; and here she was going to see Lord Clane, a completely unknown factor. Thinking about it from that viewpoint, she felt astonished. What possible danger, she asked herself again and again, could a mutation be to her?

Even as those thoughts infuriated the surface of her mind, deep inside she knew better. There was something here. *Something.* The old man would never bother with a nonentity. He was either quiet with the quietness of weariness, or utterly impatient. Young people particularly enraged him easily, and if Clane was an exception, then there was a reason.

From a distance, Clane's residence looked small. There was brush in the foreground, and a solid wall of trees across the entire eight-hundred-foot front of the estate. The house peaked a few feet above a mantle of pines and evergreens. As her chair drew nearer it, Lydia decided it was a three-story building, which was certainly minuscule beside the palaces of the other Linns. Her bearers puffed up a hill, trotted past a pleasant arbor of trees, and came after a little to a low, massive fence that had not been visible from below. Lydia, always alert for military obstacles, had her chair put down. She climbed out, conscious that a cool, sweet breeze was blowing where, a moment before, had been only the dead heat of a stifling summer day. The air was rich with the perfume of trees and green things.

She walked slowly along the fence, noting that it was skillfully hidden from the street below by an unbroken hedge, although it showed through at this close range. She recognized the material as similar to that of which the temples of the scientists was constructed, only there was no visible lead lining. She estimated the height of the fence at three feet, and its thickness about three and a half. It was fat and squat and defensively useless.

When I was young, she thought, *I could have jumped over it myself.*

She returned to the chair, annoyed because she couldn't fathom its purpose, and yet couldn't quite believe it had no purpose. It was even more disconcerting to discover a hundred feet farther along the walk that the gate was not a closure but an opening in the wall, and that there was no guard in sight. In a minute more, the bearers had carried her inside, through a tunnel of interwoven shrubs shadowed by towering trees, and then to an open lawn. That was where the real surprise began.

"Stop!" said the Lady Leader Lydia.

An enormous combination meadow and garden spread from the edge of the trees. She had an eye for size, and, without consciously thinking about it, she guessed that fifteen acres were visible from her vantage point. A gracious stream meandered diagonally across the meadow. Along its banks scores of guest homes had been built, low, sleek, be-windowed structures, each with its overhanging shade trees. The house, a square-built affair, towered to her right. At the far end of the grounds were five spaceships neatly laid out side by side. And everywhere were people. Men and women singly and in groups, sitting in chairs, walking, working, reading, writing, drawing and painting. Thoughtfully, Lydia walked over to a painter, who sat with his easel and palette a scant dozen yards from her. He was painting the scene before him, and he paid no attention to her. She was not accustomed to being ignored. She said sharply:

"What is all this?" She waved one arm to take in the activities of the estate. "What is going on here?"

The young man shrugged. He dabbed thoughtfully at the scene he was painting, then, still without looking up, said:

"Here, madam, you have the center of Linn. Here the thought and opinion of the empire is created and cast into molds for public consumption. Ideas born here, once they are spread among the masses, become the mores of the nation and the solar system. To be invited here is an unequaled honor, for it means that your work as a scholar or artist has received the ultimate recognition that power and money can give. Madam, whoever you are, I welcome you to the intellectual center of the world. You would not be here if you had not some unsurpassed achievement to your credit. However, I beg of you, please do not tell me what it is until this evening when I shall be happy to lend you both my ears. And now, old and successful woman, good day to you."

Lydia withdrew thoughtfully. Her impulse, to have the young man stripped and lashed, yielded before a sudden desire to remain incognito as long as possible while she explored this unsuspected outdoor salon.

It was a universe of strangers. Not once did she see a face she recognized. These people, whatever their achievements, were not the publicized great men of the empire. She saw no patrons and only one man with the insignia of a knight on his coat. And when she approached him, she recognized from the alien religious symbol connected with the other markings, that his knighthood was of provincial origin.

He was standing beside a fountain near a cluster of guest homes. The fountain spewed forth a skillfully blended mixture of water and smoke. It made a pretty show, the smoke rising up in thin, steamlike clouds. As she paused beside the fountain there was a cessation of the cooling breeze, and she felt a wave of heat that reminded her of steaming hot lower town. Lydia concentrated on the man and on her desire for information.

"I'm new here," she said engagingly. "Has this center been long in existence?"

"About three years, madam. After all, our young prince is only twenty-four!"

"Prince?" asked Lydia.

The knight, a rugged faced individual of forty, was apologetic.

"I beg your pardon. It is an old word of my province, signifying a leader of high birth. I discovered on my various journeys into the pits, where the atom gods live, and where once cities existed, that the name was of legendary origin. This is according to old books I found in remnants of buildings."

Lydia said, shocked: "You went down into one of the reputed homes of the gods, where the eternal fires burn?"

The knight chuckled. "Some of them are less eternal than others, I discovered."

"But weren't you afraid of being physically damaged?"

"Madam," shrugged the other, "I am nearly fifty years old. Why should I worry if my blood is slightly damaged by the aura of the gods?"

Lydia hesitated, interested. But she had let herself be drawn from her purpose. "Prince," she repeated now, grimly. Applied to Clane, the title had a ring she didn't like. Prince Clane. It was rather stunning to discover that there were men who thought of him as a leader. What had happened to the old prejudices against mutations? She was about to speak again when, for the first time, she actually looked at the fountain.

She pulled back with a gasp. The water was bubbling. A mist of steam arose from it. Her gaze shot up to the spout, and now she saw that it was not smoke and water spewing up from it. It was boiling, steaming water. Water that roiled and rushed and roared. More hot water than she had ever seen from an artificial source. Memory came of the blackened pots in which slaves heated her daily hot water needs. And she felt a spurt of pure jealousy at the extravagant luxury of a fountain of boiling water on one's grounds.

"But how does he do it?" she gasped. "Has he tapped an underground hot spring?"

"No, madam, the water comes from the stream over there." The knight pointed. "It is brought here in tiled pipes, and then runs off into the various guest homes."

"Is there some arrangement of hot coals?"

"Nothing, madam." The knight was beginning to enjoy himself visibly. "There is an opening under the fountain, and you can look in if you wish."

Lydia wished. She was fascinated. She realized that she had let herself be distracted, but for the moment that was of secondary importance. She watched with bright eyes as the knight opened the little door in the cement, and then she stooped beside him to peer in. It took several seconds to become accustomed to the dim light inside, but finally she was able to make out the massive base of the spout, and then the six-inch pipe that ran into it. Lydia straightened slowly. The man shut the door matter-of-factly. As he turned, she asked:

"But how does it work?"

The knight shrugged. "Some say that the water gods of Mars have been friendly to him ever since they helped his late father to win the war against the Martians. You will recall that the canal waters boiled in a frightful fury, thus confusing the Martians as they were attacked. And then, again, others say that it is the atom gods helping their favorite mutation."

"Oh!" said Lydia. This was the kind of talk she could understand. She had never in her life worried about what the gods might think of her actions. And she was not going to start now. She straightened and glared imperiously at the man.

"Don't be such a fool," she said. "A man who has dared to penetrate the homes of the gods should have more sense than to repeat old wives' tales like that."

The man gaped. She turned away before he could speak, and marched off to her chair. "To the house!" she commanded her slaves.

They had her at the front entrance of the residence before it struck her that she had not learned the tremendous and precious secret of the boiling fountain.

❖ ❖ ❖

She caught Clane by surprise. She entered the house in her flamboyant manner, and by the time a slave saw her, and ran to his master's laboratory to bring the news of her coming, it was too late. She loomed in the doorway, as Clane turned from a corpse he was dissecting. To her immense disappointment he did not freeze up in one of his emotional spasms. She had expected it, and her plan was to look over the laboratory quietly and without interference.

But Clane came towards her. "Honorable grandmother," he said. And knelt to kiss her hand. He came up with an easy grace. "I hope," he said with an apparent eagerness, "that you will have the time and inclination to see my home and my work. Both have interesting features."

His whole manner was so human, so engaging, that she was disconcerted anew, not an easy emotion for her to experience. She shook off the weakness impatiently. Her first words affirmed her purpose in visiting him:

"Yes," she said, "I shall be happy to see your home. I have been intending for some years to visit you, but I have been so busy." She sighed. "The duties of statecraft can be very onerous."

The beautiful face looked properly sympathetic. A delicate hand pointed at the dead body, which those slim fingers had been working over. The soft voice informed that the purpose of the dissection was to discover the position pattern of the organs and muscles and bones.

"I have cut open dead mutations," Clane said, "and compared them with normal bodies."

Lydia could not quite follow the purpose. After all, each mutation was different, depending upon the way the god forces had affected them. She said as much. The glowing blue eyes of the mutation looked at her speculatively.

"It is commonly known," he said, "that mutations seldom live beyond the age of thirty. Naturally," he went on, with a faint smile, "since I am now within six years of that milestone, the possibility weighs upon me. Joquin, that astute old scientist, who unfortunately is now dead, believed that the deaths resulted from inner tensions, due to the manner in which mutations were treated by their fellows. He felt that if those tensions could be removed, as they have been to some extent in me, a normal span of life would follow as also would

normal intelligence. I'd better correct that. He believed that a mutation, given a chance, would be able to realize his normal *potentialities*, which might be either super- or sub-normal compared to
human beings."

Clane smiled. "So far," he said, "I have noticed nothing out of the
ordinary in myself."

Lydia thought of the boiling fountain, and felt a chill. *That old
fool, Joquin,* she thought in a cold fury. *Why didn't I pay more
attention to what he was doing? He's created an alien mind in our
midst within striking distance of the top of the power group of the
empire.*

The sense of immense disaster possibilities grew. *Death,* she
thought, *within hours after the old man is gone. No risks can be taken
with this creature.*

Suddenly, she was interested in nothing but the accessibility of
the various rooms of the house to assassins. Clane seemed to realize
her mood, for after a brief tour of the laboratory, of which she
remembered little, he began the journey from room to room. Now,
her eyes and attention sharpened. She peered into doors, examined
window arrangements, and did not fail to note with satisfaction the
universal carpeting of the floors. Meerl would be able to attack without warning sounds.

"And your bedroom?" she asked finally.

"We're coming to it," said Clane. "It's downstairs, adjoining the
laboratory. There's something else in the lab that I want to show you.
I wasn't sure at first that I would, but now"—his smile was angelic—
"I will."

❖❖❖

The corridor that led from the living room to the bedroom was
almost wide enough to be an anteroom. The walls were hung with
drapes from floor to ceiling, which was odd. Lydia, who had no inhi-
bitions, lifted one drape, and peered under it. The wall was vaguely
warm, like an ember, and it was built of temple stone. She looked at
Clane questioningly.

"I have some god metals in the house. Naturally, I am taking no
chances. There's another corridor leading from the laboratory to the
bedroom."

What interested Lydia was that neither door of the bedroom had either a lock or a bolt on it. She thought about that tensely, as she followed Clane through the anteroom that led to the laboratory. He wouldn't, it seemed to her, leave himself so unprotected forever.

The assassins must strike before he grew alarmed, the sooner the better. Regretfully, she decided it would have to wait until Tews was confirmed as heir to the throne. She grew aware that Clane had paused beside a dark box.

"Gelo Greeant," he said, "brought this to me from one of his journeys into the realms of the gods. I'm going to step inside, and you go around to the right there, and look into the dark glass. You will be amazed."

Lydia obeyed, puzzled. For a moment, after Clane had disappeared inside, the glass remained dark. Then it began to glow faintly. She retreated a step before that alien shiningness, then, remembering who she was, stood her ground. And then she screamed.

A skeleton glowed through the glass. And the shadow of a beating heart, the shadow of expanding and contracting lungs. As she watched, petrified now, the skeleton arm moved, and seemed to come towards her, but drew back again. To her paralyzed brain came at last comprehension.

She was looking at the inside of a living human being. At Clane. Abruptly, that interested her. *Clane.* Like lightning, her eyes examined his bone structure. She noticed the cluster of ribs around his heart and lungs, the special thickness of his collar bones. Her gaze flashed down towards his kidneys, but this time she was too slow. The light faded, and went out. Clane emerged from the box.

"Well," he asked, pleased, "what do you think of my little gift from the gods?"

The phraseology startled Lydia. All the way home, she thought of it. Gift from the gods! In a sense it was. The atom gods had sent their mutation a method for seeing himself, for studying his own body. What could *their* purpose be?

She had a conviction that, if the gods really existed, and if, as seemed evident, they were helping Clane, then the Deities of the Atom were again—as they had in legendary times—interfering with human affairs.

The sinking sensation that came had only one hopeful rhythm. And that was like a drumbeat inside her: Kill! And soon. *Soon!*

But the days passed. And the demands of political stability absorbed all her attention. Nevertheless, in the midst of a score of new troubles, she did not forget Clane.

The return of Tews was a triumph for his mother's diplomacy and a great moment for himself. His ship came down in the square of the pillars, and there, before an immense cheering throng, he was welcomed by the Lord Leader and the entire patronate. The parade that followed was led by a unit of five thousand glitteringly arrayed horse-mounted troops, followed by ten thousand foot soldiers, one thousand engineers and scores of mechanical engines for throwing weights and rocks at defensive barriers. Then came the Lord Leader, Lydia and Tews, and the three hundred patrons and six hundred knights of the empire. The rear of the parade was brought up by another cavalry unit of five thousand men.

From the rostrum that jutted out from the palace, the Lord Leader, his lion's voice undimmed by age, welcomed his stepson. All the lies that had ever been told about the reason for Tews' exile were coolly and grandly confirmed now. He had gone away to meditate. He had wearied of the cunnings and artifices of government. He had returned only after repeated pleadings on the part of his mother and of the Lord Leader.

"As you know," concluded the Lord Leader, "seven years ago, I was bereft of my natural heir in the moment of the greatest military triumph the empire has ever experienced, the conquest of the Martians. Today, as I stand before you, no longer young, no longer able to bear the full weight of either military or political command, it is an immeasurable relief to me to be able to tell the people with confidence and conviction: Here in this modest and unassuming member of my family, the son of my dear wife, Lydia, I ask you to put your trust. To the soldiers I say, this is no weakling. Remember the Cimbri, conquered under his skillful generalship when he was but a youth of twenty-five. Particularly, I direct my words to the hard-pressed soldiers on Venus, where false leaders have misled the island provinces of the fierce Venusian tribes to an ill-fated rebellion.

Ill-fated, I say, because as soon as possible Tews will be there with the largest army assembled by the empire since the war of the Martians. I am going to venture a prediction. I am going to predict that within two years the Venusian leaders will be hanging on long lines of posts of the type they are now using to murder prisoners. I predict that these hangings will be achieved by *Co-Lord Leader* General Tews, whom I now publicly appoint my heir and successor, and on whose behalf I now say, Take warning, all those who would have ill befall the empire. Here is the man who will confound you and your schemes."

The dazzled Tews, who had been advised by his mother to the extent of the victory she had won for him, stepped forward to acknowledge the cheers and to say a few words. "Not too much," his mother had warned him. "Be noncommittal." But Lord Tews had other plans. He had carefully thought out the pattern of his future actions, and he had one announcement to make, in addition to a ringing acceptance of the military leadership that had been offered him, and a promise that the Venusian leaders would indeed suffer the fate which the Linn of Linn had promised them, the announcement had to do with the title of Co-Lord Leader, which had been bestowed on him.

"I am sure," he told the crowd, "that you will agree with me that the title of Lord Leader belongs uniquely to the first and greatest man of Linn. I therefore request, and will hold it mandatory upon government leaders, that I be addressed as Lord Adviser. It shall be my pleasure to act as adviser to both the Lord Leader and to the patronate, and it is in this role that I wish to be known henceforth to the people of the mighty Linnan empire. Thank you for listening to me, and I now advise you that there will be games for three days in the bowls, and that free food will be served throughout the city during that time at my expense. Go and have a good time, and may the gods of the atoms bring you all good luck."

❖❖❖

During the first minute after he had finished, Lydia was appalled. Was Tews mad to have refused the title of Lord Leader? The joyful yelping of the mob soothed her a little, and then, slowly, as she followed Tews and the old man along the promenade that led from the rostrum to the palace gates, she began to realize the cleverness of the new title. Lord Adviser. Why, it would be a veritable shield against the charges of those who were always striving to rouse the people against the absolute government of the Linns. It was clear that the long exile had sharpened rather than dulled the mind of her son.

The Lord Leader, too, as the days passed, and the new character of Tews came to the fore, was having regrets. Certain restrictions, which he had imposed upon his stepson during his residence on Awai, seemed unduly severe and ill-advised in retrospect. He should not, for instance, have permitted Tews' wife to divorce him, but should instead have insisted that she accompany him.

It seemed to him now that there was only one solution. He rushed the marriage between Tews and Gudrun, and then dispatched them to Venus on their honeymoon, taking the precaution of sending a quarter of a million men along, so that the future Lord Leader could combine his love-making with war-making.

Having solved his main troubles, the Lord Leader gave himself up to the chore of aging gracefully and of thinking out ways and means whereby his other heirs might be spared from the death which the thoughtful Lydia was undoubtedly planning for them.

The Lord Leader was dying. He lay in his bed of pillows sweating out his last hours. All the wiles of the palace physician—including an ice-cold bath, a favorite remedy of his, failed to rally the stricken great man. In a few hours, the patronate was informed, and state leaders were invited to officiate at the death bed. The Linn of Linn had some years before introduced a law to the effect that no ruler was ever to be allowed to die incommunicado. It was a thoughtful precaution against poisoning, which he had considered extremely astute at the time, but which now, as he watched the crowd surging outside the open doors of his bedroom, and listened to the subdued roar of voices, seemed somewhat less than dignified.

He motioned to Lydia. She came gliding over, and nodded at his request that the door be closed. Some of the people in the bedroom looked at each other, as she shooed them away, but the mild voice of the Lord Leader urged them, and so they trooped out. It took about ten minutes to clear the room. The Lord Leader lay, then, looking sadly up at his wife. He had an unpleasant duty to perform, and the unfortunate atmosphere of imminent death made the affair not less but more sordid. He began without preliminary:

"In recent years I have frequently hinted to you about fears I have had about the health of my relatives. Your reactions have left me no recourse but to doubt that you now have left in your heart any of the tender feelings which are supposed to be the common possession of womankind."

"What's this?" said Lydia. She had her first flash of insight as to what was coming. She said grimly, "My dear husband, have you gone out of your head?"

The Lord Leader went on calmly: "For once, Lydia, I am not going to speak in diplomatic language. Do not go through with your plans to have my relatives assassinated as soon as I am dead."

The language was too strong for the woman. The color deserted her cheeks, and she was suddenly as pale as lead. "I," she breathed, "kill your kin!"

The once steel-gray, now watery eyes stared at her with remorseless purpose. "I have put Jerrin and Draid beyond your reach. They are in command of powerful armies, and my will leaves explicit instructions about their future. Some of the men, who are administrators, are likewise protected to some extent. The women are not so fortunate. My own two daughters are safe, I think. The elder is childless and without ambition, and Gudrun is now the wife of Tews. But I want a promise from you that you will not attempt to harm her, and that you will similarly refrain from taking any action against her three children, by her first marriage. I want your promise to include the children of my two cousins, my brother and sister, and all their descendants, and finally I want a promise from you about the Lady Tania, her two daughters, and her son, Lord Clane."

"Clane!" said Lydia. Her mind had started working as he talked. It leaped past the immense insult she was being offered, past all the names, to that one individual. She spoke the name again, more loudly "*Clane!*"

Her eyes were distorted pools. She glared at her husband with a bitter intensity. "And what," she said, "makes you think, who suspect me capable of such crimes, that I would keep such a promise to a dead man?"

The old man was suddenly less bleak. "Because, Lydia," he said quietly, "you are more than just a mother protecting her young. You are the Lady Leader whose political sagacity and general intelligence made possible the virtually united empire, which Tews will now inherit. You are at heart an honest woman, and if you made me a promise I think you would keep it."

She knew he was merely hoping now. And her calmness came back. She watched him with bright eyes, conscious of how weak was the power of a dying man, no matter how desperately he strove to fasten his desires and wishes upon his descendants.

"Very well, my old darling," she soothed him, "I will make you the promise you wish. I guarantee not to murder any of these people you have mentioned."

❖ ❖ ❖

The Lord Leader gazed at her in despair. He had, he realized, not remotely touched her. This woman's basic integrity—and he knew it was there—could no longer be reached through her emotions. He abandoned that line immediately.

"Lydia," he said, "don't anger Clane by trying to kill him."

"Anger him!" said Lydia. She spoke sharply, because the phrase was so unexpected. She gazed at her husband with a startled wonder, as if she couldn't be quite sure that she had heard him correctly. She repeated the words slowly, listening to them as if she somehow might catch their secret meaning: "Anger him?"

"You must realize," said the Lord Leader, "that you have from fifteen to twenty years of life to endure after my death, provided you hoard your physical energies. If you spend those years trying to run the world through Tews, you will quickly and quite properly be discarded by him. That is something which is not yet clear to you, and so I advise you to reorientate yourself. You must seek your power through other men. Jerrin will not need you, and Draid needs only Jerrin. Tews can and will dispense with you. That leaves Clane, of the great men. He can use you. Through him, therefore, you will be able to retain a measure of your power."

Her gaze was on his mouth every moment that he talked. She listened as his voice grew weaker, and finally trailed into nothingness. In the silence that fell between them, Lydia sat comprehending at last, so it seemed to her. This was Clane talking through his dying grandfather. This was Clane's cunning appeal to the fears she might have for her own future. The Clane who had frustrated her designs on the slave girl, Selk, was now desperately striving to anticipate her designs on him.

Deep inside her, as she sat there watching the old man die, she laughed. Three months before, recognizing the signals of internal disintegration in her husband, she had insisted that Tews be recalled from Venus, and Jerrin appointed in his place. Her skill in timing was now bearing fruit, and it was working out even better than she had hoped. It would be at least a week before Tews' spaceship would arrive at Linn. During that week the widow Lydia would be all-powerful.

It was possible that she would have to abandon her plans against some of the other members of the family. But they at least were human. It was Clane, the alien, the creature, the nonhuman, who must be destroyed at any cost.

She had one week in which she could, if necessary, use three whole legions and a hundred spaceships to smash him and the gods that had made him.

The long, tense conversation had dimmed the spark of life in the Lord Leader. Ten minutes before sunset, the great throngs outside saw the gates open, and Lydia leaning on the arms of two old patrons came dragging out, followed by a crowd of noblemen. In a moment it was general knowledge that the Linn of Linn was dead.

Darkness settled over a city that for fifty years had known no other ruler.

❖❖❖

Lydia wakened lazily on the morrow of the death of the Lord Leader. She stretched and yawned deliciously, reveling in the cool, clean sheets. Then she opened her eyes, and stared at the ceiling. Bright sunlight was pouring through open windows, and Dalat hovered at the end of the bed.

"You asked to be wakened early, honorable lady," she said.

There was a note of respect in her voice that Lydia had never noticed before. Her mind poised, pondering the imponderable difference. And then she got it. The Linn was dead. For one week, she was not the legal but the *de facto* head of the city and state. None would dare to oppose the mother of the new Leader—uh, the Lord Adviser Tews. Glowing, Lydia sat up in the bed.

"Has there been any word yet from Meerl?"

"None, gracious lady."

She frowned over that. Her assassin had formed a relationship with her, which she had first accepted reluctantly, then, recognizing its value, with smiling grace. He had access to her bedroom at all hours of the day or night. And it was rather surprising that he to whom she had entrusted such an important errand, should not have reported long since.

Dalat was speaking again. "I think, madam, you should inform him, however, that it is unwise for him to have parcels delivered here addressed to himself in your care."

Lydia was climbing out of bed. She looked up, astounded and angry.

"Why, the insolent fool, has he done that? Let me see the parcel."

She tore off the wrapping, furiously. And found herself staring down at a vase filled with ashes. A note was tied around the lip of the vase. Puzzled, she turned it over and read:

❖ ❖ ❖

Dear Madam:

Your assassin was too moist. The atom gods, once roused, become frantic in the presence of moisture.

Signed, Uranium
For the council of gods.

❖ ❖ ❖

CRASH! The sound of the vase smashing on the floor shocked her out of a blur of numbness. Wide-eyed, she stared down at the little pile of ashes amid the broken pieces of pottery. With tense fingers she reached down, and picked up the note. This time, not the meaning of the note, but the signature, snatched at her attention: *Uranium.*

It was like a dash of cold water. With bleak eyes, she gazed at the ashes of what had been Meerl, her most trustworthy assassin. She realized consciously that she felt this death more keenly than that of her husband. The old man had hung on too long. So long as life continued in his bones, he had the power to make changes. When he had finally breathed his last, she had breathed easily for the first time in years, as if a weight had lifted from her soul.

But now—a new weight began to settle in its place, and her breath came in quick gasps. She kicked viciously at the ashes, as if she would shove the meaning of them out of her life. How could Meerl have failed? Meerl, the cautious, the skillful, Meerl the bold and brave and daring!

"Dalat!"

"Yes, Lady?"

With narrowed eyes and pursed lips, Lydia considered the action she was contemplating. But not for long.

"Call Colonel Maljan. Tell him to come at once."

She had one week to kill a man. It was time to come out into the open.

❖ ❖ ❖

Lydia had herself carried to the foot of the hill that led up to the estate of Lord Clane. She wore a heavy veil and used as carriers slaves who had never appeared with her in public, and an old, unmarked chair of one of her ladies in waiting. Her eyes, that peered out of this excellent disguise, were bright with excitement.

The morning was unnaturally hot. Blasts of warm air came sweeping down the hill from the direction of Clane's house. And, after a little, she saw that the soldiers one hundred yards up the hill, had stopped. The pause grew long and puzzling, and she was just about to climb out of the chair, when she saw Maljan coming towards her. The dark-eyed, hawk-nosed officer was sweating visibly.

"Madam," he said, "we cannot get near that fence up there. It seems to be on fire."

"I can see no flame." Curtly.

"It isn't that kind of fire."

Lydia was amazed to see that the man was trembling with fright. "There's something unnatural up there," he said. "I don't like it."

She came out of her chair then, the chill of defeat settling upon her. "Are you an idiot?" she snarled. "If you can't get past the fence, drop men from spaceships into the grounds."

"I've already sent for them," he said, "but—"

"BUT!" said Lydia, and it was a curse. "I'll go up and have a look at that fence myself."

She went up, and stopped short where the soldiers were gasping on the ground. The heat had already blasted at her, but at that point it took her breath away. She felt as if her lungs would sear inside her. In a minute her throat was ash dry.

She stooped behind a bush. But it was no good. She saw that the leaves had seared and darkened. And then she was retreating behind a little knoblike depression in the hill. She crouched behind it, too appalled to think. She grew aware of Maljan working up towards her. He arrived, gasping, and it was several seconds before he could speak. Then he pointed up.

"The ships!" he said.

She watched them creep in low over the trees. They listed a little as they crossed the fence, then sank out of sight behind the trees that hid the meadow of Clane's estate. Five ships in all came into sight and disappeared over the rim of the estate. Lydia was keenly aware that their arrival relieved the soldiers sprawling helplessly all around her.

"Tell the men to get down the hill," she commanded hoarsely, and made the hastiest retreat of all.

The street below was still almost deserted. A few people had paused to watch in a puzzled fashion the activities of the soldiers, but they moved on when commanded to do so by guards who had been posted in the road.

It was something to know that the campaign was still a private affair.

❖ ❖ ❖

She waited. No sound came from beyond the trees where the ships had gone. It was as if they had fallen over some precipice into an abyss of silence. Half an hour went by, and then, abruptly, a ship came into sight. Lydia caught her breath, then watched the machine float towards them over the trees, and settle in the road below. A man in uniform came out. Maljan waved at him, and ran over to meet him. The conversation that followed was very earnest. At last Maljan turned, and with evident reluctance came towards her. He said in a low tone:

"The house itself is offering an impregnable heat barrier. But they have talked to Lord Clane. He wants to speak to you."

She took that with a tense thoughtfulness. The realization had already penetrated deep that this stalemate might go on for days.

If I could get near him, she decided, remorselessly, *by pretending to consider his proposals—*

It seemed to work perfectly. By the time the spaceship lifted her over the fence, the heat that exuded from the walls of the house had died away to a bearable temperature. And, incredibly, Clane agreed that she could bring a dozen soldiers into the house as guards.

As she entered the house, she had her first sense of eeriness. There was no one around, not a slave, not a movement of life. She headed in the direction of the bedroom, more slowly with each step. The first grudging admiration came. It seemed unbelievable that his preparations could have been so thorough as to include the evacuation of all his slaves. And yet it all fitted. Not once in her dealings with him had he made a mistake.

"Grandmother, I wouldn't come any closer."

She stopped short. She saw that she had come to within a yard of the corridor that led to his bedroom. Clane was standing at the far end, and he seemed to be quite alone and undefended.

"Come any nearer," he said, "and death will strike you automatically."

She could see nothing unusual. The corridor was much as she remembered it. The drapes had been taken down from the walls, revealing the temple stone underneath. And yet, standing there, she felt a faint warmth, unnatural and, suddenly, deadly. It was only with an effort that she threw off the feeling. She parted her lips to give the command, but Clane spoke first:

"Grandmother, do nothing rash. Consider, before you defy the powers of the atom. Has what happened today not yet penetrated to your intelligence? Surely, you can see that whom the gods love no mortal can harm."

The woman was bleak with her purpose. "You have misquoted the old saying," she said drably. "Whom the gods love die young."

And yet, once more, she hesitated. The stunning thing was that he continued to stand there less than thirty feet away, unarmed, unprotected, a faint smile on his lips. How far he has come, she thought. His nervous affliction, conquered now. And what a marvelously beautiful face, so calm, so confident.

Confident! Could it be that there *were* gods?

Could it be?

"Grandmother, I warn you, make no move. If you must prove that the gods will strike on my behalf, send your soldiers. BUT DO NOT MOVE YOURSELF."

She felt weak, her legs numb. The conviction that was pouring through her, the certainty that he was not bluffing brought a parallel realization that she could not back down. And yet she must.

She recognized that there was insanity in her terrible indecision. And knew, then, that she was not a person who was capable of conscious suicide. Therefore, quit, retreat, accept the reality of rout.

She parted her lips to give the order to retire when it happened.

❖ ❖ ❖

What motive impelled the soldier to action was never clear. Perhaps he grew impatient. Perhaps he felt there would be promotion for him. Whatever the reason, he suddenly cried out, "I'll get his gizzard for you!" And leaped forward.

He had not gone more than a half dozen feet past Lydia when he began to disintegrate. He crumpled like an empty sack. Where he had been, a mist of ashes floated lazily to the floor.

There was one burst of heat, then. It came in a gust of unearthly hot wind, barely touched Lydia, who had instinctively jerked aside, but struck the soldiers behind her. There was a hideous masculine squalling and whimpering, followed by a mad scramble. A door slammed, and she was alone. She straightened, conscious that the air from the corridor was still blowing hot. She remained cautiously where she was, and called:

"Clane!"

The answer came instantly. "Yes, grandmother?"

For a moment, then, she hesitated, experiencing all the agony of a general about to surrender. At last, slowly:

"What do you want?"

"An end to attacks on me. Full political co-operation, but people must remain unaware of it as long as we can possibly manage it."

"Oh!"

She began to breathe easier. She had had a fear that he would demand public recognition.

"And if I don't?" she said at last.

"Death!"

It was quietly spoken. The woman did not even think to doubt. She was being given a chance. But there was one thing more, one tremendous thing more.

"Clane, is your ultimate goal the Lord Leadership?"

"No!"

His answer was too prompt. She felt a thrill of disbelief, a sick conviction that he was lying. But she was glad after a moment that he had denied. In a sense it bound him. Her thoughts soared to all the possibilities of the situation, then came down again to the sober necessity of this instant.

"Very well," she said, and it was little more than a sigh, "I accept."

Back at the palace, she sent an assassin to perform an essential operation against the one outsider who knew the Lady Lydia had suffered a major defeat. It was late afternoon when the double report came in: The exciting information that Tews had landed sooner than anticipated, and was even then on his way to the palace. And the satisfying words that Colonel Maljan lay dead in an alleyway with a knife in one of his kidneys.

It was only then that it struck her that she was now in the exact position that her dead husband had advised for her own safety and well-being.

Tears and the realization of her great loss came as late as that.

Home of the Gods

At first the land below was a shadow seen through mist. As the three spaceships of Lord Clane Linn's expedition settled through the two thousand mile atmosphere, the vagueness went out of the scene. Mountains looking like maps rather than territories took form. The vast sea to the north sank beyond the far horizon of swamps and marshes, hills and forests. The reality grew wilder and wilder, but the pit was directly ahead now, an enormous black hole on a long narrow plain.

The ships settled to the ground on a green meadow half a mile from the nearest edge of the pit, which lay to the northeast. Some six hundred men and women, three hundred of them slaves, emerged from the vessels, and a vast amount of equipment was unloaded. By nightfall habitations had been erected for Clane and the three slave women who attended him, for two knights and for three temple scientists and five scholars not connected with a religious organization. In addition a corral had been built for the slaves, and the two companies of soldiers were encamped in a half circle around the main camp.

Sentries were posted, and the spaceships withdrew to a height of about five hundred feet. All night long, a score of fires, tended by trusted slaves, brightened the darkness. Dawn came uneventfully, and slowly the camp took up the activities of a new day. Clane did not remain to direct it. Immediately after breakfast, horses were saddled; and he and twenty-five men, including a dozen armed soldiers, set out for the nearby home of the gods.

They were all rank unbelievers, but they had proceeded only a few hundred yards when Clane noticed that one of the riders was as pale as lead. He reined up beside him.

"Breakfast upset you?" he asked gently. "Better go back to camp
and rest today."

Most of those who were destined to continue watched the lucky
man trot off out of sight into the brush.

The evenness of the land began to break. Gashes opened in the
earth at their feet, and ran off at a slant towards the pit, which was
still not visible beyond the trees. Straight were those gashes, too
straight; as if long ago irresistible objects had hurtled up out of the
pit each at a different angle, each tearing the intervening earth as it
darted up out of the hell below.

Clane had a theory about the pits. Atomic warfare by an immeasurably superior civilization. Atomic bombs that set up a reaction in
the ground where they landed, and only gradually wore themselves
out in the resisting soil, concrete and steel of vast cities. For centuries
the remnants roiled and flared with deadly activity. How long? No
one knew. He had an idea that if star maps of the period could be
located an estimate of the time gap might be possible. The period
involved must be very great, for several men that he knew had visited pits on Earth without ill effects.

The god fires were dying down. It was time for intellectually bold
men to begin exploring. Those who came first would find the treasures. Most of the pits on Earth were absolutely barren affairs over-
grown with weeds and brush. A few showed structures in their
depths, half buried buildings, tattered walls, mysterious caverns. Into
these a handful of men had ventured—and brought back odd
mechanical creations, some obviously wrecks, a few that actually
worked, all tantalizing in their suggestion of a science marvelous
beyond anything known to the temple scholars.

It was this pit on Venus, which they were now approaching,
that had always excited the imagination of the adventurers. For
years visitors had crouched behind lead or concrete barriers and
peered with periscopes into the fantastic depths below. The nameless city that had been there must have been built into the bowels
of the earth. For the bottom was a mass of concrete embankments, honeycombed with black holes that seemed to lead down
into remoter depths.

Clane's reverie died down. A soldier in front of him let out a shout, reined in his horse and pointed ahead. Clane urged his horse up to the rise on top of which the man had halted. And reined in *his* horse.

He was looking down a gently sloping grassy embankment. It ran along for about a hundred feet. And then there was a low concrete fence.

Beyond was the pit.

At first they were careful. They used the shelter of the fence as a barrier to any radiation that might be coming up from below. Clane was the exception. From the beginning he stood upright, and peered downward through his glasses into the vista of distance below. Slowly, the others lost their caution, and finally all except two artists were standing boldly on their feet gazing into the most famous home of the gods.

It was not a clear morning. A faint mist crawled along hiding most of the bottom of the pit. But it was possible, with the aid of glasses, to make out contours, and to see the far precipice nearly seven miles away.

About midmorning, the mists cleared noticeably, and the great sun of Venus shone down into the hole, picking out every detail not hidden by distance. The artists, who had already sketched the main outlines, settled down to work in earnest. They had been selected for their ability to draw maps, and the watchful Clane saw that they were doing a good job. His own patience, product of his isolated upbringing, was even greater than theirs. All through that day he examined the bottom of the pit with his glasses, and compared the reality with the developing drawings on the drawing boards.

By late afternoon, the job was complete. And the results satisfied every hope he had had. There were no less than three routes for getting out of the pit on foot in case of an emergency. And every tree and cave opening below was clearly marked in its relation to other trees and openings. Lines of shrubs were sketched in, and each map was drawn to scale.

That night, too, passed without incident. The following morning Clane signaled one of the spaceships to come down, and, shortly after breakfast, the two temple scientists, one knight, three artists, a dozen soldiers, a crew of fifteen and himself climbed aboard. The ship floated lightly clear of the ground. And, a few minutes later, nosed over the edge of the pit, and headed downward.

They made no attempt to land, but simply cruised around searching for radioactive areas. Round and round at a height that varied between five hundred feet and a daring two hundred feet. It was daring. The spaceship was their sole instrument for detecting the presence of atomic energy. Long ago, it had been discovered that when a spaceship passed directly above another spaceship, the one that was on top suffered a severe curtailment of its motive power. Immediately it would start to fall.

In the case of spaceships, the two ships would usually be moving along so swiftly that they would be past each other almost immediately. Quickly, then, the disabled ship would right itself and proceed on its way.

Several attempts had been made by military scientists to utilize the method to bring down enemy spaceships. The attempts, however, were strictly limited by the fact that a ship which remained five hundred feet above the source of energy endured so slight a hindrance that it didn't matter.

Nine times their ship made the telltale dip, and then, for as long as was necessary they would cruise over and over the area trying to define its limits, locating it on their maps, marking off first the danger zone, then the twilight zone and finally the safety zone. The final measure was the weakness or strength of the impulse.

The day ended, with that phase of their work still uncompleted. And it was not until noon the next day that details were finally finished. Since it was too late to make a landing, they returned to camp and spent the afternoon sleeping off their accumulated fatigue.

It was decided that the first landing would be made by one hundred men, and that they would take with them supplies for two weeks. The site of the landing was selected by Clane after consultation with the knights and the scientists. From the air it looked like a large concrete structure with roof and walls still intact, but its main feature was that it was located near one of the routes by which the people on foot could leave the pit. And it was surrounded by more than a score of cavelike openings.

❖❖❖

His first impression was of intense silence. Then he stepped out of the ship onto the floor of the pit. And there was a kind of pleasure in listening to the scrambling sounds of the men who followed him. The morning air quickly echoed to the uproar of a hundred men breathing, walking, moving—and unloading supplies.

Less than an hour after he first set foot into the soft soil of the pit, Clane watched the spaceship lift from the ground, and climb rapidly up above five hundred feet. At that safety height it leveled off, and began its watchful cruise back and forth above the explorers.

Once again no hasty moves were made. Tents were set up and a rough defense marked off. The food was sealed off behind a pile of concrete. Shortly before noon, after an early lunch, Clane, one knight, one temple scientist and six soldiers left the encampment and walked towards the "building" which, among other things, had drawn them to the area.

Seen from this near vantage point it was not a building at all, but an upjutment of concrete and metal, a remnant of what had once been a man-made burrow into the depths of the earth, a monument to the futility of seeking safety by mechanical rather than intellectual and moral means. The sight of it depressed Clane. For a millennium it had stood here, first in a seething ocean of unsettled energy, and now amid a great silence it waited for the return of man.

He paused to examine the door, then motioned two soldiers to push at it. They were unable to budge it, and so, waving them aside, he edged gingerly past the rusted door jamb. And was inside.

He found himself in a narrow hallway, which ran along for about eight feet, and then there was another door. A closed door this time. The floor was concrete, the walls and ceiling concrete, but the door ahead was metal. Clane and the knight, a big man with black eyes, shoved it open with scarcely an effort, though it creaked rustily as they did.

They stood there, startled. The interior was not dark as they had expected, but dimly lighted. The luminous glow came from a series of small bulbs in the ceiling. The bulbs were not transparent, but coated with an opaque coppery substance. The light shone through the coating.

Nothing like it had ever been seen in Linn or elsewhere. After a blank period, Clane wondered if the lights had turned on when they opened the door. They discussed it briefly, then shut the door. Nothing happened. They opened the door again, but the lights did not even flicker.

They had obviously been burning for centuries.

❖❖❖

With a genuine effort, he suppressed the impulse to have the treasures taken down immediately and taken to the camp. The deathly silence, the air of immense antiquity brought the sane realization that there was no necessity to act swiftly here. He was first on this scene.

Very slowly, almost reluctantly, he turned his attention from the ceiling to the room itself. A wrecked table stood in one corner. In front of it stood a chair with one leg broken and a single strand of wood where the seat had been. In the adjoining corner was a pile of rubble, including a skull and some vaguely recognizable ribs which merged into a powdery skeleton. The relict of what had once been a human being lay on top of a rather long, all-metal rod. There was nothing else in the room.

Clane strode forward, and eased the rod from under the skeleton. The movement, slight though it was, was too much for the bone structure. The skull and the ribs dissolved into powder, and a faint white mist hovered for a moment, then settled to the floor.

He stepped back gingerly, and, still holding the weapon, passed through the door, and along the narrow hallway, and so out into the open.

❖❖❖

The outside scene was different. He had been gone from it fifteen minutes at most, but in that interval a change had taken place. The spaceship that had brought them was still cruising around overhead. But a second spaceship was in the act of settling down beside the camp.

It squashed down with a crackling of brush and an "harumph!" sound of air squeezing out from the indentation it made in the ground. The door opened, and, as Clane headed for the camp, three men emerged from it. One wore the uniform of an aid-de-camp to supreme headquarters, and it was he who handed Clane a dispatch pouch.

The pouch contained a single letter from his elder brother, Lord Jerrin, commander-in-chief of Linnan armies on Venus. In the will of the late Lord Leader, Jerrin had been designated to become co-ruler with Tews when he attained the age of thirty, his sphere of administration to be the planets. His powers in Linn were to be strictly secondary to those of Tews. His letter was curt:

Honorable brother:

It has come to my attention that you have arrived on Venus. I need hardly point out to you that the presence of a mutation here at this critical period of the war against the rebels is bound to have an adverse effect. I have been told that your request for this trip was personally granted by the Lord Adviser Tews. If you are not aware of the intricate motives that might inspire Tews to grant such permission, then you are not alert to the possible disasters that might befall our branch of the family. It is my wish and command that you return to Earth at once.

As Clane looked up from the letter, he saw that the commander of the spaceship which had brought the messenger, was silently signaling to him. He walked over and drew the captain aside.

"I didn't want to worry you," the man said, "but perhaps I had better inform you that this morning, shortly after your expedition entered the pit, we saw a very large body of men riding along several miles to the northeast of the pit. They have shown no inclination to move in this direction, but they scattered when we swooped over them, which means that they are Venusian rebels."

Clane stood frowning for a moment, then nodded his acceptance of the information. He turned away, into his spacious tent, to write an answer to his brother that would hold off the crisis between *them* until the greater crisis that had brought him to Venus shattered Jerrin's disapproval of his presence.

That crisis was due to break over Jerrin's still unsuspecting head in just about one week.

In high government and military circles in Linn and on Venus, the succession of battles with the Venusian tribesmen of the three central islands were called by their proper name: war! For propaganda purposes, the word, rebellion, was paraded at every opportunity. It was a necessary illusion. The enemy fought with the ferocity of a people who had tasted slavery. To rouse the soldiery to an equal pitch of anger and hatred there was nothing that quite matched the term, rebel.

Men who had faced hideous dangers in the swamps and marshes could scarcely restrain themselves at the thought that traitors to the empire were causing all the trouble. Lord Jerrin, an eminently fair man, who admired a bold and resourceful opponent, for once made no attempt to discourage the false impression. He recognized that the Linnans were the oppressors, and at times it made him physically ill that so many men must die to enforce a continued subjection. But he recognized, too, that there was no alternative.

The Venusians were the second most dangerous race in the solar system, second only to the Linnans. The two peoples had fought each other for three hundred and fifty years, and it was not until the armies of Raheinl had landed on Uxta, the main island of Venus some sixty years before that a victory of any proportions was scored. The young military genius was only eighteen at the time of the battle of the Casuna marsh. Swift conquest of two other islands followed, but then his dazzled followers in Linn provoked the civil war that finally ended after nearly eight years in the execution of Raheinl by the Lord Leader. The latter proceeded with a cold ferocity to capture four more island strongholds of the Venusians. In each one he set up a separate government, revived old languages, suppressed the common language—and so strove to make the islanders think of themselves as separate peoples.

For years they seemed to—and then, abruptly, in one organized uprising they seized the main cities of the five main islands. And discovered that the Lord Leader had been more astute than they imagined.

The military strongholds were not in the cities, as they had assumed, and as their spies had reported. The centers of Linnan power were located in an immense series of small forts located in the marshes. These forts had always seemed weak outposts, designed to discourage raiders rather than rebellions. And no Venusian had ever bothered to count the number of them. The showy city forts, which were elaborately attacked turned out to be virtual hollow shells. By the time the Venusians rallied to attack the forts in the marshes it was too late for the surprise to be effective. Reinforcements were on the way from Earth. What had been planned as an all-conquering coup became a drawn-out war. And long ago, the awful empty feeling had come to the Venusians that they couldn't win. Month after month the vise of steel weapons, backed by fleets of spaceships and smaller craft tightened noticeably around the ever narrowing areas which they controlled. Food was becoming more scarce, and a poor crop year was in prospect. The men were grim and tense, the women cried a great deal and made much of their children, who had caught the emotional overtones of the atmosphere of fear.

Terror bred cruelty. Captive Linnans were hanged from posts, their feet dangling only a few inches from the ground. The distorted dead faces of the victims glared at the distorted hate-filled faces of their murderers.

The living knew that each account would be paid in rape and death. They were exacting their own payments in advance.

The situation was actually much more involved than it appeared. Some six months before, the prospect of an imminent triumph for Jerrin had penetrated to the Lord Adviser Tews. He pondered the situation with a painful understanding of how the emotions of the crowd might be seduced by so momentous a victory. After considerable thought he resurrected a request Jerrin had made more than a year before for reinforcements. At the time Tews had considered it expedient to hasten the Venusian war to a quick end, but second thought brought an idea. With a pomp of public concern for Jerrin he presented the request to the patronate and added his urgent recommendations that at least three legions be assembled to assist "our hardpressed forces against a skillful and cunning enemy."

He could have added, but didn't, that he intended to deliver the reinforcements and so participate in the victory. The patronate would not dare to refuse to vote him a triumph co-equal with that already being planned for Jerrin. He discussed his projected trip with his mother, the Lady Lydia, and, in accordance with her political agreement with Clane, she duly passed the information on to the mutation.

Lydia had no sense of betraying her son. She had no such intention. But she knew that the fact that Tews was going to Venus would soon be common knowledge, and so, sardonically, she reported to Clane less than two weeks before Tews was due to leave.

His reaction startled her. The very next day he requested an audience with Tews. And the latter, who had adopted an affable manner with the late Lord Leader's grandchildren, did not think of refusing Clane's request for permission to organize an expedition for Venus.

He was surprised when the expedition departed within one week of the request, but he thought that over too, and found it good.

The presence of Clane on Venus would embarrass Jerrin. The birth of a mutation twenty-five years before into the ruling family of Linn had caused a sensation. His existence had dimmed the superstitions about such semihumans, but the fears of the ignorant were merely confused. Under the proper circumstances people would still stone them—and soldiers would become panicky at the thought of the bad luck that struck an army, the rank and file of which saw a mutation just before a battle.

He explained his thoughts to Lydia, adding, "It will give me a chance to discover whether Jerrin was implicated in any way in the three plots against me that I have put down in the past year. And if he was, I can make use of the presence of Clane."

Lydia said nothing, but the falseness of the logic disturbed her. She, too, had once planned against Clane. For months now, she had questioned the blind impulse of mother love that had made her slave and conspire to bring Tews to power. Under Tews, the government creaked along indecisively while he writhed and twisted in a curious and ungraceful parody of modest pretense at establishing a more liberal government. His plans of transition were too vague. An old tactician herself, it seemed to her that she could recognize a developing hypocrite when she saw one.

"He's beginning to savor the sweetness of power," she thought, "and he realizes he's talked too much."

The possibilities made her uneasy. It was natural for a politician to fool others, but there was something ugly and dangerous about a politician who fooled himself. Fortunately, little that was dangerous could happen on Venus. Her own investigations had convinced her that the conspiracies against Tews had involved no important families, and besides Jerrin was not a man who would force political issues. He would be irritated by the arrival of Tews. He would see exactly what Tews wanted, but he would do nothing about it.

After the departure of Tews and his three legions, she settled herself to the routine tasks of governing for him. She had a number of ideas for re-establishing firmer control over the patronate, and there were about a hundred people whom she had wanted to kill for quite a long while.

During the entire period of the crisis on Venus, life in Linn went on with absolute normalcy.

Tews took up his quarters in the palace of the long-dead Venusian emperor, Heerkel, across town from the military headquarters of Jerrin. It was an error of the kind that startles and starts history. The endless parade of generals and other officers that streamed in and out of Mered passed him by. A few astute individuals made a point of taking the long journey across the city, but even some of those were in obvious haste, and could scarcely tolerate the slow ceremoniousness of an interview with their ruler.

A great war was being fought. Officers in from the front lines took it for granted that their attitude would be understood. They felt remote from the peaceful pomp of Linn itself. Only the men who had occasion to make trips to Earth comprehended the vast indifference of the populations to the war on Venus. To the people at home it was a far-away frontier affair. Such engagements had been fought continuously from the time of their childhood, only every once in a while the scene changed.

His virtual isolation sharpened the suspicions with which Tews had landed. And frightened him. He hadn't realized how widespread was the disaffection. The plot must be well advanced, so advanced that thousands of officers knew about it, and were taking no chances on being caught with the man who, they must have decided, would be the loser. They probably looked around them at the enormous armies under the command of Jerrin. And knew that no one could defeat the man who had achieved the loyalty of so many legions of superb soldiers.

Swift, decisive action, it seemed to Tews, was essential. When

Jerrin paid him a formal visit a week after his arrival, he was startled
at the cold way in which Tews rejected his request that the reinforcements be sent to the front for a final smashing drive against the
marsh-bound armies of the Venusians.

"And what," said Tews, noting with satisfaction the other's dis-
concertment, "would you do should you gain the victory which you
anticipate?"

❖❖❖

The subject of the question, rather than the tone, encouraged the
startled Jerrin. He had had many thoughts about the shape of the
coming victory, and after a moment he decided that that was actually
why Tews had come to Venus, to discuss the political aspects of conquest. The other man's manner he decided to attribute to Tews'
assumption of power. This was the new leader's way of reacting to his
high position.

Briefly, Jerrin outlined his ideas. Execution of certain leaders
directly responsible for the policy of murdering prisoners, enslave-
ment only of those men who had participated intimately in the carrying out of the executions. But all the rest to be allowed to live without molestation, and in fact to return to their homes in a normal
fashion. At first each island would be administered as a separate
colony, but even during the first phase the common language would
be restored and free trade permitted among the islands. The second
phase, to begin in about five years, and widely publicized in advance,
should be the establishment of responsible government on the separate islands, but those governments would be part of the empire, and
would support the occupation troops. The third phase should start
ten years after that, and would include the organization of one central all-Venusian administration for the islands, with a federal system
of government. And this system, too, would have no troops of its
own, and would be organized entirely within the framework of the
empire.

Five years later, the fourth and final phase could begin. All families with a twenty year record of achievement and loyalty could
apply for Linnan-Venusian citizenship, with all the privileges and
opportunities for self-advancement that went with it.

"It is sometimes forgotten," said Jerrin, "that Linn began as a city state, which conquered neighboring cities, and held its power in them by a gradual extension of citizenship. There is no reason why this system should not be extended to the planets with equal success."

He finished, "All around us is proof that the system of absolute subjection employed during the past fifty years has been a complete failure. The time has come for new and more progressive statesmanship."

Tews almost stood up in his agitation, as he listened to the scheme. He could see the whole picture now. The late Lord Leader had in effect willed the planets to Jerrin; and this was Jerrin's plan for welding his inheritance into a powerful military stronghold, capable, if necessary, of conquering Linn itself.

Tews smiled a cold smile. *Not yet, Jerrin,* he thought. *I'm still absolute ruler, and for three years yet what I say is what will happen. Besides, your plan might interfere with my determination to re-establish the republic at an opportune moment. I'm pretty sure that you, with all your liberalistic talk, have no intention of restoring constitutional government. It is that ideal which must be maintained at all costs.*

Aloud, he said, "I will take your recommendations under advisement. But now, it is my wish that in future all promotions be channeled through me. Any commands that you issue to commanding officers in the field are to be sent here for my perusal, and I will send them on."

He finished with finality, "The reason for this is that I wish to familiarize myself with the present positions of all units and with the names of the men in charge of them. That is all. It has been a privilege to have had this conversation with you. Good day, sir."

Move number one was as drastic as that.

It was only the beginning. As the orders and documents began to arrive, Tews studied them with the assiduity of a clerk. His mind reveled in paper work, and the excitement of his purpose made every detail important and interesting.

He knew this Venusian war. For two years he had sat in a palace some hundred miles farther back, and acted the role of commander-in-chief, now filled by Jerrin. His problem, therefore, did not include the necessity of learning the situation from the beginning. He had merely to familiarize himself with the developments during the past year and a half. And, while numerous, they were not insurmountable.

From the first day, he was able to accomplish his primary purpose: replacement of doubtful officers with one after another of the horde of sycophants he had brought with him from Linn. Tews felt an occasional twinge of shame at the device, but he justified it on the grounds of necessity. A man contending with conspiring generals must take recourse to devious means. The important thing was to make sure that the army was not used against himself, the Lord Adviser, the lawful heir of Linn, the only man whose ultimate purposes were not autocratic and selfish.

As a secondary precaution, he altered several of Jerrin's troop dispositions. These had to do with legions that Jerrin had brought with him from Mars, and which presumably might be especially loyal to him personally. It would be just as well if he didn't know their exact location during the next few critical weeks.

On the twelfth day he received from a spy the information he had been waiting. Jerrin, who had gone to the front on an inspection tour two days before was returning to Mered. Tews actually had only a hour's warning. He was still setting the stage for the anticipated interview when Jerrin was announced. Tews smiled at the assembled courtiers. He spoke in a loud voice:

"Inform his excellency that I am engaged at the moment but that if he will wait a little I shall be happy to receive him."

The remark, together with the knowing smile that went with it, started a flutter of sensation through the room. It was unfortunate that Jerrin had failed to wait for his message to be delivered, but was already halfway across the room. He did not pause until he was standing in front of Tews. The latter regarded him with an indolent insolence.

"Well, what is it?"

Jerrin said quietly, "It is my unpleasant duty, my Lord Adviser, to inform you that it will be necessary to evacuate all civilians from Mered without delay. As a result of rank carelessness on the part of certain front-line officers, the Venusians have achieved a breakthrough north of the city. There will be fighting in Mered before morning."

Some of the ladies, and not a few of the gentlemen who were present uttered alarmed noises, and there was a general movement toward exits. A bellow from Tews stopped the disgraceful stampede. He settled heavily back in his chair. He smiled a twisted smile.

"I hope," he said, "that the negligent officers have been properly punished."

"Thirty-seven of them," said Jerrin, "have been executed. Here is a list of their names, which you might examine at your leisure."

Tews sat up. "Executed!" He had a sudden awful suspicion that Jerrin would not lightly have executed men who had long been under his command. With a jerk he tore the seal from the document and raced his gaze down the column. Every name on it was that of one of his satellite-replacements of the past twelve days.

Very slowly, he raised his eyes, and stared at the younger man. Their gazes met and held. The flinty blue eyes of Tews glared with an awful rage. The steel gray eyes of Jerrin were remorseless with contempt and disgust.

"Your most gracious excellency," he said in a soft voice, "one of my Martian legions has been cut to pieces. The carefully built-up strategy and envelopment of the past year is wiped out. It is my opinion that the men responsible for that had better get off of Venus, and back to their pleasures in Linn—or what they have feared so foolishly will really transpire."

He realized immediately it was a wild statement. His words stiffened Tews. For a moment the big man's heavy face was a mask of tensed anger, then with a terrible effort he suppressed his fury. He straightened:

"In view of the seriousness of the situation," he said, "I will remain in Mered and take charge of the forces on this front until further notice. You will surrender your headquarters to my officers tomorrow morning."

"If your officers," said Jerrin, "come to my headquarters, they will be whipped into the streets. And that applies to *anyone* from this section of the city."

He turned and walked out of the room. He had not a clear idea in his head as to what he was going to do about the fantastic crisis that had arisen.

❖❖❖

Clane spent those three weeks, when the Venusian front was collapsing, exploring a myriad of holes in the pit. And, although the threat from the wandering parties of Venusians did not materialize, he moved his entire party into the pit for safety's sake. Guards were posted at the three main routes leading down into the abyss, and two spaceships maintained a continuous vigil over the countryside around the pit, and over the pit itself.

None of the precautions was an absolute guarantee of safety, but they added up fairly well. Any attempt of a large body of troops to come down and attack the camp would be so involved an affair that there would be plenty of time to embark everyone in spaceships, and depart.

It was not the only thing in their favor. After sixty years under Linnan rule, and although they themselves worshiped a sea god called Submerne, the Venusians respected the Linnan atom gods. It was doubtful if they would risk divine displeasure by penetrating into one of the pit homes of the gods.

And so the six hundred people in the pit were cut off from the universe by barriers of the mind as well as by the sheer inaccessibility of the pit. Yet they were not isolated. Daily one of the spaceships made the trip to Mered, and when it floated back into the depths of the pit Clane would go aboard and knock on door after door inside. Each time he would be cautiously admitted by a man or woman, and the two would hold a private conference. His spies never saw each other. They were always returned to Mered at dusk, and landed one by one in various parts of the city.

The spies were not all mercenaries. There were men in the highest walks of the empire who regarded the Linn mutation as the logical heir of the late Lord Leader. To them Tews was merely a stopgap who could be put out of the way at the proper time. Again and again such individuals, who belonged to other groups, had secretly turncoated after meeting Clane, and become valuable sources of information for him.

Clane knew his situation better than his well-wishers. However much he might impress intelligent people the fact was that a mutation could not become ruler of the empire. Long ago, accordingly, he had abandoned some early ambitions in that direction, retaining only two main political purposes:

He was alive and in a position of advantage because his family was one of the power groups in Linn. Though he had no friends among his own kin, he was tolerated by them because of the blood relationship. It was to his interest that they remained in high position. In crises he must do everything possible to help them.

That was purpose number one. Purpose number two was to participate in some way in all the major political moves made in the Linnan empire, and it was rooted in an ambition that he could never hope to realize. He wanted to be a general. War in its practical aspects, as he had observed it from afar, seemed to him crude and unintelligent. From early childhood he had studied battle strategy and tactics with the intention of reducing the confusion to a point where battles could be won by little more than irresistible maneuver.

It was a pleasure to combine purposes number one and two.

He arrived in Mered on the day following the clash between Tews and Jerrin, and took up residence in a house which he had long ago thoughtfully reserved for himself and his retinue. He made the move as unobtrusively as possible, but he did not delude himself that his coming would be unremarked.

Other men, too, were diabolically clever. Other men maintained armies of spies, as he did. All plans that depended upon secrecy possessed the fatal flaw of fragility. And the fact that they sometimes succeeded merely proved that a given victim was not himself an able man. It was one of the pleasures of life to be able to make all the preparations necessary to an enterprise within the sight and hearing of one's opponent.

Without haste he set about making them.

❖ ❖ ❖

When Tews was first informed of Clane's arrival in Mered, about an hour after the event, his interest was dim. More important—or so they seemed—reports were arriving steadily from other sources about the troop dispositions Jerrin was making for the defense of the city. What puzzled Tews was that some of the information came from Jerrin in the form of copies of the orders he was sending out.

Was the man trying to re-establish relations by ignoring the fact that a break had taken place? It was an unexpected maneuver, and it could only mean that the crisis had come before Jerrin was ready. Tews smiled coldly as he arrived at that conclusion. His prompt action had thrown the opposition into confusion. It should not be difficult to seize Jerrin's headquarters the following morning with his three legions, and so end the mutiny.

By three o'clock Tews had sent out the necessary orders. At four, a very special spy of his, the impoverished son of a knight, reported that Clane had sent a messenger to Jerrin, requesting an interview that evening. Almost simultaneously other spies reported on the activity that was taking place at Clane's residence. Among other things several small round objects wrapped in canvas were brought from the spaceship into the house. More than a ton of finely ground copper dust was carried in sacks into a cement outhouse. And finally a cube of material of the type used to build temples was carefully lowered to the ground. It must have been hot as well as heavy, because the slaves who took it into the house used slings and lead-lined asbestos gloves.

Tews pondered the facts, and the very meaninglessness of them alarmed him. He suddenly remembered vague stories he had heard about the mutation, stories to which he had hitherto paid no attention.

It was not a moment to take chances.

Ordering a guard of fifty men to attend him, he set out for Clane's Mered home.

His first sight of the place startled Tews. The spaceship which, according to his reports, had flown away, was back. Suspended from a thick cable attached to its lower beam was a large gondola of the type slung under spaceships when additional soldiers were to be transported swiftly. They were used in space to carry freight only.

Now, it lay on the ground, and slaves swarmed over it. Not until he was on the estate itself did Tews see what they were doing. Each man had a canvas bag of copper dust suspended around his neck, and some kind of liquid chemical was being used to work the copper dust into the semitransparent hull of the carrier.

Tews climbed out of his chair, a big, plump man with piercing blue eyes. He walked slowly around the gondola, and the longer he looked the more senseless was the proceeding.

And, oddly, nobody paid the slightest attention to him. There were guards around, but they seemed to have received no instructions about spectators. They lounged in various positions, smoking, exchanging coarse jests, and otherwise quite unaware that the Lord Adviser of Linn was in their midst.

Tews did not enlighten them. He was puzzled and undecided, as he walked slowly towards the house. Again, no effort was made to interfere with his passage. In the large inner hallway, several temple scientists were talking and laughing. They glanced at him curiously, but it did not seem to occur to them that he did not belong.

Tews said softly, "Is Lord Clane inside?"

One of the scientists half turned, then nodded over his shoulder, casually. "You'll find him in the den working on the benediction."

There were more scientists in the living room. Tews frowned inwardly as he saw them. He had come prepared for drastic action, if necessary. But it would be indiscreet to arrest Clane with so many temple scientists as witnesses. Besides, there were too many guards.

Not that he could imagine any reason for an arrest. This looked like a religious ceremony, being readied here.

He found Clane in the den, a medium sized room leading onto a patio. Clane's back was to him, and he was bending intently over a cube of temple building material. Tews recognized it from the description his spies had given him as the "hot," heavy object that the sweating slaves had handled so carefully in transporting it from the spaceship.

On the table near the "cube" were six half balls of coppery substance.

Tews had not time to look at them closely, for Clane turned to see who had come in. He straightened with a smile.

"Your excellency," he said. He bowed. He came forward. "This is a pleasure."

Tews was disappointed. He had heard that the mutation could be surprised into a condition of extreme nervousness, as the result of his affliction. There was no nervousness. It was obvious that this pale, intense, fragile looking young man had overcome his childish weakness. Or else he was calm with the calmness of a clear conscience. Tews began to feel better. Whatever the explanation there seemed nothing dangerous here.

"I was passing by," he said, "and, having been informed of your presence in Mered, decided to, uh, drop in." He waved a hand. "What is all this? This gondola and such."

Clane bowed again, but his expression was grave when he straightened, his eyes sorrowful.

"As your excellency is aware," he said, "some ten thousand officers and men of the fourth Martian legion were captured by the Venusians. This morning the Venusians were observed to be erecting thousands of posts on which they intend to hang these brave, unfortunate men, without"—he suddenly sounded indignant—"without so much as a religious ceremony."

He went on quietly, "The gondola will be towed over to the scene of the hanging, and a benediction will be spoken over it from the spaceship at the moment that the men are dying." He sighed heavily. "It is unfortunately all that we can do."

He finished: "I am going tonight to ask my brother, Jerrin, for permission to perform this merciful act since I am informed that nothing else can be."

All the vague fears that had troubled the Lord Adviser were gone as if they had never existed. He nodded sanctimoniously. "I am sure," he said, "that the noble Jerrin will grant your worthy request."

He hesitated, anxious now to leave; and yet— He looked around, conscious that he should take nothing for granted. He walked over to the table and stared frowningly down at the hollow half balls that lay there. They were very possibly the round objects that had been brought in from the spaceship wrapped in canvas. And now they had been cut in half, or opened. The balls were not completely empty. Each one contained a fragile appearing internal structure, which seemed to come to a focus in the center. But whatever had been supported by the spidery web of transparent stuff was not now visible.

Tews did not look very hard. These were details for temple scientists.

Once more he turned away—and saw a metallic rod standing against the near wall. He walked over and picked it up. Its lightness startled him. It was, he estimated, about four feet long, and the thin end was startlingly bright, a jewel rather than a metallic brightness.

Tews turned to look questioningly at Clane. The young man came over.

"We are all hoping," he said, "that this rod, which we found in the pit of the gods, is the legendary rod of fire. According to the legend, a basic requirement was that the wielder be pure in heart, and that, if he was, the gods would at their own discretion, but under certain circumstances, activate the rod."

Tews nodded soberly, and put the thing back where he had found it.

"It is with pleasure," he said, "that I find you taking these interests in religious matters. I think it important that a member of our illustrious family should attain high rank in the temples, and I wish to make clear that no matter what happens"—he paused significantly—"*no matter what happens*, you may count me as your protector and friend."

He returned to Heerkel's palace, but, being a careful, thoughtful man, who knew all too well that other people were not always as pure in heart as they pretended, he left his spies to watch out for possible subversive activity.

He learned in due course that Clane had been invited for dinner by Jerrin, but had been received with that cold formality which had long distinguished the relationship between the two brothers. One of the slave waiters, bribed by a spy, reported that once, during the meal, Clane urged that a hundred spaceships be withdrawn from patrols and assigned to some task which was not clear to the slave.

There was something else about opening up the battle lines to the northeast, but this was so vague that the Lord Adviser did not think of it again until, shortly after midnight, he was roused from sleep by the desperate cries of men, and the clash of metal outside his bedroom.

Before he could more than sit up, the door burst open, and swarms of Venusian soldiers poured inside.

The battle lines to the northeast had been opened up.

❖ ❖ ❖

It was the third night of his captivity, the hanging night. Tews quivered as the guards came for him about an hour after dusk, and led him out into the fire-lit darkness. He was to be first. As his body swung aloft, twenty thousand Venusians would tug on the ropes around the necks of ten thousand Linnan soldiers. The writhings and twistings that would follow were expected to last ten or more minutes.

The night upon which Tews gazed with glazed eyes was like nothing he had ever seen. Uncountably numerous fires burned on a vast plain. In the near distance he could see the great post upon which he was to be executed. The other posts began just beyond it. There were rows of them, and they had been set up less than five feet apart, with the rows ten feet from each other, to make room for camp fires that lighted the scene.

The doomed men were already at their posts, tied hand and foot, the ropes around their necks. Tews could only see the first row with any clearness. They were all officers, that first line of victims; and they stood at ease almost to a man. Some were chatting with those near them, as Tews was led up, but the conversation stopped as they saw him.

Never in his life had Tews seen such consternation flare into so many faces at once. There were cries of horror, groans of incredulous despair.

Tews did not expect to be recognized, but it was possible the men had been taunted with his identity. Their eyes were curious, but his three-day beard and the night with its flickering fire shadows gave them little opportunity to be sure.

No one said anything as he mounted the scaffold. Tews himself stood stiff and pale as the rope was fitted around his neck. He had ordered many a man to be hanged in his time. It was a different and thrilling sensation to be the victim not the judge.

The passion of anger that came was rooted in a comprehension that had been gathering in his brain for three days: the comprehension that he wouldn't be where he was if he had actually believed that an insurrection was in progress. Instead, he had *counted* on Jerrin maintaining his forces against the enemy, while his three legions seized control from Jerrin.

Deep down inside, he had believed in Jerrin's honesty.

He had sought to humiliate Jerrin, so that he could nullify the rightful honors of a young man with whom he did not wish to share the power of the state.

His desperate fury grew out of the consciousness—too late—that

Jerrin had in reality been plotting against him.

That chaos of thought would have raged on but for one thing: At that moment he happened to glance down, and there, below the platform, with a group of Venusian leaders, stood Clane.

❖ ❖ ❖

The shock was too great to take all in one mental jump. Tews glared down at the slim young man, and the picture was absolutely clear now. There had been a treasonable deal between Jerrin and the Venusians.

He saw that the mutation was in his temple scientist fatigue gown, and that he carried the four foot metal "rod of fire." That brought a memory. He had forgotten all about the benediction in the sky. He looked up, but the blackness was unrelieved. If the ship and the gondola were up there they were part of the night, invisible and unattainable.

His feverish gaze flashed down again at the mutation. He braced himself, but before he could speak, Clane said:

"Your excellency, let us waste no time with recriminations. Your death would renew the civil war in Linn. That is the last thing we desire, as we shall prove tonight, beyond all your suspicions."

Tews had hold of himself suddenly. With a flare of logic, he examined the chances of a rescue. There was none. If spaceships should try to land troops, the Venusians need merely pull on their ropes, and hang the bound men—and then turn their vast, assembled army to hold off the scattered attacks launched from scores of spaceships. That was one maneuver they had undoubtedly prepared against; and since it was the only possible hope, and *it* couldn't take place, then Clane's words were a meaningless fraud.

He forgot that, for the Venusian emperor, a grim-faced man of fifty or so was climbing the platform steps. He stood there for minutes while silence gradually fell on the enormous crowds. Then he stepped to the front group of megaphones and spoke in the common language of Venus:

"Fellow Venusians, on this night of our vengeance for all the crimes that have been committed against us by the empire of Linn, we have with us an agent of the commanding general of our vile enemy. He has come to us with an offer, and I want him to come up here and tell it to you, so that you can laugh in his face as I did."

There was a mass shriek from the darkness: "Hang him! Hang him, too!"

Tews was chilled by that fierce cry, but he was forced to admire the cunning of the Venusian leader. Here was a man whose followers must many times have doubted his wisdom in fighting the war to a finish. His face, even in those shadows, showed the savage lines of obstinacy, of a badly worried general, who knew what criticism could be. What an opportunity this was for gaining public support.

❖❖❖

Clane was climbing the steps. He waited until silence once more was restored, and then said in a surprisingly strong voice:

"The atom gods of Linn, whose agent I am, are weary of this war. I call upon them to end it NOW!"

The Venusian emperor started towards him. "That isn't what you were going to say," he cried. "You—"

He stopped. Because the sun came out.

The sun came out. Several hours had passed, since it had sunk behind the flaming horizon of the northern sea. Now, in one leap it had jumped to the sky directly overhead.

The scene of so many imminent deaths stood out as in the brightness of noon. All the posts with their victims still standing beneath them, the hundreds of thousands of Venusian spectators, the great plain with the now visible coastal city in the distance—were brilliantly lighted.

The shadows began on the other side of the plain. The city could only be seen by vague light reflections. The sea beyond to the north and the mountains to the south were as deep as ever in blackness.

Seeing that darkness, Tews realized that it was not the sun at all above, but an incredible ball of fire, a source of light that, in this cubic mile of space equaled the sun in magnitude of light.

The gods of Linn had answered the call made to them.

His realization ended. There was a cry from scores of thousands of throats, a cry stranger and more horrible than any sound that Tews had ever heard. There was fear in it, and despair, and an awful reverence. Men and women alike started to sink to their knees.

At that moment the extent of the defeat that was here penetrated to the Venusian leader. He let out a terrible cry of his own—and leaped towards the catch that would release the trapdoor on which Tews stood. From the corner of one eye, Tews saw Clane bring up the rod of fire.

There was no fire, but the emperor dissolved. Tews could never afterwards decide what actually happened, yet he had a persistent memory of a human being literally turning into liquid stuff. Liquid that collapsed onto the platform, and burned a hole through the wood. The picture was so impossible that he closed his eyes, and never again quite admitted the reality to himself.

When he opened his eyes again, spaceships were coming down from the sky. To the now prostrate Venusians, the sudden appearance of fifty thousand Linnan soldiers among them must have seemed like a miracle as great as the two they had already witnessed.

An entire reserve army was captured that night, and, though the war on other islands dragged on and on, the great island of Uxta was completely captured within a few weeks.

Clane's words had been proved beyond all suspicions.

On a cloudy afternoon a week later, Clane was among the distinguished Linnans who attended the departure of the flotilla of ships, which was to accompany the Lord Adviser Tews back to Earth.

Tews and his retinue arrived, and as he came up to the platform, a group of temple Initiates burst into a paroxysm of singing. The Lord Adviser stopped, and stood for a minute, a faint smile on his face, listening.

The return to Earth, quietly suggested by Clane, suited him completely. He would take with him the first tidings of the Venusian victory. He would have time to scotch any rumors that the Lord Adviser himself had been humiliatingly captured. And, above all, he would be the one who would insist upon full triumph honors for Jerrin.

He was amazed that he had temporarily forgotten his old cunnings about things like that. As he climbed aboard the flagship, the Initiates broke into a new spasm of sound.

It was clear that the atom gods, too, were satisfied.

The Barbarian

The only warning was a steely glinting of metal in the early morning sky.

The invaders swooped down on the city of Linn in three hundred spaceships. There must have been advance spying, for they landed in force at the gates that were heavily guarded and at the main troop barracks inside the city.

From each ship debouched two hundred odd men.

"Sixty thousand soldiers!" said Lord Adviser Tews after he had studied the reports.

He issued instructions for the defense of the palace, and sent a carrier pigeon to the three legions encamped outside the city ordering two of them to attack when ready. And then he sat pale but composed watching the spectacle from a window which overlooked the hazy vastness of Linn proper.

Everything was vague and unreal. Most of the invading ships had disappeared behind large buildings. A few lay in the open, but they looked dead. It was hard to grasp that vicious fighting was going on in their vicinity.

At nine o'clock a messenger arrived from the Lady Lydia, Tews' aging mother:

❖ ❖ ❖

Dear Son:

Have you any news? Who is attacking us? Is it a limited assault or an invasion of the empire? Have you contacted Clane?

L.

❖ ❖ ❖

The first prisoner was brought in while Tews was scowling over the unpalatable suggestion that he seek the advice of his mutation cousin. The prisoner, a bearded giant, proudly confessed that he was from Europa, one of the moons of Jupiter, and that he feared neither man nor god.

The man's size and obvious physical prowess startled Tews. But his naïve outlook on life was cheering. Subsequent prisoners had similar physical and mental characteristics. And so, long before noon, Tews had a fairly clear picture of the situation.

This was a barbarian invasion from Europa. It was obviously for loot only. And, unless he acted swiftly, Linn would be divested in a few days of treasures garnered over the centuries.

Bloodthirsty commands flowed from Tews' lips. Put all prisoners to the sword. Destroy their ships, their weapons, their clothing. Leave not one vestige of their presence to pollute the eternal city.

The morning ran its slow course. Tews considered making an inspection of the city escorted by the palace cavalry. But abandoned the plan when he realized it would be impossible for commanders to send him reports if he was on the move.

For the same reason he could not transfer his headquarters to a less clearly marked building.

Just before noon, the relieving report arrived that two of three camp legions were attacking in force at the main gates.

The news steadied him. He began to think in terms of broader, more basic information about what had happened. He sat somber while the court historian delivered a brief lecture on Europa.

❖ ❖ ❖

The amazing thing to Tews was how little was known about that remote moon of Jupiter. It had been inhabited from legendary times by fiercely quarreling tribes. Its vast atmosphere was said to have been created artificially with the help of the atom gods by the scientists of the golden age. And, like all the artificial atmospheres, it contained a high proportion of the gas, teneol, which admitted sunlight, but did not allow heat to escape into space.

Starting about five years before, travelers had begun to bring out reports of a leader named Czinczar who was ruthlessly welding all the hating factions of the planet into one nation.

Czinczar. The name had a sinister rhythm to it, a ring of leashed violence, a harsh, metallike tintinnabulation. If such a man and his followers escaped with even a fraction of the portable wealth of Linn, the inhabited solar system would echo with the exploit. The government of Lord Adviser Tews might tumble like a house of cards.

Tews had been hesitating. There was a plan in his mind that would work better if carried out in the dead of night. But that meant giving the attackers precious extra hours for loot.

He decided not to wait, but dispatched a command to the third— still unengaged—camp legion to enter the tunnel that led into the Central Palace.

As a precaution, and with the hope of distracting the enemy leader, he sent a message to Czinczar in the care of a captured barbarian officer. In it he pointed out the foolishness of an attack that could only result in bloody reprisals on Europa itself, and suggested that there was still time for an honorable withdrawal.

There was only one thing wrong with all these schemings. Czinczar had concentrated a large force of his own for the purpose of capturing the Imperial party. And had held back in the hope that he would learn definitely whether or not the Lord Adviser was inside the palace.

The released prisoner, who delivered Tews' message, established his presence inside.

The attack in force that followed captured the Central Palace and everyone in it, and surprised the legionnaires who were beginning to emerge from the secret passageway. Czinczar's men poured all the oil in the large palace tanks into the downward sloping passageway, and set it afire.

Thus died an entire legion of men.

That night a hundred reserve barbarian spaceships landed behind the Linnan soldiers besieging the gates. And in the morning, when the barbarians inside the city launched an attack, the two remaining legions were cut to pieces.

Of these events the Lord Adviser Tews knew nothing. His skull had been turned over the previous day to Czinczar's favorite goldsmith, to be plated with Linnan gold, and shaped into a goblet to celebrate the greatest victory of the century.

❖ ❖ ❖

To Lord Clane Linn, going over his accounts on his country estate, the news of the fall of Linn came as a special shock.

With unimportant exceptions, all his atomic material was in Linn.

He dismissed the messenger, who had rashly shouted the news as he entered the door of the accounting department. And then sat at his desk—and realized that he had better accept for the time being the figures of his slave bookkeepers on the condition of the estate.

As he glanced around the room after announcing the postponement, it seemed to him that at least one of the slaves showed visible relief.

He did not delay, but called the man before him instantly. He had an inexorable system in dealing with slaves, a system inherited from his long dead mentor, Joquin, along with the estate itself. Integrity, hard work, loyalty, and a positive attitude produced better conditions, shorter working hours, more freedom of action, after thirty the right to marry, after forty legal freedom.

Laziness and other negative attitudes such as cheating were punished by a set pattern of demotions.

Clane could not even imagine a better system. And now, in spite of his personal anxieties, he carried out the precept of Joquin as it applied to a situation where no immediate evidence was available. He told the man, Oorag, what had aroused his suspicions, and asked him if they were justified.

"If you are guilty and confess," he said, "you will receive only one demotion. If you do not confess and you are later proven guilty, there will be three demotions, which means physical labor, as you know."

The slave, a big man, shrugged, and said with a sneer:

"By the time Czinczar is finished with you Linnans, you will be working for me."

"Field labor," said Clane curtly, "for three months, ten hours a day."

He was astonished. Again and again, he had noticed this self-destructive instinct in people. Men and women in the highest and lowest walks of life yielded to the instinct to say something devastating for the sake of a momentary defiance or thrill of superiority.

As the slave was led out by guards, he shouted a final insult over his shoulder:

"You wretched mutation, you'll be where you belong when

Czinczar gets here."

Clane forbore an answer. He considered it doubtful that the new conqueror had been selected by fate to punish all the evildoers of Linn according to their desserts. It would take too long. He put the thought out of his mind, and walked to the doorway. There he paused, and faced the dozen trusted slaves who sat at their various desks.

"Do nothing rash," he said slowly in a clear voice, "any of you. If you harbor emotions similar to those expressed by Oorag, restrain yourselves. The fall of one city in a surprise attack is meaningless."

He hesitated. He was, he realized, appealing to their cautious instincts, but his reason told him that in a great crisis men did not always consider all the potentialities.

"I am aware," he said finally, "there is no great pleasure in being a slave, though it has advantages—economic security, free craft training. But Oorag's wild words are a proof that, if young slaves were free to do as they pleased, they would constitute a jarring if not revolutionary factor in the community. It is unfortunately true that people of different races can only gradually learn to live together."

He went out, dissatisfied with his argument, but unable to see the flaw in it, if there was one.

He had no doubt whatsoever that here in this defiance of Oorag, the whole problem of a slave empire had shown itself in miniature. If Czinczar were to conquer any important portion of Earth, a slave uprising would follow automatically.

There were far too many slaves, far too many for safety, in the Linnan empire.

❖❖❖

Outside, he saw his first refugees. They were coming down near the main granaries in a variety of colorful skyscooters.

Clane watched them for a moment, trying to picture their departure from Linn. The amazing thing was that they had waited till the forenoon of the second day. People must simply have refused to believe that the city was in danger, though, of course, early fugitives could have fled in different directions. And so not come near the estate.

Clane emerged decisively out of his reverie. He called a slave, and dispatched him to the scene of the arrivals with a command to his personal guards:

"Tell these people who have rapid transportation to keep moving. Here, eighty miles from Linn, we shall take care only of the foot-weary."

Briskly now, he went into his official residence, and called the commanding officer of his troops.

"I want volunteers," he explained, "particularly men with strong religious beliefs, who on this second night after the invasion are prepared to fly into Linn and remove all the transportable equipment from my laboratory."

His plan, as he outlined it finally to some forty volunteers, was simplicity itself. In the confusion of taking over a vast city, it would probably be several days before the barbarian army would actually occupy all the important residences. Particularly, on these early days, they might miss a house situated, as was his, behind a barrier of trees.

If by some unfortunate chance it was already occupied, it would probably be so loosely held that bold men could easily kill every alien on the premises, and so accomplish their purpose.

Clane hoped so, violently.

"I want to impress upon you," he said, "the importance of this task. As all of you know, I am a member of the temple hierarchy. I have been instructed with sacred god metals and sacred equipment, including material taken from the very homes of the gods.

"It would be a disaster if these precious relics were to fall into unclean hands. I, therefore, charge you that, if you should by some mischance be captured, do not reveal the real purpose of your presence. Say that you came to rescue your owner's private property. Even admit that you were very foolish to sacrifice yourself for such a reason."

Clane finished: "And finally," he said, "no matter what time of the night you return, I wish to be awakened immediately."

❖ ❖ ❖

When they had gone out to prepare for the mission, Clane dispatched one of his private spaceships to the nearby city of Goram, and asked the commander there, a friend of his, what kind of counteraction was being prepared against the invader.

"Are the authorities in the cities and towns," he asked, "showing that they understand the patterns of action required of them in a major emergency? Or must the old law be explained to them from the beginning?"

The answer arrived in the shortest possible time, something under forty minutes. The general placed his force at Clane's command, and advised that he had dispatched messengers to every major city on earth, in the name of "his excellency, Lord Clane Linn, ranking survivor on Earth of the noble Tews, the late Lord Adviser, who perished at the head of his troops, defending the city of Linn from the foul and murderous surprise attack launched by a barbarian horde of beastlike men, who seek to destroy the fairest civilization that has ever existed."

There was more in the same vein, but it was not the excess of verbiage that startled Clane. It was the offer itself, and the implications. *In his name*, an army was being organized.

He had from childhood taken it for granted that soldiers regarded mutations as bad luck. Even the presence of a mutation on a field, it was said, could demoralize entire legions.

After rereading the message, he walked slowly to the full length mirror in the adjoining bathroom, and stared at his image.

He was dressed in the fairly presentable reading gown of a temple scientist. Like all his temple clothing, the cloth folds of this concealed his "differences" from casual view. An observer would have to be very acute to see how carefully the cloak was drawn around his neck, and how tightly the arm ends were tied together at his wrists.

It would take three months to advise Lord Jerrin on Venus, and four to reach Lord Draid on Mars, both planets being near the far side of the Sun from Earth. It would require almost, though not quite, twice as long to receive back a message from them.

Only a member of the ruling family could possibly win the support of the diversified elements of the empire. Of the Lord Adviser's immediate family, there was the venerable Lady Lydia—too old; and there was Lord Clane, younger brother of Jerrin, grandson of the late Lord Leader.

For not less than six months accordingly he could be the legitimate Lord Leader of Linn.

❖❖❖

The afternoon of that second day of the invasion waned slowly. Great ships began to arrive, bringing soldiers. By dusk, more than a thousand men were encamped along the road to the city Linn, and by the riverside. Darting small craft and wary full-sized spaceships floated overhead, and foot patrols were out, guarding all the approaches to the estate.

The roads themselves were virtually deserted. It was too soon for the mobs from Linn, which airscooter scouts reported were fleeing the captured city by the gates that, at mid-afternoon, were still open.

During the last hour before dark, the air patrols reported that the gates were being shut one by one. And that the stream of refugees was dwindling to a trickle near the darkening city.

All through that last hour, the sky was free of scooters transporting refugees.

It was clear that the people who could afford the costly machines were either already safe, or had waited too long, possibly in the hope of succoring some absent member of the family.

At midnight, the volunteers departed on their dangerous mission in ten scooters and one spaceship. As a first gesture of his new authority, Clane augmented their forces by adding a hundred soldiers from the regular army.

He watched the shadowy ships depart, then hurried to attend a meeting of those general officers who had had time to arrive. A dozen men climbed to their feet as he entered. They saluted, then stood at attention.

Clane stopped short. He had intended to be calm, matter-of-fact, pretend even to himself that what was happening was natural.

The feeling wasn't like that. An emotion came, familiar but terrifying. He could feel it tangling up the remoter reflexes of his nervous system as of old, the beginning of the dangerous childish panic, product of his early, horrible days as a tormented mutation.

The muscles of his face worked. Three times he swallowed hard. Then, with a stiff gesture, he returned the salute. And, walking hastily to the head of the table, sat down.

The acting Lord Leader of Linn was in conference with his general staff.

❖❖❖

Clane waited till they had seated themselves, then asked for brief reports as to available troops. He noted down the figures given by each man for his province, and at the end added up the columns.

"With four provinces still to be heard from," he announced, "we have a total of eighteen thousand trained soldiers, six thousand partly trained reserves, and some five hundred thousand able-bodied civilians. The—"

He stopped. The confidence went out of him. "Is that all?" he asked sharply.

"Your excellency," said his friend, Morkid, "the Linnan empire maintains normally a standing army of one million men. On Earth by far the greatest forces were stationed in or near the city of Linn, and they have been annihilated. Some four hundred thousand men are still on Venus, and slightly more than two hundred thousand on Mars."

Clane, who had been mentally adding up the figures given, said quickly:

"That doesn't add up to a million men."

Morkid nodded, gravely. "For the first time in years, the army is understrength. The conquest of Venus seemed to eliminate all potential enemies of Linn, and Lord Adviser Tews considered it a good time to economize."

"I see," said Clane.

He felt pale and bloodless, like a man who has suddenly discovered that he cannot walk by himself.

Lydia climbed heavily out of her sedan chair, conscious of how old and unattractive she must seem to the grinning barbarians in the courtyard. She didn't let it worry her too much. She had been old a long time now, and her image in a mirror no longer shocked her. The important thing was that her request for an interview had been granted by Czinczar after she had, at his insistence, withdrawn the proviso that she be given a safe conduct.

The old woman smiled mirthlessly. She no longer valued highly the combination of skin and bones that was her body. But there was exhilaration to the realization that she was probably going to her death. Despite her age, and some self-disgust, she felt reluctant to accept oblivion. But Clane had asked her to take the risk.

It vaguely amazed Lydia that the idea of the mutation holding the Lord Leadership did not dismay her any more. She had her own private reasons for believing Clane capable.

She walked slowly along the familiar hallways, through the gleaming archways and across rooms that glittered with the treasure of the Linn family. Everywhere were the big, bearded young men who had come from far Europa to conquer an empire about which they could only have heard by hearsay. Looking at them, she felt justified in all the pitiless actions she had taken in her day. They were, it seemed to the grim old woman, living personifications of the chaos that she had fought against all her life.

As she entered the throne room, the darker thoughts faded from her mind. She glanced around with sharp eyes for the mysterious leader.

There was no one on or near the throne.

Groups of men stood around talking. In one of the groups was a tall, graceful, young man, different from all the others in the room. They were bearded. He was clean shaven.

He saw her, and stopped listening to what one of his companions was saying, stopped so noticeably that a silence fell on the group.

The silence communicated itself to other groups. After no more than a minute, the roomful of men had faced about and was staring at her, waiting for their commander to speak.

Lydia waited also, examining him swiftly. Czinczar was not a handsome man, but he had an appearance of strength, always a form of good looks.

And yet, it was not enough. This barbarian world was full of strong-looking men. Lydia, who had expected outstanding qualities, was puzzled.

His face was rather sensitive than brutal, which was unusual. But still not enough to account for the fact that he was absolute lord of an enormous undisciplined horde.

The great man came forward. "Lady," he said, "you have asked to see me."

And then she knew his power. In all her long life, she had never heard a baritone voice so resonant, so wonderfully beautiful, so assured of command.

It changed him. She realized suddenly that she had been mistaken about his looks. She had sought normal clean-cut handsomeness.

This man was beautiful.

The first fear came to her. A voice like that, a personality. . . like that.

She had a vision of this man persuading the Linnan empire to do his will. Mobs hypnotized. The greatest men bewitched.

She broke the spell with an effort of will. She said:

"You are Czinczar?"

"I am Czinczar."

The definite identification gave Lydia another though briefer, pause. But this time she recovered more swiftly. And this time, too, her recovery was complete.

Her eyes narrowed. She stared at the great man with a developing hostility.

"I can see," she said acridly, "that my purpose in coming to see you is going to fail."

"Naturally." Czinczar inclined his head, shrugged.

He did not ask her what was her purpose. He seemed incurious. He stood politely, waiting for her to finish what she had to say.

"Until I saw you," said Lydia grimly, "I took it for granted that you were an astute general. Now, I see that you consider yourself a man of destiny. I can already see you being lowered into your grave."

There was an angry murmur from the other men in the room. Czinczar waved them into silence.

"Madam," he said, "such remarks are offensive to my officers. State your case, and then I will decide what to do with you."

Lydia nodded, but she noted that he did not say that he was offended. She sighed inwardly. She had her mental picture now of this man, and it depressed her. All through known history these natural leaders had been spewed up by the inarticulate masses. They had a will in them to rule or die. But the fact that they frequently died young made no great difference. Their impact on their times was colossal.

Such a man could, even in his death throes, drag long established dynasties with him.

Already, he had killed the legal ruler of Linn, and struck a staggering blow at the heart of the empire. By a military freak, it was true—but history accepted such accidents without a qualm.

Lydia said quietly, "I shall be brief, since you are no doubt planning high policy and further military campaigns. I have come here at the request of my grandson, Lord Clane Linn."

"The mutation!" Czinczar nodded. His remark was noncommittal, an identification not a comment.

Lydia felt an inward shock that Czinczar's knowledge of the ruling faction should extend to Clane, who had tried to keep himself in the background of Linnan life.

She dared not pause to consider the potentialities. She went on quietly:

"Lord Clane is a temple scientist, and, as such, he has for many years been engaged in humanitarian scientific experiments. Most of his equipment, unfortunately, is here in Linn."

Lydia shrugged. "It is quite valueless to you and your men, but it would be a great loss to civilization if it was destroyed or casually removed. Lord Clane therefore requests that you permit him to send slaves to his town house to remove these scientific instruments to his country estate. In return—"

"Yes," echoed Czinczar, "in return—"

His tone was ever so faintly derisive; and Lydia had a sudden realization that he was playing with her. It was not a possibility that she could pay attention to.

"In return," she said, "he will pay you in precious metals and jewels any reasonable price which you care to name."

Having finished, she took a deep breath. And waited.

❖ ❖ ❖

There was a thoughtful expression on the barbarian leader's face.

"I have heard," he said, "of Lord Clane's experiments with the so-called"—he hesitated—"god metals of Linn. Very curious stories, some of them; and as soon as I am free from my military duties I intend to examine this laboratory with my own eyes.

"You may tell your grandson," he went on with a tone of finality, "that his little scheme to retrieve the greatest treasures in the entire Linnan empire was hopeless from the beginning. Five spaceships descended in the first few minutes of the attack on the estate of Lord Clane, to insure that the mysterious weapons there were not used against my invading fleet, and I consider it a great misfortune that he himself was absent in the country at the time.

"You may tell him that we were not caught by surprise by his midnight attempt two days ago to remove the equipment, and that his worst fears as to its fate are justified."

He finished, "It is a great relief to know that most of his equipment is safely in our hands."

Lydia said nothing. The phrase, "You may tell him," had had a profound chemical effect on her body. She hadn't realized she was so tense. It seemed to her that, if she spoke, she would reveal her own tremendous personal relief.

"*You may tell him—*" There could be only one interpretation. She was going to be allowed to depart.

Once more she waited.

Czinczar walked forward until he was standing directly in front of her. Something of his barbarous origin, so carefully suppressed until now, came into his manner. A hint of sneer, the contempt of a physically strong man for decadence, a feeling of genuine basic superiority to the refinement that was in Lydia. When he spoke, he showed that he was consciously aware that he was granting mercy:

"Old woman," he said, "I am letting you go because you did me a great favor a few years ago, when you maneuvered your son, Lord Tews, into the, what did he call it, Lord Advisership. That move, and that alone, gave me the chance I needed to make my attack on the vast Linnan empire."

He smiled. "You may depart, bearing that thought in mind."

Long ago, Lydia had condemned the sentimental action that had brought Tews into supreme power. But it was a different matter to realize that, far out in interplanetary space, a man had analyzed the move as a major Linnan disaster.

She went out without another word.

❖ ❖ ❖

Czinczar slowly climbed the hill leading up to the low, ugly fence that fronted Lord Clane's town house. He paused at the fence, recognized the temple building material of which it was composed—and then walked on thoughtfully.

With the same narrow-eyed interest a few minutes later, he stared at the gushing fountain of boiling water.

He beckoned finally the engineer who had directed the construction of the spaceships that had brought his army to Earth.

"How does it work?"

The designer examined the base of the fountain. He was in no hurry, a big fattish man with a reputation for telling jokes so coarse that strong men winced with shame. He had already set up house in one of the great palaces with three Linnan girls as mistresses and a hundred Linnan men and women as slaves. He was a happy man, with little personal conceit and very little pride as yet to restrain his movements.

He located the opening into the fountain, and knelt in the dirt like any worker. In that, however, he was not unique. Czinczar knelt beside him, little realizing how his actions shocked the high born Linnans who belonged to his personal slave retinue.

The two men peered into the gloom.

"Temple building material," said Meewan, the designer.

Czinczar nodded. They climbed to their feet without further comment, for these were matters which they had discussed at length over a period of several years.

At the house, a few minutes later, the leader and his henchman both lifted the heavy draperies that covered the walls of a corridor leading into the main laboratory. Like the fence outside, the walls were warm as from some inner heat.

Temple building material! Once again, there was no comment passed between them. They walked on into the laboratory proper; and now they looked at each other in amazement.

The room had been noticeably enlarged from its original size. A great section had been torn out of one wall, and the gap, although it was completely filled in, was still rough and unfinished.

But that was only the environment. On almost every square yard of the vast new floor were machines opaque and machines transparent, machines big and small, some apparently complete, others unmistakably mere fragments.

For a moment there was a distinct sense of too much to see. Czinczar walked forward speculatively, glancing at several of the transparent articles with an eye that tried to skim the essentials of shape and inner design.

At no time, during those first moments, did he have any intention of pausing for a detailed examination.

And then, out of the corner of his eye, he caught a movement.

A glow. He bent down, and peered into a long partly transparent metal case, roughly shaped like a coffin, even as to the colorful and costly looking lining. The inside, however, curved down to form a narrow channel.

Along this channel rolled a ball of light.

It turned over sedately, taking approximately one minute to cover the distance to the far side. With the same lack of haste, it paused, seemed to meditate on its next action, and then, with immense deliberation began its return journey.

The very meaninglessness of the movement fascinated Czinczar. He extended his hand gingerly to within an inch of the ball. Nothing happened. He drew back, and pursed his lips. In spite of his attack on Linn, he was not a man who took risks.

He beckoned towards a guard. "Bring a slave," he said.

Under his direction a former Linnan nobleman, perspiring from every pore, extended his finger and touched the moving ball.

His finger went in as if there was nothing there.

He drew back, startled. But the inexorable Czinczar was not through with him. Once more the reluctant, though no longer quite so fearful, finger penetrated the moving ball.

The ball rolled into it, through it, beyond it.

Czinczar motioned the slave aside, and stood looking at him thoughtfully. There must have been something of his purpose in his face, for the man gave forth a low cry of horror:

"Master, I understand nothing of what I have seen. Nothing. Nothing."

"Kill him!" said Czinczar.

He turned, scowling, back to the machine. "There must be," he said, and there was a stubborn note in his glorious voice, "some reason for its movements, for—its existence."

Half an hour later, he was still examining it.

❖❖❖

There was an old saying in the Linnan army to the effect that, during his first month, a trainee, if put into battle, caused the death of his trained companions. During the second month, he hindered retreats made necessary by his presence. And during the third month he was just good enough to get himself killed in the first engagement.

Clane, watching a group of trainees after several weeks of drilling, experienced all the agony of realizing how true the adage was.

Learning to fire a bow effectively required complex integration of mind and body. Infighting with swords had to include the capacity for co-operating with companions. And effective spear fighting was an art in itself.

The plan he outlined that night to the full general staff was an attempt to cover up against the weakness. It was a frank determination to use unfit men as first-line defense troops.

He put in a word for the unfit: "Do not overexercise them. Get them out into the open air, and simply teach them the first elements of how to use weapons. First, bows and arrows, then spears, and finally swords."

He paused, and, looking around the table, mentally measured the ability of the audience to assess his next statement. He said slowly:

"If two months from now our position is as desperate as I anticipate, there is one other possibility which I will then explore. It has to do with one of several machines of the gods which I removed last year from a pit of the gods, and which Czinczar captured when he effectively occupied my town. But nothing can be done for two months."

❖❖❖

After the meeting, long into the night, he examined reports on the cities of Nouris and Gulf, which had fallen virtually without a fight. As the barbarians attacked, the slaves simply rose up and murdered their masters. A supplementary general staff report recommended mass execution for all able-bodied slaves.

The uneasy Clane took that problem to bed with him.

FREEDOM FOR LOYAL SERVANTS

❖❖❖

By order of his excellency, the acting Lord Leader of Linn, temple scientist, beloved of the Atomic Gods themselves, it is hereby commanded, and so it shall be forevermore:

GREETINGS to all those good men and women who have quietly and efficiently served the empire in atonement for sins of leaders who rashly led them into hopeless wars against the god-protected Linnan empire—here is the chance for complete freedom which you have earned by your actions and attitudes during past years.

The empire has been attacked by a cruel and barbarous invader. His reign of terror cannot but be temporary, for invincible forces are gathering against him. An army of a million men is on the way from Mars and Venus, and here on Earth irresistible forces totaling more than two million men are already organizing for battle.

The enemy himself numbers less than sixty thousand soldiers. To this small army, which gained its initial victory by a surprise and base attack, a few foolish men and women have rashly attached themselves. All the women unless they are convicted of major crimes, will be spared. For the men who have already gone over to the enemy, there is but one hope: Escape immediately from the barbarian enemy, and REPORT TO THE CONCENTRATION CAMPS listed at the bottom of this proclamation. There will be no guards at the camps, but weekly roll calls will be made. And every man whose name appears regularly on these rolls will be granted full freedom when the enemy is defeated.

For hardened recalcitrants, the penalty is death.

To those men and women still loyally serving at their appointed tasks, I, Lord Clane, acting Lord Leader of Linn, give the following commands:

All women and children will remain at their present residences, continuing to serve as in the past.

All men report to their masters, and say, "It is my intention to take advantage of the offer of Lord Clane. Give me a week's food, so that I, too, may report to a concentration camp."

Having done this, and having received the food, leave at once. DO NOT DELAY A SINGLE HOUR.

If for some reason your master is not at home, take the food and go without permission. No one will hinder you in your departure from the city.

Any man to whom this order applies, who is found lurking within any city or town twenty-four hours after this proclamation is posted, will be suspected of treasonable intent.

The penalty is death.

Any man, who after one week, is found within a fifty-mile radius of a city, will be suspected of treasonable intent.

The penalty is death.

To save yourself, go to a concentration camp, and appear regularly for roll call. If the barbarians attack your camp, scatter into the forests and hills and hide, or go to another camp.

Adequate food rations will be supplied all camps.

All those of proven loyalty will receive freedom when the war is over. They will immediately have the right to marry. Settlement land will be opened up. After five years, citizenship rights, granted alien immigrants, will be available on application.

After three years, new citizens may own unpaid servants.

BE WISE—BE SAFE—BE FREE

It was a document that had its weak points. But Clane spent most of one day arguing its merits to a group of doubtful officers. He pointed out that it would be impossible to keep secret a general order for mass execution. A majority of the slaves would escape, and then they would really be dangerous.

He admitted the proclamation was full of lies. A million slaves in Linn alone had gone over to Czinczar, many of them highly trained soldiers. Czinczar could use them to garrison any city he might capture, and thus have his own army free for battle. It was Morkid, sardonic and scathing, who ended the argument late in the afternoon.

"Gentlemen," he said, "you do not seem to be aware that our commander-in-chief, the acting Lord Leader of Linn, has at one stroke cut through all our illusions and false hopes, and penetrated straight to the roots of the situation in which we find ourselves. What is clear by the very nature of our discussion is that we have no choice."

His voice went up: "In this period when disaster is so imminent, we are fortunate in having as our leader a genius of the first rank, who has already set us on the only military path that can lead to victory.

"Gentlemen"—his voice rang with the tribute—"I give you Lord Clane Linn, acting Lord Leader of Linn."

The clapping lasted for five minutes.

Clane watched the battle for Goram from a patrol craft, that darted from strong point to strong point. Enemy squadrons tried again and again to close in on him, but his own machine was faster and more maneuverable.

The familiar trick of getting above him was tried, an old device in patrol craft and spaceship fighting. But the expected energy flow upward did not take place. His small vessel did not even sag, which was normally the minimum reaction when two sources of atomic energy operated in a gravity line.

The efforts worried Clane. Czinczar was, of course, aware by this time that his enemy knew more about the metals of the gods than he or his technicians. But it would be unfortunate if they should conclude from the actions of this one craft that Clane himself was inside.

He wanted to see this battle.

In spite of everything, minute by minute, he saw it.

The defense was tough, tougher than he had anticipated from the fact that four more cities had fallen in the past four weeks.

The unfit were fighting grimly for their lives. Arrows took a toll of the attackers. Spears, awkwardly but desperately manipulated, inflicted wounds and sometimes death.

The sword fighting stage was the worst. The muscular and powerful barbarians, once they penetrated the weapons that could attack them from a distance, made short work of their weaker adversaries.

The first line was down, devastated, defeated. The second line battle began. Barbarian reserves came forward, and were met by waves of arrows that darkened the sky—and took their toll when they struck the advancing groups of men.

Hoarse cries of pain, curses, and shrieks of the desperately wounded, the agonized horror of Linnans suddenly cut off, and doomed rose up to the ears of those in the darting small craft.

The defenders strove to stay together. That was a part of their instructions. Retreat slowly to the central squares—which were strongly held against a surprise rear attack. Retreat, and at the last minute spaceships would land to rescue the hard pressed, but theoretically still intact army of what had once been able-bodied civilians.

After a month and a half of training, they were too valuable to sacrifice in a last ditch fight.

As it was, their dogged resistance was shaping the pattern of the war. Surely, Czinczar, counting his men after each battle, must already be having his own private doubts. His army as a whole, augmented by the unrepentant among the slaves, was increasing daily. But the larger the army grew the smaller was his chance of controlling it.

But there was no doubt about this battle, or this city. As the dark tide of night slipped in from the east, victory fires began to burn in all the important streets. The smoke wreathed into the sky and blood-red flames licked up into the blackness.

The Linnans below, at this very moment enduring the beginning of a barbarian occupation, would not be in a humor to appreciate that their grudgingly accepted defeat represented a possible turning point in the war.

The time had come to decide when and where and under what conditions the main Linnan force would be thrown into a decisive battle for the control of the planet.

And there was another decision, too, involving an immensely risky attempt to get near a certain atomic machine. Clane shifted uneasily in his seat, and drew his cloak more tightly around his shoulders.

He had no illusions about what one easily killable man could do even with phenomenal weapons. Besides, he had received a disturbing note from Czinczar, which contained only one sentence, a question:

"Have you ever wondered, my Lord Clane, how the civilization of the golden age was so *completely* destroyed?"

It was a problem about which the mutation, Clane, had pondered many times.

But it had never occurred to him that the answer might be known to a barbarian from a remote moon of Jupiter.

❖ ❖ ❖

The moment the news arrived, Czinczar headed for Linn. He was met on the roof of the central palace by Meewan. The big man had a smile on his plump, good-fellow face.

"Your theory was right," he said admiringly. "You thought he would take a chance at the critical period of the invasion. And he arrived this morning."

"Tell me exactly how you accepted his services."

The golden voice spoke softly. The strange face was thoughtful as the other man gave his detailed account. There seemed no end to his interest. When the story was finished, he asked question after question. Each answer seemed merely to stimulate new questions. Meewan said finally, querulously:

"Your excellency, what are you doubtful about?"

That stopped him, for he had not realized how tense he was. After all, he told himself, the situation was simple enough. He had issued an open invitation for temple scientists to come and take care of "some god metal relics" which had fallen into possession of the conquerors. It was a cleverly worded request, designed to win general approval from the defeated even as it drew *the* temple scientist to his own undoing.

Its only stipulation, very guardedly worded, was that in return for the privilege of sharing the "safeguarding of the relics," experiments should be continued as if no war was being waged.

"The gods," Czinczar had said sanctimoniously in the invitation, "are above the petty quarrels of mankind."

Apparently, at least one of its purposes was accomplished. The mutation himself had applied for the job. Czinczar meditated cautiously on tactics.

"Bring him here," he said finally. "We can't take any risks of his having established control over anything at his house. We know too little and he too much."

While he waited, he examined the rod of force—which was one of the few workable instruments that had been found in the house. He was not a man who accepted past truths as final. The fact that it had worked a week ago did not mean that it would work now.

He tested it from a great window, pointing it at the upper foliage of a nearby tree.

No sound, no visible light spewed forth—but the upper section of the tree crashed down onto a pathway below.

Czinczar experienced the satisfaction of a logical man whose logic had proved correct. It was not an uncommon satisfaction. From the early days when he had been a back country transcriber of messages to the days of his rise to power, he had taken risks which seemed necessary, no more, no less.

Even now he could not be sure that the atomic wizard, Lord Clane, would not defeat him by some decisive wile. For several minutes, he pondered that, and then ordered a box brought in from the ice room of the palace. The contents of the box had come all the way from Europa packed in ice.

He was indicating to the slaves where to place the box when an officer burst breathlessly into the throne room.

"Excellency," he cried. "Hundreds of spaceships. It's an attack."

Standing at the window a moment later, watching the ships settling down, Czinczar realized that his hazy suspicions had been correct.

The appearance of Clane in the city was part of a planned maneuver, which would now run its deadly course.

It was a pleasure to know that Lord Clane himself was caught in a trap.

❖ ❖ ❖

Czinczar wasted no time watching a battle which he could not hope to see from the palace in any important detail. Nor did he have the feeling Tews had had months earlier, that it was necessary for commanders to know where he was in the early stages of the engagement.

It was nice for a general to get reports, and there was a thrill in giving a "Stand fast" order to troops already fighting for their lives. But it was quite unnecessary.

Czinczar issued quick instructions about the box, and wrote a note for Meewan. Then he rode with a strong escort to the headquarters of the reserve army in the middle of the city.

The reserve contained a barbarian core, but, like the main defense forces of the city, it was overwhelmingly made up of slaves. Czinczar's arrival was greeted by a roar of excitement. The cheers did not die down until long after he had entered the building.

He talked over the situation with some of the slave officers, and found them calm and confident. According to their estimates sixty thousand Linnan soldiers had landed in the first wave. The fact that that was exactly the number of barbarians who had originally invaded the city did not seem to occur to the slaves. But the comparison struck Czinczar sharply. He wondered if it was designed to have some symbolic meaning.

The possibility made him sardonic. Not symbols but swords spoke the language of victory.

As the afternoon dragged on, the Linnan attack was being held everywhere. The box was delivered from the palace about three. It was dripping badly, and since there was no long any immediate danger, Czinczar sent a messenger to Meewan.

At three-thirty Meewan came in grinning broadly. He was followed by slave Linnans carrying a sedan chair. In the chair, bound hand and food, was the acting Lord Leader of Linn.

There was complete silence as the chair was set down, and the slaves withdrew.

❖❖❖

Clane studied the barbarian leader with a genuine interest. His grandmother's opinion of the man had impressed him more than he cared to admit. The question was, could this strong-looking, fine-looking military genius be panicked into thinking that the atom gods existed? Panicked now, during the next half hour?

Fortunately, for the first time in his career as an atomic scientist, he had behind him the greatest power ever developed by the wizards of the fabulous days of the legends. He saw that the impersonal expression on the other's face was transforming into the beginning of contempt.

"By the god pits," said Czinczar in disgust, "you Linnans are all the same—weaklings every one."

Clane said nothing. He had looked often with regret into mirrors that showed him exactly what Czinczar was seeing: A slim, young man with a face that was white and womanish and . . . well, it couldn't be helped.

Czinczar's face changed again. There was suddenly irony in it.

"I am speaking," he asked politely, "to Lord Clane Linn? We have not made a mistake."

Clane couldn't let the opening pass. "No mistake," he said quietly. "I came into Linn for the sole purpose of talking to you while the battle was on. And here I am."

It must have sounded ridiculous, coming from a man bound as he was. The near guards guffawed, and Meewan giggled. Only Czinczar showed no sign. And his marvelous voice was as steady as steel as he said:

"I have not the time to flirt with words, nor the inclination. I can see that you are counting on something to save you, and I presume it has something to do with your knowledge of atomic energy."

He fingered the rod of force suggestively. "So far as I can see, we can kill you in less than a second whenever we desire."

Clane shook his head. "You are in error. It is quite impossible for you to kill me."

There was a sound from Meewan. The engineer came forward.

"Czinczar," he said darkly, "this man is intolerable. Give me permission to slap his face, and we shall see if his atom gods protect him from indignity."

Czinczar waved him aside. But he stared down at the prisoner with eyes that were unnormally bright. The swiftness with which tension had come into the room amazed him. And, incredibly, it was the prisoner who had seized the advantage—"Impossible to kill me!" In one sentence he dared them to make the attempt.

As he stood hesitating, an officer came in with a report. Except for a tiny note, everything was favorable. The note was about prisoners: "All have been told that a great miracle will win the battle for the Linnans. I mention this for what it is worth—"

Czinczar returned to his prisoner, and there was a crinkle of a frown in his forehead. He had been careful in his handling of Clane as a matter of common sense, not because he anticipated disaster. But now, quite frankly, he admitted to himself that the man was not reacting normally.

The words Clane had spoken had a ring in them, a conviction that could no longer be ignored. The purpose of his own invasion of the Linnan empire could be in danger. He said urgently:

"I have something to show you. No attempt will be made to kill you until you have seen it. For your part, do nothing hasty, take no action, whatever power you have, until you have gazed with understanding."

He was aware of Meewan giving him an astounded glance. "Power!" exclaimed the designer, and it was like a curse. "The power *he* has!"

Czinczar paid no attention. This was his own special secret, and there could be no delay.

"Guards," he said, "bring that box over here."

It was soaking wet when they brought it. It left a dirty trail of water on the priceless rug, and a pool began to accumulate immediately where it was set down.

There was a delay while sweating men pried off the top. Even the guards at far doors strained to see the contents.

A gasp of horror broke the tension of waiting.

What was inside was about eight feet long. Its width was indeterminable, for there seemed to be folds in its body that gave an impression of great size. It had obviously died only a short time before it was packed in the ice.

It looked fresh, almost alive.

It lay there in its case of ice, unhuman, staring with sightless, baleful eyes at the ornate ceiling.

Clane looked up finally into Czinczar's waiting eyes. He said slowly:

"Why are you showing this to me?"

"It would be a grave error," said Czinczar, "for either of us to destroy each other's armies."

"You are asking for mercy?"

That was too strong to take. The barbarian showed his teeth in a snarl. "I am asking for common sense," he said.

"It's impossible," said Clane. "The people must have their revenge. In victory, they will accept nothing less than your death."

❖❖❖

The words brought an obscene curse from Meewan. "Czinczar," he shouted, "what is all this nonsense? I have never seen you like this. I follow no man who accepts defeat in advance. I'll show you what we'll do with this . . . this—"

He broke off: "Guards, put a spear into him."

Nobody moved. The soldiers looked uneasily at Czinczar, who nodded coolly.

"Go right ahead," he said. "If he can be killed, I'd like to know."

Still nobody moved. It was apparently too mild an order, or something of the leader's tension had communicated to the men. They looked at each other, and they were standing there doubtfully when Meewan snatched a sword from one of them, and turned towards the bound man.

That was as far as he got.

Where he had been was a ball of light.

"Try," came the voice of Clane, "to use the rod of force against me." A fateful pause. "Try. It won't kill you."

Czinczar raised the rod of force, and pressed the activator.

Nothing happened—Wait! The ball of light was growing brighter.

Clane's voice split the silence tantalizingly: "Do you still not believe in the gods?"

"I am surprised," said Czinczar, "that you do not fear the spread of superstition more than the spread of knowledge. We so-called barbarians," he said proudly, "despise you for your attempt to fence in the human spirit. We are free thinkers, and all your atomic energy will fail in the end to imprison us."

He shrugged. "As for your control over that ball, I do not pretend to understand it."

At last, he had shocked the mutation out of his ice-cold manner. "You actually," said Clane incredulously, "do not believe in the atom gods?"

"Guards," shouted Czinczar piercingly, "attack him from every side."

The ball of light flickered but did not seem to move.

There were no guards.

"Now do you believe?" Clane asked.

The barbarian looked haggard and old. But he shook his head.

"I have lost the war," he mumbled. "Only that I recognize. It is up to you to take up the mantle which has fallen from my shoulders."

The smaller man gazed at him wonderingly. And then, the bonds fell from him as if they did not exist. He stood up, and now that crown among all the jewels of the ages rode above his head in a matchlessly perfect rhythm with his movement.

Czinczar said stubbornly, "It would be a mistake to kill any able bodied man, slave or otherwise."

Clane said, "The gods demand absolute surrender."

Czinczar said in fury, "You fool, I am offering you the solar system. Has this monster in the box not changed your mind in the slightest degree?"

"It has."

"But then—"

"I do not," said Clane, "believe in joint leadership arrangements."

A pause. Then:

"You have come far—who once used his power merely to stay alive."

"Yes," said Clane, "I have come far."

"Will you promise to try for the Lord Leadership?"

"I," Clane said, "can promise nothing."

They looked at each other, two men who almost understood each other. It was Czinczar who broke the silence:

"I make an absolute surrender," he said, "to you, and you alone, of all my forces—in the belief that you have the courage and common sense to shirk none of your new duties as Protector of the Solar System.

"It was a role," he finished somewhat unnecessarily, "that I originally intended for myself."

❖❖❖

In a well-guarded room in a remote suburb of Linn, a core of energy rolled sedately back and forth along a narrow path. In all the solar system there was nothing else like that core. It looked small, but that was an illusion of man's senses. The books that described it, and the men who had written the books, knew but a part of its secrets.

They knew that the micro-universe inside it pulsed with a multiform of minus forces. It reacted to cosmic rays and atomic energy like some insatiable sponge. No sub-molecular energy released in its presence could escape it. And the moment it reached its own strange variation of critical mass it could start a meson chain reaction in anything it touched.

One weakness it had—and men had seized upon that in their own greedy fashion—it imitated thought. Or so it seemed.

So—it—seemed.

Part II:
The Wizard of Linn

1

In the deceptive darkness of space, the alien ship moved with only an occasional glint of reflected sunlight to show its presence. It paused for many months to study the moons of Jupiter, and the Riss-creatures aboard neither concealed the presence of their ship, nor made a particular display of it or of themselves.

A score of times, Riss exploring parties ran into human beings. Their policy on such occasions was invariable. They killed every human who saw them. Once, on remote Titan, the hilly nature of the terrain with its innumerable caves enabled a man to evade the net they spread for him. That night, after he had had ample time to reach the nearest village, an atomic bomb engulfed the entire area.

For what it was worth, the policy paid off. Despite the casual way their ship flew over towns and villages, only the vaguest reports of the presence of a big ship were spread. And for long no one suspected that the ship was not occupied by human beings.

Their precautions could not alter the natural order of life and death. Some hours out of Titan, a Riss workman who was repairing a minor break in an instrument on the outer skin of the spaceship, was struck by a meteor. By an immense coincidence, the flying object was moving in the same direction as the ship and at approximately the same speed. The workman was killed by the blow, and swept out into space. On Europa, the largest moon, a Riss one-man exploring craft made its automatic return to the mother ship but without its pilot aboard. Its speedometer registered more than a thousand miles of flight, and those who tried to follow its curving back trail found themselves over mountains so precipitous that the search was swiftly abandoned.

Surprisingly, both bodies were found, the former by meteor miners from Europa, the latter by troops engaged in grueling maneuvers preliminary to Czinczar's invasion of Earth. Both monstrosities were brought to the leader; and, putting together various reports he had heard, he made an unusually accurate guess as to the origin of the strange beings.

His attack on Earth took place a few months later while the alien ship was still in the vicinity of Europa. And his defeat at the hands of Lord Clane Linn followed. The machine from the stars continued its unhurried voyage of exploration. It arrived on Mars less than a month after Lord Jerrin and his army embarked for Earth, and another month went by before its presence was reported to the Linnan military governor on Mars.

A descendant of the great Raheinl, he was a proud young man, who dismissed the first account as a tale of simple imagination, all too common in these regions where education had fallen a victim of protracted wars. But when the second report came in from another section, it struck him that this might be the Martian version of the barbarian invasion. He acted swiftly and decisively.

Police spaceships and patrol craft scoured the atmosphere. And, since the alien made no effort to avoid being seen, contact was established almost immediately. Two of the police craft were destroyed by great flares of energy. The other ships, observing the catastrophe from a distance, withdrew hastily.

If the Riss noticed that they were now in a more highly mechanized part of the solar system, they did not by their actions let it disturb them. If they guessed that in these regions their action meant war, they seemed equally unaware of that.

The governor dispatched a warning to Earth, and then set about organizing his forces. For two weeks his patrol craft did nothing but watch, and the picture that came through was very satisfactory to the grim young man. The enemy, it appeared, was sending out exploring parties in small ships. It was these, on the fifteenth day, that the human-manned ships attacked in swarms.

The technique of assault had been very carefully worked out. In every case an attempt was made to ram the Riss craft. Four of the attacks were successful. The smashed "lift" boats glittered in the dull afternoon light as they fell to the flat earth below. Swiftly, spaceships darted down, drew the fallen machines aboard, and hastily took off for widely separated landing fields.

It was a major victory, greater even than was immediately suspected. The enemy reacted the following morning. The city of Gadre blew up in a colossal explosion that sent a mushroom of smoke billowing up to obscure the atmosphere for a hundred miles.

The ferocity of the counterattack ended the war on Mars. The alien was left strictly alone thereafter. The youthful Raheinl, stunned by the violence of the response, ordered the evacuation of the larger cities, and dispatched another of a long series of warning reports to Earth. He also sent along for examination the two largest and least damaged of the enemy small craft which he had captured.

It was about a month later that he ceased to receive reports of the ship's presence inside the Martian atmosphere. He concluded that it had departed for Earth, and made out his final report on that basis. He was relieved.

The problem would now be faced by those who were in the best position to know if it could be handled at all.

Jerrin put down the first report from Mars as his wife Lilidel entered the room. He rose to his feet, and gravely assisted her and the babe-in-arms she carried—their seventh child—to a chair. Then, uneasily, he returned to his own chair. He had an idea that he was going to hear more about a certain person.

Lilidel began at once. And, as he had expected, it *was* about his brother, Clane. He listened politely, with a sense of dissatisfaction in her, a feeling of exasperation that came to him whenever she tried to influence his judgment for emotional reasons. When she had gone on for several minutes, he interposed gently:

"My dear, if Clane had wanted to seize control, he had two whole months between the end of the barbarian war and my return."

She waited respectfully while he spoke. Lilidel—he had to confess it—was a remarkable wife. Dutiful, good, gracious, discreet, and with an unblemished past, she was, as she had pointed out many times, a model among the women of noble birth.

Jerrin could not help wondering at times what it was about her that annoyed him. It made him unhappy that he had to have thoughts like that. Because, considered in individual segments, her character was perfect. And yet, the woman-as-a-whole irritated him at times to the point of distraction. Once more, he spoke:

"We have to recognize that Clane conducted the barbarian invasion campaign with remarkable skill. I still don't quite see how it was done."

He realized immediately that he had said the wrong thing. It was a mistake, according to Lilidel, to be too generous with appreciation for the merits of other men. Clane had only performed his duty. There was no reason why he should not retreat now into private life, and restrict his ambition for the good of the family and of the state.

Jerrin listened unhappily. He was seriously dissatisfied with the way he had acted towards his brother's victory. At the very least, a Triumph should have been offered Clane. And yet, his advisers in the Patronate had persuaded him that such recognition would be highly dangerous.

When he spoke again, his reply seemed to be a direct answer to Lilidel. Actually, it was partly a defensive reaction to all the people who had held down his natural impulse to give credit where it was due. He said:

"My dear, if some of the things I've heard about Clane are true, then he could seize control of the government at any time. And I should like to point out one more thing: The idea that the Lord Advisership is now a rightful property of my branch of the family is an illusion. We may hold it, but power slips from a person's grasp even as he thinks he has it firmly gripped. I have here"—he picked up the report from Mars—"a most disturbing message from General Raheinl—"

He was not allowed to change the subject as easily as that. It seemed that if he did not have any ambition for himself, at least he could think of his own offspring. It appeared that it was up to him to insure that his eldest son was confirmed in the succession. Young Calaj was now seventeen years of age, and the plan for him should be made clear at an early date. Jerrin cut her off at last.

"I've been intending to tell you. I have to make a tour of inspection in the provinces, and I am scheduled to leave this afternoon. We'd better postpone this discussion till I return."

Lilidel put in a final word on the subject of how fortunate he was to have a wife who accepted his ever more frequent absences with a heavy but understanding heart.

2

Somebody said, "Look!"

There was so much amazement and wonder in the word that Lord Jerrin whirled involuntarily. All around him, men were craning their necks, staring up at the sky.

He turned his gaze to follow that collective stare. And he felt a flame-like shock. The ship up there was enormous beyond all his previous experience. He guessed, from his detailed knowledge of the limitations of spaceship construction on Earth, that it was not of the solar system. His mind flashed back to the messages that had come from his military governor on Mars. For a moment then a feeling of imminent disaster seized him.

His courage flooded back with a rush. He estimated that the stranger was a third of a mile in length. His sharp eyes picked out, and noted for future reference, details of construction dissimilar to anything he had ever seen before. As he watched, the great machine floated by silently. It seemed to be about three miles above the ground, and its speed could not have been very great, because after a minute it was still visible in the distance. It disappeared finally beyond the mists of the eastern horizon.

Before it was out of sight, Jerrin was giving his orders. He had still to receive the message about the destruction of the Martian city Gadre, but he was more cautious than Raheinl had been. The fleet of spaceships and smaller craft which he sent after the stranger had strict orders to keep at a distance.

The preliminary defensive measures taken, Lord Jerrin returned to the City of Linn, and settled down to await reports. By morning, half a dozen messages had arrived, but they added nothing of importance to what he had personally observed. What did count was the arrival about noon of a letter from Lord Clane.

❖❖❖

Your Excellency:

I earnestly urge that you order the evacuation from the large cities of all forces and equipment necessary to the defense of the realm.

It is vital that this ship from another sun be destroyed. There is some reason to believe that those aboard are descendants of the same beings who destroyed the legendary civilization of Earth. Riss they were called.

I request that there be a meeting between us as soon as possible. I have a number of valuable suggestions to make concerning the tactics to be employed against the enemy.

Clane

Jerrin read the note several times, and tried to picture the details of the evacuation that his brother was recommending. Considered in its practical details, the enterprise seemed so vast that he put the letter aside angrily. Later he bethought himself, and sent a reply.

Most Excellent Brother:

All necessary and practicable precautions are being taken. I shall be most happy to have a visit from you at any time.

Jerrin,

Lord Adviser of Linn

When that had been sent off, he wondered for the first time how Clane had learned so quickly of the interstellar ship. It seemed far-fetched that he also could have seen it personally. The incident was merely one more confirmation of his suspicions that there were supporters of Clane in every branch of the service including, apparently, his own staff.

By evening, when the reports about the ship were coming in steadily, the bitterness of his feeling against his mutation brother yielded to the need for a careful study of the mountain pile of evidence.

Now, the alien ship was crossing the ocean. Then it was over the mountains. Next, it stopped for an hour above the city of Goram. A hundred small craft emerged from it, and spent the daylight hours exploring the nearby hills.

In spite of Jerrin's orders that none of the visitor's "lift" boats be interfered with, two incidents occurred. They took place at widely separated points, but were similar in outcome. Both resulted from Earth patrol boats venturing within a mile of one of the small enemy vessels.

Observers reported flashes of blue fire. The Earth craft burst into flame and crashed, killing their occupants.

The news, when it reached him, shook Jerrin. But it confirmed him in a plan that had been growing on him. He had been waiting to hear from Mars the outcome of Raheinl's plan. (He took it for granted that the ship which had come to Earth was the same one that had been on Mars. And that it had merely made the journey from the fourth planet to the third one more swiftly than the spaceship which undoubtedly was bringing the report of the Martian governor.) But now it seemed to him the answer was clear.

The alien had come from another star. Soon, it would go back home. Therefore, since those aboard were making no attempt to communicate with him, they should be allowed to carry on as they pleased. Meanwhile, the Linnan fleet would strengthen its defenses, and be ready for a crisis. When he communicated these instructions to his chief of staff, the officer stroked his mustache, and said finally:

"What do you mean—strengthen our defenses? In what way? Have more spears and arrows manufactured?"

Jerrin hesitated. Put in that way, his plan sounded blurred. He said at last, "Be alert. Be ready for sacrifices."

He didn't know what he meant by that, either.

The second day went by while his sense of inadequacy grew. The following morning the officer in charge of the men and women watching Lord Clane and his chief supporters reported that the mutation was moving all his equipment out of his residence in the city of Linn.

Jerrin considered that in a gathering anger. It was exactly the kind of incident that could start a panic, if it became known. He was still seething when a second note arrived from his brother.

❖❖❖

Dear Jerrin:
I have received the news of the Martian disaster, and I urge you to

order the evacuation of Linn and other cities.

   I tell you, sir, this ship must be destroyed before it leaves Earth.

                 Clane

❖❖❖

It was a sharp letter. Its curtness brought the color flooding to Jerrin's lean, tanned cheeks. And for more than a minute the tone, and not the contents, absorbed his full attention. Then he thought, "Martian disaster!"

Holding himself calm, he sent a courier to the field where the official ships from Mars always landed. The courier returned empty-handed.

"No ship has arrived from Mars for more than a week, your excellency."

Jerrin paced the floor of the palace reception room. He was amazed, and concerned to realize that he believed that Clane had received information which the government did not have. He recognized that the mutation had revealed a personal secret in letting him know by this indirect method that he had a faster means of communication with the planets. The willingness to let that secret out seemed significant now.

And yet, he could not make up his mind to accept all the implications in good faith.

He was still worrying about it when Lilidel came in. As usual, she brought one of the children with her.

❖❖❖

Jerrin studied her absently as she talked. She was no longer the great beauty he had married, though her remarkably even features remained almost unchanged from the day he had first met her.

Not her face, but her body showed the marks of the years that had gone by, and the children she had borne. Jerrin was not unreasonably critical. He only wished his wife's character had altered as little as her body. He said presently, patiently:

"I want to make one thing clear. A man who cannot protect the empire cannot hold his office. I suggest that you cease worrying about the succession of our Calaj, and seriously consider the desperate position we are in as a result of the presence of this strange ship."

Quickly, he told her of the messages he had received from Clane. When he had finished, the woman was pale.

"This is what I feared," she said in a tensed voice. "I knew he had a scheme afoot."

The egocentricity of the remark startled him. He pointed out that Clane could hardly be considered responsible for the appearance of the ship. Lilidel brushed the explanation aside.

"What reason he uses doesn't matter," she said impatiently. "When a man has a purpose, any reason is good."

She was going on in the same vein when Jerrin cut her off. "Are you insane?" he said violently. "Let me inform you, madam, that I will not tolerate such nonsense in my presence. If you wish to chatter about Clane's conspiracies against the state, please don't do it to me." His anger aroused by her illogicalness, he forgot for the moment his own suspicions of Clane.

Lilidel stared at him with hurt eyes. "You've never talked to me like this before," she sniffled. She clutched the little girl tightly against her, as if to protect herself from further thrusts.

The action also served to call attention to the presence of the child. There was a pattern to the movement that abruptly pulled Jerrin back along the years, to all the other occasions when she had brought one of their children whenever she came to him with a complaint or a request. *Or a request.* The shock of the thought that came was terrific. He had always been proud of the fact that Lilidel, unlike the scheming consorts of rulers of other days, had never used her relationship with him for private purposes.

Now, he had a flashing picture of the *thousands* of times she had come to him to forward the interests of some individual. She had suggested appointments to positions of varying importance, all the way up to governorships. In her quiet way she had promoted a fantastic number of decrees, orders, and laws, only a fraction of which could possibly have originated in her own mind.

He saw her, suddenly, as the spokesman for a group that had been ruling the provinces he commanded by taking advantage of his preoccupation with military affairs. Through him they had set up a vast organization subservient to their interests. And it was they who wanted to turn him against Clane.

The extent of the betrayal sobered him. It was hard to believe that Lilidel could be aware of the implications of what she had done and was doing. It was easier to believe that her character, too, had been analyzed by clever men, and that she was being used. Unquestionably, however, she must be playing the game consciously as far as she understood it. He did not doubt that she loved her children.

The problem was too great to be acted on immediately. Jerrin said quietly: "Please leave me. I have no desire to talk to you harshly. You caught me at a bad moment."

When she had gone, he stood for a long time undecided, his mind again on Clane's message. At last he thought: *The truth is, I have no solution to the problem of the invading ship. It's time to find out if Clane has.*

His message to his brother was brief and to the point: "Let us meet. Name date, place and conditions."

Clane's reply was, "Will you order the evacuation of all large cities immediately? And then will you come if I send a ship for you?"

"Yes," Jerrin answered back.

3

There was no sign of Clane when the Lord Adviser's party arrived at the spaceship. Jerrin accepted the implication of that with a grim smile, but there were murmurs of annoyance from his staff. The tension ended as an officer in general's uniform came hurrying down the gangplank. He came up quickly, saluted, and stood at attention, waiting for permission to speak. Jerrin gave it. The man said quickly, apologetically:

"Your excellency, Lord Clane sends his sincere regrets that he was unable to complete certain preliminaries. We are to pick him up at his estate, and he will wait upon you the moment he comes aboard."

Jerrin was mollified. He was no stickler for rules, but he did not have to be told that people who deliberately broke them were expressing unspoken purposes and thoughts, which, on the government level, could mean open rebellion. He was glad that Clane had chosen this way to express his purposes. He was fulfilling the minimum of amenities.

Jerrin was not so indelicate as to inquire the nature of the "preliminaries" that had caused the delay. He took it for granted that they existed only in the imagination.

From a porthole of his apartment, a few minutes later, he watched the land recede below, and it was then that his first alarm came, the first realization that perhaps he had been hasty in risking himself aboard this ship without a large guardian fleet. It seemed hard to believe that his brother would risk a major civil war, and yet such things had happened before.

He could not bring himself to admit openly that he might have walked into a trap, so he did not inform the officers of his party of his suspicions.

He began to feel better when the ship started its descent towards Clane's estate landing field. Later, as he watched his brother coming across the field, the anxiety faded even more. He grew curious as he saw that the men behind Clane were carrying an elongated, trough-like metal object. There was something in the trough that shone, and it seemed to be moving back and forth in a very slow fashion. It was out of his line of vision before he could decide what it was. It looked like a glass ball.

In a short time the ship was in the air again, and presently an officer arrived with Clane's request for an audience. Jerrin granted the request at once. He was puzzled. Just where was this ship heading?

He had been sitting down; but as Clane entered he rose to his feet. The apartment was ideally constructed for a man of rank to receive homage from lesser mortals. From the anteroom, where the entrance was, three steps led up to the larger reception room beyond. At the top of these steps, as if it was a throne dais, Jerrin waited. With narrowed eyes and pursed lips, he watched his brother come toward him.

He had noticed from the porthole that Clane, as usual, wore temple clothing. Now, he had a moment to observe the effect in greater detail. Even in those spare surroundings, he looked drab and unassuming. In that room, with its dozen staff officers in their blue and silver uniforms, he seemed so terribly out of place that, suddenly, the older man could not believe that here was a threat to his own position.

The rigid hostility went out of Jerrin's body. A wave of pity and understanding swept over him. He knew only too well how carefully that clothing covered the other's mutated shoulders and arms and chest.

I remember, he thought, *when I was one of a gang of kids that used to strip him and jeer at him.*

That was long ago now, more than twenty years. But the memory brought a feeling of guilt. His uncertainty ended. With an impulsive friendliness, he strode down the steps and put his great, strong arms around Clane's slim body.

"Dear brother," he said, "I am glad to see you."

He stepped back after a moment, feeling much better, less cynical, and very much more convinced that this delicate brother of his would never compete with him for power. He spoke again:

"May I inquire where we are heading?"

Clane smiled. His face was fuller than it had been the last time Jerrin had seen him. Some of the angelic womanlike quality of it was yielding to a firmer, more masculine appearance. Even the smile was assured, but just for a moment it gave him the appearance of being beautiful rather than handsome. He was thirty-three years old, but there was still no sign that he had ever shaved.

He said now: "According to my latest reports, the invader is at present 'lying to' over a chain of mountains about a hundred miles from here. I want you to witness an attack I am planning to make against the ship."

It took all the rest of the journey for the full import of that to penetrate.

❖ ❖ ❖

At no time did Jerrin clearly realize what was happening. He stood on the ground, and watched Clane examine the enemy ship, which was about three miles distant, a shape in the mist. Clane came over to him finally, and said in a troubled voice:

"Our problem is the possibility of failure."

Jerrin said nothing.

Clane continued, "If my use of the Temple metals fails to destroy the ship, then they may take counter action."

The reference to the god metals irritated Jerrin. His own feeling about the Temples, and of the religion they taught, was from the viewpoint of a soldier. The ideas involved were useful in promoting discipline among the rank and file. He had no sense of cynicism about it. He had never given thought to religion of itself. Now, he felt a kind of pressure on him. He could not escape the conviction that Clane and the others took it for granted that there was something in the religion. He had heard vague accounts of Clane's activities in the past, but in his austere and active existence, with each day devoted to an immense total of administrative tasks, there had never been time to consider the obscure tales of magic that occasionally came his way. He felt uneasy now, for he regarded these things as of a kind with other superstitions that he had heard.

Apparently, he was about to be given an exhibition of these hitherto concealed powers, and he felt disturbed. *I never should*, he thought, *have allowed myself to become involved with these metaphysicians.*

He waited unhappily.

Clane was eying him thoughtfully. "I want you to witness this," he said. "Because on the basis of it, I hope to have your support of a major attack."

Jerrin said quickly, "You expect this attack to fail?"

Clane nodded. "I have no weapons better than those that were available during the Golden Age. And if the best weapons of that great scientific era were unable to stave off the destruction that our ancestors barely survived, then I don't see how we can be successful with odds and ends of their science."

He added, "I have an idea that the enemy ship is constructed of materials in which no pattern of destruction can be established."

The meaning of that shocked Jerrin. "Am I to understand that this first attack is being undertaken with the purpose of convincing me to support a *second* attack? And that it is this second attack you are building your hopes on?"

Clane hesitated, then nodded. "Yes," he said.

"What is the nature of your second plan?" Jerrin asked.

He grew pale as Clane outlined it. "You want us to risk the fleet merely as a support?"

Clane said simply, "What else is it good for?"

Jerrin was trembling, but he held his voice calm. "The role you have in mind for yourself to some extent shows how seriously you regard this matter. But, brother, you are asking me to risk the state. If you fail, they'll destroy cities."

Clane said, "The ship cannot be allowed to return home."

"Why not? It seems the simplest solution. They'll leave sooner or later."

Clane was tense. "Something happened," he said. "It was not a completely successful war for them thousands of years ago. They were driven off then, apparently not aware that they had caused irreparable damage to the solar system by destroying all its cities. If this ship gets back now, and reports that we are virtually helpless, they'll return in force."

"But why?" said Jerrin. "Why should they bother us?"

"Land."

The blood rushed to Jerrin's face, and he had a vision then of the fight that had taken place long ago. The desperate, deadly, merciless war of two races, utterly alien to each other, one seeking to seize, the other to hold, a planetary system. The picture was sufficient. He felt himself stiffening to the hard necessities. He straightened.

"Very well," he said in a ringing voice, "I wish to see this experiment. Proceed."

❖❖❖

The metal case with the silvery ball rolling back and forth in it was brought to the center of the glade. It was the object Jerrin had watched them bring aboard at Clane's estate. He walked over to it, and stood looking down at it.

The ball rolled sedately first to one end, and then back again to the other. Its movement seemed without meaning. Jerrin put his hand down, glanced up to see if Clane objected to his action; and when Clane merely stood watching him, lowered his finger gingerly into the path of that glistening sphere.

He expected it to be shoved out of the way by a solid metal weight.

The ball rolled through it.

Into it, through it, beyond it. There was no feeling at all, no sensation of substance. It was as if he had held his hand in empty air.

Repelled by its alienness, Jerrin drew back. "What is it?" he said with distaste.

The faintest of smiles came into Clane's face. "You're asking the wrong type of question," he said.

Jerrin was momentarily baffled, and then he remembered his military training. "What does it do?"

"It absorbs any energy directed at it. It converts all matter that it touches into energy, and then absorbs the energy."

"It didn't convert my finger into energy."

"It's safe to handle while it's in its case. It probably has a limitation on the amount of energy it will absorb, though I have yet to find what it is. That's what gives me hope that it just might be useful against the enemy."

"You're going to use it against *them?*"

Incredibly, it hadn't occurred to him that this was the weapon. He stared down at it, shocked; and the feeling—which had briefly gone away—that he was being made a fool of in some obscure fashion, returned. Jerrin looked around him unhappily. An armor-plated battleship a third of a mile long floated in the mists to the southeast. Down here, a dozen men stood in a forest glade. Nearby, lay the small, open-decked craft which had brought them from their own spaceship some ten miles away. The craft was unarmed except for a score of bowmen and spearmen.

Jerrin controlled himself. "When are you going to attack?"

"Now!"

Jerrin parted his lips to speak again, when he noticed that the silvery ball was gone from its case. With a start he looked up— and froze as he saw that it was floating in the air above Clane's head.

It was brighter now, and danced and blurred, and quivered like something alive. It was a shiningness, insubstantial yet palpable. Feather-light, it floated above the mutation's head, riding with his movements.

"Watch the ship!" Clane pointed.

The words and the movement were like a signal. The "ball" was abruptly gone from above his head. Jerrin saw it momentarily, high in the sky, a gleam against the dark bulk of the great ship. There was a flash of shiningness, and then the fantastic thing was back over Clane's head.

High above them, the great ship rode its invisible anchors, apparently unharmed.

Jerrin said with disappointment, "It didn't work?"

Clane waved at him, a spasmodic movement of his hand. "Wait!" he said. "There may be a counterattack."

The silence that followed did not last long.

A rim of fire appeared along a line of the ship running from the nose to the tail. Miles away in the forest, thunder rolled. It came near, and grew louder. A quarter of a mile away through the brush, there was a bright splash of fire, and then it was a quarter of a mile beyond them, on the other side.

Jerrin noticed that for just a moment while the thunder and flame threatened them, the ball was gone from above Clane. When he looked again, it was back in position, dancing, bobbing, blurring. Clane must have caught his distracted gaze, for he said:

"They couldn't locate us, so they plotted a curve, and struck at intervals along that line. The question is, will they notice that there was no explosion at one of the probable centers of the attack against them?"

Jerrin guessed then that the enemy had plotted an accurate curve, and by some magic science had picked their exact position as one of the areas to attack.

And apparently the shining sphere had absorbed the energy of the attacking force.

He waited, tense.

After five minutes, there was still no sign of a further attack. At the end of twenty minutes, Clane said with satisfaction, "They seem to be satisfied with their counterattack. At least we know they're not superhuman. Let's go."

They boarded the small craft, slid along for a while slowly under a spread of tree branches, then turned through a narrow pass and so into a valley from which the big ship was not visible. As they picked up speed, Clane spoke again:

"I'd like to have a look at those captured craft that Raheinl sent you from Mars. The sooner we act the better. There may be retaliations."

Jerrin had been thinking about that, thinking of how deeply he was committed. An attack had been made, the enemy advised by active means that his presence was resented. The war was on, and there was no turning back.

He asked quietly, "When do you plan to make your second attack?"

4

The invading ship had fortunately not come nearer to the city of Linn than about a hundred and fifty miles. So it was natural that its first victim should not be the capital. A large midland city received the first blow.

The bomb was dropped approximately twenty hours after Clane's attempt to destroy the alien with the sphere. It dropped on a city that had been evacuated except for street patrols and the looters who made the patrols necessary. Dense clouds of smoke hid the damage and the disaster.

Less than half an hour later, a second city was struck by one of the colossal bombs, and the poisonous smoke rose up in its toadstool shape, infinitely deadly and irresistible.

The third city was struck an hour later, and the fourth shortly after noon. There was a pause then, and a host of small craft were seen to emerge from the giant. They explored the outer edges of the four gigantic smoke areas, and flew tantalizingly near Linnan patrol craft, as if trying to draw their fire.

When the news of this maneuver was brought to Clane, he sent a message to Jerrin:

Most Excellent Lord Leader:

It would appear that they were severely surprised by our attack yesterday, and are now trying to draw the fire of more such weapons as I turned against them, possibly with the hope of finding out exactly how much strength we can muster against them.

Having examined the machines captured from them by Raheinl, I am happy to report that one needs only minor repairs, and that we can launch our attack possibly tomorrow night.

> *Yours in hope,*
> *Clane*

Certain characteristics of the alien patrol craft puzzled Clane. As he supervised the work of the mechanics, he had to force himself by effort of will to concentrate on the coarser aspects of the task.

"If I have time," he told himself, "I'll investigate that attachment to the steering device."

The two machines lay side by side in one of his underground workshops. Each was approximately fifty feet long, and basically of very simple design. Their atomic motors were different from those in Linnan ships only in that they were more compact. The principle was the same. A block of treated metal exploded under control in rocket chambers.

For thousands of years machines thus powered had been flying through the atmosphere of the planets.

Jerrin arrived early in the afternoon of the day set for the attack. He was pale and earnest, and subdued. "Seventeen cities," he reported to Clane, "have now been destroyed. They are certainly inviting us to do everything we can."

Clane led him to the controls of the craft that had been repaired. "I've been experimenting," he said, "with a little attachment they have geared to the controls."

He bent down. "I have a map here," he said. "I want you to mark on it where the enemy ship now is, according to the latest reports."

Jerrin shrugged. "That's easy. It's lying to over—"

"*Don't tell me!*" Clane's words were quick and sharp, and had the desired effect. Jerrin gazed at him questioningly. Clane continued, "I have an idea in connection with this thing, so put your mark—and don't show it to me."

The older man accepted the map, and touched it with the point of a pencil as closely as possible to the exact location of the ship. He stepped back, and waited. Clane touched a button.

There was a faint throb as the motors sounded in the vast emptiness of the underground chamber. Under their feet, the craft turned slowly on its revolving platform, and steadied. The sound of the motors died away. Clane straightened.

"The nose is now pointing north by northeast. Draw a line on the map in that direction from this cavern."

Jerrin drew the line silently. It passed within a millimeter of the point where he had made his mark. "I don't understand," he said slowly. "You mean that this craft *knows* where the mother ship is?"

"It seems so, in a purely mechanical fashion of course."

"Then, very likely, the mother ship knows where it is."

Clane frowned. "It could be, but I doubt it. It would be quite complicated, and somewhat unnecessary, under normal circumstances, to keep track of hundreds of small craft. The small craft, however, must be able to return to the big machine."

He added, "If they knew where this craft was, I think they would have made some effort to get it back."

Jerrin shook his head. "The matter seems of minor importance. After all, we can locate the invader whenever we want to."

Clane said nothing to that. He had studied detailed reports of how these small ships entered into and emerged from their parent. And for hours now, a possibility had been growing on him.

It was not something that could be explained to a practical man. The whole concept of automatic machinery was as new as it was dazzling.

❖ ❖ ❖

Zero hour was near.

It grew darker as they waited in the shelter of a mountain. Earlier, there had been desultory conversation between them, but now they were silent. From the men in the rear there came only an occasional mutter of sound.

The plan was made. The fleet had its orders. It was now only a matter of carrying out the attack itself.

"Halloo-oo!"

The call floated down from the rim of the peak. Jerrin straightened, and then, stepping close, embraced his brother. The darkness hid his tears. "Good luck," he said, "and forgive me for all the things that I have done or said or thought against you."

He stepped down into the darkness, where his own soldiers waited.

The mechanism of the captured Riss-craft functioned smoothly. Like a shadow, the machine rose, climbed, and flitted over the mountain top. Almost immediately, they were in the center of the battle.

The Linnan spaceships were attacking in groups of a hundred, and they came in waves. They were manned by skeleton crews, and they had two purposes: Engage if possible all the enemy's defenses by diving nose first into the torpedo-shaped invader. That was the first purpose.

It was believed the aliens would not care to have their interstellar ship rammed by hundreds of projectiles weighing thousands of tons each.

The second purpose of the attackers was for each crew to leave its ship in a small escape craft a few moments before contact. The theory was that the air would be so filled with lifeboats that the enemy would not notice their own captured machine approaching.

Clane's energy-absorbing sphere was expected to handle any direct attacks.

The sky flashed with flame. Everywhere, Linnan spaceships were burning and falling. Clane saw no lifeboats, however, and the first sick feeling that the men were not getting away, came. There was nothing to do, however, but go ahead.

The crash of Linnan spaceships striking the metal walls of the invader was almost continuous now; and there was no longer any doubt that the enemy's defenses were not capable of coping with such a complicated attack.

Clane thought tensely: "They'll have to leave. We won't have time to get near." It was a possibility that hadn't occurred to him, earlier.

He had taken it for granted that the big ship would be able to shrug off the Linnan attack without difficulty, and without moving from its position. Instead, it was being seriously hurt.

Beside him, his commanding officer whispered, "I think I see an opening."

Clane peered where the man was pointing, and saw it, too. He felt a chill, for it was directly ahead. Unmistakably, his craft was aiming toward it—or was being drawn toward it. It was possible that the automatic controls of his small machine had activated a door in the mother ship and that they would be able to enter without resistance. His own plan had been to force an entry with a tiny bomb, and it seemed to him he still preferred that method. The problem now was, was this a trap of those aboard, or was the process so automatic that no one paid any attention to newcomers?

It was a chance he had to take. The greatest danger was that the giant machine would start moving.

The light of the air lock proved deceptively dim. He was estimating that it was still more than a hundred feet away when there was a click. The machine slowed sharply, and he saw a blur of dully colored gray walls slide by on either side.

Doors flowed shut behind them and, in front, another set glided open. The small craft, with its thirty-five men aboard, moved sedately forward—and was inside the ship from the stars.

❖ ❖ ❖

At his camp headquarters, where he had taken his family for refuge, Jerrin waited.

"They're still inside." That was the terse report from his chief field officer.

After nearly eighteen hours, the reality was a virtual death sentence. Jerrin blamed himself. "I should never have allowed him to go," he told Lilidel. "It's ridiculous that a member of our family should participate in direct assaults."

He had taken part in more than a hundred direct assaults himself, but he ignored that now. He also ignored the fact that only the man who controlled the energy sphere—Clane himself—could possibly carry out the attack that the latter had outlined to him.

Jerrin paced the floor of his headquarters study; and it was several minutes before he noticed that, for once, Lilidel had nothing to say. Jerrin stared at her narrowly, realizing grimly that she and those behind her were not displeased at what had happened.

"My dear," he said finally, "Clane's failure will have repercussions on the whole state. It will mark the beginning and not the end of our troubles."

Still she said nothing. And he saw that in this crisis she was not able to comprehend the issues. She had her own purposes, the purposes of a mother and of the agent of the group that worked through her. His mind went back to the choice the old Lady Lydia, his grandmother, had made in persuading her aging husband that *her* son should be the heir of Linn.

"I must make sure," Jerrin decided, "that the succession is never in Lilidel's giving. It's just about time, also, that I take more interest in the children. I can no longer trust what she has done with them."

That applied particularly to Calaj, his eldest son.

He looked again at his wife, and parted his lips to tell her that, if Clane was alive, he had the power to take over the government at will. He didn't say it. It would serve no useful purpose. In the first place she wouldn't believe it, and in the second it was not completely true. Government depended partly on the co-operation of the governed; and there were factors against Clane of which, fortunately— he was convinced—Clane himself was aware.

The meetings between them had made an amicable co-operation possible. Only an emergency, he was sure, would now alter the shape of things political in Linn.

I shall have to make a will, he thought. *If anything happened to me, if I should die—there must be no confusion.*

He felt oppressed. For a second time in less than a year, disaster had struck at the heart of the empire. First, Czinczar, the barbarian, and now the aliens. From the air he had seen the refugees streaming out of the concealing smoke of cities bombed before they were completely evacuated, and he was conscious of his inadequacy in the face of such a colossal catastrophe. It was that that decided him.

❖ ❖ ❖

"I refuse," he said, "to believe that Clane has failed. If he has, then we are lost. And my awareness of that fact emphasizes once again his importance in a crisis. He is the only person qualified to handle a major emergency involving atomic energy. If he is still alive, I intend to do as follows."

She listened wide eyed as he explained about the will he planned to write. Abruptly, her face twisted with fury. "Why, you're mad," she breathed. "Are you serious? You're going to disinherit your own son?"

He gazed at her bleakly. "My dear," he said, "I want to make one thing clear to you and to your private army, for now and always. So long as I am the Lord Adviser, the state will not be regarded as a property which my children automatically inherit. It is too soon to decide whether Calaj has the qualities necessary for leadership. My impression of him is that he is an exceedingly emotional youth who gets his own way far too often. There is no sign yet of that stability which I have, which Clane has, and which even Tews had to some degree."

The woman's face was softening. She came over to him. "I can see you're tired, darling. Please don't do anything rash until this crisis is past. I'll bring you a cup of tea—strong, the way you like it."

She brought the tea with trembling fingers, and went out with tears in her eyes. The liquid seemed unusually bitter even for his taste, but he sipped it as he began to dictate, first the will, then the letter to Clane. He recognized that he was taking a lot for granted, but his mood continued dark. And it was not until he had sealed the two articles, and put them among his public papers, that he realized that the strain of the past few days had affected his body. He felt very tired, even a little feverish.

He dismissed his secretary, and lay down on a cot under the window. Twenty minutes passed, and a door opened softly, so softly that the sleeper seemed undisturbed. Lilidel came in, took the cup in which the tea had been, and tiptoed out.

It was about an hour later when the intense silence of the room was again broken. The outer door was flung open. A staff officer burst across the threshold.

"Your excellency," he began breathlessly, "the invader has arrived above the camp."

The slim, uniformed body on the cot did not stir.

5

When Clane's "lift" boat came to rest inside the enemy ship, he saw after a moment that they were firmly held in a kind of metal incasement. The nose of the machine and half the body were buried in that enveloping cradle. All around him were other small craft similarly incased.

The craft had apparently slipped automatically into its own pigeonhole. And there was only one problem. Would the officer at the controls of the big machine notice that the lifeboat just in was one which had been captured on Mars by the human beings?

If he noticed, he gave no sign during the vital first minutes that followed.

There were high steps where the casement of the "pigeonhole" ended. Up these steps Clane and his men climbed. They came to an empty corridor. Clane stopped short, hesitated, drew a deep breath— and sent the sphere on its death mission.

It flashed out of sight, came back, disappeared again, and once more came back. For a third time, then, it glided off like a stroke of lightning.

This time it returned—sated.

They found no living creature of any kind. They wandered for hours before they were finally convinced that the huge ship had been captured during those few seconds by a simple process. The sphere had absorbed every alien being aboard. As soon as he was positive, Clane headed for the massive control room.

He was just in time to witness a strange mechanical phenomenon. A huge glassy plate, which had been lightless and soundless when he first passed through the control room, glittered with light flashes and stuttered with apparently meaningless sounds.

Clane took up a position behind a barrier, and, with the sphere bobbing above his head, watched alertly.

Abruptly, the lights on the plate steadied. A shape took form on it, and Clane was shaken as he recognized that the creature was of the same species as the monster that Czinczar had brought from Europa.

Only this one was alive in some curious picture fashion.

The creature stared from the plate into the control room, and it was nearly a minute before his gaze touched Clane. He said something in a series of low-pitched sounds that had no meaning for the mutant. Two other individuals came out of the vagueness behind him, and they also stared through the plate.

One of them gestured in unmistakable command, and roared something. There was a click, and the screen went blank. The sounds continued for a few seconds, and then they also faded.

Hesitantly, Clane ventured farther into the control room. He was trying to understand what he had seen. A picture of living aliens focused from some far place on a shining plate. It was a hard idea to grasp, but he had the sinking conviction that other living aliens now knew what had happened to the first of their ships to reach Earth.

In one mental jump he had to try to comprehend the possibility that communication could be established by other means than smoke signals, light flashes from strategically located mirrors, and courier ships. What he had seen indicated that such communication was possible not only over the face of a planet, but across the gulf in space between stars.

It changed everything. It changed the whole situation. Capture of this one ship actually meant nothing. Other aliens knew that the defense forces of the solar system had failed to protect their cities. They would be puzzled by the seizure of their ship, but it was doubtful if they would be seriously alarmed.

What one ship had almost accomplished, a fleet would surely be able to do—effortlessly. That would be their attitude; and Clane, swiftly estimating the defense possibilities of the solar system, did not doubt the ability of a powerful force of enemy ships to do anything they pleased.

The entire distance-vision incident was enormously significant. Gloomily, he began to study the control system of the big machine. Nearly four hours went by before he was satisfied that he could guide it for atmospheric travel.

Certain functions of the intricate control board baffled him completely. It would take time and study to master this ship.

He headed the ship for Jerrin's headquarters.

He landed in a lifeboat that trailed the fluttering victory flags of Linn, and in a few minutes was admitted to where Jerrin lay dead.

That was about an hour after the body was discovered.

❖ ❖ ❖

As he gazed down at his dead brother, Lord Clane noticed almost immediately the evidence of poisoning. Shocked, he stepped back from the cot, and looked down at the scene, trying to assess it as a whole.

The widow Lilidel was on her knees with one arm flung in an

apparent agony of grief over the corpse. She seemed anxious rather than grieved, and there was just a hint of calculation in the way her eyes were narrowed. She was tearless.

The tableau interested Clane. He had had innumerable reports about the group that had used this woman to influence Jerrin, and there was a time when he had even intended to warn Jerrin against her.

He found himself wondering where her eldest son, the incredible Calaj, was.

It required only a moment for that wonder to focus into a sharp picture of the potentialities of this situation. He had a sudden vision of Calaj already on his way to Golomb, the little town outside Linn to which the Patronate as well as other government departments had been transferred. Given advance warning, the group behind Lilidel— many well-known Patrons among them—might seize the occasion to proclaim the boy Lord Adviser.

There was explosive material here for a bloody struggle for power. Unless the right action were taken, rumors would spread that Jerrin had been murdered. Some of the rumors would point to the widow, others at Clane himself. Supporters of his own who had reluctantly accepted the noble Jerrin would very possibly refuse to agree that a youth of seventeen should be put into power by their worst enemies. Civil war was not improbable.

Jerrin's secretary, General Marak—a secret Clane supporter— touched Clane's arm, and whispered in his ear. "Your excellency, here are copies of very important documents. I would not swear that the originals are still available."

A minute later Clane was reading his brother's last will. Then he read the personal letter, of which the essential sentence was, "I intrust my dear wife and children to your care."

Clane turned and gazed at the widow. Her eyes met his briefly, flashed with hatred; and then she lowered them, and thereafter gave no sign that she was aware of his presence.

He guessed that his appearance on the scene was unexpected.

It was time for decision. And yet, he hesitated. He glanced at the high staff officers in the room, all Jerrin men, and still he could not make up his mind. He had a picture in his brain larger than anything that was happening in this room—or on this planet. A picture of a mighty alien fleet heading from some far star system to avenge the capture of their exploring ship. Of course that would be only an additional incitement. Their real purpose would be to destroy every human being in the solar system, and seize all of man's planets— while men fought each other for the petty stakes of governmental power.

❖❖❖

With fingers that trembled slightly, Clane folded the two documents and put them in his pocket. Standing here in the presence of his dead brother, so recently become a friend, he hated the political knowledge that made him think automatically, *I'll have to try to get the originals, in case I ever want to use them.*

The revulsion grew stronger. With narrowing eyes and grim face, he gazed not only at this scene before him, but at the world of Linn outside—the intricate association of direct vision and sharp, perceptive memory, the scene he was seeing and all the scenes he had ever witnessed. He remembered his own schemes over the years, his emotional joy in political maneuvering; and now, in one burst of insight, recognized it all for the childish nonsense it had been.

His lips moved. Under his breath he murmured, "Beloved brother, I am shamed, for I knew enough to know better."

It seemed to him, then, that Jerrin had been a greater man than he. All his life, Jerrin had treated politics and politicians with disdain, devoting himself to the hard realities of a military man in an age when war was inescapable.

"Can I do less?" The question quivered in his mind like a flung knife vibrating in the flesh.

Then he saw that he was being sentimental in making comparisons. For his problem was on a level that Jerrin could hardly even have imagined. There was power here for him if he wanted it. All the schemes of Lilidel and her group could not stop him from seizing control by sheer force. Without shame, without modesty, he recognized that he was *the* man of science in Linn.

Clearly, sharply, he perceived his pre-eminence, the enormous stability of his mind, the acuteness of his understanding. Somehow he had it, and others hadn't. It made it necessary now for him to reject the highest office in the land—because he had a duty to the whole race of man. A duty that grew out of his knowledge of the titanic danger.

He could expect no one else to evaluate the extent of that danger, least of all this venal, childish woman and those behind her.

Abruptly, angrily decisive, Clane turned and beckoned General Marak. The latter came forward quickly. To him, Clane whispered, "I would advise you to leave this room with me. I could not otherwise answer for the life of a man who knows what is in these documents." He tapped his pocket, where the copy of Jerrin's will reposed.

It was unfortunate, but that was the grim reality. Intrigue and sudden death.

Without a word to any of the others present, he turned and left the room, Marak following close behind. His problem would be to restrain his more ardent followers from trying to seize power in his name.

And save a world that was almost mindless with corruption.

❖❖❖

A few hours later, he landed at his estate. His guards' captain met him.

"Your excellency," he said curtly, "the sphere and its container have been stolen."

"The sphere gone!" said Clane. His spirit sagged like a lead weight.

In a few minutes, he had the story. The guards of the sphere had apparently been ambushed by a larger force.

The captain finished, "When they didn't get back here on schedule, I investigated personally. I found their bodies at the bottom of a canyon. All of them were dead."

Clane's mind was already beyond the crime, seeking the culprit. And swiftly, he focused on one man.

"Czinczar," he said aloud, savagely.

6

For Czinczar and his men, defeat at the hands of Lord Clane a few months previously had not been a complete disaster. Before actually ordering his army to surrender, that remarkable logician examined his situation.

At the worst, he himself would not be killed immediately but would be saved for public execution. His men, of course, would be sold into slavery—unless he could persuade Lord Clane to let the army remain a unit. To do that, he must convince the mutation that such a force might be useful to him.

Since his reasoning was soundly based, everything happened as he had hoped it would. Clane transferred the barbarian army, together with a number of crack rebel slave units, to an easily defendable mountain territory. Having regained control of the invincible sphere of energy, the mutation considered himself in control of the situation. He even suspected correctly that Czinczar had held a number of spaceships out in space, where they could still be contacted.

At the time he informed the barbarian leader, "These ships could provide you with transportation to return to your planet. But I warn you, make no such move without my permission. You must know that I can seek you out and destroy you at any time."

Czinczar had no doubt of it. And besides, he had no desire to return to Europa. Great events were in the making, and he intended to be in the center of them.

He began his preparations boldly.

Single spaceships were fitted out for forays. The men assigned to them shouted their disapproval when informed they must shave off their beards, but the leader was adamant. Singly and in the dark of night, spaceships landed at carefully selected points as far as possible from the city of Linn. Out of them sprang bare-faced men dressed like ordinary Linnans. They killed men only, slaves as well as Linnans—and helped themselves over a period of many months to vast supplies of grain, fruit, vegetables, meat, and all the metal and wood that an army might need.

The prisoners had been assigned a minimum existence diet by Clane. Within a week of the surrender they were eating off the fat of the land. From every fire on the mountains came the odor of roasting meat. Within a few weeks there were several women to attend to each fire. Czinczar issued orders that only slave women should be brought to the camp, and that any Linnan women captured by mistake should be killed.

Everyone agreed that this was wise, but suspiciously no women were executed. It seemed clear to Czinczar that the Linnan women, when informed of the alternatives, were only too anxious to masquerade as slaves. And so the purpose of the bloodthirsty threat was served. A huge camp, that might have been disorderly in the extreme, operated for months on a high level of efficiency.

And, because of the tremendous dislocation of normal Linnan life, first as a result of the barbarian invasion and then because of the alien invader, their violent actions went almost unnoticed; their existence was almost literally unsuspected.

The arrival of the invader made possible even bolder activity. In broad daylight barbarian ships would land at the outskirts of cities, and in small groups penetrate past the guardposts without being challenged. These small spying units brought back information from widely scattered points to one of the keenest military minds of the age. As a result, Czinczar knew before the event that an attack was going to be made against the invading ship. And he also knew the nature of it.

❖❖❖

On the night of the attack, he was fully aware of the tremendous issues at stake. He personally accompanied the men who crouched within bow and arrow range of the coffinlike structure which acted as a container for the sphere of energy. He waited until the sphere vanished into the darkness toward the gigantic enemy ship. Then he gave his command. The little group of barbarians swept down upon the half hundred guards around the container.

The darkness echoed with the horrified cries of men bloodily surprised by a superior force. But silence followed swiftly. The barbarians disposed of the dead guards by rolling them over a nearby cliff. Then they settled themselves tensely to wait for the sphere.

It came suddenly. One instant there was nothing; the next, the silver ball was rolling sedately to and fro. Czinczar gazed down at it, startled. It was not the first time he had seen it, but now he realized some of its powers.

Aloud, he said, "Bring the telescope. I might as well have a look inside this thing while we're waiting."

That was a new idea; and the method used was very rough. Two men poked the long, narrow telescope into the outer "skin" of the sphere, and then walked along at a steady pace beside it. It was a problem in timing, and Czinczar's part was the most difficult. He walked beside the telescope, one eye glued to the eyepiece; and the trick was to establish a rhythm of backward and forward movement.

His first view was so different from anything he might have expected that his vision blurred, and he fell out of step. He organized himself, and looked again. Oddly, the surprise was almost as great, as if his mind had already rejected what it first saw.

He saw a starry universe. He stepped back in confusion, striving to grasp the awful magnitude, the fantastic reality. Then once more he fell in step, and gazed. By the time he straightened up again, he was trying to interpret what he had seen.

The sphere, he decided, was a "hole" in space. Baffled, he stared down at it, as it rolled back and forth. How could a silvery ball-like object be an opening into anything?

He motioned the men to take the telescope away, and then punched his finger into the sphere. He felt nothing at all, no resistance, no sensation.

The finger swelled a little finally, and he remembered that meteor miners had proved space was not cold, but that it was vital to wear an air-tight pressure suit. Lack of pressure would have caused his finger to bloat.

He wondered if he had reached into some depth of space. A finger poking out of nowhere into a vacuum. Thoughtfully, he walked away from the sphere and sat down on a rock. In the east, the sky was beginning to lighten, but still he sat there, still his men waited in vain for the order to leave. He intended to give Clane every opportunity of using the sphere against the aliens.

As the sun edged over the jagged horizon, he stood up briskly, and had the container and the sphere transported to a waiting ship. The vessel had instructions to climb right out of the atmosphere, and take up an orbit around Earth.

Czinczar remembered sharply how Clane had had to come to the city of Linn to make use of the sphere against himself. And there was the fact that each time it was used, it had to be transported near the object against which it was to be employed.

Accordingly, the greatest weapon ever conceived was in his possession.

❖❖❖

He was not satisfied. Restlessly, he paced the room which was his headquarters, and over and over again examined the facts of his position. Years ago, he had discovered the basic secret of power and success. And now, because the pattern was not complete, he was uneasy.

Men came and went from his room. Spies bringing information. The invading ship was captured. Jerrin was dead. Clane had refused to take advantage of the death, and had instructed his supporters not to oppose the plan to make Calaj the Lord Adviser.

When the man who brought that latest bit of news had gone, Czinczar shook his head in wonder, and for the first time in all these months something of his terrible tension let up. He himself wouldn't have had the courage *not* to seize power at such an opportune moment. Nor could he visualize the logic of it—even so, the actuality seemed superhuman.

It made him indecisive. He had intended to make an effort to seize the gigantic invader ship when Clane was not on it. With clock-like precision his men completed the preliminaries—but he did not give the final order.

On the sixth day after the death of Jerrin, a messenger came from Clane commanding him aboard the captured giant. Czinczar suspected the worst, but he had no alternative short of open resistance. Since that would quickly bring the main Linnan armies against him, he decided to trust himself to Clane, and to his own analysis of the situation.

At the appointed hour, accordingly, Czinczar and his staff flew in a strongly escorted patrol vessel to Clane's estate. The alien ship floated high above, as they stepped to the ground.

A few guards lounged around. Nowhere was there sign of a force large enough to defend the battleship from a determined air attack. Looking up, Czinczar saw that several dozen air locks were open in the ship, and that a thin but steady traffic moved to and from the openings. It was a picture that his spies had reported in considerable detail, and it baffled Czinczar now as it had earlier. The ship looked helpless, wide open to assault. The very extent of that helplessness had made him hesitate. It was still hard to credit that Clane could be so negligent, but now the barbarian leader silently cursed himself for his failure to take advantage of a military possibility.

For the first time in his grim career he had missed an opportunity. He had a premonition of disaster.

He watched with narrowed eyes, as one of Clane's officers came up. The man saluted the barbarian commanders with stiff formality, and then bowed to Czinczar.

"Your excellency, will you and your staff please follow me?"

Czinczar expected to be led toward the estate residence, which was visible over a low hill about a third of a mile to the south. Instead, the Linnan officer guided them to a small stone building half hidden among thick undergrowth. Once more he saluted and bowed.

"If you will step inside one by one," he said, "so that the machine can take a"—he hesitated over the word—"photograph of you." He added hurriedly, "Lord Clane asked me to assure you that this is essential; otherwise it would be impossible for you to approach the *Solar Star*."

Czinczar said nothing, nor did he immediately allow himself to examine the meaning of the words. He motioned his officers to go in ahead of him, and watched curiously as each man in turn entered, disappeared for a moment, and then came into sight and through the door. Since he did not ask them, they all knew better than to volunteer information.

Presently, it was his turn. Unhurriedly, Czinczar stepped through the door. He found himself in a room that was bare except for a chair and a table, and the instrument that rested on the table. The chair was occupied by an officer, who rose to his feet and bowed, as Czinczar entered.

The barbarian acknowledged the greeting, then stared curiously at the instrument. It looked as if it had been torn from its metal casing. The metal was fused where it had been cut with torches. Czinczar noted the point in passing, saw also that the machine itself seemed to consist principally of a telescopelike protuberance complete with lens. He turned to the attendant.

"What does it do?" he asked.

The officer was polite. "According to Lord Clane, sir, it takes photographs."

"But that's only another word for portrait," said Czinczar. "Do you mean the machine has made a portrait of me? If so, where is it?"

The attendant's cheeks were slightly flushed. "Your excellency," he confessed, "I know nothing more. Lord Clane asked me to refer all interrogators to him personally." He added, somewhat pointedly, "I believe that he will expect you, now that you are through here."

Czinczar was persistent. "I didn't see you do anything."

"It's automatic, sir. Anyone who stands in front of it is photographed."

"If such a photograph," said the barbarian, "is necessary before I can approach the ship, how was it that Lord Clane and his men were able to enter the vessel a week ago, and capture it, without having their photographs taken?"

It was a rhetorical question, and he scarcely heard the other's protestation of ignorance. Silently, he left the little building, and followed the first officer to a larger liftboat, which was in the act of settling to the ground half a hundred feet distant.

In a few minutes they were whisked up to one of the openings. The liftboat glided through, and gently nosed into a slot. Czinczar stepped out with the others, hesitated as he saw the double lines of guards drawn up to receive them, and then, with the chill of the welcome already upon him, walked wordlessly along a corridor towards a huge door. As he crossed the threshold, and saw the tremendous gallows that had been erected against the far wall, he stopped involuntarily.

The pause was momentary. Imperturbably, he walked forward, straight to the foot of the gallows. He sat down on a lower step, pulled out a notebook, and began to write a farewell address. He was still writing it when, out of the corner of his eyes, he saw Clane come in. He stood up, and bowed.

The slim young man came over to him, and without any preliminaries said, "Czinczar, you have a simple choice. Produce the sphere, or hang."

❖❖❖

"Sphere?" said the barbarian finally. He hoped he sounded properly surprised, but he did not doubt the seriousness of his situation. There were rough minutes ahead.

Clane made an impatient gesture, hesitated, and then grew visibly calmer. "Czinczar," he said slowly, "your skillful reorganization of your forces the last few months had just about decided me to use you in a major enterprise."

The barbarian bowed once more, but his eyes narrowed at the revelation that his activities were known to the mutation. Czinczar neither underestimated nor overestimated the fact. He recognized both the weakness and strength of Lord Clane's position. The great weakness was that he depended too much on himself. He was at the mercy of people who had little or no idea of the relative importance of his possessions or his actions.

And so, during the barbarian assault on Linn, the attackers had seized Clane's house with all its valuable scientific equipment, including the sphere of force. Not knowing the tremendous potentialities of the sphere, they had made the mistake of trying to use it and the other equipment as bait to trap Clane. And thus had let him get near it—and trapped themselves.

The secrecy that made such things possible was a form of strength. But, obviously, once the pattern was understood, the solution was simple. Watch Clane's movements. He could not be everywhere at once. Like other human beings, he needed sleep: he had to take time off for eating. It was impossible for him to be alert continuously.

The fact that he had allowed the barbarian force to reorganize was no evidence that he was capable of foreseeing all the possible eventualities of such an act. His successful capture of the sphere was evidence of that.

Once more, it was Clane who broke the silence. "As you know," he said, "I have defended you from the fate that is normally dealt out to individuals who have the audacity to invade Linn. The policy of executing such leaders may or may not be a deterrent on other adventurers; possibly it is. I saved you from it, and one of your first acts is to betray me by stealing a weapon which you have not the knowledge to use yourself."

It seemed to Czinczar that it was time to make a denial. "I don't know what you're talking about," he protested in his most open-faced fashion. "Has the sphere been stolen?"

Clane seemed not to hear. He went on grimly, "I cannot say honestly that I have ever admired you. You have discovered a simple technique of power, and you keep following the pattern. I personally am opposed to so much killing, and I really believe it is possible to reach the heights of power in *any* state, however governed, without stabbing a single person in the back."

He paused; he took a step backward. His eyes were merciless as they stared straight into Czinczar's. He said curtly, "Enough of this talk. Do you yield up the sphere, or do you hang?"

Czinczar shrugged. The pressure of the deadly threat tensed every muscle in his body. But in his tremendously logical way he had analyzed the potentialities of his theft of the sphere; and he still stood by that analysis.

"I know nothing of this," he said quietly. "I have not got the sphere. I did not even know it was stolen until this minute. What is this enterprise on which you planned to use me? I'm sure we can come to an agreement."

"There are no agreements," said Clane coldly, "until I get the sphere." He went on, "However, I see that you are convinced that I won't hang the man who has it, so let us proceed to the actuality. Will you climb the gibbet yourself, or do you need assistance?"

Since there could be no effective opposition, Czinczar turned around, climbed the steps to the top of the gallows, and without waiting for the hangman to help him, slipped the rope over his head. He was pale now, in spite of his confidence. For the first time it struck him that the dazzling career of Czinczar, the one-time scribe who had made himself absolute ruler of the barbarians of Europa, was about to end.

He saw that Clane had motioned the executioner, a Linnan noncommissioned officer, to come forward. The man took up his position beside the lever that would open the trapdoor, and turned to watch Clane, who had raised his arm. The mutation stood tautly in that striking position, and said:

"A last chance, Czinczar. The sphere or death."

"I haven't got it," said Czinczar in a steady voice, but with finality.

Inexorably, Clane's arm swept down. Czinczar felt the trap under him collapse. And then—

He was falling.

7

He dropped about a foot, and landed so jarringly that his body vibrated with pain. The tears started to his eyes. He blinked them away. When his vision cleared, he saw that he was standing on a second trapdoor, which had been built below the first.

He grew aware of scuffling somewhere near. He glanced around. His staff officers were struggling with the Linnan guards, trying to reach him. Czinczar hesitated, wondering if perhaps he and they should not attempt to make a fight to the death.

He shook his head, ever so slightly. The fact that he was still alive underlined his own hard convictions. He raised his golden voice, and presently the barbarian officers ceased their struggles, and stood sullenly looking up at him.

Czinczar spoke directly at them, indirectly at Clane. "If my life is really in danger," he said with resonant positivity, "it will be because Lord Clane has lost his good sense. That would apply even if I had the sphere—"

He realized that Clane would regard the words as an admission, and he glanced coolly at the mutation, inviting comment. Clane scowled; but he picked up the challenge after a moment.

"Suppose that you did have the sphere," he said mildly, "why does that protect you?"

"Because," said Czinczar, and his golden voice had never been steadier, "if I have it, so long as I am alive, you would still have a chance of getting it back. If I die, then that chance goes forever."

"If you had it," said Clane in a grim but ironic voice, "why would you want to hold on to it, knowing that you cannot make any use of it?"

"I would first have to make an investigation," was the barbarian's reply. "After all, you learned how to use it without having any previous knowledge of its operation."

"I had a book," Clane flashed, "and besides I have some knowledge of the nature and structure of matter and energy."

"Perhaps," said Czinczar coolly, "I could get hold of the book—such things do happen."

"I memorized this particular book," said Clane, "and then destroyed it."

Czinczar was politely incredulous. "Perhaps, my agents could discover the place where you burned it," he said. "Or, if I sent them into the homes of the gods, they might find another book."

He realized that tension was building up again, and that no verbal byplay would settle this argument. Clane was stiffening, his eyes narrowing. "Czinczar," he said sharply, "*if* you had this sphere, and you knew that you couldn't ever find out how to use it, would you still hold on to it, knowing the danger that is building up for the human race?"

The barbarian drew a deep breath. He expected a violent reaction. "Yes," he said.

"Why?" Clane was visibly holding himself under control.

"Because," said Czinczar, "I have no confidence in a man who refuses repeatedly to accept power, and who thus rejects the only means by which he can control and direct the defense against a possible invader. And, besides, the sphere is obviously worthless against the Riss."

Clane seemed not to hear that last. "Suppose I told you that I refused to take power because I have a plan of much greater scope."

"I recognize power," said Czinczar flatly, "not the grandiose schemes of a man who is now virtually impotent."

"My plan," said Clane, "if of such scope that I dare not tell it to a man of your rigid attitudes, for fear that you would regard it as impractical. For once I don't think your imagination could appreciate the possibilities."

"Try me."

"When I have the sphere," said Clane, "and not one second before. As for my being impotent, please note that I have the ship."

Czinczar was scornful. "What are you going to do with it—attack the legal government and make the people love you? That isn't the way a mutation can operate. For you and for your group the moment for taking over the government is past. It will probably not come again until the Riss attack, and by then anything you can do may be too late."

He went on, in an even more violent tone, "Lord Clane, you have been a grave disappointment to me. Your failure has placed my troops and myself in grave danger, because very soon now the *legal* government of Linn will demand that you turn us over, and of course you will also be required to turn over the ship. If you refuse, then for the first time in your life you will be out in the open as a rebel. From that moment on, your days are numbered."

Clane was smiling humorlessly. "I can see," he said, "that you are at your old game of political intrigue, and I am utterly impatient with such childish nonsense. The human race is in deadly danger, and I refuse to argue with anyone who plots and schemes for advantage under such circumstances. Men must mature or die."

He turned aside, and said something to one of the officers who stood near him. The man nodded, and once more Clane faced Czinczar.

The barbarian braced himself for the next step of torture.

Clane said curtly, "Please remove the noose from around your neck, and come over to the tank in the corner to your left."

As he slipped the rope over his head, Czinczar studied the tank. It was a large concrete affair, and he had noticed it when he first came in. It looked enigmatic; he couldn't imagine its purpose.

He was thinking furiously as he came down from the gallows. He said to Clane, "I'm really very persuadable. Why not tell me your plan? I can't give you the sphere as evidence of my good faith because I haven't got it."

Clane merely shook his head impatiently. Czinczar accepted the rejection, and said matter-of-factly, "Do I climb into the tank?"

Clane said: "Take a look inside, and you'll see the arrangement."

Czinczar climbed up curiously, and looked down. The tank was quite deep, and it was empty. At the bottom was a simple hand pump, and there were two chains with clamps fastened to rings imbedded in the concrete floor.

He lowered himself gingerly into the tank, and waited for instructions. He looked up and saw that Clane was looking down at him over the edge.

"Fasten the chain clamps around your ankles," instructed the mutation.

Czinczar did so. They clicked shut with a metallic finality. The metal felt heavy against his flesh and even uncomfortable.

"The chains," explained the mutation, "will hold you down to the bottom of the tank, so that when the water comes in you'll have to pump it out if you want to prevent yourself from drowning." He added, "You can see the approach is very simple. The pump operates easily. The choice you make will be entirely your own. You live or die by your own effort, and at any time you can stop the entire process by agreeing to turn over the sphere. There comes the water now."

It swirled around Czinczar's legs, bubbling up noisily. It was lukewarm, so it felt rather pleasant. Czinczar sat down on the floor, and glanced up at Clane.

"May I make a request?" he asked.

"Does it include handing over the sphere?"

"No."

"Then I'm not interested."

"It's the pump," said Czinczar. "Its presence makes me unhappy. Will you please have it taken out?"

Clane shook his head. "A few minutes from now you might be very happy to have it there." Nevertheless, there was an anxious look in his eyes as he spoke. The reaction was clearly one that he had not expected.

He finished, "If you change your mind at any time, you'll find that the pump can quickly reduce the level of the water."

Czinczar did not answer. The water was swirling around his neck. In a minute it closed over his mouth. He found himself involuntarily relaxing so that he could float up a little. He tensed with the expectation of the physical horror that was now only minutes away.

Presently, he was standing up, and he could feel the weight of the chain on his ankles. There was no doubt but that he had reached the limit of that particular method of escaping. And still the water surged higher.

It came up to his mouth again, then his nose. He held his breath as it rose up over his eyes and covered his head. And then, abruptly, he couldn't hold it any longer. Explosively he exhaled— and inhaled.

There was a knifelike pain in his chest, but that was all. The water tasted flat and unpleasant, not as if he was drinking it. Finally, there was no sensation at all. Darkness closed over his consciousness.

❖ ❖ ❖

When he came to, he was lying over a barrel. He had never felt more miserable in his life. And they were still squeezing water out of him.

He was coughing. Every explosive discharge wracked his body. The pain of returning life was immeasurably greater than the pain of death. But even he realized presently that he would live.

They carried him to a cot, and there after an hour or so, he began to feel normal again. Clane came in alone, pulled up a chair, and sat silently regarding him.

"Czinczar," he said at last, "I am reluctantly compelled to admire your bravery. I despise the animallike astuteness behind it."

Czinczar waited. He refused to believe that his travail was over.

"You have proved once more," said the mutation bitterly, "that a courageous man who is prepared to take calculated risks on the low level of political intrigue can conquer even death. I hate the stupid logic which makes you feel that you have to keep the sphere. If you persist in that madness, we are all dead men."

"If I had this sphere," said Czinczar, "then the logical thing for you to do in a moment of crisis would be for you to forget self and tell me how to work it."

Czinczar spoke in a precise tone, conscious of how dangerous the statement was. It was his first admission by implication of his own vast ambitions. For it was obvious that if he ever learned how to use the sphere, he would thereafter be in a position to seize power at will, and take control of any state.

It also implied that, according to his analysis of Clane's character, the other might actually allow him to have control of the sphere in an emergency involving the destiny of the human race as distinct from any nation.

Clane was shaking his head. "It won't happen, my friend. I do not expect that the sphere will ever again by itself be useful against the Riss. I won't tell you why."

Czinczar was silent. He had hoped, not too optimistically, that somewhere along the line he would receive a clue about the operation of the sphere. But the information he was getting made the problem seem more, not less, difficult.

Clane continued, "It might appear that I was very careless with the sphere. But long ago I discovered that I could not be everywhere at once. And of course, I repeat, it's quite useless to anyone else. It works on the basis of a mathematical formula relating to the release of atomic energy, and I question whether anyone in the solar system other than myself even knows that there is such a formula."

❖❖❖

Czinczar had his clue, and it was bitter to take. He said at last, "What are your plans for me, as of this moment?"

Clane hesitated. When he finally spoke, there was an edge of fire in his tone. "For the past few months," he said, "I have tolerated your murderous forays because I question whether we could have got together such a vast total of food and other supplies by any legal method in my control."

He paused, then continued, "I question also whether it would have been possible to get so many women together without using methods similar to yours. For my purposes, the women are as important as the food."

Once more he paused. And Czinczar had time to feel chagrined. He had thought he knew something of the intricate workings of this man's mind. But now, briefly, he was beyond his depth, and he had the empty conviction that he had been outplayed at his own devious game.

It was a startling thought that his secret forays would now be used for the benefit of Clane's plan. The mutation continued:

"Here is what I want you to do. Tomorrow, the *Solar Star* will fly over to your camp. You will begin to load your equipment aboard the lower decks—there are twenty of them, each capable of holding about ten thousand people and their supplies; so there'll be plenty of room for your entire army and the women."

Czinczar said: "Once I have such a force aboard, what's to prevent me from taking over the ship?"

Clane smiled grimly. "The twenty upper decks are already occupied by a well armed Linnan army group, all young married men accompanied by their wives. Except on the officer level, there will be no liaison between the two groups. In fact, except for an entrance from your headquarters all connecting doors will be sealed."

Czinczar nodded, half to himself. It sounded effective. Every defense of that kind could of course be overcome by bold and astute planning. But that scarcely concerned him now. There was an implication here of a tremendous journey about to be undertaken, and that dominated his thought.

"Where are we going?" he asked sharply. "To one of the outer moons?"

"Wait and see," said Clane coolly.

He stood up, with a frown. "Enough of this. You have your instructions. I have to make a vital journey to the capitol. I want you and your forces to be aboard and ready for flight one week from today. And if you can for once rise above the moronic military idiocy that guides your reasoning, bring the sphere along." His tone was one of suppressed anger.

Czinczar stared at him thoughtfully. "My friend," he said, "you're being emotional. There *is* no escape from political intrigue. This that you suddenly despise is the human environment. The environment of human passion, human ambition. There never has been, and never will be any other climate for you to operate in. A man succeeds or fails to the extent that he can understand and control the unrelenting drives of others of his kind. If he tries to abandon intrigue, the tide will wash over him and his plans as if they never existed. Beware."

He finished automatically, "I haven't got the sphere."

8

The arrow came out of the darkness, whizzed past Clane's head, and lodged in the shoulder of a guardsman.

The man screamed throatily, and clutched at the thin, vibrating wand. A companion leaped to his aid. Other soldiers dived into the alleyway. There was the sound of squealing, almost feminine in its high-pitched alarm and annoyance. Presently, a group of soldiers stalked out of the darkness, dragging a slim, resisting, boyish form.

The injured man, meanwhile, succeeded in tearing the arrow from his flesh. More frightened than damaged, he stood there cursing in a deep, bass voice.

Men were hurrying back from farther along the street. Torches flamed and guttered in the night wind. In that smoky, malodorous atmosphere, the changing patterns of dim light gave only flashing glimpses of faces and bodies. Clane stood silent, displeased with the milling excitement. Presently, when the turmoil showed no sign of abating, he called to an officer, and in a minute a path was cleared for him. Along it the guards dragged the prisoner.

Somebody shouted, "It's a woman!"

The discovery echoed back among the men. Curses of amazement sounded. The woman, or boy—it was hard to decide which in that dim light—ceased struggling. And then settled the question of gender by speaking.

"Let me go, you filthy rats! I'll have you whipped for this. I wish to speak to Lord Clane."

The voice, despite its vicious tone, was feminine. What was more surprising, the accent was that cultivated at the schools where young ladies of noble birth were taught.

The recognition startled Clane out of the icy calm into which the attempt on his life had thrown him. He took it for granted that the attempt *had* been on him, and not on the guard who had actually been struck. He assumed automatically that the assassin was an agent of the group behind Lilidel.

The names of her immediate superiors would have to be wheedled out of her, now that the assassination had failed. That was a natural development, and it concerned him only incidentally. What disturbed him was that she had evidently not considered the serious consequences of her act. In accepting the assignment, she couldn't have known a long established method of dealing with woman assassins. They were turned over to the soldiers.

He stared at her with troubled eyes. It was probably an illusion of the unsteady light, but she seemed little more than a child. At a maximum, he put her age at eighteen. Her eyes gleamed with the passionate fire of a willful youngster. Her mouth was full and sensuous.

He shrugged as he realized that he was yielding her up in his own mind to the punishment established by long practice. He who had recently set himself against so many old customs, could not now afford to offend his own private guard. Slowly, he stiffened to the inevitabilities of the situation.

Because he was angry at her for the decision she was forcing on him, he said with grim curtness, "Who are you?"

"I won't talk here," she said.

"What's your name?"

She hesitated; then, apparently recognizing the hostility in his voice, she said sullenly, "Madelina Corgay."

The identification gave him his second major pause. For it was an old and famous name in Linn. Generals and Patrons had borne that name into the field of battle and with it had signed the laws of the country. The father of this girl, Clane recalled, had died fighting on Mars, a year before. As a war hero, his daughter's action would be excused.

Clane was chagrined to realize that he was already thinking of the political repercussions. But it would be folly to blind himself to the fact that this incident could be highly dangerous to him. He shook his head angrily. With Calaj already voted Lord Adviser, and scheduled to make his triumphal entry into this capital city of Linn tomorrow morning, the young man's supporters might well make an issue of an affair like this. And yet he had to take into account the expectations of the guards, who would not be interested in excuses. Fortunately, an intermediate decision was possible.

"Bring her along," he said. "I shall question her when we reach out destination."

No one demurred. It was expected that there would be a period of questioning. The crisis would come later.

Clane gave the necessary orders. Presently the procession was moving again along the street.

❖❖❖

Several weeks had gone by since the capture of the invading ship, and it was more than six months since the defeat of Czinczar and his barbarian army from Europa, that distant and little known moon of Jupiter. The Linnan world was still in the process of settling down from those two near catastrophes. But already the survivors were forgetting how great the danger had been. From all parts of the empire the ever-louder voices of discontent echoed.

Commercial interests protested that Czinczar never had been a real threat. And that in any event the danger had been a product of gross negligence by the government. Jerrin had overruled previous objections, but now that Jerrin was dead there was a determined movement under way to nullify the decree which Clane had proclaimed during the barbarian invasion, freeing all loyal slaves. The feverish fury of numberless individuals dispossessed of valuable servants mounted with each passing day. And several ugly rumors had come to Clane that there would probably have been no disasters in the first place if a mutation had not been tolerated for so long in the family of the lord leaders.

That was a direct attack at himself, and one which he could not fight by any means known to him. This was particularly true since he had prevented his supporters from opposing the Patronate vote that gave the Lord Advisership to young Calaj.

Alarmed by the direction the public rage was taking, several of Clane's adherents had already regretted that they had allowed him to persuade them. It was now necessary, they claimed, for him to act before the Lord Adviser Calaj actually arrived in the capital.

It was just such a scheme that had brought Clane on this night journey through the streets of sleeping Linn. A *coup d'etat* was being planned—so the report had come to him upon his arrival in the city only a few hours before—the object of which was to proclaim him Lord Leader.

On his arrival at the palace of the Patron Saronatt, where the conspirators had set up their headquarters, Clane called the leaders to one of the three apartments that were immediately assigned to him. From the beginning, his attitude was under attack. He listened, startled, as former staunch supporters of his assailed his stand in language more violent than any he had ever had used against him. There were sneers and furious tirades. His fear of an alien invasion, when not openly derided, was attacked on the grounds that only as Lord Leader would he be in a position to defend the state. The arguments were much the same as Czinczar's, and were held with equal determination.

Shortly after 3 a.m., a famous Patron denounced his leadership. "I have been invited," he said savagely, "to join the Lilidel group and I shall accept. I'm through with this cautious coward." That was the beginning. The scramble to desert a sinking ship started then. At four o'clock, when Clane started to speak, his audience had dwindled to a score of men, mostly military leaders who had fought with him against Czinczar. And even they, he saw, were not too friendly. For their benefit, he discussed briefly and austerely the possible nature of the coming Riss attack. He did not tell them what his plans were, but he did offer them an emotional satisfaction.

"Our opponents," he said, "do not, in my opinion, realize as yet what they are doing in promoting this particular mother's boy to the rank of Lord Adviser. Children are concerned with the people around them, not with individuals whom they never meet. Just imagine a child that is now in a position to get its own willful way *every* time." He stood up, and looked around the little group grimly. He said, "I leave this thought with you."

He returned to his own residence, more shaken by the trend of events than he cared to admit. He was on his way to his bedroom when he was reminded by his guards' captain of the assassin.

❖❖❖

Clane hesitated. He was tired, and sick of problems. He was not even sure that he was interested in finding out who wanted him dead. Even some of his old supporters might now feel that he was dangerous to them alive. What decided him in the end was his general attitude of curiosity. He attributed his larger success to a habit of quick and thorough investigation of anything that seemed to affect his interest. He ordered the girl brought before him.

She came into the room boldly, spurning the attempt of the guards to lead her in like a prisoner. Seen in the bright light of the oil lamps, she looked older than his earlier impression of her had indicated. He guessed that she was twenty-two or three, or even twenty-five. She was beautiful, by his standards. Her features had the even lines of good looks and keen intelligence. The effect was marred only by the unmistakable insolence of her expression. But he realized that was not necessarily a fault. It was she who spoke first.

"If you think," she said, "that I am the usual type of assassin, you are quite mistaken."

Clane bowed ironically. "I am sure," he said, "that all assassins are unusual."

"I shot at you to attract your attention," she said.

Clane thought back to the moment of the attack. The arrow as he remembered it, had swished by about a foot from his head. For a skilled archer it was a bad shot. The question was, how skillful was she? And how much had the darkness affected her aim. The woman spoke again.

"I belong to the Martian Generals' Archery Club, and two weeks before Czinczar's attack I was runner-up in the championship matches. That's what decided me to take the risk. I was sure I could prove to you that I could have hit you."

Clane said satirically, "Couldn't you have chosen some other method of attracting my attention?"

"Not," she flashed, "if I expected to hold it."

Clane stiffened. This was verbal byplay, and he was not interested. "I'm afraid this is beyond me," he said. "And I'm afraid, too, that we will have to follow a more orthodox method of questioning, and assume the usual reasons for the attack."

He paused, curious in spite of himself. "Just why did you want to attract my attention?"

"I want to marry you," she said.

Clane, who had been standing, walked to a chair and sat down. There was a long silence.

He stared at her with bright eyes that concealed more turmoil than he cared to admit even to himself. He hadn't expected to have his hard crust of worldliness penetrated. He had the distinct and unhappy feeling that if he spoke his voice would tremble. And yet it was natural that he should have a strong reaction.

This young woman belonged to a part of Linn that he had considered forever beyond his reach. She was a part of the society that, except for a few men, had ignored the mutation member of the family of the late Lord Leader Linn. The fact that a girl of her station had decided to try to marry him merely proved that she saw him as a way to power for herself. If the night just passed was evidence, then that might be an error of judgment on her part. But her action was the first break in the dike of social opposition. Politically speaking, she could be very valuable to him.

Clane groaned inwardly as he realized that once more he was evaluating a situation in terms of its advantages to his purposes. He sighed, and made up his mind. He called to the guards captain:

"You will assign an apartment to the Lady Madelina Corgay. She will be our guest until further notice. See to it that she is well protected."

With that, he went to bed. He left instructions as to when he should be roused, and lay awake for a while turning over in his mind his plans for the day. Over and above everything else was the visit he wanted to make to the Central Palace to have another look at the monster that Czinczar had brought to Earth.

It would be important that somebody know something about the physical side of man's deadly enemy.

9

Lord Clane awoke about midmorning to the sound of distant singing. It puzzled him for a moment, and then he remembered that today the Lord Adviser Calaj was arriving, and that a fete had been proclaimed.

He ate a hasty breakfast, and then set out for the Central Palace in a patrol boat. As they started to float down for a landing, the pilot sent back a message with one of the guards:

"Your excellency, the Square is filled with people."

Clane ordered, "Land on a side street, and we'll walk the rest of the way."

They landed without incident, and wound their way among the dancers and the musicians. They passed swaying groups of singing men and women; and Clane, who had never failed to marvel at the antics of human beings, observed them in genuine wonder.

They were celebrating the accession to power of a youth whom they did not know. Sweet voices, raucous voices, good-natured yelling, women wiggling their hips coquettishly, men snatching at bare arms, kissing any pair of feminine lips that happened to be passing—it was in its own way a fascinating show. But in view of the danger that had been so narrowly averted, and of the impending invasion, it was a scene that had implications of disaster.

Physically grown men and women were acting like children, accepting as their ruler a boy whose only apparent qualification was that he was the son of the great Lord Jerrin. Here was so great a love of the childish things of life that all human life was imperiled.

His thought reached that point—and was violently interrupted. "It's that dastardly little priest!" a voice shouted.

The words were flung back among the crowd. There were angry cries of "Evil One!" "Mutation!" "Devil Priest!" The dancing in the near distance came to a stop, and there was a sullen surging of a mass of people to get nearer to him. Somebody yelled: "It's Lord Clane, the man responsible for all our troubles."

A furious murmur swept the throng. Beside Clane, the guards captain quietly motioned to the two dozen guards. The powerful men pressed forward, hands on swords and daggers. Clane, who had been watching the incident develop, stepped forward, a twisted smile on his lips. He raised his arm, and for just a moment received the silence he wanted. He called out in his most resonant voice:

"Long live the new Lord Adviser Calaj."

With that, he reached into a pouch, which he had carried for years for just such a moment as this, and brought it out clutching a handful of silver coins. With a flick of his wrist he tossed the money up into air. The metal glinted in the sun, and came down over a wide area about twenty feet away. Even before it landed another handful sparkled in the air in the opposite direction.

Once more, he called, more cynically this time, "Long live the Lord Adviser Calaj."

The crowd wasn't listening. There were shrieks as people stampeded after the money. Even after Clane's party was clear of the danger, he could hear cries of, "Give it to me, it's mine!" "You wretch, you stepped on my hand!" Feet scuffled, fists smacked audibly on the morning air.

❖ ❖ ❖

The incident made him bitter. Once again, he had been forced to rely on a technique for handling masses of people. Simple, effective, cunning, it was a part of the vast fund of information he had about the man in the street.

In spite of his tremendous desire to dissociate himself from such cheap trickeries, he couldn't do it. He recalled what Czinczar had said. He shook his head. There must be some way of arousing people to the fact that this was the eleventh hour of man's destiny. And that for once all men must put aside personal ambition and act in unison against an enemy so ferocious that he refused even to communicate with human beings.

But how? What could he say or do that would strike the vital spark? He who was spending *his* time and energy studying the machines aboard the Riss battleship, a task so colossal and so important that all else paled into insignificance beside it?

Yet here he was, on his way to the palace to do personally what should have been a routine job for one or more subordinates. It wasn't, of course. No one else was qualified for either of the two tasks that had to be done, the political and the scientific. A few years before, he had belatedly started an advanced school for science students; but he'd been too busy to give it proper attention. Politics. Wars. Intrigue. People to see. Spy reports to study. Property management. Exploration. Experiments. New ideas. Each twenty-four hours had gone by like a flash, leaving an ever accumulating variety of things to attend to. One man could do only so much. And now that the crisis was here, he felt the reality of that.

He was still thinking about it when he arrived at the palace gate. The time he noted with automatic attention to detail, was a few minutes before noon. The question in his mind was, would he be allowed inside?

It turned out not to be a problem at all. A distracted captain of the guard admitted him and his staff. Clane headed straight for the refrigeration room. He had no difficulty in finding the body of the dead Riss which Czinczar had brought with him from Europa.

❖ ❖ ❖

The elongated body of the unhuman creature did not act kindly to the thawing. As the water began to drip from the brown-stained, leathery folds of its skin, an unwholesome stench rose from it. In the beginning, the odor was faint. But it grew stronger.

As the butchers he had brought along sawed it into sections, Clane took the pieces and dictated first to one, then to another of his two secretaries. When he was finished with a segment, he handed it to an artist, who drew a lifelike picture of it with sure, rapid strokes.

As the afternoon waned, the odor thickened until it seemed to permeate every crevice of the room. And still Clane examined and dictated, examined and dictated. Gas flames and test tubes were brought into action. Juices from glands, liquid from the circulatory system of the thing, and fluid from the spinal column were tested with various chemicals, separated into their components, described, named and illustrated for future reference.

Once, when he put his fingers into a sticky goo and tasted it, one of the secretaries fainted. Another time he tried to feed a piece of it to a rat in a cage. The animal, purposely kept hungry, pounced on it—and died a few minutes later, convulsively.

Clane dictated: "The flesh, on examination, proved to be predominantly a complex protein structure, so complex in fact that it seemed doubtful if it would be edible by any animal of Earth origin. Rat, to which it was fed, died in 3.08 minutes."

Shortly after the dinner hour, he had the parts of the body returned to the box and put back into the ice room. The task completed, he hesitated. Because it was only the first of his two purposes. The other one required his knowledge of how to ride roughshod over another's will.

Once again, he was back in the role he hated. And there was no alternative.

He sent his party home, and inquired the way to Calaj's apartment. The official he spoke to recognized him, and put his hands to his head, as he said:

"Oh, your excellency, the confusion today is fantastic. We are all worn out."

He quieted long enough to give Clane the directions he desired. There were guards at the entrance of Calaj's apartment, but they sprang to attention when he said, "I am Lord Clane Linn, uncle of the Lord Adviser."

"Shall we announce you, your excellency?" one asked doubtfully.

"No." Clane was cool and positive. "I'll just go in."

He entered.

There was a little alcove, then a large outer room. As he glanced around him curiously, Clane saw Calaj standing on his head beside an open window. He was exhibiting his skill for the benefit of a Martian slave girl. The girl giggled, and then she turned away, and saw Clane. She froze.

She said something, and Calaj came tumbling down out of his upside down pose. He must have heard his mother express fears about Lord Clane, because he turned pale when he saw who it was.

"Uncle!" he said. And Clane did not miss the overtones of alarm in the voice. Calaj was hypnotized by his own anxiety.

In a sense the boy's fears were justified. Clane had no time to waste. He had come to the palace with two objectives, and he had brought along his rod of energy for emergencies. One objective—the examination of the Riss—was accomplished. The other depended on Calaj.

Clane felt remorseless. According to the reports of his spies, this boy was abnormal. If that was so, then he could not be saved. Often in the past, Clane had taken children and grown-ups to a private asylum, and there with all his knowledge had tried to untangle their minds. In vain.

This was no time to hope for success, where so often he had failed before.

Calaj had to be sacrificed. And Lilidel. And all that group behind her.

Destroyed by the madman they had raised to power.

"My boy," said Clane, "I have received instruction from the gods about you. They love you—but you must do their will."

"They love *me*?" said Calaj. His eyes were wide.

"They love you," said Clane firmly. "Why else do you think you were allowed to attain the height of power? Surely, you do not think that any human could have made you Lord Adviser without their permission."

"No, no, of course not."

"Listen, carefully," said Clane, "here are *their* instructions for your future actions. Repeat them after me. You must rule in your own right."

"I must rule in my own right." His voice was dull.

"Let no one in the palace advise you on affairs of state. Whatever you decide will be as the decision of the gods."

Calaj repeated the words with a rising inflection. And then he blinked. "Not even mother?" he asked, amazed.

"Especially not mother," said Clane.

He went on, "You will need new people around you. Be careful for a while, but gradually appoint men of your own choice. Disregard those recommended by your mother and her friends. And now, I have a document here—"

❖ ❖ ❖

Arrived at home, he wasted no time. "I am leaving at once," he told the heads of the various departments of his household staff. "You will probably not hear from me for a long time. You will conduct yourselves and the estate as in the past."

The guards captain said, "What about the assassin?"

Clane hesitated; then, "I suppose the men are expectant?"

"That they are, sir."

Clane said steadily, "I regard this custom of turning a woman assassin over to the soldiery as a barbarous practice, and it will not take place. First, it would be very dangerous for us all since her family is friendly with the new Lord Adviser. You might stress that point to the men, and then say—"

He made his offer of compensation. It was so generous that there was no doubt of it being accepted. He finished, "The offer holds for one year. And captain—"

"Yes, sir?"

Clane parted his lips to make his next announcement, then closed them. It was more than just another move in the complex game he was playing, and yet, the political color was there, too.

I've got to rise above all this pettiness, he told himself. In spite of what Czinczar had said, there was more to statesmanship than animal cunning. It all seemed so obvious; so essential. Because if he also played only the game the others were playing, there would be no hope.

His very determination stiffened him. He said quietly: "You may pass the word along to the company officers that the Lady Madelina Corgay will in future be known as the Lady Madelina Linn. All ranks will treat her accordingly."

"*Yes*, sir. Congratulations, your excellency."

"The marriage will take place today," Clane finished.

10

"But what did you sign?" Lilidel raged. "What was in the document?"

She paced the floor of his apartment in a frenzy of distress. Calaj watched her sullenly, annoyed at her critical attitude. She was the one person who could make him feel like a small boy, and he was silently furious at her for reminding him once again that he should have read what he had signed.

He was not anxious to think about Clane's appearance at the palace five weeks before, and it was annoying that the incident remained as fresh in his mother's mind as the day it had happened. "Why should I read the document?" he protested. "It was just one more paper. You people are always bringing me something to sign; what's one more? And anyway, he's my uncle, and after all, he didn't make any trouble about my becoming Lord Adviser."

"We can't let him get away with it," Lilidel said. "You can just picture him laughing to himself, thinking we're afraid to act against him openly."

That also was the latest of an endless repetition. Psychoneurotic Calaj could not help wondering if his mother was not a little crazy.

Lilidel raged on: "We've sent queries to all the governors, with instructions to scrutinize official documents, with particular emphasis on checking back with us on anything relating to the military establishment.

"Of course"—her tone grew bitter—"asking some of those people to co-operate is like talking to a blank wall. They pay about as much attention to us as if they were the government and we merely hirelings."

Calaj shifted uneasily. His mother's assumption of the word "we" rankled. She had no official position, and yet she acted as if she was the Lord Adviser, and he only her son and heir. He remembered, not for the first time, that Clane had said something about asserting himself. The trouble was, how could he possibly ever dare to oppose his mother and all these dominating people?

It's time I did something, he thought.

Aloud he said: "But what's the good of all this? Our spies report that he isn't at any of his estates." He added, with a sly dig that had become one of his defenses against his mother's dominance, "You'll have to locate him before you do anything against him publicly, and even then I'd hold Traggen in front of me, if I were you. As head of the camp legions, Traggen should do the dangerous work." Calaj stood up. "Well, I think I'll drop over to the games."

He sauntered out.

Lilidel watched him depart uneasily. She was not aware that, in Clane's estimation, her action of poisoning Jerrin had set up conflicts inside her that were not resolvable. But, in spite of the murder, way in the back of her mind, she applied her dead husband's standards of dignity to the great position which Calaj now had.

It had been a tremendous shock to her when Calaj had insisted that the festival celebrating his appointment be extended beyond the three days originally set for it, free to the people, but at colossal expense to the government. The games were still continuing, his interest in them unabated.

Already, there had been even more disturbing incidents. A group of youths, returning with Calaj from the games to the palace, were astounded to hear him suddenly burst out: "I could kill all of you! *Guards, kill them!*" The third time he shrieked the order the nearest guard, a big brute of a man, noticed one of Calaj's companions had his hand on a half-drawn sword. In one synchronized movement, he slashed at the boy with his saber, nearly cutting him in two. In the resulting confusion, nine of the eleven young noblemen were slaughtered. The remaining two escaped by taking to their heels.

Lilidel had had no alternative but to report it as an attempted assassination. At her insistence, the two boys who had escaped were dragged through the streets at the end of hooks, and eventually impaled against the pilings of the river's edge.

Standing there in his apartment—where she had to come these days, if she hoped to see him—Lilidel had the unhappy conviction that what had happened was only the beginning.

During the weeks that followed, she discovered that Traggen had selected several companies of bully boys to act as Calaj's personal guards, and that the men had orders to accept the slightest command given by the Lord Adviser. She could not help suspecting Traggen's motives, but she could find no fault openly with his orders. It was natural that the Lord Adviser Calaj should have automatic obedience to his commands. What was unnatural were the commands that Calaj gave, and all too obviously Traggen the schemer could have no direct control over that.

Month after month, the stories trickled in to her. Hundreds of people were disappearing, never to be heard of again. Their places were swiftly filled by newcomers who knew nothing of what had gone before, or else dismissed as nonsense the vague stories they had heard.

Everywhere in Linn, people in every walk of life intrigued to gain access to the Lord Adviser. The yearning will of thousands of social climbers to become a part of the palace circle was a pressure that never ended. For generations, that had been the road to power and position. But now, success in such a purpose precipitated the individual into a nightmare.

All the trappings and ornamentation that each person's heart craved were there. He attended banquets that consisted almost entirely of out-of-season delicacies, and rare and costly foods from the planets. Each night, the palace ballroom was awhirl with gaily attired dancers. On the surface everything was as it should be.

Usually, the first few incidents failed to alarm the individual. Someone in the crowd would cry out in fear and pain; and it was often difficult to find out what had happened.

Besides, it was happening to someone else. It seemed remote and without personal meaning, and that was true even when it took place close by. The guards—so it was reported to Lilidel—had developed a skillful technique of snatching up the dead body, pressing in close around it, and racing out of the nearest door.

In the beginning it was hard for any particular person to imagine that such a thing could ever happen to him. But the strain began to tell. No one who was accepted in high government circles dared to withdraw from active social life. But Lilidel began to notice that her listeners were no longer completely sympathetic to her blurred references to the danger of assassination. Too many Linnan families were in mourning for a son or daughter who had been casually killed by Calaj's butchers.

A year and three weeks went by.

One day Lilidel's ceaseless search for a clue to the nature of the document Calaj had signed for Clane was rewarded. A paragraph in a routine letter from a provincial governor was brought to her attention. It read:

"Will you please convey to his excellency, the Lord Adviser, my appreciation of the precautions the government has taken to insure the safety of the populace in the event of another invader bombing out cities. We of Reean, who have before us always the awful example of what happened to our neighbor city of Mura, are perhaps in a better position to understand the practical brilliance of what is being done. In my opinion, more than anything else this has established the reputation of the Lord Adviser among people who formerly might have considered him too young for his high office. The breadth of statesmanship revealed, the firm determination, the break with precedent—as you know farm people are usually the least patriotic and the most commercially minded of the populace in an emergency—are all proof that the New Lord Adviser is a man of remarkable insight and character."

That was all there was, but it was enough for Lilidel. A week of careful inquiry produced the picture of what had happened, and was still happening.

Everywhere except around Linn, city people had been organized and assigned to nearby farms. Until further notice, and under heavy penalties, they were ordered to spend ten percent of their incomes to construct living quarters—and an icehouse for food storage—on the farms to which they were to go if an emergency was proclaimed.

The buildings were to be so constructed that they could be converted into granaries, but for three years they were to remain empty. The city people would do the building, and they were to visit their farm once a month as a group in order to familiarize themselves with the environment.

At the end of three years, the farmer could buy the buildings at fifty percent of the cost of materials—but with no charge for labor— but he could not tear them down for another ten years. The food in the icehouse remained the property of the city people, but must be disposed of by the end of the fifth year.

Lilidel satisfied herself that this was indeed the result of the document which Calaj had signed for Clane, and then she consulted agricultural experts. They were amazed. One of them said dazedly:

"But you don't do that kind of thing to farmers. They won't stand for it. They won't co-operate. And the least we can do now is to *give* them the buildings at the end of the three years."

Lilidel was about to agree with the indictment of the plan, when she remembered—it kept slipping her mind—that Calaj was supposed to have sponsored it.

"Nonsense!" she brushed aside the objections. "We will proceed exactly as we have in the past."

She added, "And, of course, we will now extend it to include the city Linn."

She told Calaj afterwards, triumphantly, "The beauty of it is that Lord Clane has actually strengthened your position." She hesitated. There was one thing wrong with her victory. After more than a year there was still no sign of the mutation. He had vanished as completely as if he had died and been buried. Victory—when the loser did not know you had won—lacked savor.

"But what's all this about?" Calaj asked peevishly. "What are the precautions against?"

"Oh, there was some invading ship here from one of the little known outer planets. Your father worried a great deal about it, but when the fleet attacked they had little or no trouble driving it away. I suppose we should have pursued them and declared war, but you can't be fighting the barbarians all the time. The important thing is not the precautions but that the people seem to approve of them. And they think you're responsible."

Calaj said: "But I only signed one paper." It was a point that had been bothering him for some time in a curious irksome fashion.

His mother stared at him, baffled. She sometimes had difficulty following her son's associations. "What do you mean?"

Calaj shrugged. "The reports say that official orders were posted up in every district with my name and seal signed to them. But I only signed one."

Lilidel was white. "Forgeries," she whispered. "Why, if they can do that—" She broke off. "Come to think of it, the one sent us did look odd."

Trembling, she sent for it, and presently they were bending over the document. "It's my signature all right," said Calaj. "And that's the seal."

"And there were hundreds like this," whispered Lilidel, overwhelmed.

She had never before seen a Photostat.

❖ ❖ ❖

A week later, she was still undecided as to whether she should feel satisfied or dissatisfied about the situation when a terrible report reached her. Hundreds of gigantic spaceships were hovering over the mountain areas of Earth. From each one of them thousands of monsters were being landed.

The Riss had arrived.

11

Lord Clane was very much alive indeed. At the appointed hour, more than a year before, he had sent a peremptory order to all sections of the giant ship, and then settled himself at the controls.

The *Solar Star* began to lift. The initial movement was normal enough, but the difference showed within a few minutes. It grew dark with extreme rapidity. The acceleration made the men in the control room look at each other with sickly grins.

Clane noticed the reaction, but he stayed on his couch beside the touch controls. He had a hollow feeling at the pit of his stomach, but only he knew their destination.

After three hours he reduced that tensing acceleration to one gravity, and went up to his own apartment for dinner. Conscious of the difficulties that thousands of people in the decks below would have in preparing their meals, he waited an hour and a half before again applying acceleration.

Five hours ticked by before once more he reduced the acceleration to one gravity, and allowed another hour and a half for the preparation and consumption of food. The next period of acceleration was four hours. At that time he reduced the tremendous pressure briefly while his new instructions were circulated.

"The people aboard this ship," he ordered, "will now sleep for seven hours. Acceleration will be somewhat greater than normal but not so great as it has been. Be sure and take advantage of the opportunity."

For the first time then he allowed his officers to transmit the pattern of travel to their subordinates, and so on through the ship: "Two (breakfast), three (acceleration), one and a half (dinner), five (acceleration), one and a half (supper), four (acceleration), seven (sleep)." The extra time for breakfast allowed for dressing and toilette.

"This," said Madelina, "is silly."

Clane studied her as she sat across the breakfast table from him. It was their fourth morning of living in the spaceship. He had wondered how the pressure of acceleration, and the dreary routine would affect her. For several meal periods now, he had been finding out. As a wife, Madelina was as outspoken as she had been while a captive. It was time she found out the truth.

She looked at him now, her dark eyes flashing. "I see no reason whatever," she said, "for us to run away. You've got to be bold in this world, Clane. Maybe that's why you've never got anywhere."

Her casual dismissal of all his achievements startled Clane. But there was an even more disturbing implication behind her words. After thirty years of being a free agent, he must now adjust himself to the presence of somebody who could talk to him in this critical but undiscriminating fashion. Most unsatisfactory of all, intellectually, was his own reaction to her presence.

Gratitude! A woman of the Linnan aristocracy had sought him out to marry him. She was little more than a child, impulsive, impatient, undisciplined, lacking the experience and training that alone would give balance to her judgments. But he was grateful to her nonetheless. And anxious. Suppose she grew impatient and decided she had made a mistake. He did not doubt that she would leave him, lightly, disdainfully, perhaps seeking some other protector aboard the ship. Czinczar? It was not a possibility he cared to consider.

It was time she found out that this was not just a flight from Lilidel. He said, "After breakfast, why don't you come up to the control room with me. There's an all glass room next to it from which you can get a wonderful view of the stars."

Madelina shrugged. "I've seen the sun before in space."

It seemed to be a rejection, and Clane wasn't sure whether he should be relieved or unhappy. And then, an hour later, just as he was about to increase the acceleration, she came into the control room.

"Where's this viewing room?" she said cheerfully.

Clane saw several officers look at each other significantly. Silently furious, Clane walked towards her. Her action was inexcusable, since he had told her what the pattern of flight would be.

"This way," he said.

She must have noticed the suppressed anger in his voice. But she merely smiled sweetly, and walked in the direction he indicated. She stopped as she came to the door of the viewing room. He heard the hissing intake of her breath, and then she had moved forward and out of sight. When Clane came to the door, he saw that she was already standing with her face pressed against the transparent wall.

❖ ❖ ❖

Seemingly inches beyond was the great dark itself. Silently, Clane took up a position beside her. His anger was unabated. For this visit of Madelina's, casually calculated to be annoying, fitted in with all the more foolish things that human beings were doing on Earth on the eve of disaster. Each day that went by, it grew clearer that the interrelationships of human beings was inextricably bound up with the Riss danger itself. It was not two or more, but one complex problem.

With a dark awareness of how intricate was this alien war, Clane waited for Madelina's reaction.

The viewing room was unique from the transparent sections in other parts of the ship in that the "glass" bulged out. From where they stood, it was possible to look both forward and backward. Almost directly behind the ship, a very bright star was visible.

Clane said in a low tone: "Madelina, you've made a fool of me before my own staff, coming up like this."

Madelina did not look around, but her shoulders lifted ever so slightly, defiantly. She said: "I think this whole flight is ridiculous. You men ought to be ashamed of yourselves, running away. Personally, I won't have anything to do with it."

She turned impulsively, but there was an intense expression on her face. "Now, look, Clane," she said, "I'm not going to embarrass you again, so don't worry. You see, I know I'm going to be good for you. You're too careful. You don't realize that life is short, and you've got to cut corners and do things fast and without fear. There's only one thing I'm scared of, and that is that I'll miss something, some experience, some vital part of being alive."

She went on earnestly: "Clane, I tell you this trip is a mistake. We should go back and boldly take up residence on the estate. Certainly, we must take precautions against danger, but even if we do get caught in one of Lilidel's traps, I'm ready. I love life, but I'm not going to live it on my knees."

Once more she broke her thought abruptly. "What planet are we going to? Mars, or Venus?"

"Neither."

"One of the moons, perhaps? If it's somewhere interesting, Clane, I might feel less impatient. After all, a girl ought to have a nice honeymoon." She pointed at the bright star behind them. "What planet is that?"

"It's the Sun," said Clane.

He helped her presently to one of the nearby couches, and returned to the control room.

A few minutes later, the *Solar Star* was plunging at tremendously increased acceleration through a space that grew darker with each passing hour.

❖❖❖

It was during the supper hour on the fifth day that Clane was informed that Czinczar desired an audience. He hesitated, fighting an instant impatience. Another human hurdle, and an important one.

"Bring him in," he ordered finally.

The barbarian leader came in thoughtfully and accepted the chair to which Clane motioned him. His face was a study of conflicting emotions, but his voice was steady when he finally spoke.

"You madman!" he said.

Clane smiled. "That's what I thought your reaction would be."

Czinczar brushed aside the remark with an angry gesture. "What's the logic behind such a move?"

"Hope."

The barbarian's lips curled. "You've given up the political control of a planet, the enormous geographical distances of Earth to which men can retreat in case of an emergency—for a dream."

Clane said, "This matter of political control is an obsession with you, Czinczar. In the face of a Riss invasion, it is a meaningless achievement. This is not a problem that will be solved in the solar system."

"Nor by a man whose first thought is to escape from danger into outer space," Czinczar sneered.

Clane smiled again, more grimly this time. "If you knew what plans I have, you would swallow those words."

Czinczar shrugged. "Just where are we going?" he asked at last.

Clane told him, "It's a star I located on an old star map of this part of the galaxy."

Having used those magic words, he had to hold himself calm. "Galaxy", other "stars"—even to him who had discovered so much of the science of the days of old, there were new meanings here, emotional excitements on a level beyond anything he had ever known.

"It's about sixty-five light-years from Sol," he said steadily.

He watched Czinczar to see if the fantastic distance he had named had any meaning. But the barbarian seemed to be involved in a mental conflict. He looked up finally, his face twisted.

"Men—out there?" Even after a minute of silence, he sounded astounded.

Clane said earnestly, "I want you to picture the golden age of science, Czinczar. Surely, this idea is not new to you, who brought the first Riss body to Linn. Long ago, man's civilization attained a stature that has never since been equaled. In those marvelous days, ships not only went to other planets, but to other stars.

"Then the aliens came. A bitter war ensued. The civilization of the solar system was virtually buried with the destruction of *all* its cities. But out in space, colonies escaped, and continued to develop scientifically beyond anything now known on Earth."

The young man climbed to his feet. "Your excellency," he said in a formal tone, "in my opinion you have by your actions destroyed the solar system. In leaving the Linnan Empire in the control of a mad youth and his murderess-mother, you have at one stroke handed the fate of the known human race over to a government that will be thrown into confusion at the moment the Riss attack, and will remain in a state of confusion until the end. Your imaginative flight is illogical in the first place because, if other men had found a means of fighting the Riss, they would by this time have contacted the people of Earth."

Clane hesitated; then, "There are several possible answers to that. Colonies don't build interstellar ships. Or if these have, then by the time they developed them they had forgotten that Earth existed. Or at least forgotten where it was in space."

Czinczar controlled himself with a visible effort. "Your excellency," he said, "I urge you to turn back. I also believe in imagination, or I would never have achieved my present position. Nor would I have dared to take the enormous risk of attacking Linn. If I had thought you would make this flight into darkness, I would not have surrendered to you, sphere or no sphere."

Clane said, "Czinczar, you're a great disappointment to me. In a curious—I suppose illogical fashion—I counted on your seeing the importance of forgetting all irrelevant personal ambition. I counted on you denying yourself the pleasure which you obtain from military combat—you have some scheme, I know, of fighting a purely defensive war against the Riss. All that, I say, I expect you to forgo in this crisis. And what do I find?"

He made a movement with his hand that expressed some of his own fury at the petty things that Czinczar had done. "From the beginning you have plotted primarily for personal advantage. You have forced other men to take defensive action against you—"

"The idea being, of course," sneered Czinczar, "that these other individuals were not doing any plotting of their own, and would not have intrigued against each other if I had not come on the scene."

Clane said quietly, "Each man must forget his own schemes, his own desires, for the duration. There can be no exceptions."

Czinczar was cold and contemptuous. "Harping on the same old subject, aren't you? Well, I refuse to talk further to a person who has lost his good sense because of a childish, naïve dream. The able man who abdicates his own ideas betrays himself and his state. He must fight for his own convictions against the firmly held ideas of other men. I am convinced that, having adopted such a juvenile attitude, all your plans are now suspect."

He stalked to the door, turned. "Don't forget, the reason the Riss are attacking the solar system must be because there are a limited number of habitable planets in the area of space that can be reached by their ships. I hope you're sure that *we* will find a habitable planet when we reach our destination about—" He paused, abruptly tense. "How long will it take?"

"Something over a year," said Clane.

Czinczar groaned. "Madness," he muttered. "Utter madness!"

❖❖❖

He went out, leaving Clane disturbed and upset. The barbarian leader was unquestionably one of the outstanding military logicians of the age, a bold and careful man who had probably examined the entire Riss situation with a minute attention to detail. No fear of unknown distances would influence his decisions.

And yet, his analysis must be wrong. Czinczar simply did not have the understanding of science that alone made possible a considered judgment. All his courage, his calculated risks, and his military skill would merely delay the enemy, not defeat him.

If the answer was not available out in space, then there was no answer.

12

A week of routine flight went by. At first Clane held himself aloof from some of the precautions that he would in the past have taken against a man like Czinczar.

"If intrigue is ever going to end," he told himself, not for the first time, "then somebody has to take the first step. You have to show people that you trust them."

One little point jarred on him. During that week, it grew in his mind to uneasy proportions. The point was simple. Czinczar had stated unequivocally that he would not co-operate.

Abruptly, on the sixth day, that recollection broke through Clane's reserve. He began to spy on Czinczar. He was intensely disappointed, though, he realized bitterly, not basically surprised, to discover that massive military preparations were under way in the lower half of the ship.

The discovery depressed Clane because Czinczar clearly counted on his own precautions to prevent any spying. It showed up his ignorance of science. His actual preparations were skillful and bold. He had readied Riss-type explosives he had discovered in one of the holds. Crews with battering rams had been trained to smash down connecting doors which the explosive failed to shatter. The entire barbarian army—a magnificent array of fighters—was divided into groups of a size more suitable for battle in a confined area.

The date of the attack was set by Czinczar for the sleep period of the eighth "night."

Twelve hours before the attack was scheduled, Clane invited the barbarian leader to come up and inspect Riss weapons. He recognized that he was up to his old tricks. He told himself defensively that what he hoped for could only be achieved gradually. In the meantime, he must accept the old environment of human machinations that he knew so well.

There was a delay of several hours, while Czinczar discussed the timing of the invitation with his general staff. Finally, he sent a messenger to Clane accepting the offer. But the attack was not called off.

Czinczar arrived at the appointed time with two engineer officers. He ignored Clane's extended hand, saying curtly, "You surely don't expect me to be friendly to a man who tortured me."

"But didn't kill you," Clane pointed out with a faint smile.

"That," said Czinczar, "is because you hope to make use of my forces. Since that involves my own abilities, I must have a picture of the possibilities of our situation, so that I can start training my men. Let us proceed."

Clane felt vaguely sorry for the great man. He was so obviously unaware of what he was up against.

It emphasized—if emphasis were needed—how little he was qualified to judge the hard realities of the Riss war.

It grew clear from the barbarian's next words that he had specific ideas as to what weapons he wanted to see. He said, "Before coming aboard, I was 'photographed' by a machine. That was subsequently done to everyone. What was the purpose?"

Clane led the way to a special weapon control room, with its huge chairs and oversized equipment. He remained in the background while the barbarian engineers exclaimed over the glittering machines and instruments. Czinczar evidently shared their amazement, for he looked around soberly, and then said:

"I can see that the Riss are scientifically our superiors in every department."

Clane said nothing. Weeks ago, that had been his reaction, too. Now, he wasn't so sure. Involuntarily, he glanced down at the floor. It was covered by a finely woven fiber mat. In looking under the mat—as he had done as a matter of course—he had found that once there had been another floor covering, a plastic coating of some kind. It was all gone except for chips and fragments.

His workmen had been unable to remove those pieces. The material defied steel chisels.

To Clane, that suggested this was an old ship. The plastic had deteriorated unevenly over the centuries—*and the Riss didn't know how to replace it.*

There was other evidence. Some of the control switches were dummies. In tracing their leads, he had come to empty rooms which looked as if they had once contained machines.

The implications were titanic. The Riss, too, had an unbalanced civilization. More fortunate than man, they had been able to continue to build interstellar ships. Or perhaps they were actually using ships that had fought in the deadly war fifty centuries ago, and simply did not know how to rebuild some of the machines in them.

That gave Clane his picture. Two races struggling up out of the abysmal night, with the Riss far in the lead in the race for scientific advantage.

As of now, their advantage was overwhelming. Man would go down in the first major engagement.

Czinczar was speaking again. "I expect you to stop me if I do anything wrong."

He seemed to have forgotten the protector "photographing" machine. He settled himself in one after the other of the huge control chairs, and began to manipulate dials. With each move he asked questions, while the engineers took notes. "What does this do? And this? And this?" He listened intently, and the answer never seemed too detailed for him. Several times, in spite of extensive explanation, he shook his head and frankly admitted, "I don't understand how that works."

Clane refrained from making an even more extensive admission. He had taken most of these machines apart, and put them together again. But just how they worked was a problem on a different level of understanding. He had made attempts to duplicate apparently simple looking plates and circuits, with completely negative results.

Fortunately, the great ship's storerooms were packed with duplicates, so extensive experiments were still possible.

Czinczar was beginning to understand purposes now. His gaze moved quickly along the tremendous instrument board; and it was not surprising that he walked over to the "protector" machine, and stared down at it. At this control end, it bore no resemblance to the telescopic "photographic" machine, which had taken his "picture." Obviously, he stared down at the array of locks that were rigidly clamped over every dial.

Clane came forward. "This is it," he said.

❖ ❖ ❖

Clane began by giving some idea of the intricate science involved, and of the advanced mechanical arrangement.

"As you may or may not know," he said, "the ninety-odd chemical elements in the periodic system are made of atoms, which in turn are complex structures involving nuclei and orbital particles. The outer particle 'ring' of each atom is of first importance in any chemical reaction. Where the outer 'rings' of two elements are very similar, it is difficult to separate them chemically.

"Naturally, clusters of such atoms are in a state of turmoil. They send out a constant barrage of radiation on different energy levels. It would seem at first thought that at each particle level, the radiation of one object would be exactly similar to the same energy radiation from another body. According to the Riss diagrams I have examined—and there are some very interesting films aboard to illustrate the text—these radiations differ on a basis of spacing and timing. They exist in a different space-time. I confess that's been a hard formulation for me to grasp."

He paused. It was the first time he had talked of this to anyone; and he was conscious of a tension of excitement inside him. Sometimes, when he thought of the colossal treasure-house of science he had captured along with the Riss ship, the emotional impact threatened to overwhelm him. That was the feeling he had to fight now. He went on finally, huskily:

"This machine"—he pointed at the "protector" instrument board—"sends out a stream of radiation, which permeates the space-time in and around the ship. The radiation runs up and down the scale of energy several hundred thousand times a second. Whenever it resonates—that is, enters the space-time of some other radiation—the temperature of the affected object goes up. This happens to all except 'protected' atoms.

"The nature of the 'protection' is basically simple. When you were photographed, a pattern was set up in a series of tubes here, whereby your position in space was thereafter recognized. This recognition could be used either to single you out for destruction from among billions of other objects, or it could be used to 'protect' you. As of this moment, the radiation skips over you and me and the other people in this ship. It skips over every object in the ship by the process of recognizing them and rejecting them several hundred thousand times a second."

Clane finished, "This is one of the most deadly weapons ever invented for use against flesh and blood creatures. If I had known they had something like this aboard, I would not have considered making an attack. Every man in the spaceships that took part in the battle was killed. Not just a percentage of them, but every single Linnan in the part of the fleet that actually attacked. My men and I escaped because the Riss patrol boat we were in had a 'protector' camera aboard, which automatically 'photographed' us. Apparently, they used it so that the liftboats could bring specimens to the ship."

The account completed, he waited. He was not too surprised at the prolonged silence. Finally, Czinczar said, "Does it operate only against living matter?"

"It's set that way."

"But it could be used against inanimate objects? You either deliberately or unconsciously implied that in your use of such words as 'object'."

Clane hesitated. Not for the first time, he was startled at the discernment of the barbarian leader. He shrugged finally, and admitted the fact. "Frankly, I don't quite see how it can effectively be used against inorganic matter. It raises the temperature of the entire affected area about sixty degrees. That's fatal for life organisms, but even a tree would survive it."

"You would say then that this instrument could not destroy our planet?"

"I don't see how."

"That," said Czinczar, "is what I wanted to know."

His tone indicated that he had guessed the purpose of the long explanation. His eyes met Clane's, and there was a sardonic light in them.

"You'll have to try again," he said. "I don't scare easily."

❖❖❖

He seemed dissatisfied with the limitations of his rebuttal. For he hesitated, glanced at his engineers, parted his lips to speak, and then apparently changed his mind. Silently, he settled himself into the next chair, and began to manipulate the dials of the weapon controlled from it.

Clane held back his disappointment. He intended to come back to the matter, and he had a feeling that Czinczar did too. While he waited, he explained the new weapon.

It operated on a molecular level. It was definitely not radioactive. It seemed to set up a terrific agitation in the molecules of an object. Result: the object burned with a blue-white heat, dissolving quickly into its component gases. It could be used against organic or inorganic matter, but it was a limited weapon in that it had to be aimed and held briefly on its target. He had still to find out if it could be used automatically.

Clane continued, "I've merely tested it. I haven't had time to examine it." He paused ever so briefly, then finished deliberately, "I gave most of my attention to the 'protector' device. It's existence nullifies everything we've got."

Czinczar said quickly, "And the sphere nullifies it."

He looked around, and squarely met Clane's determined gaze. "Think, your excellency, if they try to land, the sphere not only decimates them; it destroys every single Riss in the vicinity."

"All they have to do," said Clane bleakly, "is fly low over one of our cities with this 'protector' device on, and every person in that city dies. A hundred ships could wipe out the population of Earth in a given time."

Czinczar was facing him now. "Then why did they use atomic bombs against the cities they destroyed?" His tone challenged Clane to give a logical answer.

Clane said slowly, "I think it's a weapon they developed since the war that originally destroyed man's civilization. I don't think they wanted us to find out about it from an exploring ship. Its potentialities can be partially nullified by evacuating cities and scattering the population."

Czinczar shook his head. "Your answer is not complete enough. An irresistible weapon doesn't have to be concealed. You say you've tested it. Knowing your thoroughness I'm going to guess that you know its range."

"About two and a half miles," said Clane without hesitation.

"Since it has a range," said Czinczar, "it obviously must be more effective at one mile than at two."

Clane nodded. "The nearer to the ship the higher the temperature it produces. At two and a half miles it is still fatal, but the individual may be in agony for several hours before death comes."

"What happens when a barrier is placed between it and its intended victims?"

"The men in the Linnan fleet," said Clane, "were protected by several inches of metal, but everyone of them died."

"According to your account," flashed Czinczar, "they should have died when they were still more than two miles from the invader. Actually, all of them got close enough for them to ram the big ship. If the ship had been out of control for the full two miles, only a few of them would have reached their objective."

Clane said irritably, "All right, suppose a small portion of the population successfully burrows out of reach of this weapon. A thousand or ten thousand people survive to fight on. Surely, that is not a satisfactory solution. The Riss could ignore them almost completely."

Czinczar climbed to his feet. "Your excellency," he said angrily, "it is clear that you and I do not understand each other."

To Clane, something else was clear. The argument had reached a critical stage.

❖❖❖

"Your excellency," Czinczar began, "I am predominantly a military man, you are a scientist. To me, your fear that people may be killed has little or no meaning. People are always being killed, if not in wars, then by other methods. But the wars are ever present, so we need look no further."

He went on grimly, "It is the essential nature of a military man that he must think in terms of percentage losses. Only the skillful leaders must be protected. During a war the death of a first-class military strategist can be a national disaster. The resulting defeat may mean slavery by one means or another for the entire population. In an alien war it can mean the extermination of the race."

Clane parted his lips at that point to interrupt, changed his mind, and then thought better of that, and said dryly, "And who shall decide on the importance of the man? He himself?" He broke off. "Go on," he urged.

Czinczar shrugged angrily. "In certain rigid governmental structures, a single man may lose every battle and still remain in power. But a brave and determined general with enough supporters can break through such an egocentric pattern, and seize control of the defense forces. That situation existed in Linn for one person—yourself." Contemptuously, "You lost your nerve."

"Proceed," said Clane coolly.

"The importance of the leader," said Czinczar, "constitutes one principle of warfare. Another one, even more basic, is that you do not surrender your land to the invader except for specific military purposes, and in the belief that you are actually strengthening your position. Usually, you make him pay a price for it."

Clane said, "If we exchanged one man for two Riss, we would exterminate ourselves, and the natural increase on one or two Riss planets would make up the Riss losses in a single year. Actually, at a conservative estimate, we would lose ten of our own people for every Riss we killed."

"You can't prove that," Czinczar snapped. He waved a hand in annoyance. "Never mind." He went on, "You are wrong in believing that I oppose such a journey as this. But I believe it's too soon. The solar system must be defended first. We must show these aliens that they cannot make a successful landing on any of our planets. Later, when we have established our lines of defense, when we know where and under what terms we can fight, when the populace is trained to the conditions under which the battle must be waged, then and only then can we trust other individuals to carry on."

His eyes were glowing, his face was set in hard lines, his lips tightly drawn together. "There," he said, "you have my argument."

He sat down, and gazed at Clane expectantly. The latter hesitated. So far as he could see, nothing new or important had been brought out. He had considered every one of Czinczar's points long ago, and found them inadequate to the situation. He said finally, slowly:

"In the first place, I reject the notion that one or two men are indispensable to the human race, even if they have managed by political cunning to convince a large following that the group can obtain power through them. I have personally told many individuals how I think a war against the Riss would have to be fought. In a crisis, these gentlemen will make their counsel felt."

"Too late," interjected Czinczar.

Clane went on, "This war between Riss and human cannot be won by making a stand on a single planet, or in a single sun system. I am not even sure that an attempt should be made to win it. There you have my second point."

Czinczar said, "I am a great proponent of the limited objective— provided the enemy concurs."

"Thirdly," said Clane, "we will not operate on the basis that half the population, or three quarters of it, is expendable. Leaders with such notions are criminally irresponsible."

Czinczar laughed, harshly. "A good military man accepts the potentialities of his situation. He makes what sacrifices are necessary. Since the alternative in this situation is utter disaster, then the sacrifice of three quarters *or more* of the population is not something that is in the control of the individual leader."

Clane said, "I am sure that I can trust even Lilidel to maintain herself within those elastic limitations. And now"—his tone changed—"before I make my fourth point, I want you to examine this part of the weapon control board." He indicated a section which they had not yet inspected.

❖ ❖ ❖

Czinczar gave him a sharp look, and then settled down into one of the chairs. His first touch on a dial brought a picture onto a large screen on the wall in front of him. He frowned at a scene in space.

"A window?" he asked doubtfully.

Clane urged, "Go on."

The barbarian moved quickly from instrument to instrument. He grew abruptly tense when he came to those that showed the inside of the ship. In silence, he adjusted more dials, and watched the scenes that unfolded on the plates, and listened to the dialogue that came from concealed loud speakers.

People talking—in their rooms, along corridors, in the great community kitchens. Talking, unaware that they were being observed. Those all-seeing viewers peered in at lovers, and at the headquarters of Czinczar in the barbarian section of the ship. They showed the preparations that had been made by the barbarians for their assault. Everywhere, the evidence was brought to light.

At last, he seemed to have enough. He shut off the instrument he had been manipulating, and sat for nearly a minute with his back to Clane. Finally, he stood up, turned, and gazed at Clane with steady eyes. "What is your fourth point?" he asked.

Clane stared at him, suddenly gloomy. Because he was back on the childish level. In spite of his desire to raise the entire undertaking to a plane where it was above politics, above the need for force, inexorably it had sunk to that level. And now, he had no recourse but to act accordingly. He said:

"Very simple. We are on our way to another star. In my egocentric fashion, I have somehow entrenched myself in a position of command. So long as I am in that position, the journey continues. If I should find my control seriously threatened, I would be reluctantly compelled to tamper with the 'protective' machine on a level where it might damage any conspirators. Do I make myself clear?"

The barbarian stared at him with icy hostility. "Perfectly," he said.

He turned with a shrug. "Let us proceed with the inspection."

There was no further discussion. So far as Clane was concerned, it was a defeat for both of them.

13

One year and eighteen days went by. The giant ship approached the end of its journey.

Twin planets, like two large moons, swam in the blackness ahead. It seemed clear from their size and their distance from each other—they looked about the same diameter—that they revolved one around the other, and that the two of them together followed an eccentric orbit around the hot blue star that was their sun.

The *Solar Star* approached them on a line almost equidistant from each planet. Ranking technical officers—both barbarian and

Linnan—gathered in the viewing room. From where he stood near Czinczar, Clane could hear the comments.

"Undoubtedly, both have atmospheres."

"I can see continents and oceans on both of them."

"Look, that must be a mountain. See the shadow it casts."

Clane listened silently. Most of the remarks confirmed his own impressions. He had had a few other thoughts that no one had yet mentioned, but they would come to them, he felt sure.

He waited for additional comments, and presently, as he had expected, they came. A man said, "You'd think we'd have caught the glint of a ship before this. There must be a steady stream of traffic between the two planets."

Another man said, "I've been watching the dark areas of the right side of each planet, where it's night now. I have yet to see the lights of a city."

The murmur of conversation ended abruptly. More than a dozen pairs of eyes turned to stare at Clane. The mutation smiled faintly, and turned to Czinczar.

"They're expecting me to guarantee them that we'll find human beings down there," he murmured in a low, amused tone. The barbarian leader shrugged coldly.

Clane faced his mixed, partly hostile staff. "Gentlemen," he said, "consider the following possibilities. Cities are vulnerable to the aliens; therefore there are no cities. It is much too soon to say that there is no periodic traffic between the two planets."

He walked over and made some adjustments on the auxiliary steering gear. The ship began to turn gradually in its course. Unmistakably, it headed for the planet that had been to their right a few moments before.

No one made any comment on the choice. One planet of these twins seemed as good as the other—especially as both could be visited in a matter of days by this tremendously swift ship.

❖ ❖ ❖

The ship entered the atmosphere of Twin One, as someone suggested they call it, at a sedate speed. On Clane's star map, the two planets had names of their own—Outland and Inland—but the mutation did not mention the fact. The machine sped down toward sea level, and gradually straightened its course until it was moving along about three miles above a hilly wilderness that glinted with streams. As far as the eye could see there was forest or green meadow.

The men looked at each other. Clane walked over to Czinczar and, standing beside him, stared somberly down at the virgin land below. Czinczar spoke first, "It's too bad the aliens didn't find this planet. They could have it without a fight."

Clane laughed abruptly. It was a curiously harsh sound, that startled him. "Czinczar," he said after a moment, "there won't be any fight on Earth either unless the inhabitants of Twin One or Twin Two can provide us with superior weapons."

The barbarian said nothing. He must have sensed something of Clane's intense disappointment.

Somebody shouted, "There's a village!"

Clane counted nineteen houses set rather widely apart, and then a sprinkling of houses even farther from each other. About a hundred acres of trees evenly spaced suggested an orchard, and there were fields of green stuff.

He saw no moving dots which, at three miles, was not too surprising. Human beings did not show up well from a height.

They were past. The houses blurred into the mist behind them, but their existence had already communicated a warmth of excitement to the men in the viewing room. A babble of conversation broke out.

Clane said to Czinczar: "Suppose that this planet was inhabited by an agricultural society. With an army no larger than the one aboard, we could take control. Then, even if we failed to find weapons to stop the invaders, we could have a nucleus of civilization here."

Czinczar maintained a sour silence, and the two men stood without speaking for a long moment. Then Clane said: "Let's see what we find below. Everything may be different than it seems to be."

He changed the subject. "How do you think we should approach them?"

They decided to go in force into several villages. There *had* been several but now the largest was composed of twenty-eight houses, with a scattering of others in the vicinity. It was agreed that individual spies could not possibly infiltrate into such small groups. The individual spy was fine for cities like Linn, where foreigners arrived daily from all parts of the solar system. Here, any new man would be regarded as a stranger. There would very likely be language difficulties so serious as to prevent immediate communication.

Only a force large enough to handle opposition or hostility would be in a position to obtain important information.

The decision made, Clane commanded, "Six patrol vessels will leave immediately. Three Europan, three Linnan." He added, "Good luck."

Groups of men had been training for such expeditions for many months.

As Clane watched them prepare to depart, he said: "I would suggest that we all come back here in four hours. At that time we may have a report."

❖❖❖

Clane was back in the view room a few minutes before the time set. He arrived in a room that buzzed with excitement, and it took several minutes to realize what had happened. All except one of the patrol commanders had reported back, and something was wrong.

Quickly, he brought order out of chaos. "One by one," he said sharply, "make your reports." He turned to Czinczar, "One of your men first." The barbarian nodded to one of his patrol leaders.

The officer began unhappily, "We found everything as might be expected in a small rural community. They were human beings, all right, and they seemed simple enough, very like our own people. As Lord Clane instructed, we took no hostile action, simply came down and looked around. Everybody was friendly. There were no language problems at all, although we did most of the talking at first. As soon as they realized what we wanted, a man and a woman showed us around. The houses were of simple construction, a little better furnished than we might have expected, but no machinery that we could see.

"Here's what we learned. This planet is called Outland, and its companion Inland. One of the women said she had a sister living on Inland, and she admitted that she visited there occasionally, but I couldn't find out where the spaceships took off. The twin planets are very similar, and life is exclusively farm or village. The name Earth, or Linn, or solar system seemed to be completely unfamiliar to them.

"Naturally, we were beginning to relax a bit. You know what our men are like, high-spirited, and with an eye for a good-looking woman."

The man paused; and Clane glanced quickly at Czinczar to see how the leader would respond to that. The ability of the barbarian leader to control his men had always fascinated Clane. Now, as he watched, Czinczar, slowly and deliberately, winked. It was a startling acceptance of a coarse innuendo by a man who was normally without crudeness. But the result was immediately evident. The officer brightened. Enthusiasm came into his voice.

"Roodge," he said, "is quite a man in his own way. He picked up one of the younger women and carried her off into the bushes. She giggled, and didn't make any fuss, so I decided not to interfere."

"What happened then?"

"I watched the reaction of the other people. They were quite unconcerned. Mind you, I should have known that something was wrong when Roodge came back in less than a minute with a funny look on his face. I figured the girl had got away from him, but I said nothing because I didn't want the men laughing at him. And the silly fool didn't help matters any by keeping his mouth shut."

Czinczar was patient. "Go on."

❖ ❖ ❖

The reporting officer continued in a doleful tone. "We asked more questions. I wondered if they knew about the aliens. When I described them, one of the men said, 'Oh, you mean the Riss.' Just like that. He went on to say that they occasionally traded with the Riss."

Clane broke in. "They trade with them?" he said sharply.

The officer turned to him, glanced back at Czinczar who nodded as much as to say it was all right for him to answer the question, and then faced Clane again. "That's what he said, your excellency. And I'm sure they recognized the description."

Clane was astounded. For a moment, he abandoned his questioning, and paced up and down before the officer. He stopped finally, and gazed at the group as a whole.

"But that would mean," he said in a puzzled voice, "that they've found some method of neutralizing these Riss. Why would the Riss let them alone and yet come to the solar system and refuse even to communicate with human beings there?" He shook his head. "I refuse to believe that they have really solved the problem of Riss aggression. That problem will never be solved by the human beings of one planet alone."

No one said anything. And presently Clane once again faced the patrol commander. "Continue," he said curtly.

"I knew you'd want to question these people personally," said the officer, "so I suggested that a woman and a man come along and have a look at the ship. I figured it'd be better to take them by persuasion than by force, though naturally if the first didn't work, then it'd have to be the other."

"Naturally."

"Well, our guides agreed to come, made no objection, and in fact seemed kind of interested in a childlike way—the way our own people might have been."

"Go on, go on."

"We started up. On the way, Roodge edged over to the woman and before I realized what was up made a pass at her. At least, that's the way I heard it. I didn't see the incident. I heard the uproar. When I looked around, the man and woman were gone."

Clane looked at him blankly for a moment; and then, "How high up were you?" he asked.

"About two miles."

"Did you look down over the edge? Of the patrol boat, I mean?"

"Within a few seconds. I thought they might have—jumped."

"Or been pushed?" Czinczar added.

The officer nodded. "Knowing the quick impulses of our simple people, yes, I thought of that."

It seemed to Clane that the remark was well phrased. The "quick" impulses of the simple folk in Czinczar's part of the ship had resulted during the voyage in the murder of twelve hundred and ninety men and three hundred and seventy-two women. In each case Czinczar's judges had sentenced the killer to a hundred lashes to be given at the rate of ten every day for ten days. In the beginning it had seemed to Clane that a few hangings would act as deterrent, but statistics had proved that only three men so whipped had become second offenders. The lashes apparently penetrated deep, but only into the hides of those who received them.

The officer was finishing his account. "Well, that's about all, sir. Except that Roodge admitted to me that his first girl had vanished just like the second."

Each of the other four patrol leaders reported experiences that were similar in substance, varying only in details. All had tried to bring back guests. In two cases the invitations had been rejected, and they had attempted to imprison a man and a woman. One couple had gone up about a mile and then apparently tired of the "game" and vanished. The third officer described how a Roodge-type man of his troop had offended the woman he'd tried to bring. The fourth commander had actually succeeded in getting his "prisoners" aboard. He sounded aggrieved.

"I thought they got themselves lost in the crowd, and my men are still looking for them. But I guess they took one look at the swarm of people in the corridors, and went home."

His words completed the accounts. With only one patrol still to report, the picture seemed fairly complete.

❖❖❖

Clane was frowning over the unexplained details when there was a commotion at the door. The sixth patrol commander burst into the room. Even at a distance, he looked pale and agitated.

"Out of the way," he cried to the officers around the door. "Quick, I have important news."

A path was made for him, and he raced along it, and paused in front of Clane. "Excellency," he gasped, "I was questioning the villagers I was assigned to when one of them mentioned that there was a Riss ship like ours—he definitely said like ours—just outside the atmosphere of the other planet. Inland, he called it."

Clane nodded casually. At such moments as this he felt at his best. He walked over to Czinczar, and said: "I think we should disembark all aboard except our fighting crews, landings to be made on the night side in widely separated uninhabited areas. After a year in confined quarters, everybody needs a chance to get down to a planet again."

"What about the Riss ship?" Czinczar asked.

"Nothing. We remain alert, but avoid battle." His eyes flashed with abrupt excitement. He said tensely: "Czinczar, there's something here for us. I foresee difficulties. We've got to make the most sustained and concentrated effort of our existence. I'm going to make a personal investigation of the village life below."

Czinczar was frowning, but he nodded presently. "In connection with being alert," he said, "how about some of my officers staying on duty up here along with your own? There would be a certain rivalry which would make for wakefulness."

The high excitement in Clane died. He studied the barbarian leader thoughtfully. Finally, he nodded. "With certain precautions to prevent any attempt to take over the ship," he said, "that sounds reasonable."

They smiled at each other humorlessly, two men who understood each other.

14

The landing was without incident. Clane stepped down to the grass, and paused to take a deep breath of air. It had an ever so slight acrid odor, and he guessed the presence of minute quantities of chlorine. This was unusual, considering that gas's natural proclivity for combining other substances.

It suggested the presence of a natural chlorine-producing chemical process.

What interested him was that the chlorine content might explain the faint over-all mistiness of the air. It even looked a little green, it seemed to him suddenly.

He laughed, and put it out of his mind.

The first house of the village stood about a hundred yards away. It was a single-story structure, rather sprawling, and made of wood.

His whole being quivered with eagerness. But he held himself calm. He spent the day on a folding chair near the boat. He paid no direct attention to the Outlanders. Whenever he noticed an individual or a group doing anything, he made a note of it in his journal. He established a north-south-east-west orientation for the village, and recorded the comings and going of the villagers.

The air grew cooler as night drew near, but he merely slipped on a coat and maintained his watch. Lights came on in the houses. They were too bright to be candles or oil lamps, but he couldn't decide from his distance exactly what they were.

Starting about two hours after dark, the lights winked out one by one. Soon, the village was in total darkness. Clane wrote down, "They seem to be unafraid. There's not even a watchman posted."

He tested that. Accompanied by two husky barbarians, he spent two hours wandering among the buildings. The blackness was complete. There was no sound except the pad of their own feet, and the occasional grunt of one of the soldiers. The movements and the sounds didn't seem to disturb the villagers. No one came out to investigate.

Clane retreated at last to the boat, and entered his closed cabin. In bed he read his day's journal, and heard the vague noises of the soldiers bedding down outside in their sleeping bags. And then, as the silence lengthened, he clicked off the boat's electric lights.

He slept uneasily, tensely aware of his purpose and his need, desperate to take action. He awakened at dawn, ate a hearty breakfast, and then once more settled down to observe the passing show. A woman walked by. She gazed stolidly at the men around the boat, giggled as one of the soldiers whistled at her, and then was lost to sight among the trees.

Some men, laughing and talking, went off to the orchard to the north, and picked fruit. Clane could see them on their ladders filling small pails. About noon, struck by a discrepancy in their actions, he left the vicinity of the boat, and moved nearer to them.

His arrival was unfortunately timed. As he came up, the men as of one accord put down their pails, and headed toward the village.

To his question, one of them replied, "Lunch!"

They all nodded in a friendly fashion, and walked off, leaving Clane alone in the orchard. He strode to the nearest pail, and as he half expected, it was empty.

All the pails were empty.

❖❖❖

The great blue sun was directly overhead. The air was warm and pleasant, but not hot. A mild breeze was blowing, and there was the feel of timeless summer in the quiet peacefulness around him.

But the pails were empty.

Clane spent some forty minutes exploring the orchard. And there was no bin anywhere, no place where the fruit could have been carried. Baffled, he climbed one of the ladders, and carefully filled a pail.

He was wary, though he didn't know what he expected would happen. Nothing happened. The pail held twenty-one of the golden fruits. And that was the trouble. It held them. Clane took the fruit and the container back to the liftboat, set it down on the ground, and began a systematic investigation.

He found nothing unusual. No gadgets, no buttons, no levers, no attachments of any kind. The pail seemed to be an ordinary metal container, and at the moment it contained substantial, non-disappearing fruit. He took up one of the yellow things, and bit into it. It tasted deliciously sweet and juicy, but the flavor was unfamiliar.

He was eating it thoughtfully, when one of the men came for the pail.

"You want the fruit?" the villager asked. He was obviously prepared to have him keep it.

Clane began slowly to take out the fruit, one at a time. As he did so, he studied the other. The fellow was dressed in rough slacks and an open-necked shirt. He was clean-shaven, and he looked washed. He seemed about thirty-five.

Clane paused in his manipulations. "What's your name?" he asked.

The man grinned. "Marden."

"Good name," said Clane.

Marden looked pleased. Then he grew serious. "But I must have the pail," he said. "More picking to do."

Clane took another fruit from the container, then asked deliberately: "Why do you pick fruit?"

Marden shrugged. "Everybody has to do his share."

"Why?"

Marden frowned at Clane. He looked for a moment as if he

wasn't sure that he had heard correctly. "That isn't a very smart question," he said at last.

❖❖❖

Clane assumed ruefully that the story would now spread that a stupid man from the ship was asking silly questions. It couldn't be helped. "Why," he persisted, "do you feel that you have to work? Why not let others work, and you just lie around."

"And not do my share?" The shock in Marden's tone was unmistakable. His outer defenses were penetrated. "But then I wouldn't have a right to the food."

"Would anyone stop you from eating?"

"N-no"

"Would anyone punish you?"

"Punish?" Marden looked puzzled. His face cleared. "You mean, would anyone be angry with me?"

Clane let that go. He had his man on the run. He was getting a basic philosophy of life here, one so ingrained that the people involved were not even aware that there could be any other attitude.

"Look at me," he said. He pointed up at the ship which was a blur in the sky. "I own part of that."

"You live there?" said Marden.

Clane ignored the misunderstanding. "And look at me down here," he said. "I sit all day in this chair, and do nothing."

"You work with that thing." The villager pointed at Clane's journal lying on the ground.

"That's not work. I do that for my own amusement." Clane was feeling just a little baffled himself. He said hastily, "When I'm hungry, do I do anything myself? No. I have these men bring me something to eat. Isn't that much better than having to do it yourself?"

Marden said: "You went out into the garden, and picked your own fruit."

"I picked *your* fruit," said Clane.

"But you picked it with your own hands," said the man triumphantly.

Clane bit his lip. "I didn't have to do that," he explained patiently. "I was curious about what you did with the fruit you picked."

He kept his voice deliberately casual, as he asked the next question. "What do you do with it?" he said.

Marden seemed puzzled for a moment, and then he nodded his understanding. "You mean the fruit we picked. We sent that to Inland this time." He pointed at the massive planet just coming up over the eastern horizon. "They've had a poor crop in—" He named a locality the name for which Clane didn't catch. Then he nodded with an air of "Is-that-all-you-wanted-to-know?" and picked up the pail.

"Want the rest of this fruit?" he asked.

Clane shook his head.

Marden smiled cheerfully and, pail in hand, walked off briskly. "Got to get to work," he called over his shoulder.

Clane let him go about twenty feet; and then called after him, "Wait a minute!"

He climbed hastily to his feet, and as the wondering Marden turned, he walked over to him. There was something about the way the man was swinging the pail that—

As he came up, he saw that he had not been mistaken. There had been about eight of the fruit in the bottom of the pail. They were gone.

Without another word, Clane returned to his chair.

❖ ❖ ❖

The afternoon dragged. Clane looked up along the rolling hills to the west with their bright green garments and their endless pink flowers. The scene was idyllic, but he had no patience. He was a man with a purpose; and he was beginning to realize his problem.

There was a solution here; and yet already he had the conviction that the human beings of Outland and Inland were obstacles as great or greater than he had found in Linn.

Unhappily, he bent down and picked a pink flower, one of the scores that grew all around him. Without looking at it, he broke it into little pieces, which he dropped absently to the ground.

A faint odor of chlorine irritated his nostrils. Clane glanced down at the broken pieces of flower, and then sniffed his fingers where the juice had squeezed from the flower's stem.

The chlorine was unmistakably present.

He made a note of it in his journal, stimulated. The potentialities were dazzling, and yet—he shook his head. It was not the answer.

Night came. As soon as the lights were on in all the houses, he ate his own evening meal. And then, accompanied by two of the barbarians, he started his rounds. The first window that he peered in showed nine people sitting around on couches and chairs talking to each other with considerable animation.

It seemed an unusual number of occupants for that house. Clane thought: "Visitors from Inland?" It was not, he realized seriously, impossible.

From where he stood, he was unable to see the source of the room's light. He moved around to the window on the far side. Just for a moment, then, he thought of the light as something that hung down from the ceiling.

His eyes adjusted swiftly to the fantastic reality. There was no cord and no transparent container. This light had no resemblance to the ones aboard the Riss ship.

It hung in midair, and it glowed with a fiery brilliance.

He tried to think of it as an atomic light. But the atomic lights that he had worked with needed containers.

There was nothing like that here. The light hung near the ceiling, a tiny globe of brightness. He guessed its diameter at three inches.

He moved from house to house. In one place a man was reading with the light shining over his shoulder. In another it hovered over a woman who was washing. As he watched, she took the clothes out of the tub, shook the tub as if she was rinsing it, and then a moment later put the clothes back into steaming water.

Clane couldn't be sure, but he suspected that she had emptied the dirty water from the tub, refilled it with scalding water—possibly from a hot spring somewhere—and all in the space of a minute resumed her task.

He couldn't help wondering what she did with the clothing when she finished. Did she step "through" to where the sun was shining, hang up her clothes, and have them beautifully sun-dried when she woke up in the morning?

He was prepared to believe that that was exactly what would happen.

She seemed in no hurry, so he moved on. He came presently to the home of Marden. He walked to the door slowly, thinking: "These people are friendly, and without guile. They have no government. There's no intrigue. Here, if anywhere, an honest approach will win us what we want."

Oddly, even as he knocked on the door, it seemed to him there was a flaw in his reasoning.

It made him abruptly tense again.

15

Marden opened the door. He looked relaxed and easygoing, and there was no doubt about his good nature, for he did not hesitate. He smiled and said in a friendly, half humorous tone:

"Ah, the man who does not work. Come in."

There was a suggestion of tolerant superiority in the comment, but Clane was not offended. He paused in the center of the room, and glanced around expectantly. When he had looked through the window, a woman had been present. Now, there was no sign of her.

From behind him, Marden said: "When my wife heard your knock, she went visiting."

Clane turned. "She knew it was me?" he asked.

Marden nodded, and said: "Naturally." He added, "And, of course, she saw you at the window."

The words were simply spoken, but their frankness was disarmingly devastating. Clane had a momentary picture of himself as these villagers must see him. A slim, priestly peeping Tom who prowled around their homes in the dead of night and who asked stupid questions.

It was not a pleasant picture, and it seemed to him that his best reply was to be equally frank. He said: "Marden, we're puzzled by you people. May I sit down and talk to you?"

Marden silently indicated a chair. Clane sank into it and sat frowning for a moment, organizing his thoughts. He looked up finally.

"We're from Earth," he said. "We're from the planet where all human beings originally came from, including your people."

Marden looked at him. His gaze was polite. He seemed to be say-ing, "If you say so, that's the way it must have been. I don't have to believe you, of course."

Clane said quietly: "Do you believe that?"

Marden smiled. "Nobody here remembers such a connection; but it may be as you say."

"Do you have a written history?"

The villager hesitated. "It begins about three hundred years ago. Before that is blankness."

Clane said: "We're both human beings. We speak the same lan-guage. It seems logical, doesn't it?"

Marden said: "Oh, language." He laughed.

Clane studied him, puzzled. He recognized that the villager could not accept an abstract idea which did not fit in with his previous con-cepts.

Clane said: "This method you have of moving yourself and your goods from Outland to Inland, and anywhere else on either planet— have you always been able to do that?"

"Why, of course. It's the best way."

"How do you do it?"

"Why, we just—" Marden stopped, and a curious blankness came over his face; he finished weakly—"do it."

That was what Clane had thought. Aloud, he said: "Marden, I can't do it, and I'd like to be able to. Can you explain it to me sim-ply?"

The man shook his head. "It's not something you explain. You just do it."

"But when did you learn? How old were you the first time you did it?"

"About nine."

"Why couldn't you do it before then?"

"I was too young. I hadn't had time to learn it."

"Who taught you?"

"Oh, my parents."

"How did they teach you?"

"It wasn't exactly teaching." Marden looked unhappy. "I just did what they did. It's really very simple."

Clane had no doubt of it, since they could all do it, apparently without even thinking about it. He eyed the other anxiously, and realized that he was pressing the man harder than appeared on the surface. Marden had never had thoughts like this before, and he didn't like them.

Hastily, Clane changed the subject. There was a far more vital question to be asked, a question that struck to the very root of all this.

❖❖❖

He asked it. "Marden," he said, "why don't the Riss take over the planets Outland and Inland?"

He explained about the attack on Earth, the use of atomic bombs, the refusal to communicate, and the possibility of future danger. As he described what had happened, he watched the villager for reactions. And saw with disappointment that the man was not capable of grasping the picture as a whole.

He had a mental picture then that shook him. Suppose these people had the answer to the Riss menace. Suppose that here on this quiet planet was all that men of Earth would need to win their deadly war.

And couldn't get it because—

Marden said: "The Riss don't bother us. Why should they?"

"There must be a reason for that," said Clane. He continued urgently, "Marden, we've got to find out what that reason is. Even for you, that's important. Something is holding them back. Until you know what it is, you can never really feel secure."

Marden shrugged. He had the bored look of a man who had jumped to a surface conclusion about something that did not fit into his own ideas. He said tolerantly: "You Earth people are not very smart, asking all these silly questions."

And that was actually the end of the interview. Clane remained many minutes longer, but Marden no longer took him seriously. His answers were polite and meaningless.

Yes, they traded with the Riss. It was the natural thing to do. The twin planets gave them their food surplus, and in return they took what they wanted of the articles aboard the Riss ship. The Riss didn't really have very much that the Outlanders and Inlanders wanted. But there was always something. Little things—like this.

He got up, and brought Clane a machine-made plastic ornament, the figure of an animal. It was cheaply made, worth a few sesterces at most. Clane examined it, nonplussed. He was trying to imagine two planets giving their food surplus to nonhumans in return for useless trinkets. It didn't explain why the Riss hadn't taken over the system, but for the first time he could understand the contempt which the aliens must feel for human beings.

He took his leave, finally, conscious that he had ruined himself with Marden, and that his next move must be through someone else.

❖❖❖

He radioed Czinczar, requesting him to come down. In spite of his sense of urgency, he cautiously suggested that the barbarian wait until twilight of the following evening. Clane slept somewhat easier that night, but he was awake at dawn. He spent the day in the folding chair, analyzing the possibilities of the situation. It was one of the longest days of his life.

Czinczar came down shortly before dusk. He brought two of his secretaries, and he listened to Clane's account in silence. The mutation was intent, and it was several minutes before he noticed the barbarian leader's satirical expression. Czinczar said:

"Your excellency, are you suggesting that we trick this Outlander?"

Clane was still concentrated on his own purposes. He began, "It's a matter of taking into account certain things that have already happened, and the simple character of Mard—"

He stopped. He heard Czinczar say, "Exactly. I approve of your analysis. I think the idea is excellent." Ever so slightly, Clane shook his head, rejecting the cynical overtones of the other's praise. But he was startled, too.

For nearly twenty-four hours he had planned the pattern of this night's interview. And not once had it struck him that he was playing his old, astute role. There was cunning in what he had in mind, based on a sharp understanding of the difficulty of communicating with these Outlanders. Based, also, on his conviction that there was no time to waste.

"Shall we proceed?" asked Czinczar.

Silently, Clane led the way. He decided not to be ashamed of his failure to live up to the ideals which he considered vital to final success. After all, he was operating in a new environment.

But it mustn't happen again.

Marden received them graciously. His eyes widened a little as he heard Czinczar's wonderful golden voice, and thereafter he listened with a profound respect whenever the barbarian leader spoke. The reaction was in line with Clane's thinking. One of his personal problems on Earth had been that he was of slight build, that because of certain mutational differences in his physical structure, he wore the drab concealing clothing of a priest of the atom gods. What strength he showed was intellectual, and that did not impress other people until they realized its implications. Which always took time.

Not once during the entire evening did Marden intimate even indirectly that his interrogator was asking silly questions.

Czinczar began by praising the two planets and their peoples. He called Outland and Inland two examples of Paradise. He eulogized the economic system. The people were wonderful, the most highly civilized he had ever run into. Here things were done as they should be done. Here life was lived as people dreamed of living it. Here was intelligence carried to the uttermost pinnacle of wisdom.

Clane listened gloomily. He had to admit it was well done. Czinczar was talking to the villager as if he was a primitive savage. There appeared to be no doubt of it. The villager was taking in every word of praise with evident delight.

Czinczar said: "We are like children at your feet, Marden, eager to learn, respectful, anxious to begin the long climb to the heights where you and the people of the twin planets live in a glorious harmony. We realize that the goal is possibly unattainable in our own lifetime. But we hope that our children may share the perfection with your children.

"Perhaps you will give us a little of your time this evening, and tell us at your own discretion a little of what you believe in, of the thoughts that go through your mind, the hopes you have. Tell me, do you have a national symbol, a flag, a plant of some kind, a coat of arms?"

He paused, and abruptly sat down on the floor, motioning the two secretaries and Clane to do the same. It was an unrehearsed action, but Clane obliged promptly. Czinczar went on:

"While you relax in that chair, Marden, we sit at your feet and listen respectfully."

❖ ❖ ❖

Marden walked over, and sat down. He shifted uneasily and then, as if he had suddenly come to a decision, leaned back against the cushions. He was obviously embarrassed by the godlike role that had been thrust upon him, but it was apparent that he could see reasons for accepting it.

"I had not thought of this before," he said, "but it is true; I can see that now."

He added, "I do not quite know what you mean by 'flag' or a plant as a national symbol. I can sense part of the idea but—" He hesitated.

Czinczar said: "Do you have seasons?"

"Yes."

"There are times when the trees and plants bloom, and times when the leaves fall off?"

"That happens to some of them."

"Do you have a rainy season?"

"Yes."

"What do you call it?"

"Winter."

"Do you celebrate the coming of the rain?"

Marden's face lighted with understanding. "Oh, no. The ending of it, not the beginning. The appearance of the first chlorodel anywhere on the planets. We have dancing then, and feasting."

Czinczar nodded casually. "Is that an old custom, or a new one?" He added, "All this may seem unimportant to you, but we are so anxious to catch the spirit of your idyllic existence."

"It's a very old custom," said Marden.

He shrugged regretfully. "But we have nothing such as you mentioned. No national symbols."

As the evening progressed, the villager seemed equally unaware that he was actually answering questions. He took the customs for granted. They were not symbols to him. That was the way things *were*.

It was all so natural and so universally practiced. The possibility that other peoples might have other customs simply did not penetrate.

And so, it was established beyond reasonable doubt that the Outlander and Inlander symbol of life was the pink chlorine flower, chlorodel. That each year people visited the underground caverns. That they put a little square box on the table when they ate, and tapped on it when they didn't care to eat much. That they had always given their spare food to the Riss.

One point that came out was especially interesting. There were old, buried cities, Marden admitted. Or rather, ruins of cities. It was years since anything of importance had been found in any of them.

Czinczar talked around that cautiously for a few moments, and then looked at Clane questioningly. That too, was part of their previous arrangement. Clane nodded.

❖ ❖ ❖

The barbarian leader climbed to his feet. He bowed to the villager. "Oh, noble man of Outland, we have a great favor to ask of you. Would you transport us by your wonderful method to such a city on a hemisphere of this planet where the sun is shining?"

"Now?" said Marden. His voice was casual. He didn't sound opposed to the idea.

"We need not stay long. We just wish to look."

Marden stood up. He was frowning thoughtfully. "Let me see— which city? Oh, I know—where the ship is."

Clane had been tensing himself against he knew not what. He was annoyed to realize that he was just a little anxious. And then—

Afterwards, he tried to analyze what happened. There was a flash, a roundness of light. It was gone so swiftly that he couldn't be sure of just what he had seen. And then, all around was the brightness of day. Almost directly overhead hung the blue sun of the twin planets.

They were standing in the middle of a wilderness of broken stones and twisted metal. As far as the eye could see was a growth of shrubbery and trees. As Clane watched—that was his role; to pretend to be a subordinate—Czinczar walked over to a section of concrete piling and kicked at a thick piece of wood that lay on the ground.

The hard boot made a hollow sound in that silence. But the wood did not budge. It was firmly embedded in the soil.

Czinczar came back to Marden. "Has any digging been done in this or other cities recently?"

Marden looked surprised. "Who would want to dig in such stuff as this?"

"Of course," said Czinczar quickly. He hesitated. He seemed about to say something else, and then in a curious fashion, he stiffened. His head tilted sharply. Clane followed his gaze, and was surprised to see the *Solar Star* overhead.

That is, for a split instant, he thought it was their own ship.

He realized the truth. He said, "The Riss!"

From nearby, Marden said mildly: "Oh, yes, I thought you might be interested in seeing it, which is why I brought you to this city. The Riss were very interested when we told them you were here in a ship like theirs. They decided to come to Outland to have a look. From something I sensed in your attitude—it seemed to me you might like to see their ship first."

There was a moment, then, when even Clane was disconcerted. Czinczar spoke first. He turned calmly to the Outlander. "We accept your judgment about the uselessness of looking further at these ruins. Let's go back to your house."

Clane caught a final glimpse of the Riss battleship. It was disappearing into the mists above the eastern horizon.

He presumed that it was heading unerringly toward the *Solar Star*.

16

As he had done for the journey from Marden's house to the ruins of the ancient Outland city, Clane unconsciously tensed himself for the return trip. Once more, there was the flashing ball of light. This time it seemed even briefer than before.

Then he was in Marden's living room. At the door Clane, who was the last to leave the house, paused. He asked: "Marden, I'm curious. Why did you tell the Riss that we were here?"

Marden looked surprised, and then the look came into his face.

Another foolish question, his expression intimated. He said: "Sooner or later, they ask us if anything is happening. Naturally, we tell them."

Clane said: "Do they speak your language, or do you speak theirs?"

The Outlander laughed. "You keep talking about language," he said. He shrugged. "We and the Riss understand each other, that's all."

The others were moving off into the darkness. Czinczar had paused, and was looking back. Clane stayed where he was. "Do you go aboard the Riss ship, or do they come to the ground?" he asked.

He waited stiffly. There was a purpose in his mind that vibrated with cunning. But he was too angry to be ashamed. The Outlanders' action in telling the Riss of the presence of the *Solar Star* had shocked him. It set the pattern now for his deadly plan.

Marden said: "We go aboard. They have some kind of a round thing which they point at us, and then it's safe."

Clane said deliberately: "How many of your people have had this thing pointed at them?"

"Oh, a few hundred." He started to close the door. "Bedtime," he said.

Clane was beginning to cool off. It struck him that the whole problem needed thinking out. Perhaps he was being hasty in judging these people.

It would serve no useful purpose to risk attacking the enemy ship.

He accepted Marden's dismissal. A few minutes later, he was in a liftboat heading back to his own section of the *Solar Star*. Presently, the ship was moving at a sharp slant up the umbral cone of the night-side of Outland.

❖❖❖

A messenger arrived from Czinczar's headquarters. "Great Czinczar requests an interview."

Clane said slowly: "Tell his excellency that I should like him to prepare a written interpretation of what we found out from Marden."

He was getting ready for bed some time later when a second messenger arrived with a written request.

Dear Lord Clane:
 It is time to discuss our next move.
                            Czinczar.

The trouble, Clane thought grimly, was that he had no plans. There was a great secret here; but it was not to be had by any method he could think of. The human beings of the twin planets could possible save the race. And yet he was already convinced they wouldn't.

They refused to recognize that there was a problem. Pressed too hard, they got angry, the neurotic anger of someone whose basic attitudes are being attacked. Nor was there such a thing as forcing them. Their method of transportation nullified all the old techniques of persuasion by threat and violence. That left cunning.

Which brought him back to his first thought: He had no real plans. He wrote:

Your excellency:
 I should like to sleep over this matter.
                            Clane.

He sealed it, dismissed the messenger, and went to bed. At first he couldn't sleep. He kept tossing and turning, and once in a long while he dozed, only to jerk awake with a start. His conscience burdened him. Unless he could think of something, the trip was a failure. He was up against the stone wall of one fact. Neither Marden nor his compatriots could even begin to understand what was wanted. That was especially baffling because, from all indications, they could read minds.

He slept finally. In the morning, he dictated a note to Czinczar:

Your excellency:
 My idea is that we should exchange views and information before we meet to discuss future plans.
                            Clane.

The answer to that was:

Dear Lord Clane:

I have the feeling that you are evading this discussion because you have no plans. However, since the long journey has now been made, let us by all means consider the possibilities. Will you please name for me the actual information which you think we have obtained?

Czinczar.

Dear Czinczar:

The chlorodel is the "national" flower, because it gives off a gas which makes the air unbreathable to the Riss.

The reference to knocking on a little box in the center of the table when they were not hungry probably dates back to the radioactivity period after the great war. The little box was a detector, and many a time they must have gone hungry because the instrument indicated the food was radioactive.

The annual visit to the caverns derives from the same period.

They give the Riss their surplus food without remembering that that must have started as a form of tribute to a conqueror. In this connection, I would say that only certain foods would be usable by the Riss because of their somewhat different chemical make-up.

Clane.

Your excellency:

Do you seriously claim that the chlorodel can create an unbreathable atmosphere for the Riss? Then we have our answer. We need look no further. Let us hurry back to the solar system, and plant this flower until its perfume is diluted in every molecule of the air of every habitable planet or moon.

Czinczar.

Clane sighed when he read that. The problem of the barbarian leader, pragmatist extraordinary, remained as difficult of solution as all the other riddles.

He ate breakfast while he considered his reply. He took the ship down near the atmosphere of the planet, and spent nearly an hour looking for the Riss battleship, without success. By the time he was satisfied that it was not in the vicinity of Marden's village, another note had arrived from Czinczar.

❖❖❖

Dear Lord Clane:

Your failure to reply to my last letter indicates that you do not accept the implications of your discovery about the chlorodel. Let us meet at once and discuss this entire problem.

Czinczar.

❖❖❖

Clane wrote:

❖❖❖

Dear Czinczar:

I am sorry to see you jumping at a solution which can have no meaning in the larger sense. The Riss-human struggle will not be resolved by the use of a defensive gas. If the Riss ever believed that a campaign was under way to poison the atmospheres of planets against them, they would take counter-measures. They could use radioactive poisons on a planetary scale, or some other gas development as inimical to man as the chlorodel seems to be to the Riss.

The fact that long ago the Outland-Inland Twins defended themselves in that way is not conclusive. The Riss could accept isolated activity. This would be especially true during the confusion that existed toward the end of the Riss-human war. By the time they discovered what the people of the Twins had done, the limited character of the action would be evident. The Riss would accordingly be in an exploratory frame of mind. Even as it was, they must have made threats so terrible that a tribute agreement was made.

I repeat, this is not a final answer. Far from it. In my earnest opinion, it would be the signal for an attempt to destroy the solar system.

Clane.

❖❖❖

Dear Lord Clane:

I am astounded by your purely intellectual approach to these matters. We defend our planets by any and every means at our disposal. Let us meet immediately to discuss the only course now open to us: to return to Earth with a shipload of chlorodel plants for replanting.

Czinczar.

❖❖❖

Dear Lord Clane:

I have received no answer to my communication delivered three hours ago. Please let me hear from you.

Czinczar.

❖❖❖

Dear Lord Clane:

I am amazed that you have failed to reply to my last two notes. I realize of course that you have no answer, because what can our next move possibly be except return to Earth? The alternative would be to continue our blind search through space for another planet inhabited by human beings. Am I right in believing that the star map which brought us to Outland does not show any other stars as having habitable planets?

Czinczar.

❖❖❖

Dear Lord Clane:

This situation is now becoming ridiculous. Your failure to reply to my notes is a reflection on our relationship. If you do not answer this letter, I shall refuse to have any further communication with you.

Czinczar.

❖❖❖

Lord Clane did not see that note or the previous ones until some time later. He was paying another visit to Marden.

❖❖❖

The interview began unsatisfactorily. The place was bad. Marden was busy picking fruit when Clane stopped under the tree where he was working. He looked down, and he was visibly impatient with the "fool" who had been bothering him for so long now.

He said: "The Riss ship waited for about an hour. Then it moved on. I see this pleases you."

It did indeed. Clane said steadily: "After our trouble with the Riss, we have no desire to meet them. In our opinion they would attack us on sight."

Marden kept on picking fruit. "We have had no trouble with the Riss, ever."

Clane said: "Why should you? You give them everything you own."

Marden had evidently been doing some thinking about the previous conversation on that. He said coldly: "We do not keep from
others what we do not need ourselves." He spoke tartly.

Clane said serenely: "So long as you keep down your population,
learn nothing of science, and pay tribute, you will be left alone. All
this, provided the chlorodel does not wither away. At that point, the
Riss would land, and you would learn what their friendship was
worth."

It was a dangerous comment. He made it because it was time
such thoughts were circulated among these people. Nevertheless,
Clane quickly changed the subject.

"Why didn't you tell us you could read minds?" he asked.

"You didn't ask," said Marden. "Besides—"

"Besides what?"

"It doesn't work well with you. You people don't think clearly."

"You mean, we think differently?"

Marden dismissed that. "There's only one way to think," he said
impatiently. "I find that it's easier to use spoken language with you,
and search your minds for the right word when I might otherwise be
at a loss. All those who have dealt with you feel the same way." He
seemed to think that settled the matter.

Clane said: "You don't really speak our language? You learn it by
getting some of our thoughts as we speak?"

"Yes."

Clane nodded. Many things were becoming much clearer. Here
was a human colony that had carried on to new heights of scientific
development long after the connection between Earth and Outland
was broken. The reasons for their subsequent decadence were probably intricate: Disruption of commerce with other man-inhabited
planets. Destruction of tens of thousands of their own factories.
Irreplaceable gaps in the ranks of their technicians. The deadly pressure of Riss threats. Inexorably, that combination had added up to
the present static state.

Clane said: "Does the reading of minds have any relation to your
method of transportation?"

Marden sounded surprised. "Why, of course. You learn them at
the same time, though it takes longer."

He climbed down from the tree, carrying his pail. "All this time while you've been talking, there's been a question in the back of your mind. It's your main reason for this visit. I can't quite make it out, but if you will ask it, I'll answer as best I can, and then I can go to lunch."

Clane took out his star map. "Have you ever seen one of these?"

Marden smiled. "At night, I look up into the sky, and there it is."

"Apart from that?"

"I have seen occasional thoughts about such maps in the minds of the Riss."

Clane held the map up for him. "Here is your sun," he said. He pointed. Then brought his finger down. "And here is ours. Can you use the knowledge in my mind about such things to orient yourself to this map, and point out to me which is the nearest Riss sun?"

There was a long silence. Marden studied the map. "It's hard," he sighed. "But I think it's this one."

Clane marked it with trembling fingers, then said huskily, "Marden, be as sure as you can. If you're wrong, and we go there, we will have wasted half a year or more. Millions of people may die."

"It's either this one or this one," said Marden. He pointed at a star about an inch from the other one.

Clane shook his head. "That one's a hundred light-years, and this one about twenty."

"Then it's the close one. I have no impression of the distance being very great."

"Thank you," said Clane. "I'm sorry to have been such a nuisance."

Marden shrugged.

"Good-by," said Clane.

He turned and headed back to the liftboat.

17

Back on the ship, he read Czinczar's letters with an unhappy sense of more trouble to come. He ate lunch, and then, bracing himself, invited the angry barbarian for a conference.

He included an apology in his letter. He explained where he had been, though not his purpose in visiting Marden.

That account he saved until Czinczar and he were alone together. When he had finished, the great man sat for a long time saying not a word. He seemed unutterably nonplussed. At last, he said in a mild tone: "You have no faith in the chlorodel plant?"

Clane said: "I see it as a weapon of last resort. We mustn't use it till we are sure we understand all the possible repercussions."

Czinczar sighed. "Your action in producing the chlorodel as a weapon had decided me that this journey was worthwhile after all. Now you yourself devaluate it, and suggest that we extend our trip to take in the planets of another star."

He brought up one hand, as if he would use it somehow to make his protest more effective. He seemed to realize the futility of that, for he spoke again.

"I confess it baffles me. What can you possibly hope to gain by going to a Riss planet?"

Clane said earnestly: "If Marden is right, it would take us three months. Actually, the Riss star is almost, though not quite, as near to Earth as this one." He paused. He was anxious to have moral support for the journey. He went on, "I honestly believe it is our duty to investigate the potentialities of taking counteraction against man's deadly enemy. This war will not be won on the defensive."

He saw that Czinczar was looking straight at him. The barbarian said: "If Marden is right—that's a damning phrase." He shook his head in visible despair. "I give up. Anybody who will order a ship as big and important as this one to make a trip on the strength of Marden's memory of what he saw in the mind of a Riss—"

He broke off. "Surely, there must be maps aboard the Solar Star."

Clane hesitated. This was a sore point with him. He said carefully: "We had an unfortunate accident at the time we took over the ship. Everyone was in an exploring frame of mind, and one of the men wandered into the map room. Can you guess the rest?"

"They'd set energy traps for interlopers."

"He was killed, of course," Clane nodded drably. "It was a lesson for us all. I discovered that all the main control and mechanical departments were similarly mined. We used condemned slaves to do

the dangerous work, promising them freedom if they were successful. Result: Only one other accident."

"What was that?" asked the ever-curious Czinczar.

"The interstellar television communicator," Clane replied. He
broke off. "I regret as much as you do that we have to make our next
move on the basis of Marden's memory."

He hesitated, then made his appeal. "Czinczar," he said slowly,
"although I have apparently ignored your opinions on this journey, I
do have a high respect for them. I sincerely believe you are being too
narrowly practical. You are too bound to the solar system. I don't
think you realize how much you think of it as a home that must be
defended to the death. But never mind that. What I have to say to
you is no longer based strictly on logic, or even on whether or not we
are in agreement.

"I ask for your support because, first, I am the commander of this
ship for better or worse; second, if we do come to a Riss planet I
intend us to take enormous risks—and that will require your fullest
cooperation; third, in spite of all your doubts, you yourself feel that
the discovery of the chlorodel plant partially justifies the journey so
far. I disagree with that, but at least it goes to show that there are
secrets to be discovered out here."

He finished quietly: "That's all I have to say. What's your
answer?"

Czinczar said: "In our correspondence, and in our present discussion, neither you nor I have referred to the Outlander method of
transportation. What is your reason for not mentioning it? Don't you
think it has any value?"

The very extent of the thoughts he had had on the subject held
Clane momentarily silent. He said finally, "It would be a terrific
advantage, but I can't see it as being decisive—as it now stands.
Besides, we can't get it."

He explained the efforts he had made, and the impossibility of
gaining the secret from the mercurial inhabitants. He finished:

"I do have a plan about it. My idea is that we leave behind young
couples to whom children were born during the trip. Their instructions will be to try to have their youngsters trained by the
Outlanders. That will take nine years."

"I see." Czinczar frowned at the floor, finally stood up. "If there's any fighting to do when we get to the Riss planet, call on me. Is that what you mean by support?"

Clane smiled wanly, and also stood up. "I suppose so," he said. "I suppose so."

Lord Clane Linn walked slowly to the weapon control room after separating from Czinczar. For a long time, he sat in one of the giant chairs, idly manipulating a viewing instrument. Finally, he shook his head. The unpleasant fact was that Czinczar's doubts about accepting Marden's directions had convinced him. Such a trip still had to be made, but not on such a flimsy basis.

Unfortunately, the only other idea he had was so wild—and dangerous—he still hadn't mentioned it to anyone. Even Czinczar had not suggested an attack on the other Riss battleship.

Six hours went by. And then a message arrived from the barbarian leader.

Dear Lord Clane:
The ship is not accelerating. What's the matter? If we are going on this journey, we should be on our way.
                    Czinczar.

Clane bit his lips over the letter. He did not answer it immediately, but its arrival stiffened him to the need for a decision. *At least,* he thought, *I could go down again, and see Marden.*

It was already dark when he landed in the village. Marden opened the door with the reluctance of a man who knew in advance who his visitor was, and was not interested.

"I thought you were leaving," he said.

"I have a favor to ask," said Clane.

Marden peered through the slit of the door, polite from habit.

"We have to try to come to an agreement with the Riss," said Clane. "Do you think one of your people—of those who are allowed aboard the Riss ship—would be willing to help my emissaries meet the Riss?"

Marden laughed, as at a private joke: "Oh, yes, Guylan would."

"Guylan?"

"When he learned of the enmity between you and the Riss, he thought something should be done to bring you together." Marden's tone suggested that Guylan was a little simple about such things. He finished, "I'll talk to him about this in the morning."

Clane urged, "Why not now?" He had to fight his impatience. "All this is very serious, Marden. If our two ships should meet, there might be a big battle. It's not too late in the evening yet. Could you possibly contact him for me immediately?"

He tried to hide his anxiety. There was just a chance that Marden would realize his real intentions. He was counting on their intricacy, and their mechanical aspects, to baffle the Outlander's suspicions. He saw that the man seemed doubtful.

"There's something about your purpose—" Marden began. He shook his head. "But then you people don't think straight, do you?" He seemed to be talking to himself. "This fear of yours," he said aloud thoughtfully. Once more he failed to finish a sentence. "Just a minute," he said.

He disappeared into the house. Not one, but several minutes went by. Then he came to the door with a tall, thin, mild-faced man.

"This is Guylan," he said. He added, "Good night." He closed the door.

❖ ❖ ❖

The battle began in the hours of darkness before the dawn. In the weapon control room, Clane sat in a chair at the back of the room. From that vantage point he could see all the viewing plates.

High on the "forward" screen, the Riss battleship was clearly visible. Like a monstrous torpedo, it was silhouetted against the dark sky of Outland.

All the plates were on infrared light control, and visibility was amazingly sharp.

A hand tugged at Clane's arm. It was Guylan. "Is it time?" the Outlander asked anxiously.

Clane hesitated, and glanced at the thirty volunteers waiting in the corridor outside. They had been training for hours, and there was such a thing as letting too much tension build up. They had their instructions. All he had to do was give the signal.

His hesitation ended. "All right, Guylan," he said.

He did not look to see what the reaction was, but touched a button that flicked on a light in front of the man controlling the molecular weapon. The officer paused to aim along a sighting device, and then released the firing pin.

He held the aiming device steady.

A line of fire crept along the length of the enemy battleship. The effect was beyond Clane's anticipation. The flame licked high and bright. The night came alive with the coruscating fury of that immense fire. The dark land below sparkled with reflected glare.

And still there was no answering fire. Clane stole a glance at the corridor, where the volunteers had waited. It was empty.

A shout brought his gaze back to the Riss ship. "It's falling!" somebody yelled.

It was, slowly and majestically, one end tilted down, and the other end came up. It made a complete somersault in the first five miles of its fall, and then began to spin faster. The man manipulating the screen on which it had been visible lost sight of it for a few seconds. When he brought it into focus again, it was ten miles nearer the ground, and still falling.

It struck the ground with a curious effect. The soil did not seem solid, but acted as a liquid might. The ship went into it for about a third of its length.

That was their only indication of how tremendous the impact had been.

The weapon officers were cheering wildly. Clane said nothing. He was trembling, but mass enthusiasm was something in which he was constitutionally incapable of joining. He caught a movement out of the corner of one eye. He turned. It was Guylan.

The Outlander had a hurt expression on his face. "You didn't play fair," he said, as soon as he could make himself heard. "I thought this was supposed to be an attempt to be friendly."

It was a moment for guilt feelings, a time to think of abandoned ideals. Clane shook his head. He felt sorry for the Outlander, but he was not apologetic. "We had to be prepared for an attack," he said. "You can't fool with beings who bombed Earth cities."

"But it was you who attacked," Guylan protested. "The moment

I put your men aboard each one ran for some machine, and exploded something."

"The Riss have other ships," said Clane diplomatically. "Thousands of them. We have only this one. To make them talk to us, we have to get them where they can't get away."

"But they're all dead," Guylan said plaintively. "The fall killed everybody aboard."

Clane tried to hold down his feeling of triumph. "It did strike the ground rather hard," he admitted.

He realized that the conversation was getting nowhere. "See here, Guylan, this whole business is deadly, and you're looking at it from too narrow a viewpoint. We want to make contact with the Riss. So far, they haven't let us. If you'll look into my mind, you'll see that that's true."

Guylan said unhappily after a moment, "I guess that's so all right, but I didn't realize before what you were going to do. There was something in your mind but—"

❖ ❖ ❖

Clane could understand a part of the other's dilemma. All his life Guylan had taken for granted that he knew what was going on in other people's minds. But he had not been able to grasp the notion that thirty men could attack a gigantic battleship with tens of thousands of powerful beings aboard. And that that small number of individuals would set off booby traps which the Riss had designed to protect their secrets in the event a ship ever fell into the possession of an enemy. The concept involved mechanical understanding. Accordingly, it was beyond Guylan and his fellows. Lacking the knowledge, lacking the complex associations, their mind-reading ability was of no use to them in this situation.

Clane saw that the man was genuinely dispirited. He said quickly: "Look, Guylan, I want to show you something."

Guylan said glumly: "I think I'd better go home."

"This is important," said Clane. He tugged gently at the other's sleeve. Guylan allowed himself to be led to the "protector" instrument. Clane indicated the main switch. "Did you see one of our men shut this off by pushing it like this?" He grasped the instrument, and plunged it deep into its socket. It locked into position.

Guylan shook his head. "No, I don't remember."

Clane said earnestly: "We've got to make sure of that." He explained how the "protector" worked, and that any Outlander who wandered near the ship would die. "You've got to go aboard, Guylan, and shut that off."

Guylan said in surprise: "Is this the thing that they guarded me against, and the others who were allowed aboard?"

"This is it. It kills everything in a two and a half mile range."

Guylan frowned. "Why didn't it kill the men I took aboard?"

Clane swallowed hard. "Guylan," he said gently, "have you ever seen a man burned alive?"

"I've heard of it."

"Did he die right away?"

"No. He ran around madly."

"Exactly," said Clane grimly. "Guylan, those volunteers started to burn all through their bodies the moment they got aboard. But they didn't die right away. They gambled on getting that machine shut off in time."

It didn't work exactly like that. But it was too difficult to explain what happened to the metabolism of a human being when the temperature in every cell of his body suddenly went up sixty degrees.

The Outlander said uneasily: "I'd better hurry. Somebody might get hurt."

He vanished. That made Clane jump. It was the first time he had actually seen it happen, and it gave him an eerie feeling. Abruptly, Guylan was standing beside him again.

"It's off," he said. He seemed relieved.

Clane held out his hand. "Guylan," he said warmly, "I want to thank you."

The Outlander shook his head. He had evidently been doing some thinking. "No," he said, "that was all unfair. You treated the Riss unfairly." A stubborn expression grew into his mild face. "Don't ever ask me to do you another favor."

"Thank you just the same."

Afterwards, Clane thought: *First, I'll go aboard, and get the maps, and then—*

He had to struggle against the tremendous excitement that was in him. He pictured the message he would send to Czinczar just before breakfast. Abruptly, he couldn't restrain himself. He sat down, and with quivering hand dashed off the message:

❖❖❖

Dear Czinczar:

You will be happy to know that we have successfully engaged the enemy warship. Our victory includes capture of his ship, and destruction of all Riss aboard. It is interesting to note that captured maps identified the nearest Riss star as the one picked by Marden.

Clane.

❖❖❖

As it turned out, the final sentence of the note had to be rewritten before the message was delivered. The captured maps proved that Marden knew nothing about the direction of stars. The Riss sun was about three months away, but in exactly the opposite direction.

By the following evening, the *Solar Star* was on its way.

18

The first squall from the boy came faintly to Clane's ears through the thick panels of the bedroom door. The sound of it electrified him. He had already ordered acceleration down to one G. Now, he went to the laboratory that adjoined the control room, intending to work. But a great weariness was upon him. For the first time, he realized how tense he had been, how tired he was. He lay down on the cot and fell asleep immediately.

It was morning when he awakened. He went to Madelina's and his apartment, and at his request the baby was shown to him. He examined it carefully for indications that his own mutational characteristics had been passed on, but there was no sign of anything out of the normal. It baffled him. Not for the first time, he had a sense of frustration. He knew so little in a world where there was so much to know.

He wondered if there might be neural similarities between the child and himself. He hoped so. For he did not doubt his own greatness. His history proved that he was perceptive as few men had ever been. And he was just beginning to suspect that he was also super-normally stable.

He'd have to watch the child for indications that the two of them were—different.

Except for its structural normalcy, the appearance of the baby gave him no aesthetic satisfaction. It was about as ugly a child as he had ever had the misfortune to look upon, and he was startled when the head nurse crooned: "Such a beautiful child."

He supposed that it might turn into one since Madelina was an extremely good-looking girl. And he presumed that the child's normalcy proved that her side of the family would dominate it physically.

Looking down at the child as it was being clothed again after its bath, he grew sad. He had been worried about the possibility of mutational changes, and he was happy that there were none. But he could already imagine the boy being ashamed of his father.

That thought ended when a nurse came out of the bedroom and told him that Madelina was awake and was asking for him. He found her cheerful and full of plans.

"You know," she said, "I never before realized what wonderfully considerate people we have with us. The women have been just marvelous to me."

He gazed thoughtfully at her as she talked. During the long voyage, Madelina had undergone profound psychological adjustments. There had been an incident involving an assassin of Lilidel's who had somehow got aboard in the guise of a soldier. The would-be killer never guessed how hopeless his purpose was. On approaching their apartment he set off alarms; and so Clane had deliberately invited Madelina to be in at the death. The man's desperate will to live had affected her tremendously. From that moment, she ceased to talk of death as something she could take or leave alone.

He listened now, happy in the change that had taken place, as she praised several of the servants individually. She broke off abruptly. "Oh, I almost forgot. You know how hard it's been for us to decide on his name—well, I dreamed it: Braden. Just think that over for a minute. Braden Linn."

Clane accepted the name after a moment's hesitation. A child's first name should be individual, to distinguish him from other's of his line. There would have to be a string of second names, of course, to honor the famous men of both families. It was an old custom, and one of which he approved, this giving of many family names. It reminded the bearer of the past history of his line. It brought a sense of continuity of life, and gave the proud possessor a feeling of belonging; a will to do as well as, or better, than his namesake. Even he, who had so many physical reasons for not having that sense of belonging, had felt the pressure of the many names that had been bestowed upon him at the hour of his christening.

The full name finally given to the new baby was Braden Jerrin Garlan Joquin Dold Corgay Linn.

It was two weeks after the birth that the *Solar Star* came to its second destination in space.

❖ ❖ ❖

Clane entered the conference room briskly. Now, at last there was no reason for inner conflicts. An enemy planet was already bright in the darkness ahead of them.

It was time to prepare for action.

First, he made his prepared speech, stressing the value of courage. His eyes studied the faces of the men as he talked, watching for signs of cynicism. He didn't expect too much of that. These were earnest men, conscious of the reality of their mission.

Some of them, he saw, appeared puzzled by the tenor of his talk. There was a time when he would have yielded to that gathering impatience. No more. In every great objective the leader must start from the beginning, first evoking the emotional attitude necessary to success. In the past he'd assumed automatically that soldiers took courage for granted. They did, but only if they were reminded. And even then, on the general staff level, there was resistance from individuals.

Having completed his diatribe on courage, he launched into the explanation of his purpose. He hadn't gone far before he began to notice the reactions.

The officers, barbarians as well as Linnans, were almost uniformly pale. Only Czinczar was frowning with a sudden thoughtful air, his eyes narrowed with calculation.

"But, your excellency," one of the Linnans protested, "this is a major Riss planet. They'll have hundreds of ships to our one."

Clane held himself cool. It was an old experience with him now to realize that only he had reasoned out the situation as a whole. He said gently: "Gentlemen, I hope we are all agreed that this ship and those aboard must take risks to the limits of good sense."

"Yes, but this is madness." It was General Marik, now Clane's private secretary. "As soon as they discover us—" He paused, as if he had been struck by a new thought. He said, "Or do you expect that we will not be discovered?"

Clane smiled. "We'll make sure that we are. My plan is to land most of the"—he hesitated, and bit his lip; he'd almost said "barbarian," then he went on—"Europan army, and establish a bridgehead."

The faces of the barbarian officers took on a sick expression, and almost everyone in the room looked appalled. Once more, the exception was Czinczar. Clane was aware of the barbarian leader watching him with bright eyes, in which the light of understanding was beginning to dawn. Clane stood up.

❖❖❖

"Gentlemen," he chided, "you will refrain from frightening the troops with your all too obvious dismay. Our approach to this problem is soundly based. Spaceships are *not* destroyed in space. They cannot even maintain contact with each other when those aboard are friendly to each other, and make every effort to keep together. So you may be sure that the Riss will not contact us as long as we keep moving.

"As for the landing, it is the oldest reality of military history that a bridgehead can always be established and held for a time. And no one has *ever* figured out a method of preventing an enemy from landing somewhere on a planet."

He broke off. "But now, enough of argument. We have our purpose. Now, we come to what is far more important, the intricate details of carrying out that purpose."

He explained his own ideas, and then, before throwing the meeting open to general discussion, finished, "In everything, we must follow the rule of the calculated risk. We must be aware at all times that there will be sacrifices. But in my opinion, no plan can be acceptable which does not offer some hope of saving a fairly large percentage of the bridgehead army."

Czinczar was the first to get up. "What," he asked, "is the exact purpose of the landing?"

"To see what reaction it brings, how strong the reaction is, how they attack, with what weapons? In short, how do the Riss plan to defend their planet?"

"Isn't it possible," Czinczar asked, "that this information was known to the ancient humans who fought the great Riss-human war?"

"Perhaps." Clane hesitated, not sure whether this was the moment to offer his own estimate of that past war, and its conduct. He decided finally that it wasn't. He said: "I found no books on the war itself, so I can't answer your question."

Czinczar looked at him steadily for several seconds, and then finished: "Naturally, I am in favor of the landing. Here are my ideas on your plan—"

The discussion continued on that practical level. There were no further objections to the landing itself.

19

They came down on the dried-out, uneven hillside of what might have been a dead sea. Rock formations tangled that unpleasant and desolate terrain. The air was thin and cold in the morning, but by noon the heat had become a blistering thing.

The men were grumbling even as they set up their tents. Clane was aware of many a scowl sent in his direction as he flew slowly along within a few feet of the ground. And a dozen times when his ship came silently over a rock formation before dipping down into the next valley, he overheard fearful comments from big men whose courage in battle could be counted on.

Periodically, he landed to inspect the protector and molecular energy devices he had ordered set up. The protectors were the same instruments that had killed every man of the skeleton crews aboard the Linnan warships in the attack that had originally enabled him to seize the *Solar Star*. The molecular weapons had burned great gashes in the second Riss ship. He made sure that the destructive limit of each weapon was set at extreme range, and then he flew on.

He stood finally beside Czinczar, gazing out toward the bleak horizon. The barbarian was silent. Clane turned and gave his final instructions:

"Send out raiding parties. If you get any prisoners, report to me immediately."

Czinczar rubbed his chin. "Suppose they drop atomic bombs on us?"

Clane did not answer at once. From the hillside, he could see some of the tents. Most of them were hidden in the hollows behind crooked rock formations. But here and there he could see the thin, unsteady lines. They reached to the horizon and beyond—over thirty miles in each direction from where they stood.

An atomic bomb would kill everybody in its immediate vicinity. The titan wind would tear down every tent. The radiation, that deadly stuff, would bounce from the hard, glittering rock, and kill only the few men who were directly exposed.

That was for a bomb exploding at ground level. If it exploded in the air, if for instance the automatic controls of the molecular weapons forced it to explode at a height of twenty miles, the effect would be compressive. But at twenty miles the air pressure would not be too deadly, particularly for men who had orders to burrow into the rock under their tents, and *orders* that two of the four men assigned to each tent must always be in the rock burrow. The other two men of each unit were expected to be alert. It was presumed that they would hastily take cover if a Riss ship appeared overhead.

Clane explained his picture, and finished, "If they drop a bomb on us, why, we'll drop one or two on their cities."

His surface coldness yielded to his inner exultation. He laughed softly, and said, "No, no, my friend. I'm beginning to grasp the problem of two hostile civilizations in this vast universe. There's never been anything like it, before human and Riss collided. No planet can be defended. All planets can be attacked; everybody is vulnerable—and this time, here on one of their home planets, we have the least to lose."

He held out his hand. "Good luck to you, Great Czinczar. I'm sure you will do your usual thorough job."

Czinczar gazed down at the proffered hand for several seconds, and finally took it. "You can count on me, sir," he said.

He hesitated. "I'm sorry," he said slowly, "that I didn't give you the sphere."

The frank admission shocked Clane. The loss of the sphere had been a major disaster, and only the terrible will power of the barbarian leader had restrained him finally from forcing the issue to a conclusion. Even then he had realized his need for such a man as Czinczar. He could not bring himself to say that it didn't matter. But since the confession implied that the sphere would be available on Earth, he said nothing.

❖ ❖ ❖

Back on the *Solar Star*, he guided the ship from the weapon control room. A dozen men stood behind him, watching the various screens, ready to call his attention to any point that he himself might miss.

They cruised over cities—all of them were in mountain areas—and it didn't take very long to discover that they were being evacuated. Endless streams of small craft poured from each metropolitan area, unloaded their burden of refugees, and came back for more.

The spectacle exhilarated the other officers. "By all the atom gods," one man exulted, "we've got those skunks on the run."

Somebody urged, "Let's drop some bombs on them—and watch them scurry."

Clane said nothing, simply shook his head. He was not surprised at the virulence of the hatred. For two days he watched it swell and surge around him, and still it showed no signs of diminishing.

"I've got to change these automatic hate patterns," he told himself. But that was for later.

During those two days, he received periodic radio reports from Czinczar. Patrols had been sent out. That was one message. About half of them were back by the time the second report arrived.

"It appears," said Czinczar, "that an army is gathering around us. There is much activity on every side, and our patrol craft have been burned down by ground artillery at heights as great as eighteen miles. So far there has been no attack made on any of our machines from the air. It looks as if they are trying to contain us. Our men have captured no prisoners as yet."

The third report was brief. "Some air activity. No prisoners. Shall we try to go into one of their camps?"

Clane's answer to that was, "No!"

Seen from a great height, the problem of the Riss planet fascinated him. It seemed clear that a sharp clash was imminent. Considering how many individual Riss there were on the planet, it was hard to realize why not one had yet been captured.

As he flew over another city on the third day, and saw that it was still debouching refugees, he pondered a possibility. Send a patrol craft down. Intercept a refugee craft, burn the machine, and capture those aboard.

After some thought, he rejected that. In the first place, the Riss machines kept to lanes. That suggested there were "protector" instruments spotted all along the route. No human being could hope to penetrate that line of death. That was also the reason why he refused to consider Czinczar's suggestion that patrols be sent into the enemy camps. The camps also would be protected.

The risk to a few men was quite unimportant, of course. But there was another reason for not testing the danger. He wanted reactions from the Riss. It was they who must force issues against the invader; and by the very nature of the issues they brought up, show what they feared.

On the third day, accordingly, his advice to Czinczar was still, "Wait and follow the pattern."

The passing of that night brought no unexpected developments. By mid-morning, Clane was observing that the refugee traffic had diminished to a trickle of trucking craft. He could imagine the tremendous relief that must be sweeping the populace. They probably believed that they had won the first phase of the engagement, or else regarded the assailant as too foolish to appreciate the advantage he had had.

Let them think what they pleased. Having achieved the safety of wide dispersement, they must now be ready for an active second phase. He was not mistaken in his analysis. Shortly before dark that afternoon, Czinczar sent the long awaited word: "Prisoner captured. When will you be down?"

"Tomorrow," Clane replied.

He spent the rest of the day, and part of the night considering the potentialities. His plans were ready about midnight. At that time he addressed a hundred group captains. It was a very sharp, determined speech. When he had finished, the men were pale, but they cheered him lustily. Toward the end of the question period, one of them asked:

"Your excellency, are we to understand that you are planning to be on the ground tomorrow?"

Clane hesitated, then nodded.

The man said earnestly: "I'm sure I speak for my colleagues when I say to you: reconsider. We have talked all this out among us many times during these long months, and it is our opinion that the life of everyone aboard this ship depends upon your excellency remaining alive. No great expedition has ever before been so completely dependent on the knowledge or leadership of one man."

Clane bowed. "Thank you. I shall try to merit the trust reposed in me." He shook his head. "As for your suggestion, I must reject it. I feel that it is necessary for me to question the prisoner we have captured. Why? Because on Earth I dissected the body of one of these beings, and I am probably the only person who knows enough about him for the interview to have any meaning."

"Sir," said the man, "what about Czinczar? We've heard reports of his astuteness."

Clane smiled grimly, "I'm afraid Czinczar will also have to be present at the interview." He broke off. "I'm sorry, gentlemen, this argument must cease. For once, the commander must take as great a risk as any of his soldiers. I thought that was one of the dreams of lower ranks."

That brought another cheer, and the meeting broke up a few minutes later with everyone in good humor.

❖ ❖ ❖

"I don't like this," said Czinczar.

Actually, Clane didn't either. He sat down in a chair, and surveyed the prisoner. "Let's think this over for a while," he said slowly.

The Riss stood proudly—at least that was the impression he gave—in front of his human captors. Clane watched him unhurriedly, preternaturally aware of a number of possibilities. The Riss was about twelve feet from him. He towered like a giant above the powerful barbarian soldiers, and theoretically he could leap forward and tear any individual limb from limb before himself succumbing to an attack.

It was not a point that need be taken too seriously, but still there was such a thing as being prepared for any eventuality. Surreptitiously, he moved his rod of energy into a handier position for defense.

Czinczar said, "It was a little too obvious. The men, of course, were jubilant at catching him, but naturally I asked detailed questions. There's no doubt in my mind that he sought captivity."

Clane accepted the analysis. It was an example of the alertness he expected from the brilliant barbarian leader. And besides, it was the eventuality that had made him take so many precautions.

Theoretically, everything he had done might prove unnecessary. Conversely, if his anxiety was justified, then the precautions would merely provide a first line of defense. In war, the best plans were subject to unbearable friction.

Clane took out his notebook, and began to draw. He was not an artist, but presently he handed the rough sketch to a member of his staff who was. The man examined the picture, and then secured a small drawing board from the patrol craft, and began to sketch with quick, sure strokes. When the drawing was finished, Clane motioned the artist to hand it to the Riss.

That huge monstrosity accepted the paper, board and all. He studied it with evidence of excitement, then vibrated the folds of his skin. Watching him, Clane could not decide whether he was showing approval or disapproval.

The Riss continued to study the paper, and finally reached into a fold of his skin and from some hidden receptacle drew out a large pencil. He turned the sheet the artist had used, and drew something on the blank side of the paper. When the Riss had it ready, it was Czinczar who stepped forward and took the drawing from him.

It was not, apparently, his intention to examine it, for he carried it over to Clane without glancing at what was on the paper. As he handed it to the mutation, he bent down for a moment, his back to the Riss, and whispered:

"Your excellency, do you realize that the two leaders of this expedition are concentrated here on this spot?"

Clane nodded.

20

Out of the corner of one eye, Clane caught a brilliant flash of light high in the sky. He glanced quickly around to see if anyone else had noticed it. One of the barbarian officers was craning his neck, but there was an uncertain expression in his face. He had the look of a man who couldn't be sure that what he had seen meant anything.

Clane, who had sat down so that he could, among other things, gaze upward without being too obvious about it, settled slowly back in the chair. He waited tensely for the next flash. It came abruptly. It was almost straight above, which worried him a little. But still he showed no sign.

This time, no one seemed to have observed the flash.

Clane hesitated, and then finally answered Czinczar's question with a question of his own. "Just what," he asked, "do you expect?"

The barbarian leader must have sensed the undertone of excitement in his voice. He looked sharply at Clane. He said slowly, "A Riss has allowed himself to be taken captive. He must have a purpose. That purpose could well be to insure that the forces behind him make their attack at a specific time and place. Why not at the moment and the area where the top leaders of the enemy expedition are interviewing their alien prisoner?"

Clane said, "You feel then that he would be capable of evaluating your rank and mine?" He spoke deliberately. There had been a third flash in the upper sky.

"He can put two and two together," said Czinczar. The barbarian was angry now. He seemed to be aware that he was only partly understanding what was going on. "And remember what Marden said about communicating with the Riss. That suggests they can read our minds. Besides"—he was suddenly sarcastic—"for the first time in our association, you've come like a potentate. You're the only person here sitting down. That's unusual for you on a public occasion.

And for the only time in your life that I know about, you've put on the dress clothes of a Linnan temple priest. What are you trying to do—make him realize who you are?"

"Yes," said Clane.

He spoke softly, and then he laughed out loud, exuberantly. "Czinczar," he said at last, more soberly, "this is a test of something I saw during the attack against the Riss battleship on Outland."

"What did you see?" said Czinczar.

"Our molecular weapon showed up as being far more powerful than I had imagined. It did not actually help to destroy the other ship—I used it merely to distract their attention. But it burned away more than a foot of the hard outer shell of the ship wherever it touched. I subsequently discovered that it had a range of some twenty miles, and that aboard the ship it was synchronized to automatic aiming devices."

He showed his even, white teeth, as he smiled grimly. "Czinczar," he said, "this entire area is protected by molecular weapons that will with absolute precision burn an atomic bomb out of the sky at a distance of nearly twenty miles."

The barbarian leader's strong face was dark with puzzlement. "You mean, it will explode them that far away?"

"No. It burns them. There is no nuclear explosion, but only a molecular transformation into gas. Being small, the bomb is completely dissipated, the gas is caught by crosscurrents of air and its radioactivity spread over hundreds of square miles."

He expected a strong reaction. He was not mistaken. "Lord Clane," Czinczar said with suppressed excitement, "this is tremendous. All these months we have had this remarkable defensive machine, and didn't know it."

He stopped. Then more slowly, he said, "I am not going to assume, as I did with the chlorodel, that this is the answer to our requirements. A big ship like our own could fly over a solid rank of such weapons. It might suffer serious but not crippling damage, and it could come low enough for its protective space-time resonators to exterminate everyone below. What is our defense against that? Burrowing?"

"As fast as we can," said Clane, "we dive into the individual caves that your men have been digging, and crouch under several yards of rock."

Czinczar was frowning again. "All this doesn't explain the why of this byplay with our prisoner. Are you trying to force them to an attack?"

Clane savored the opportunity briefly, then he said quietly, "The attack has been on for nearly five minutes."

Having spoken, he raised the drawing the Riss had made and pretended to study it.

❖❖❖

Around him, the wave of excitement reached its peak. Men called to each other shrilly. The echoes of the sounds receded into the distance, as other men farther away took up the cry.

During the entire period of turmoil, Clane appeared to be examining the drawings. Actually, with a singleness of purpose he watched the Riss captive.

The guards had forgotten the huge alien. They stood, craning their necks, staring up into the sky, where the flashes had become more numerous. With one word, Clane could have recalled them to their duty. But he decided against saying anything.

The question was, how would the creature react when he finally realized that the atomic attack was a complete fizzle?

For a few seconds, the monster maintained his calm, proud bearing. Then he tilted his head back, and stared earnestly up. That lasted less than half a minute. Abruptly, his gaze came down from the upper air, and he looked quickly around him. For a moment his swift eyes focused on Clane, who blinked rapidly, but did not look away.

It was an effective device. His bent head suggested that he was immersed in the drawing. By blinking his eyelids, he partially concealed the fact that his eyeballs were rolled up high into their sockets. The Riss' gaze passed over him, and the Riss made his first purposeful move.

He reached into a fold of his skin, started to draw something out—and stopped, as Clane said softly almost under his breath, "Don't do it. Stay alive! I know you came here to sacrifice yourself, but it's not necessary now. It would serve no useful purpose. Stay alive, and listen to what I have to say."

He didn't expect too much from that. Telepathic communication between an alien who could read minds and a human being who couldn't must surely be a fragile thing. Nevertheless, though he still did not look directly at the Riss, he saw that the creature continued to hesitate.

More firmly, but still under his breath, Clane said: "Remember the drawing. I still don't know what your reaction was—I can't take the time to look—but I suspect it was negative. Think that over. A first judgment isn't necessarily the best. Five thousand years ago, man and Riss nearly destroyed each other. And now, the Riss have taken actions that will start the whole struggle over again. So far we have not dropped a single bomb, nor have we used the resonator. That was deliberate. That was designed to show that this time human beings want a different arrangement. Tell your people that we come as friends."

And still it was hard to tell what the reaction was. The alien remained as he had been, one "hand" hidden in the folds of his skin. Clane did not underestimate the possibilities. In dissecting the body of the dead Riss on Earth, he had discovered natural skin pockets big enough to conceal energy rods.

He had warned Czinczar to be on guard, but had asked him not to make a search. The important thing was that the Riss feel free to act.

Beside him, Czinczar said in a monotone, "Your excellency, I think our captive is nerving himself to do something violent. I've been watching him."

So at least one other person had not forgotten the danger. Before Clane could speak, Czinczar went on, sharply, "Your excellency, I urge you to take no chances. Kill him before he pulls a surprise on us."

"No," said Clane. His voice was on a conversational level. "I intend to give him a patrol craft, if he'll accept it, and let him escape. The choice is up to him."

As he spoke, he raised his head for the first time, and gazed squarely at the Riss. The creature's huge, glittering eyes glared back at him. There seemed little doubt but that he knew what was expected of him.

The conflict between his will to live and the unconscious attitudes and beliefs that had brought him here to sacrifice himself was terrible to see. He grew visibly rigid in every muscle.

❖❖❖

There was no immediate change in that tense tableau. The Riss stood on a rock ledge looking up at Clane and Czinczar who were higher up on that barren and uneven hillside. Beyond the alien, the tents of the barbarian soldiers were partly visible among the rocks. They stretched as far as the eye could see. A minute went by. The very passage of time, it seemed to Clane, was favorable. He relaxed ever so slightly, and said to Czinczar:

"I'd like to know what he drew in answer to the drawings I had made up. Will you look at them, while I watch him? I imagine you'll have to study mine first if you hope to understand his reply."

Though he had not said so, he was also interested in the barbarian's own reaction.

Without taking his gaze from the Riss, he held up the drawing board. Czinczar took it, and said presently, "I'm looking at your drawing. There are three planets shown here. One is completely shaded. One is all white, and on the third the mountain areas are shaded, and the foothills and flat sections are white. Am I right in thinking these drawings *are* meant to represent planets?"

"Yes," said Clane.

He waited. After a little, Czinczar said: "The legend at the bottom of the sheet shows the figure of a human being, and opposite that a white rectangle, and below that a Riss with a shaded rectangle opposite his figure."

"That's the explanatory legend," said Clane.

There was a long pause, longer than Clane expected from a man so astute. And yet, on second thought, he was not surprised. It was a matter of attitudes and beliefs. It was the whole nerve process of accepting a radically new notion. The reaction that came finally did not surprise him in the slightest.

"But this is ridiculous," Czinczar said angrily. "Are you seriously suggesting that Riss and human beings share one out of every three planets?"

"That's just a guess," said Clane. He made no further attempt to justify the idea. Fifty centuries before, Riss and human had not even been prepared to share a galaxy. The mental attitude involved seemed to be one of the few things that had survived a holocaust war.

He waited. When the barbarian spoke again, there was satisfaction in his voice. "Your excellency, I am examining his answer. He has drawn three planets, all shaded in. I'd say he rejects your suggestion of sharing."

Clane said steadily: "He's had time to transmit my plan by mental telepathy. The idea may spread rather rapidly. That's all I can hope for at the moment."

❖ ❖ ❖

Actually, the basic situation was quite different from what it had been long ago. This time, men and Riss alike could look back and see the disaster that had befallen their ancestors.

This time, one man believed in co-operation.

One man, sitting here on this distant enemy planet, accepted the reality that there would be difficulties. Accepted the rigid intolerance of man and Riss alike. Knew that he would be regarded as a fool, enemy of his kind. And still he had no intention of yielding his idea

He saw himself, poised for one minute of eternity at the very apex of power. In all man's history, this moment, this combination of events, had never occurred before, and possibly never would again. A few years from now what he knew of science would be common knowledge, shared by thousands of technicians. It would have to be, if the human race hoped to survive in competition or co-operation with the Riss. Already, he had trained scores of officers. The trouble was, because of his greater background, he learned a dozen things while they learned one.

That fact shaped the difference. Therein lay the tremendous opportunity. Culturally, industrially, that was bad for the human race. Politically, it made the moment.

No one could stop him. None could deny him. He was Lord Clane Linn, potential Lord Leader, commander in chief of the *Solar Star*, the only man who understood something about all the machinery aboard. He had never felt more alert, never sharper of mind, and he hadn't been sick for years.

Czinczar cut across his thought, a note of exasperation in his voice. "Your excellency, if all your schemes didn't work out so well, I'd say you were mad. The Riss attack against us here has been tactically and strategically wrong, not well planned, not well conducted. There have been no explosions for several minutes. If I were the commander on the other side, what has already happened would be only the beginning of a major assault. Logically, there is no limit to the sacrifice a race should make in defending its planet."

He went on in a puzzled tone, "There's something about the attack that we're not seeing, a factor which they're taking into account but we're not. It's holding them back."

He broke off. He said ironically, "But what about this fellow? How can you solve the problem of the Riss galactically if you can't even persuade this one individual?"

Clane said quietly, "All he's got to do to get to a patrol ship is bring his hand out into the open, slowly, inoffensively—"

He stopped. Because the "hand" was coming out. The Riss stood for a moment, studying Clane. Then he walked over to the patrol vessel Clane had mentally indicated. Silently, they watched him get into it, and take off.

When he had gone, Czinczar said, "Well, what now?"

The barbarian leader had a habit of asking such disconcerting questions.

21

Clane returned to the *Solar Star*, and considered. What *should* the next move be?

Go home? It seemed too soon.

He spent half an hour playing with baby Braden. The child fascinated him. "Here," he thought, not for the first time, "is the secret of all progress."

At the moment Braden had no ideas of his own, no unchanging attitudes or beliefs—except possibly those that derived from the way the nurses and Madelina had handled him. There were possible subtle responses to rough or gentle treatment that should not be lightly dismissed.

But he knew nothing of his origin. He did not hate the Riss. Brought up with a young Riss, the two might even develop friendly relationships—though that was not an important solution to the Riss-human problem. It couldn't be carried out on a big enough scale. Besides, it would be limited by other associations.

He left the baby finally, and settled down in a chair in the control room. There, surrounded by the panoply of instruments that controlled great machines, he told himself, "It's a matter of integrating what I know."

He had a feeling about that. It seemed to him that virtually all the facts were now available. There was one possible exception. What Czinczar had said about the unsatisfactory extent of the Riss attack.

Frowning, he went over in his mind the sequence of events on this Riss planet. And Czinczar was right, he decided.

He was still thinking about it when the radio clerk brought him a message.

Dear Lord Clane:

More prisoners have been captured. I urge you to come down immediately. I have the missing factor.

Czinczar.

Clane made his landing shortly after lunch. Barbarian guards herded the prisoners from a small pocket in the rocky hillside.

They sidled over, skinny, bright-eyed men with a feverish look about them. They were unmistakably human. Czinczar made the introduction. His golden voice held the full flavor of the occasion.

"Your excellency, I want you to meet the descendants of the human beings who used to occupy this planet—before it was captured by the Riss five thousand years ago."

Clane had had just a moment's warning—that one look at the prisoners as they came up. It was all he needed. His mind took the impact of the introduction. He was able after a moment to study them, and it seemed to him that he had never seen such wretched looking human beings. The tallest of the group—there were eight of them—was no more than five feet three. The shortest was a little old wizened individual about four feet six. It was he who spoke.

"Hear you come from Eart'."

His accent was so different from the Linnan, that his words sounded like gibberish. Clane glanced at Czinczar, who shrugged, smiled, and said, "Say, yes."

Oddly, the meaning came through then, and thereafter a painfully slow conversation was possible.

"You're the big boy?" the creature said.

Clane thought that over, and nodded. The little old man came closer, pursed his lips, and said hoarsely, "I'm the big boy of *this* bunch."

He must have spoken too loudly. One of the other men, who had been standing by, stirred, and said, in an outraged tone, "Yeah? Listen, Glooker, you do the talkin', we do the fightin'. If there's any big boy in this bunch, it's me."

Glooker ignored the interruption, and said to Clane, "Nothin' but intrigue and complaint all the time. By the holy sphere, you can't do a thing with them."

Clane's mind jumped back to the desperate political and economic intrigue of Linn. He started to say with a smile, "I'm afraid intrigue is a common heritage of limited associative balance—" he stopped. He did a mental double-take, caught himself, and said with a tense calmness, "By the *what?*"

"The sphere. You know, it rolls up and down. It's the one thing that never changes."

Clane had complete surface control of himself again. He said, "I see. You must show it to us sometime."

He turned casually to Czinczar, "Did you know about this?"

Czinczar shook his head. "I talked to them for an hour after they were brought in, but they never mentioned it."

Clane hesitated, then drew the barbarian aside. "Brief me," he said.

The picture was ordinary enough. Man had gone underground. During the long struggle, gigantic machines had created a universe of caves. Long after the burrowing machines were meaningless hulks of metal, the caves remained.

"But," said Clane, puzzled, "how did they hold off the Riss? Just going into a cave wouldn't be enough."

Czinczar was smiling. "Your excellency," he said, "we proved the method right here on this soil." He waved at the rocky, uneven terrain, the desolation that reached to every horizon. "They had, among other things, the 'protector' device—"

Clane flashed, "You mean, they know how to make them?" He thought of his own fruitless efforts to duplicate the Riss alloys.

"It's a part of life to them," said Czinczar. "They make the right alloys as a matter of simple training. They fashion them together because . . . well . . . that's the way things are. They *know*."

Clane had a limp feeling of excitement. It was the same story over again. In Linn, spaceships existed in a bow and arrow culture. On Outland, an inconceivably advanced system of transportation, and telepathy, were accepted realities in a simple, agricultural civilization. And now here was the same evidence of scientific wonders as part of a commonplace life. A technique, if remembered and passed on from one generation to the next, was not something marvelous. It was *the* way of doing something.

Such folkways had their limitations, of course. The people did not have open minds. They resisted change. The Outlanders were extreme examples of that. The Linnans as a nation were almost equally set in their decadence. These little people were harder to judge. In their confined and desperate existence, they had little opportunity for growth. And so, because of their environment, they were as rigid as any Outlander.

The deeper meanings of such things remained as obscure as ever.

Clane broke his thought. "Let us make arrangements to visit these people in their home, tomorrow."

They flew over country that was rocky and barren at first. Abruptly, the soil grew greener. A river burst into view, and wound along among trees and heavy undergrowth. And still there was no sign of Riss habitation.

Clane commented on it to Glooker. The little man nodded. "Air's too heavy for 'em. But they won't let us have it." He spoke sourly.

The mutation nodded, but said nothing more.

The entrance to the cave surprised him. It was a huge concrete piling constructed against a hillside, plainly visible for miles. Their patrol craft came down outside the range of the resonators, and the erstwhile prisoners went forward alone into the "protected" area.

They came back, "photographed" the visitors, and soon they were being led down a brightly lighted concrete causeway. Spindly bodied men and women, pitiful child mites came out of wood and stone cubbyholes to stare with their feverish unhealthy eyes at the procession of strangers.

Clane began to feel his first admiration. The scene was almost literally out of a nightmare. And yet these half humans with their stunted bodies and their desperate, tense, anxious minds, had fought off the science and military might of the Riss empire. They had burrowed into the soil; by withdrawing into that artificial underground world, they had virtually cut themselves off from sunlight. But here they were, alive, and as active as ants in an anthill.

They squabbled, fought and intrigued. They had their own caste system. They followed old marriage customs. They lived and loved and reproduced in the very shadow of the Riss menace. Their average life expectancy was about thirty-five Earth years, as near as Clane could calculate it.

The procession came to a larger cave, which was occupied by several women and swarms of children, but only one man. Clane watched alertly as the man, a roly poly individual with thin lips and hard blue eyes ambled forward. Glooker introduced him obsequiously as Huddah, the "Boss Boy."

The mutation had his own way of measuring conceited individuals. So now he made his first attempt to control the sphere, which these little people had somewhere in this tangle of caverns.

The problem was, was the sphere close enough?

An instant after he had thought the cue, it flashed up over his head. A hundred throats screeched with wonder and awe.

There was no trouble.

❖ ❖ ❖

On the return trip, Clane ordered Czinczar to re-embark the barbarian army.

"The existence of a remnant human race on this planet," he explained, "points up emphatically what we discovered. Given certain weapons, man can survive a Riss attack. We'll take along enough 'little men' technicians to start construction on Earth of the two main weapons. As more and more people learn the process, we can count on our defenses holding."

He added, "That, of course, doesn't give us back our planets. It's unfortunate but the defense weapons will work equally well for the Riss."

He glanced sharply at Czinczar, expecting a reaction. But that barbarian's lean face was impassive. Clane hesitated, then went on, "It is my plan before we leave here to turn out millions of Photostats of my drawing, showing how we propose to solve the Riss-human hostility. We'll flutter them down over various cities and over the mountain sides, so that every Riss becomes aware of the basic idea of sharing."

Czinczar made a sound as if he were choking. Clane said quickly, "We mustn't forget the Riss also have a problem. Apparently, they need a more rarefied atmosphere than man. They can stand the dense air at sea level on Earth, and here, but for everyday living they've got to be high up. That greatly limits the habitable areas available to them. Man has not been overly sympathetic to the difficulties involved, in fact aggravated them."

Czinczar broke into speech at last, "How do you mean?"

Clane said slowly, "From all accounts, men of the golden age discovered how to release the oxygen from the crusts of otherwise barren planets and moons. Presumably, the Riss knew how to do that also, but they had a terrible disadvantage. They would want the process to stop sooner than would man. I can just imagine the glee of human beings as they forced an ever thicker atmosphere on planet after planet."

Czinczar said in a remorseless tone, "It is natural that each race fight to the limit for survival."

Clane said sharply: "That's all very well for intelligent beings who think on the animal level. Man and Riss *must* rise above it." He broke off grimly, "You understand, that we will not allow the Riss in the solar system, nor should human beings aspire to share the main Riss system. The home planets have to be inviolate."

"How are we going to get them off?" said Czinczar.

Clane made no direct answer.

❖❖❖

Back on the ship, Czinczar offered only one important objection when Clane told him they would have to make a stopover on Outland.

"What about the people of the solar system?" he asked uneasily. "For all we know, a major attack has already taken place. We do know that as of now, human beings have no resonators or energy beams to protect them."

Clane was grim. "It takes time to conquer an inhabited planet. That's what I'm counting on." He added harshly, "If we go back right now, we could only fight the Riss on equal terms. That would be bad for us, since they have the ships and the weapons and the endless equipment for making more."

"And how will the situation be changed if we go to Outland first?"

"I'm not sure." Clane spoke frankly.

"I see. Another idea at the back of your mind?"

"Yes."

Czinczar was silent for several seconds. Then his eyes showed laughter. "I support it," he said, "sight unseen."

He held out his hand. "Your excellency," he said earnestly, "I'm your man. From this moment on, no more schemes, no opposition. I salute the future Lord Leader of Linn, of whom I herewith request the rank of loyal ally."

It was an unexpectedly complete surrender. Clane blinked, and swallowed hard. Momentarily, he felt overwhelmed. Then he caught hold of himself and said with a faint smile, "I'm not Lord Leader yet. It will take time to make influential people aware of me again. There will probably be a difficult preliminary."

There was no need to elaborate on that. The politically wise barbarian nodded, his lips pursed.

Clane went on, "We now have two spheres, one in reserve on Earth—" His eyes met Czinczar's, seeking confirmation.

The latter agreed. "Yes, two. You can have the one in the solar system at any time."

Clane continued in a firm voice, "As I see it, the sphere is the primitive version of the transport system developed on Outland and Inland."

"And so—"

"Control of the cosmos." Something of the fire of the thought that was in his mind enriched his voice. "Czinczar, have you ever wondered how the Universe functions?"

The barbarian was sardonic. "I was born, I am alive, I shall die. That's my function. Can you alter the pattern?"

Clane smiled wryly. "You strike too deeply, my friend. I'm just now becoming vaguely aware of the forces that are operating inside me. They're more intricate than the physical sciences. I intend to leave them alone till I have more time."

He paused, frowning. "Perhaps that's an error. How dare a man who doesn't understand himself propose to settle the affairs of the Universe?"

He shrugged. "It can't be helped. My hope right now is that, with the sphere to help him, Marden will be able to teach me their system."

❖❖❖

Marden drew back curiously to let the men carrying the sphere and its container enter his house. They set it down, as Clane said, "Ever see anything like this before, Marden?"

Marden was smiling. The sphere rose up from the container, and took up a position over his head. "An artificial opening," he said. "I've heard of them. They were the beginning."

He added, "If I had known you had such a thing as this, I would have taught him"—he nodded at Clane—"how all this works when he first talked about it."

Clane said, "Will it help me to read minds?"

Marden was tolerant. "That will take a few years. The rest you can start doing immediately with the sphere to help you."

Afterwards, Czinczar said: "But how *do* you expect to use the sphere against the Riss? You told me yourself it would not be decisive."

Clane evaded answering. The idea in his mind was so intricate in its scientific concepts, so vast in scope, that he dared not put it into words.

Besides, there was much to do first.

❖❖❖

The trip home was long and tiring but not altogether wasted. Several dozen people aboard had gone insane, and there were any number of tangled minds and eccentric characters. Clane studied them, tried techniques of therapy on them—and again and again went back to baby Braden, the wellspring of his own interest.

It seemed to him that in the child he would find the beginning of the normalness and abnormalness of the adult.

The baby made as many movements with his left hand as with his right. He was not interested in objects held farther away than two feet. But if an article was brought closer than that, he would usually—though not always—reach for it, as often with his left hand as with his right.

Given something that he could grab hold of, he could be lifted into the air, his own strength supporting him. He did this equally with either hand, but each time used only his fingers. His thumb was still a useless appendage.

He showed marked symptoms of fear after a loud noise, a pain stimulus, or when subjected to a sudden sense of falling. Nothing else could alarm him. He was not afraid of animals or objects whether large or small, no matter how close they were brought. And he liked being stroked under his chin.

Other babies aboard, given the same tests, responded similarly.

Many times, Clane pondered his observations. "Suppose," he wondered, "that *all* babies turned out to have the same instinctive reactions as Braden and the ones I've tested. In other words, basically they don't seem to be either right-handed or left-handed. They're not afraid of the dark. Apparently, they learn these things. When? Under what conditions? How does one baby become irresponsible Calaj, another one ruthless, brilliant Czinczar, and a third a field laborer?"

There was one way, he discovered, in which Braden differed from the other babies of his own age group. When a blunt object was drawn across the bottom of his foot, all his toes flexed in one direction. Every other baby under a year old flexed the big toe upward and four downward.

The dividing line seemed to be one year of age. Of the nineteen older children Clane tested, sixteen reacted like Braden. That is, their toes all flexed in the same direction. The other three continued to react like normal babies under a year old. Each one of the three was a recognized problem child.

It was highly suggestive to Clane that Braden at four months of age should have the same responses as much older children. Was here perhaps evidence that his son had inherited the supernormal stability which he suspected in himself?

He was still deeply involved in the whole intricate problem of sanity when the *Solar Star* entered Earth's atmosphere. That was nine hundred and seventy-seven days after its departure.

22

Before landing, Clane sent out patrols. Their reports were encouraging.

His estate was unharmed, though a large and noisy refugee village had grown up starting about two miles from the house.

According to the accounts brought back by the patrol commanders, some four hundred Riss battleships were in the solar system. They had taken possession of most of the mountain areas on the various planets and moons, and were busily consolidating their positions.

There had been no effective resistance. Army units, when cornered or ordered to fight, were wiped out. Human civilians who were sighted by the enemy, or who had been unlucky enough to be on the scene of a landing, were blasted to a man.

Immediately after their arrival, the invaders had made a mass attack on nearly half a hundred cities. About two million people were caught by the hellish atomic explosions; so the report went. The rest successfully reached their farm havens, and were safe.

For more than a year, no bombs had fallen. And even in those first deadly days, not a single lowland city was attacked. The Riss concentrated their colossal bombs on foothill cities and on mountain cities located less than thirty-five hundred feet above sea level.

The stupid and the thoughtless among the refugees noted both the commissions and the omissions. And for months they had been trickling back to the undamaged centers. There was need for swift action. And yet—Clane shook his head.

And yet he operated within the limitations imposed by his human as well as enemy environment.

"We'll set up defenses around the estate first," Clane told Czinczar. "It'll take about a week to put up the resonators and the molecular weapons, and start work on the caves. While that's being done, I'll try to get my spy organization together."

Everything took time, thought and the most careful preparation.

❖❖❖

Liftboats hovered in the night. Shadowy figures stood on the ground. Small craft floated down out of the blackness towards lights arranged in a certain pattern. Such rendezvous were old in Clane's experience, and he took them calmly. For years he had dealt through agents, listened to accounts of scenes witnessed by other eyes than his own, and he had a practiced skill in building up the resulting pictures, so that many times he could see things that the spy had not noticed.

Each meeting with an agent followed the same general pattern. The individual remained in the darkness so far as other agents, also on the scene, were concerned. There were slaves present to insure that the men and women were fed, but the meal itself was handed through a narrow slit of a window to a pair of hands that reached out of the night. The meal was eaten by a shadowy human being who stood in a thin lineup of his own kind. It was seldom, however, that individuals spoke to each other.

Each agent reported first to three officers. The report was verbal and delivered out of the darkness to the officers, who themselves remained hidden by the darkness. If even one of the tribunal decided that the story merited further consideration, the spy was passed on to Clane.

The next step was precautionary. The agent was searched, if a man, by a man; if a woman, by a woman. Most of the agents were old at the game and knew each step, so that they offered no objections when they entered Clane's private patrol craft and for the first time during the interview, had to show their faces.

Gradually, in this way, as the night passed, the over-all picture of the past two and a half years came through to Clane.

The last agent finally departed, and the faint sound of their small craft was scarcely more than a whisper in the intense darkness that settled down after the false dawn. Clane returned to the spaceship and considered what he had learned.

Lilidel and Calaj knew of his return. It showed swift spy work on the part of their supporters. But the information pleased Clane. They would spread the news of his reappearance much faster than he could do.

He was not surprised to learn that Lilidel had already regarded him as a deadlier danger than the Riss. To her, government was a personal possession. The fact that she herself had no idea what to do in this national emergency meant nothing. Regardless of consequences, she intended to cling to power.

Since it would take time to reestablish his contacts, Clane presumed that she would have time to take some action. With all the thoroughness of which he was capable, he set about the task of plugging up possible loopholes in his defense system.

To begin with, he concentrated on the refugee village.

23

The business manager of his estate, a former slave, had registered for him under the refugee law. The manager, who had in his day been a high Martian government official, reported that at the time of registration, more than a year before, he had noticed nothing unusual in the way his papers had been handled. The picture he gave of hastily organized clerical staffs working in confusion was typical of other areas where the same law had been introduced— without Lilidel being aware of it—and it satisfied Clane up to a point.

Because of the acreage of his estate, he had been assigned three hundred families, totaling one thousand ninety-four persons. It was a village full of strange people. When he went down to look them over on the day after his return to the estate, it seemed to Clane that he had never seen such a motley crowd. On inquiry, he discovered that he had been assigned the inhabitants of a section of a single street. On the surface, that looked fair and seemed to indicate that his farm was being handled as objectively as were the others. There was a full quota of human beings, sensible and foolish, short and long, fat and thin, clever and stupid—an ordinary cross section of any city's population.

Clane decided not to let it go at that. It took only one assassin to kill one or more people. Such a man would need only one opportunity, whether gained by chance or design. It was too easy to kill, and no man or woman in history had ever recovered from that particular type of catastrophe.

He concentrated the attention of nearly half his spies and slowly, as the days passed and the reports came in, realized that he had given them an assignment which could never be satisfactorily completed.

He had a file made up for each family and in each file he had trained clerks enter the information that came in about individual members of the family. It became apparent that part of each person's life history was not available.

In his determination to penetrate that darkness, he organized a bulletin board newspaper, full of chatty information about the doings and backgrounds of the members of the group. As the new village grew, his spies, taking on the role of friendly reporters, interviewed each adult and each child over ten years old, ostensibly for the bulletin. Some of the spies considered the age limit too low, but Clane was insistent. The history of Linn, particularly of more ancient times, was full of accounts of the bravery of very young people in times of emergency.

His hope was that he might isolate the assassin. He looked for hesitation and reluctance in answering questions. He wanted the diffident refugee marked off as a person who had possibly murderous reasons for withholding information.

As it turned out, the agent listed as suspects seventeen men and nine women. Clane had them arrested and set down in a more distant area.

And still he was not satisfied.

"It isn't," he told Madelina unhappily, "that I'm abandoning the proposition that people must rise above themselves in this crisis. But a few uncooperative individuals could cause disaster."

She patted his arm affectionately. She said, "What a man you are for worrying."

She was a slim, straight girl at this time, with a fine, sensitive face. All her emotional intensity remained, but it was concentrated now in the normal channels of husband and child. She embraced him abruptly, impulsively.

"Poor sweetheart, you have to think of so many things, don't you?"

❖❖❖

That day, also, went by without incident. Through his spies, Clane watched every horizon of human activity. The reports from Golomb, where the government was, stifled once and for all any will he might have had to cooperate with the Lilidel group.

The incredible Calaj had brought back the games. Men and animals were once more dying in the arena to provide sport for the court. At night, government buildings were converted into theaters and dance halls. Often, the merrymakers were still at play when the clerks arrived in the morning to begin work. The Lord Adviser had taken an interest in the army. Thousands of men were being drilled, so that they could assume formations which spelled out phrases like "The People Love Calaj."

Over in the mountains, a second Riss expedition arrived. Thousands of monsters disembarked. Czinczar, who reported the arrival, sent along an appeal:

❖❖❖

Your excellency:

How are you going to drive these creatures from the solar system if you do not even have control of Linn? Please take action without delay.

❖❖❖

Clane replied that he was training clerks for the first phase of government seizure. He pointed out that it was an intricate task. "A leader," he wrote, "has to work with human beings. This limits all his actions and controls his destiny. As you must know better than most people, I have tried to transcend such obstacles. I have thought in terms inviting men to do their duty to the race, and disregard such things as who shall be boss and who shall obey. I still hope that we will have such a spontaneous demonstration of will-to-cooperate for the benefit of all such as has not been seen in generations.

"At the moment, in spite of the risks, I am moving forward a step at a time. I agree with you that it is essential that I have control of the state for some years."

He had barely dispatched the message when one of his guards in a patrol craft made an emergency landing in the garden, and reported that a score of Linnan spaceships were approaching.

Even as he told of them, the dark shapes of the large naval vessels grew visible in the distance.

24

They came in four lines of five each, and settled on the ground about four and a half miles from the house. They had landed in such a way that their air locks faced away from the estate. For a while there was a great deal of activity that Clane couldn't see. He guessed that men were disembarking.

Just how many men, it was difficult to decide. On space flights, these big machines carried complements of only two hundred officers and soldiers. But on such short trips as this fifteen hundred or two thousand per ship was possible.

It quickly became apparent that a very large number of men indeed was involved, for within an hour hundreds of groups of them swarmed over the hill and began to spread out in an enveloping movement.

Clane watched them uneasily through his Riss vision system. It was one thing to have a defense system that could kill every man now approaching. It was quite another actually to kill them.

The possibility that he might have to do so brought a return of his old anger. He wondered grimly if the human race deserved to be perpctuated. As in the past, he decided in favor; and so there seemed nothing to do but to warn the approaching army.

Both the molecular beams and the resonators were set to react in their terrific fashion at two miles against all craft to which they were not attuned.

He flew alone to that perimeter, taking a loud-speaker hookup with him. He set the Riss liftboat to follow a course just within the death line.

At a hundred yards, he was not completely out of range of a good archer, but the metal walls of the machine would give ample protection.

The men nearest him were now little more than two hundred yards away. Clane rumbled out his first warning. In a clear, mechanical voice, he described the line of death, indicating trees, shrubs and other landmarks that constituted the perimeter. He urged those within hearing to send warnings to soldiers farther away. He finished that first urgent message with the words:

"Test this. Send animals across, and watch the result."

He didn't wait for their reaction, but flew on to make sure that other groups also received the same warning. When he turned back, he saw that it had stopped them about fifty yards from the demarking line. Consultations took place. Presently, messengers in small, fast ships flew from group to group. Satisfied, Clane settled to the ground, and waited.

There was another pause in the activity of the groups of soldiers, and then a small patrol ship landed among the nearest group. Traggen climbed out of it and stood with a megaphone in his hands. He started forward, but he must have known of the warnings for he stopped after proceeding less than ten yards. He raised the megaphone and shouted:

"The Lord Adviser Calaj, who is personally commanding these troops, orders you to surrender immediately."

It was interesting to Clane that as far as the eye could see there was no sign of anyone even remotely resembling the Lord Adviser Calaj. He said, "You tell his excellency, the Lord Adviser Calaj, that his uncle would like to talk to him."

Traggen said coldly, "His excellency does not talk to outlaws."

Clane said quickly, "Have I been declared an outlaw?"

Traggen hesitated. Clane did not wait for him to answer.

❖ ❖ ❖

He called, "Please inform his excellency, Lord Calaj, that unless he comes forward to talk to me, I shall ride along the perimeter here telling the truth about him to the soldiers."

Clane paused with a wry smile. "I forgot," he said, "you can't tell him that, can you? Better put it like this. Tell him that I threaten to fly along and tell *lies* about him to the soldiers."

He finished, "I'll give him ten minutes, so you'd better hurry."

Traggen hesitated, and then turned and went back to his machine. It rose from the ground, and flew back towards the ridge more than two miles away. Clane did not bother to watch it land. He flew up and down in front of the soldiers, pausing before each group to tell a ribald joke about himself. In analyzing the popularity of certain of his officers, during the barbarian war, he had assumed that no officer could actually be liked for himself alone—the average soldier simply didn't have the opportunity to find out much about the real character of his commander.

So it must be something else. He watched and listened, and finally selected a number of coarse jests which poked fun at authority. Simply by telling one or two of them, he changed the attitude toward him of most of the soldiers who heard his pep talks. According to reports, he came to be regarded as a good fellow. He wasn't, but that made no difference. The so-called humor was a magic key to their good will.

Civilians, naturally, had to be handled differently, a fact which old soldiers sometimes forgot.

The question was, would these men, who had been with Jerrin on the planets, who knew little or nothing of what Lord Clane Linn had done against Czinczar, and who were now supposed to capture him—would they also laugh at his jokes?

They did, almost to a man. Entire groups rocked with laughter. A few officers tried sternly to stop them, but they were outnumbered. At the end of ten minutes, Clane returned to his original stopping point, satisfied that he had done what he could to turn the men in his favor.

Just what good it would do was another matter.

He forgot that, for a long, strange and wonderful procession was approaching.

First of all came scores of brightly colored patrol craft. They gyrated as they flew, like a well organized pyrotechnic display. In a final chromatic swirl, they gracefully took up positions directly in front of Clane. It was skillfully, even brilliantly, done, so that not until they were stationary did he realize their new position spelled out one word. The word was "C A L A J."

And now came the most wondrous machine of all—a large, open-decked patrol ship. It was a flower float, gorgeously done up. A little ornate, perhaps, a little out of key, and rather too magnificent for its purpose—Clane assumed that its purpose was to set off the Lord Adviser.

That was an error in judgment on Calaj's part. He was hardly noticeable. He had selected a bright uniform that blended in rather well with the flowers. The red coat could have been a design of carnations or roses, or any one of a dozen flowers. The blue and yellow striped trousers were well matched by nearly half a score of similarly colored floral decorations.

It seemed clear that the new Lord Adviser had already achieved for himself the dangerous environment where no on dared to advise him.

As Clane watched, the colorful monstrosity of a ship settled to the ground. Other craft landed all around it, and presently Traggen came forward with a megaphone.

"His excellency, Lord Calaj in person, orders you to surrender."

The farce was to continue.

❖❖❖

Clane answered, loudly enough for Calaj to hear, "Tell the child in the flower box that I want to talk to him."

As Traggen turned indecisively back to the flower float, Clane saw Calaj pick up a megaphone. A moment later his shrill voice commanded nearby soldiers to go forward and seize Clane.

"Have no fear," Clane finished boldly. "His only power is that of hypnosis, and you don't have to worry about that. I've got a cage here for him. Lock him inside it, and bring him to me."

Clane smiled to himself, grimly. Calaj had apparently explained to himself why he had been so subservient the last time he and his uncle had met. Hypnosis. It was a simple method for covering up weakness.

Clane waited for the reaction to the boy's commands.

Both the soldiers of the group and their officers seemed uncertain. There was no display of dash and *élan*, no eager surge forward to show the commander in chief that here were men ready and willing to die for him. The officers gazed unhappily at Traggen, but if they expected him to help them, they were mistaken. Traggen snatched up his megaphone, and bellowed through it:

"You will obey the commands of your Lord Adviser, or suffer the consequences."

That brought action. A dozen soldiers, with one officer in command, ran toward the flower ship and removed the cage from it. A patrol vessel darted forward, and the cage was put aboard. The men climbed over the railing, and the boat darted toward Clane.

As it reached the death perimeter, there was a puff of flame. Where the boat had been, a haze of ashes settled slowly toward the ground.

"Next!" said Clane implacably.

There was a pause, and then an angry shout from Calaj. "Hypnosis," he yelled at another group of men. "Pay no attention. Go in there and get him."

The men hung back, but their officers seemed in some curious way to have accepted Calaj's explanation. Savagely, they ordered their men into patrol boats, and, being Linnan officers, they climbed in with them. Whatever blindness afflicted them, it had nothing to do with lack of courage.

This time two boats came forward, and were destroyed in that instantaneous fashion.

Clane spoke through his loudspeaker hookup into the silence: "Traggen, the atom gods will continue to defend me against all the attacks you can mount. If you want to save your legion, try to convince his excellency that I have no control over this tragedy. I can merely warn you that the gods themselves will protect me against anything that you and he and all the foolish people who raised him to power can do against me. Take heed!"

Calaj must have heard, because he shrilled: "The army will attack in one group. We'll overwhelm this traitor's hypnotic tricks."

To Clane, it was a dismaying command. He had hoped that even the boy would realize the futility of further attack. But apparently that was too much to expect. Now, it was up to him to choose between Calaj and the army. The repercussions that would follow if he were actually forced to kill the youth were unpredictable. It might seriously slow down the pattern he had set himself for taking over the government.

At the moment, one possibility remained to be explored.

He settled himself at the weapon control board of the Riss lift-boat. The aiming devices spun and pointed as he manipulated them with the deftness of much practice.

A spume of blue flame gashed the grass beside Calaj's gorgeously be-flowered craft.

❖ ❖ ❖

Through his microphone, he called derisively, "Your excellency, does it feel like hypnosis when it's this close?"

The grass was burning. Even from where Clane watched, the soil looked fused.

In the flowery float, Calaj climbed to his feet and lazily walked to the side of his craft, and looked down at the flames. Then he raised his megaphone.

"You just have to look at them," he said, "and they disappear." His voice went up: "Attack the traitor!"

It was a rather magnificent bluff. Somehow, out of the depths of confusion that was in him, the boy had dredged the outer appearance of confidence that no leader could be without if he hoped to operate with a field army.

Carefully, Clane aimed. The side of the craft opposite Calaj flared with a ravenous fire. The heat must have been terrific, for the two pilots tumbled out of their seats, and dived over the front of the boat. Their clothes were smoking.

Calaj cringed, but did not immediately budge. Clane was shaken. His hope of an easy solution was fading; and the Lord Adviser's bravery was having its effect. If Calaj were killed now, he could well be regarded as having died a hero's death.

Clane hesitated. The next step had to be the decisive one. If he aimed even a few feet too close, Calaj would either die or be desperately injured.

Clane spoke into his microphone: "Calaj," he said, "I suggest that you suddenly decide it isn't hypnosis, and say that further action must await study of the situation."

The suggestion was fortunately timed. The fire was spreading.

Most of the flowers at the front and side were burning, and the flames had caught firmly on what must be a wooden deck. A gust of smoke engulfed Calaj, and there was evidently heat in it, for he retreated a few feet, and began to cough just like any person breathing smoke instead of air.

He made the mistake, then, of putting a handkerchief over his mouth. And that seemed to convince him that his bluff could not be carried on.

With surprising dignity, he lowered himself over the side of the boat, walked clear of the fire—and arrogantly motioned Traggen to come to him.

There was a brief consultation, after which Calaj climbed into one of the colorful patrol boats that had accompanied him. The machine took off, and headed towards the distant line of spaceships. Traggen called over the commanders of the nearest groups of soldiers, and there were more consultations, after which the officers rejoined their units.

The army began to withdraw. In about an hour and a half there was not a man in sight. Just before dusk the first spaceship took off. One by one the others followed. In the gathering darkness, it was hard to decide just when the last ship departed. But one thing seemed clear. The battle was over.

He had thought the problem of Lilidel and Calaj was over also. But when he reached the house he found disaster. A stretcher had just been carried up to the patio.

On it lay the corpse of Madelina.

25

In death, she looked like a young girl asleep, her hair slightly disheveled, her body, slack, her arms limply cradling her head.

Clane looked down at her, and felt something of his own life go out of him. But his voice was steady as he asked, "How did it happen?"

"In the refugee village, half an hour ago."

Clane frowned over that, and it was several seconds before the reason for his puzzlement struck him. He said then, "But what was she doing down there?"

"A message came up inviting her to come and see a new baby."

"Oh!" said Clane. And though the other's voice went on, he heard nothing more for a time.

He was thinking drearily: *Of course, that would be the method.*

The Mother Madelina, the chatelaine of the estate, the lady bountiful—into all these roles Madelina had channeled her intense emotional nature. And the astute Lilidel, gazing from afar through the eyes and ears of her spies, had realized the potentialities. A frontal attack to distract *his* attention, and if that didn't work, at least she would have struck one deadly blow. Or perhaps the attack on him had been Calaj's idea, and Lilidel had merely utilized the opportunity.

He grew aware again of the voice of the guard's captain making his report. "Your excellency," the officer was saying, "she insisted on going. We took all possible precautions. Guards went into the house, and found the woman, her husband and the baby. When the Lady Madelina entered the bedroom, the mother of the baby said, 'Do we have to have all these soldiers in here?' Immediately, the Lady Madelina pushed the guards into the outer room, and closed the door. She must have been stabbed the moment the door was closed, for she uttered no cry. She died without knowing it."

"And the assassin?" Clane asked drably.

"We became suspicious in less than a minute. Some of our soldiers broke open the door. Others ran outside. The murderers were very skillful. The husband had gone to the back of the house where there was a patrol boat. The woman must have climbed out of the window. They were out of sight before we could commandeer another boat, or reach any of our own ships. The pursuit is already on, but I shall be surprised if it is successful."

Clane doubted it, too. "Have they been identified yet?"

"Not yet. But they must have been refugees, planted in the village for just such a purpose."

He had the grave dug on the hill where Joquin, his long dead tutor, was buried. On the headstone was engraved the epitaph:

❖❖❖

MADELINA CORGAY LINN
Beloved Wife of Clane
And Mother of Braden

❖❖❖

After the burial, he sat for a timeless period on the grass beside the grave, and for the first time considered his own responsibility in the assassination. He could have taken more precautions.

He abandoned that line quickly, for it was fruitless. One man could do only so much.

His final conclusion was simple: He was back in Linn, with all the deadly intrigue that implied. In spite of all his skill, Lilidel and Calaj had successfully worked an old trick on him. They had done so on the eve of his attempt to take over the government.

There seemed nothing to do but carry through with the plan.

❖❖❖

Lord Clane Linn set up his headquarters in a village. The village was located a mile from the outskirts of Golomb, the town where the government had taken refuge.

He established his office in a large one-story house that sprawled comfortably back from a little dirt road. There were tall trees around the house, and in their shelter many tents were swiftly erected. A huge barn at the back of the house was big enough to hold numerous small aircraft.

On the other side of the dirt road was a many-storied inn with a capacity of more than a hundred people, and dining room space to feed hundreds.

Clane set up a night and day patrol of Riss liftboats. With their terrific fire power they dominated all approaches to the village.

Guards patrolled the fields and roads. Clerks in great numbers began to arrive the first day, and each day there were more of them. Mostly, they were from his own estate, but some were hired locally. By the second day, he had organized a pool of a hundred messenger craft, and he was ready to start work.

From the beginning he made literally no mistakes intellectually. His tremendous experience stood him in good stead. On the level of action, he did the right thing almost automatically, almost without thinking.

Physically, it was a different story. He was tired all the time.

He ignored the symptoms. He forced himself to prolonged effort.

And on that second day he wrote one letter, and dispatched a hundred copies of it over the planet to men who had been his leading supporters. His words were friendly but firm. He suggested that all those in authoritative positions submit copies to him of any reports they made to the government, and that they pass on to him all official orders or documents which they, in turn, received.

His letter contained no direct suggestion that he was usurping the function of the government, but the implication must have been plain. Within a few hours answering messages began to arrive from the nearest provinces. Nearly three quarters of the replies were statements of unconditional allegiance. The rest took the same attitude but more cautiously.

Before night of that second day several score great men came personally to congratulate him on his action, and to swear that they would support him to the death.

Hour by hour the excitement and tension mounted. Clane retired late, and though he fell asleep almost immediately, he dreamed strange, terrifying dreams of his childhood. All through that long night, he tossed and turned restlessly. And in the morning he wakened with the feeling that he had not slept at all.

He emerged from his bedroom, feeling worn out even as the long day began.

He found that messages had poured in continuously throughout the hours of darkness. These were from the more remote districts. From the number of them, it seemed to Clane that each person to whom he had written must have advised dozens of other supporters in his territory.

By mid-morning the avalanche of messages made it necessary to take over part of the inn, and hurriedly to fly more clerks from his estate.

❖ ❖ ❖

Clane ate lunch with a sense of victory. From where he sat at the window of the inn restaurant, he could see men coming and going, and converted pleasure and military craft flying low over the trees. It seemed as if every minute a machine was landing or leaving.

Here and there makeshift buildings were being hastily put up, as able administrators took *all* the necessary steps to fit themselves into the pattern of his actions.

Shortly after lunch, Clane sent out his second letter, this time to governors, government officials and important personages who had not previously supported him. It was differently worded than the first. Coolly, curtly, he advised the recipients of the location of his headquarters. He ended his note with the directive:

Please be advised that duplicates of all documents which you submit to Calaj must in future be sent to me. You will also forward any messages or documents which you receive from the Calaj government, after first taking a copy for your own files.

The implications of that letter would not be lost on astute individuals. Hundreds of cautious men would size up the situation and act according to their private interests and beliefs.

The response was astounding. Within two hours not only messages but the men themselves began to arrive. Patrons, governors, military commanders, staff officers, government officials—all the rest of that day and throughout the evening, Clane's small headquarters was jammed with men eager to switch their allegiance now that they were certain there was someone to whom they could switch it.

Clane went to bed that night, more exhausted than he had been at any time since Madelina's death. But the question, the doubt, that had been in his mind for so many years, was answered, was resolved.

He had struck the spark, touched the vital chord. And men had responded—as he had hoped they would.

It was time. Oh, but it was time. It was a quarter of twelve for the race of man.

But they *had* responded. He slept tensely. And woke wondering if he would have the strength to do the ten thousand things that still had to be done. In a few, brief years all these human beings must learn to accept their great role in the stellar universe.

The parade of new supporters through his office resumed shortly after dawn. As the overcrowded conditions increased, a famous Patron suggested that Clane transfer his headquarters to Golomb into a government building of more suitable size. "It will be easier that way," he urged. "There, liaison has already been established between the various departments."

Clane agreed, and announced that he would make his move the following day.

By mid-afternoon, some of the strain was off him. Ranking officials set up offices for the sole purpose of receiving new men and assigning them to their duties. It was a task which Clane had handled almost singlehanded until then.

He began to receive reports of Lilidel's bewilderment at the way government men were disappearing from the official residence. Just when she had her first inkling of the truth, Clane did not discover. But he was not too surprised when she turned up in person on the fifth morning, less than an hour before he was due to make his move to Golomb.

The man who announced her said cynically, within her hearing, "Your excellency, a woman who claims to be your sister-in-law wants to see you."

It was a cruel remark, particularly since the man who uttered it had transferred his allegiance only the day before.

"Send her in," was all Clane said.

The woman who staggered into his office was but vaguely recognizable as Lilidel. Her face was blotched. Her eyes were wide open, too wide; and the skin around them was discolored as if she had spent a sleepless night. She was furious and terrified by turns.

"You mad man!" she shrieked. "How dare you try to take over the legal government."

The phrase obsessed her. She and Calaj *were* the "legal government." It was all she could think of, and it was not until she was persuaded to sit down that she grew calm enough for Clane to disillusion her. She listened to his words with the visible fright of a person who was being sentenced to death.

Gently, Clane explained that in a crisis governments fell because they could not help themselves. "Sometimes," he went on, "when a weak ruler does not interfere too much with the power of efficient subordinates, his government can survive a minor storm, but in time of national danger an inadequate government tumbles like a house of cards."

Towards the end of his explanation, she must have stopped listening, for she began to shout again, about what she was going to do to the traitors.

"I've ordered Traggen to execute them all," she said in a voice that trembled with the violence of her fury.

Clane shook his head, and said quietly, "I also sent an order to Traggen this morning. I ordered him to bring Calaj here to me, alive, today. Let us see whose command he will obey."

Lilidel stared at him for a moment. Then she shook her head wonderingly and mumbled, "But we're the *legal* government."

Her next action indicated what she thought Traggen's choice would be. Her eyes closed. Her head sagged. Slowly, she crumpled to the floor at Clane's feet.

❖❖❖

Calaj, when he was brought in late in the afternoon, was insolent. He sat down in a chair. He leaned back. He said, "Do the gods still love me, uncle?"

Clane was fascinated. He had watched such one-sided growth as this before. It showed how human beings responded to a new environment. For nearly three years, Calaj had been nominally Lord Adviser. With the possible exception of Lilidel, the people who had put him in power had all planned to use a naïve youth for their own purposes. How desperately they had been mistaken.

Clane wasted no time on the young monster. He had already sent Lilidel to a rest home that he maintained in a remote province. Now, under escort, he sent Calaj to join her.

There seemed no limits to the work that had to be done. The reports that came in, even when abbreviated for him, took time to read and time to understand. Gradually, however, even as he grew progressively more weary, the overall picture emerged.

From all that he could gather, the first phase of the Riss invasion was over. The arrival of a second horde of colonists, he was convinced, emphasized that the second phase was due to begin. It would be remorseless. It would be aimed at every large community. Ships with resonators need only fly low over the lands, and men would die by the millions.

Therefore—attack the Riss.

But he had caught a chest cold, which he seemed unable to throw off. Feeling sicker than he cared to admit, Clane headed for his estate. He settled down for what he intended to be a brief rest.

It seemed the worst thing he could have done. He coughed steadily, and almost choked with phlegm. His head ached until he could hardly think. At times his vision grew so blurred he could see only with the greatest difficulty.

It became impossible for him to retain solid foods. He was forced on a diet of liquids only. On the evening of the second day, sicker than he had ever been before in his life, he went to bed.

He was still convinced that all he needed was rest.

❖❖❖

This, Clane told himself shakily, *is ridiculous.*

It was morning of his third day abed. Through the open window he could hear the sounds of men working in the garden. Twice, during a period of minutes, a woman's musical laughter floated in on the still, sweet air.

His eyes ached, his body felt feverish and chilled by turns. He was miserable to the point of not caring what happened to him. He had the vague feeling that he had made a mistake in coming back to the estate; the *Solar Star* would have been a better haven. Better equipped, more trained chemists. Something might have been done for him.

The idea never came into sharp focus. It was just something he should have done. All he could do now was sweat it out.

He had a passing thought: *The trouble is, I've never been sick before. I've no experience. I didn't realize that disease weakens the mind.*

He stirred wearily, lying there in the bed. *I've got to get well*, he urged himself. *I'm the only one who can drive the Riss from Earth. If I should die—* But he dared not think of that.

Wryly, he pictured himself, the despised mutation risen to the greatest office in the empire of Linn. And in the hour of victory against a deadly enemy struck down into his bed. Here he was, held helpless by a weakness within his own body greater than any power that he could ever wield outside.

And the victory was fading, slipping, evaporating, with him.

Shaking his head, very dispirited, he turned on his side and went to sleep.

❖❖❖

He dreamed that he was a child of four back in the gardens of the Central Palace in the days of the Lord Leader Linn. And that he was being chased by the other children. In the nightmare, his one hope was that he would be able to control the sphere of energy before they could catch him.

The sphere, symbol of stupendous power, the almost godlike sphere—

Even in the dream he knew that both spheres, the one Czinczar had returned to him and the one they had taken from the little men, were far from the estate. And yet, as he ran in breathless terror, he tried to bring the sphere under his control. His mind seemed incapable of forming the cue thought.

The boys were closer. When he looked back, he could see their glittering eyes, their lips parted eagerly. Even their savage shouts floated out to him across the years, and echoed in his mind with all the old impact.

And then, just as their outstretched fingers snatched at him, just as utter despair seized on him, he spoke aloud the cue word for the sphere.

He woke up, perspiring with fear, but almost instantly he slept again. And once more the boys were after him. He realized, simply, that he had been wrong in trying to say the cue word. What he really wanted was to get to the black box that normally contained the sphere.

He reached it, and ecstatic with joy, started to climb into it. He knew—somehow he knew—if he crawled inside, the other boys would not notice him. He snuggled deep into the box—it was deeper than he remembered it—and he was sinking into a curious shadowless darkness when he thought sharply: *What am I doing here? Where is this leading me?*

Once more he woke up, more calmly this time. He thought with a bleak objectivity, *In that dream I chose death as an escape.*

For a long time, he pondered the implications. And then, very slowly and painfully, he pushed the covers aside. He sat up, nauseated but determined. *Sick or not*, he thought, *I'm getting up.*

He would go aboard the *Solar Star*. In the great chemical laboratories of the ship, he had during the long voyage found time to mix some of the drugs described in some old medical books he had found. He had tried them out first on the obviously dying, then cautiously on the sick. Some of them had been remarkably effective against respiratory diseases.

❖ ❖ ❖

A nurse came into the room. He looked up at her blurrily. "My clothes," he mumbled, "bring my clothes."

"Your excellency," she stammered, "you mustn't. You're sick. You must get back into bed."

She didn't wait for a reply. She hurried out of the room. A minute later, the estate physician came running in. He rushed over to the bed, and Clane felt himself shoved irresistibly onto his back. The sheets were drawn up over his body.

He protested with momentary fire. "Doctor, I want my clothes. I've got to go to the ship—" His voice faded to a mutter.

Above him, the blurred figure of the doctor turned to the blurred figure of the nurse. "Ship," he says. "What does he want to do? Get into a fight."

There was a pause. Then the doctor spoke again, "Nurse, bring in the other women, and give him a cold bath. I think he needs a shock."

The water felt vaguely numb, as if it was not quite reaching him. He accepted the sensation passively, but he thought with a measure of sardonicism: *I'm caught here. I can't get away. They'll watch me night and day. They know all the petty cunnings of an invalid. And somehow at this eleventh hour my rank means nothing.*

He couldn't remember being carried back to bed, but suddenly he was under the sheets again. They felt heavier now, as if more weight had been added. He wondered if they were trying to hold him down by sheer load of blankets. Above him, one of the nurses said:

"He's asleep. That's good. I think he'll be better when he wakes up."

He didn't feel as if he was sleeping. Nor was he exactly in a dream. He seemed to be standing on a green lawn, and curiously Madelina was there beside him, smiling and saying, "I'll be good for you. You need somebody like me."

He remembered that with a faint smile. His smile faded, and he turned and said to Jerrin, "I'm afraid this means that Czinczar is the next Lord Leader. The Linns are going down. All the struggle was for nothing . . . nothing—"

Far away, somebody said, "The Patronate has been advised. A Council of Nine has been set up to govern the empire—"

He was alone on the green lawn, walking in the fresh air, breathing deeply. There was a forest ahead, with shadows under the trees. Figures flitted from bole to bole. He seemed to recognize them, and yet he couldn't decide who they were.

He came to the edge of the forest, hesitated; and then, aware of Madelina close behind him, walked on into the shadows.

❖❖❖

He awakened, and opened his eyes.

It was as if vistas had sealed shut, fantastic depths receded behind him. He felt relaxed and at ease. His vision was clear, his body cool and comfortable. Clane turned his head.

Czinczar, haggard and hollow-cheeked, sat in a deep chair beside the bed. The sight of him shocked the beginning of memory in Clane. He remembered that drugs had been brought him from the ship.

He lay in bed, well but weak. And he said to Czinczar, "How long did it take?"

"Eighteen days."

The barbarian smiled wanly. "We had to fight our way in here," he said. "When I heard that you were dying, I sent an ultimatum to your doctor. When he didn't answer, I came down with three of your trained pharmacists, and an army. Since all your resonators were from the ship, and tuned to us, we just moved in."

He broke off. "How come you had such a stupid ignoramus around? After the medical work you did on the ship coming back here—"

Clane was apologetic. "I'd forgotten he was around here. I was so busy when we first came back. Besides, I was ill and lacking in sense."

A thought struck him. He stared at Czinczar with a sharper appreciation of the implications of the barbarian's presence. Here was a leader schooled in bloodthirsty tactics. And yet he had come selflessly to help his chief rival for power in the solar system.

Czinczar seemed to realize what he was thinking. "Your excellency," he said grimly, "for eighteen days I have kept a vigil beside your bed because I have no better answer to the problem of the Riss than all the fools of Linn—out there." He gestured sweepingly with one hand. He went on, "It seems incredible, but the human race can only be saved by one man, and how *he* hopes to do it I cannot even imagine."

He paused. In a curious way, he looked so tense that Clane was electrified. The barbarian nodded bleakly. "You're guessing right," he said. "The Riss war is on. And already, all the old plans I had for resisting them are beginning to look like the stupidity of a diseased mind."

He broke off. "For six days," he said simply, "hundreds of Riss battleships have been attacking human settlements of every size. I couldn't even estimate for you what the losses have been. Men and women and children are dying in agony. Unquestionably this seems to be the second and last phase."

Once more his tone changed. "Your excellency," he said harshly, "we must wipe out these monsters to the last individual."

"No!" said Clane.

He sat up slowly, conscious of his weakness. But his eyes met the other's bloodshot gaze steadily.

"Czinczar," he said, "tomorrow morning we drop a picturized ultimatum giving the Riss a month to get out of the solar system, and to accept the sharing idea as a permanent policy."

"And if they refuse?" There was a sharp doubt in the barbarian's voice. He added a protest, "Your excellency, in one month, fifty million people will be—"

Clane went on as if he hadn't heard: "Beginning about two days from now, we start destroying their forces and their civilization everywhere. The exact time depends on how soon I can get up."

He shook his head savagely at Czinczar. "Don't get alarmed. I've never felt saner. I'm ready and in position at last. I tell you, my friend, I see things that no man or brain has ever seen before. All the preliminary tests have been made, although I've still got to take some special electronic photographs."

"And then what?"

"A part at least of the innermost meaning of matter and energy will be revealed."

26

For a minute after he entered, Clane was unobserved. He took the opportunity to look over his audience.

It was a distinguished assembly gathered there in the great physics laboratory aboard the magnificent—formerly Riss, now Linnan—warship, *Solar Star*. The Temple Scientists present looked bright and clean in their white dress robes. Government officials were amazingly well garbed; they were top men, of course, and would have control of available materials.

Of all the guests, the great nobles looked the shabbiest. Their estates had been virtually taken over by hordes of refugees, and it was the common practice during the crisis to maintain an appearance of equal suffering. For some reason, as Clane had observed during the barbarian invasion, this seemed to satisfy the landless, the moneyless and the witless about equally.

People were suddenly observing him. The babble of conversation died. Lord Clane hesitated a moment longer, and then walked through the cordon of soldiers who had been assigned to protect the line of machines from curious visitors. He switched on the power in the all-energy microscope, the all-energy camera, and the other instruments that would be brought into play. And then he turned to face the guests, the last of whom were settling into their chairs.

Clane motioned the porters to bring forward the sphere and its container. When it had been set in its proper place under one of the glistening machines, he pressed a button. A television camera poked into the sphere as it rolled by, then moved backward and forward in perfect synchronization with it.

He flicked his hand over another switch; the lights went out. A huge screen glided down from the ceiling. On it appeared the stellar universe. Clane indicated the faintly glowing sphere to the right of the screen, rolling back and forth. "The scene you are gazing at is inside this," he said.

The idea must have been too new for them to grasp. Or perhaps they rejected his explanation even as he finished speaking. Nobody seemed surprised, which was not normal.

He waited till the stability of that blazing mass of stars had been established. And then, simply by thinking it so, started the entire mass into motion past the camera. At first the movement was not apparent. And then, a blazing sun swept toward them. It grew vast on the screen, and then swiftly began to slip by. A planet, tremendously nearby, touched the edge of the screen, and rolled in closer majestically. In the distance, a moon was visible. Clane identified them.

"Our earth and our moon," he said, "and that was our sun. Let's bring them into the room, shall we?"

He didn't expect them to understand that. He shut off the camera, waited till the screen was dead, and thought for an instant. There was a collective gasp from his audience. A blazing white ball about three inches in diameter flashed into view, and moved over under the microscope viewing lens. The room was abruptly as bright as day.

❖ ❖ ❖

Clane said into the deathly stillness that followed the gasp, "Although it is hard to realize, this is our sun. Although it's impossible to see them with the naked eye, all the planets are with it. Mercury, Venus, Earth, Mars, Jupiter, and so on."

He waited, and a man said in a strained voice, "But how is that possible? We're sitting here in a ship a few miles *above* Earth."

Clane did not answer. For this was one of the basic secrets of the space-time-place continuum. The Riss had isolated a by-product in their "protector" device with its resonating energy flow, that intruded momentarily into every space-time field.

But here in the sphere and *its* byproducts must be an answer closer to the final reality than any that had ever been dreamed of.

A rational cosmology? Surely, for the first time in the history of life, people were gazing into the deeps of the meaning of things. Which came first, thought of the Universe, or the Universe itself?

The answer must be intricately interwoven into the very nature of things. Size, speed, space, *place*—all are in the understanding, not the reality. A dead man has no awareness of either. A living man can gaze a billion light-years into darkness at galaxies speeding off into still greater "distances." But he cannot easily adjust to the fourth dimensional understanding that will make it possible for him to comprehend that entire universe as a momentary thought in his own mind. It would have no size other than his own estimate, no speed except in relation to himself.

"And now"—Clane turned—"we have here an earth the size of a grain of dust. That's quite big. With an all-energy range microscope we can enlarge it hundreds of millions of times. That will give us a vast globe to look at, which we can only hope to see in small segments."

He was aware of scores of eyes watching him as he bent over the instrument. He made the necessary adjustments, then straightened, and said:

"I've fitted the machine with an infra needle, which I can describe to you only by giving you some meaningless figures. The Riss used them to pierce objects of one-ten-millionth of a millimeter. I shall use it as one might use a stabbing knife."

He paused to let the mystifying words sink in. Then he said, "Now, I bring our tiny sun and its planets into position, where the microscope can be concentrated on Earth."

He peered into the instrument's eyepiece. Without looking up, he said, "I can see Earth below. It does not appear to be spinning, and yet its speed of rotation must be about twelve thousand a second. That would be in proportion to its size. I haven't figured it out, because what I intend to do will depend on automatic machinery.

"The fact that thousands of twenty-four hour days seem to be passing every second is an appearance only. There is an unbreakable relationship between ourselves and that Earth. The timing will be exact."

He went on, "You may ask, how can I possibly hope to see anything on an object moving at that terrific speed of rotation. Especially since it's making thirty circuits of the sun every 'second.' My answer is that the Riss have supplied us with all the necessary automatic devices. It's a matter of synchronization, impossible for the human mind, but simple for energy circuits. I did a little practicing on the Moon yesterday just to make sure that the theory was sound."

He straightened, picked up a pile of photographs, and carried them to the nearest person. "Start them around," he said.

He ignoring the oh-ing and ah-ing that started almost at once. Back in front of the towering microscope, he picked up the thread of his explanation.

"Speed is of little or no account when these relays are in action. This Riss camera takes millions of pictures a second. The pictures are not photographed on film, but are stored in a tube. And the way they can be used goes something like this:

"Yesterday, as you may recall, we visited the mountain cities, and looked down on them, one after another, from a safe distance. What you don't know is that I took photographs of each one and stored them in the tube."

He had been peering into the eyepiece as he spoke. Now, once more he straightened. "At this moment, the camera is taking pictures of Earth every time it passes underneath. When I press home this lever, it will take pictures only of the area of that tiny globe which compares in structure to one of the photographs I took yesterday of a Riss-controlled city."

He pressed the lever.

A shield slid between the brilliant sun and the audience, effectively dimming the screen. There was an area of brightness on the screen.

"Ah, I see it's not quite in focus," said Clane.

He made another adjustment. The result showed immediately. The bright area on the screen cleared, and became a city in a mountain setting.

A bass voice said, "Why, that's Denra."

"I thought," said Clane, "I'd give us all a ringside seat for the show."

And still, he realized, from their faint reaction, they had no idea of what was coming. It was no wonder; he had to admit that. They were witnessing the coordination of Riss and human science at its highest level—and they simply didn't have the background to grasp the stupendousness of what was about to happen.

Inexorably, he went on, "The next step is to synchronize our stabbing 'needle.' Please realize, all of you, that when used against an earth the size of a dust mote, the thrust of a 'point' one ten-millionth of a millimeter in diameter could be disastrous. The instruments must be set, accordingly, to strike a surface blow only, like this—"

On the screen, the city of Denra dissolved in a cloud of dust. Part of a mountain was indented as by a colossal hammer to a depth of about a mile.

"The beauty of it," said Clane in an even, remorseless tone, "is that there is no radioactivity, and no counterattack possible. Now, obviously we're not going to destroy our own cities unless we have to, even though they are occupied by the Riss at the moment. I think we should give the invaders a chance to think over what has happened, while we switch to another city, this time not on Earth but on the Riss planet the *Solar Star* visited. I took the necessary photographs while we were there, because even then I was thinking along these lines."

It required about a minute to bring that sun and its planets out of the sphere and under the all-energy microscope.

Clane said, "As you know, our terms have been broadcast. We used a series of pictures to tell our story. We require surrender of half the battleships that came to the solar system, cooperation in our galactic peace program—which includes mutual development of all newly discovered habitable planets and a partial sharing of many worlds already inhabited. The interstellar television mechanism, transferred from the second ship we captured, is aboard and in operation—unfortunately, the second ship itself is still out of commission. So far we have received no reply to our ultimatum. It therefore becomes necessary to convince a stubborn enemy on part of his home territory that he must co-operate or die."

He touched a button, and the Riss city on the screen dissolved as if it were made of powder. The blow seemed harder than the first one, for not only was the city squashed but the great mountain beyond it ripped apart like a piece of cloth.

"I'm setting now for an even deeper thrust," said Clane. "The reason is that we 'photographed' Riss controlled cities only on Earth and on the one Riss planet we visited. Any blows we deliver against other Riss planets marked on the captured star maps will have to be made in haphazard fashion, that is, without benefit of a preliminary 'photograph.' I think we can always hit a mountain area, but we must strike hard enough so that the effect is felt violently a hundred miles away—"

In spite of his will to calmness, his voice faltered. His audience was deathly silent, but the members could not possibly realize, as he did, the vast scope of what was happening. The Universe was tamed. Man need never again look out at the stars and feel small and insignificant. The grandeur of space-time remained as great as ever, but the veil was lifting. The days when the very mystery and size overwhelmed the wondering minds of those who gazed were not past. Yet surely it would never again be quite the same.

Clane covered his own feeling of awe by taking his time with the preliminaries to the next blow. Finally, feeling himself under control again, he said, "I imagine it will take time for them to accept the bitter reality of their defeat. We'll just have to keep on punishing them till they signal us that they are prepared to discuss terms."

Four hours went by before that signal came.

❖ ❖ ❖

A year had passed. As he walked beside Czinczar, Clane said, "It still looks ugly to me."

The two of them, Clane in a drab priestly gown and Czinczar wearing the uniform of a private in the barbarian army—a common sight around Linn these days—walked slowly up to the newly finished victory column.

Clane studied it. It stood in the great square before the Central Palace. Its construction had been voted by the Patronate, and it consisted of an enormous cube of marble on top of which an intricate scene was arranged. A man in the gown of a temple scientist stood astride two planets. High above his head, he held a third planet in his hands. He stood on his tiptoes as if reaching for something. All around his feet were other planets and some star-shaped objects.

The gown, unlike anything Clane had ever worn, was a bright gold in color. It gleamed in the afternoon sun.

The figure bore a rather striking facial resemblance to Clane, but the body was huge out of proportion to the rest of the statuary. A giant towered there.

Clane turned to speak to Czinczar, and saw that the other was watching a couple that had paused a few feet away.

"Look at that," said the man to the woman. " 'Savior of the race,' it says there. What will these ruling families think of next?"

The woman said, "Are you sure it's a member of the ruling family? Oh, there's the name up there." She moved her lips as if she were reading it to herself. Then she said, "Clane Linn. Which one is that?" They drifted off in the direction of the palace.

Clane said dryly, "Such is fame."

He saw that Czinczar was smiling. The great man was smiling. "It's a big world," he said. "Why should they know your name, or what you look like? They didn't see you do anything. Perhaps when we get a wider distribution of television, you may be recognized on every street corner."

Clane said, "I'm not arguing with you. How much thought do I give to the great men of the past? I'll divide that by ten, and assume my proper position in the hall of fame." He added, "It's good that men forget their heroes and their gods. If they didn't, life would be drab indeed for the newborn."

Czinczar said, "I'm sorry I couldn't get here in time for the unveiling. Let's sit down for a minute."

He motioned Clane to one of the hard stone benches. Presently a group of laughing girls came by. They did not even glance at the column, or at the two men who sat beneath it.

Two young men carrying artists' palettes and easels unfolded their equipment and sat down on benches across the walk from the work. They began to paint.

"What I like about it," said one, "is the way it silhouettes against the sky. If I can blur it in properly in the foreground, I think I can make a wonderful cloud scene."

"It's an atrocious work of art," said the other, "but statuary pictures have a fairly steady sale. When a new one comes along, the important thing is to get at it first. If I can place a dozen copies in the best shops, I'll have orders for hundreds of them."

They fell silent again. After several minutes, the second man came over to Clane and Czinczar. "I'm trying to draw this statue," he said, "and you two men add nothing to the scene sitting on that bench. If you don't mind, I'd like both of you to stand up and raise your right hands as if you're paying tribute to a hero. I assure you I won't take very long. I'm a fast worker, and I can sketch your likenesses in a few minutes."

He must have misread Clane's expression, for he shrugged, and said, "If you don't care to do that, I wonder if you would mind moving over to those other benches."

Czinczar glanced ironically at the Lord Leader of Linn, then he stood up. He said, "I question if my friend should pose in front of this particular statue, but I shall be very happy to do so in the position you suggested."

"Thank you," said the artist.

He went back to his easel.

THE EZWAL

Co-Operate—Or Else!

As the spaceship vanished into the steamy mists of Eristan II, Professor Jamieson drew his gun. He felt physically sick, battered, by the way he had been carried for so many long moments in the furious wind stream of the great ship. But the sense of danger held him tense there in the harness that was attached by metal cables to the now gently swaying antigravity plate above him. With narrowed eyes, he stared up at the ezwal which was peering cautiously down at him over the edge of the antigravity plate.

Its three-in-line eyes, gray as dully polished steel, gazed at him, unwinking; its massive blue head poised there alertly and—Jamieson knew—ready to jerk back the instant it read in his thoughts an intention of shooting.

"Well," said Jamieson harshly, "here we are, both of us about a hundred thousand years from our respective home planets. And we're falling down into a primitive jungle hell that you, with only your isolated life on Carson's Planet to judge by, cannot begin to imagine despite your ability to read my thoughts. Even a six-thousand-pound ezwal hasn't got a chance down there—alone!"

A great, long-fingered, claw-studded paw edged gingerly over the side of the raft, flicked down at one of the four metal cables that supported Jamieson's harness. There was a bright, steely *ping*. The cable parted like rotted twine before the ferocity of that one cutting blow.

Like a stream of blurred light, the enormous arm jerked back out of sight; and then there was only the great head and the calm, unwinking eyes peering down at him. Finally, a thought penetrated to Jamieson, a thought cool and unhurried:

"You and I, Professor Jamieson, understand each other very well. Of the hundred-odd men on your ship, only you remain alive. Out of all the human race, therefore, only you know that the ezwals of what you call Carson's Planet are not senseless beasts, but intelligent beings.

"I could have stayed on the ship, and so eventually reached home. But rather than take the slightest risk of your escaping the jungle dangers below, I took the desperate chance of jumping on top of this antigravity raft just as you were launching yourself out of the lock.

"What I cannot clearly understand is why you didn't escape while I was still battering down the control-room door. There is a blurred fear-picture in your mind, but—"

Jamieson was laughing, a jarring sound in his own ears, but there was genuine amusement in the grim thoughts that accompanied it. "You poor fool!" he choked at last. "You still don't realize what you're falling down to. While you were hammering away at that door, the ship was flying over the biggest ocean on this planet. All those glints of water down there are really continuation of the ocean, and every pool is swarming with malignant beasts.

"And, somewhere ahead of us, are the Demon Straits, a body of water about fifty miles wide that separates this ocean-jungle from the mainland beyond. Our ship will crash somewhere on that mainland, about a thousand miles from here, I should say. To reach it, we've got to cross that fifty miles of *thing*-infested sea. Now you know why I was waiting, and why you had a chance to jump onto that antigravity plate. I—"

His voice collapsed in an "*ugh*" of amazement as, with the speed of a striking snake, the ezwal twisted up, a rearing, monstrous blue shape of frightful fangs and claws that reached with hideous power at the gigantic bird that dived straight down at the shining surface of the antigravity raft.

The bird did not swoop aside. Jamieson had a brief, terrible glimpse of its merciless, protruding, glassy eyes, and of the massive, hooked, pitchfork-long claws, tensing for the thrust at the ezwal; and then—

❖ ❖ ❖

The crash set the raft tossing like a chip in stormy waters. Jamieson swung with a mad, dizzy, jerky speed from side to side. The roar of the wind from the smashing power of those mighty wings was like thunder that stunned his brain with its fury. With a gasp, he raised his gun. The red flame of it reached with blazing hunger at one of those wings. The wing turned a streaky black, collapsed; and, simultaneously, the bird was literally flung from the raft by the raging strength of the ezwal.

It plunged down, down, became a blurred dot in the mist, and was lost against the dark background of ground.

Above Jamieson, the ezwal, dangerously off balance, hung poised over the edge of the raft. Four of its combination leg-arms pawed the air uselessly; the remaining two fought with bitter effort at the metal bars on top of the raft—and won. The great body drew back, until, once again, only the massive blue head was visible. Jamieson lowered his gun in grim good humor

"You see," he said, "even a bird was almost too much for us—and I could have burned your belly open. I didn't because maybe it's beginning to penetrate your head that we've got to postpone our private quarrel, and fight together if we ever hope to get out of the hell of jungle and swamp below."

The answering thought was as cold as the sleet-gray eyes that stared down at him so steadily:

"Professor Jamieson, what you *could* have done was unimportant to me who knew what you *would* do. As for your kind offer to ally yourself with me, I repeat that I am here to see you dead, not to protect your pitiful body. You will, therefore, refrain from further desperate appeals, and meet your fate with the dignity becoming a scientist."

❖ ❖ ❖

Jamieson was silent. A thin, warm, wet wind breathed against his body, bringing the first faint, obscene odors from below. The raft was still at an immense height, but the steamy mists that clung with a limp, yet obscuring strength to this primeval land had yielded some of their opaqueness. Patches of jungle and sea that, a few minutes before, had been blurred by that all-pervading fog, showed clearer now, a terrible, patternless sprawl of dark trees alternating with water that shone and flashed in the probing sunlight.

Fantastic, incredible scene. As far as the eye could see into the remote mists to the north, there was steaming jungle and foggy, glittering ocean—the endless, deadly reality that was Eristan II. And, somewhere out there, somewhere in the dimness beyond the concealing weight of steam, those apparently interminable jungles ended abruptly in the dark, ugly swell of water that was the Demon Straits!

"So," said Jamieson at last, softly, "you think you're going to get through. All your long life, all the long generations of your ancestors, you and your kind have depended entirely on your magnificent bodies for survival. While men herded fearfully in their caves, discovering fire as a partial protection, desperately creating weapons that had never before existed, always a bare jump ahead of violent death—all those millions of years, the ezwal of Carson's Planet roamed his great, fertile continents, unafraid, matchless in strength as in intellect, needing no homes, no fires, no clothing, no weapons, no—"

"You will agree," the ezwal interrupted coolly, "that adaptation to a difficult environment must be one of the goals of the superior being. Human beings have created what they call civilization, which is actually merely a material barrier between themselves and their environment, so vast and unwieldy that keeping it going occupies the entire existence of the race. Individually, man is a frivolous, fragile, inconsequential *slave*, who tugs his mite at the wheel, and dies wretchedly of some flaw in his disease-ridden body.

"Unfortunately, this monstrous, built-up weakling with his power lusts and murderous instincts is the greatest danger extant to the sane, healthy races of the Universe. He must be prevented from contaminating his betters."

Jamieson laughed curtly. "But you will agree, I hope, that there is something wonderful about an insignificant, fearful jetsam of life fighting successfully against all odds, aspiring to all knowledge, finally attaining the very stars!"

"Nonsense!" The answer held overtones of brittle impatience. "Man and his thoughts constitute a disease. As proof, during the past few minutes, you have been offering specious arguments, apparently unbiased, actually designed to lead once more to an appeal for my assistance, an intolerable form of dishonesty.

"As further evidence I need but anticipate intellectually the moment of our landing. Assuming that I make no attempt to harm you, nevertheless your pitiful body will be instantly and, thereafter, continuously in deadly danger, while I—you must admit that, though there are beasts below physically stronger than I, the difference is not so great that my intelligence, even if it took the form of cunning flight, would more than balance the weakness. You will admit furthermore—"

"I admit nothing!" Jamieson snapped. "Except that you're going to get the surprise of your life. And you're going to regret beyond all your present capacity for emotionalism the lack of those very artificialities you despise in man. I do not mean material weapons, but—"

"What you mean is unimportant. I can see that you intend to persist in this useless, mendacious type of reasoning, and you have convinced me that you will never emerge alive from that island jungle below. Therefore—"

The same, tremendous arm that a few minutes before had torn steel chain, flashed into sight and downward in one burst of madly swift gesture.

The two remaining cables attached to Jamieson's harness parted like wet paper; and so great was the force of the blow that Jamieson was jerked a hundred feet parallel to the distant ground before his long, clenched body curved downward for its terrific fall.

A thought, cool with grim irony, struck after him:

"I notice that you are a very cautious man, professor, in that you have not only a packsack, but a parachute strapped to your back. This will enable you to reach ground safely, but your landing will be largely governed by chance. Your logical mind will doubtless enable you to visualize the situation. Good-by and—bad luck!"

❖ ❖ ❖

Jamieson strained at the thin, strong ropes of his parachute, his gaze narrowed on the scene below. Through the now almost transparent mist, and somewhat to the north, was a green-brown blaze of jungle. If he could get there—

He tugged again at the ropes, and with icy speculation watched the effect, calculated the mathematical possibilities. He was falling slowly; that would be the effect of the heavy air of this planet: pressure eighteen pounds per square inch at sea level.

Sea level! He smiled wryly, without humor. Sea level was approximately where he would be in a very few minutes.

There was, he saw, no sea immediately beneath him. A few splotches of water, yes, and a straggle of trees. The rest was a sort of clearing, except that it wasn't exactly. It had a strange, grayish, repellent appearance like—

The terrible shock of recognition drained the blood from his cheeks. His mind shrank as from an unthinkably lecherous thought. In panic he tore at the ropes, as if by sheer physical strength he would draw the tantalizingly near jungle to him. That jungle, that precious jungle! Horrors it might contain, but at least they were of the future, while that hellish stuff directly below held no future, nothing but a gray, quagmire trap, thick mud choking—

Abruptly, he saw that the solid mass of trees was beyond his reach. The parachute was less than five hundred feet above that deadly, unclean spread of mud. The jungle itself—stinking, horrible jungle, blatantly exuding the sharp, evil odors of rotting vegetation, yet suddenly the most desirable of places—was about the same distance to the northwest.

To make it would require a forty-five-degree descent. Carefully, he manipulated the rope controls of the parachute. It caught the wind like a glider; the jungle drew closer, closer—

He landed triumphantly in a tiny straggle of trees, a little island separated from the main bulk of forest by less than a hundred and fifty feet.

The island was ten feet long by eight wide; four trees, the longest about fifty feet tall, maintained a precarious existence on its soggy, wet, comparatively firm base.

Four trees, representing a total of about a hundred and eighty feet. Definitely enough length. But—his first glow of triumph began to fade—without a crane to manipulate three of those trees into place, the knowledge that they represented safety was utterly useless.

Jamieson sat down, conscious for the first time of the dull ache in his shoulders, the strained tenseness of his whole body, a sense of depressing heat. He could see the sun, a white blob barely visible through the white mists that formed the atmosphere of this deadly, fantastic land.

The blur of sun seemed to fade into remoteness; a vague darkness formed in his mind; and then a sharp, conscious thought that he had been asleep.

He opened his eyes with a start. The sun was much lower in the eastern sky and—

His mind stopped from the sheer shock of discovery. Instantly, however, it came alive, steady, cool, despite the vast, first shock of amazement.

What had happened was like some fantasy out of a fairy story. The four trees, with the tattered remains of his parachute still clinging to them, towered above him. But his plan for them had taken form while he slept.

A bridge of trees, thicker, more solid than any the little island could have produced, stretched straight and strong from the island to the mainland. There was no doubt, of course, as to who had performed that colossal feat: the ezwal was standing unconcernedly on two of its six legs, leaning manlike against the thick trunk of a gigantic tree. Its thought came:

"You need have no fear, Professor Jamieson. I have come to see your point of view. I am prepared to assist you to reach the mainland and to co-operate with you thereafter. I—"

Jamieson's deep, ungracious laughter cut off the thought. "You damned liar!" the scientist said finally. "What you mean is that you've run up against something you couldn't handle. Well, that's all right with me. So long as we understand each other, we'll get along."

❖ ❖ ❖

The snake slid heavily out of the jungle, ten feet from the mainland end of the bridge of trees, thirty feet to the right of the ezwal. Jamieson, scraping cautiously toward the center of the bridge, saw the first violent swaying of the long, luscious jungle grass—and froze where he was as the vicious, fantastic head reared into sight, followed by the first twenty feet of that thick, menacing body.

Briefly, the great head, in its swaying movement, was turned directly at him. The little pig eyes seemed to glare straight into his own stunned, brown eyes. Shock held him, sheer, unadulterated shock at the incredibly bad luck that had allowed this deadly creature to find him in such an immeasurably helpless position.

His paralysis there, under those blazing eyes, was a living, agonizing thing. Tautness struck like fire into every muscle of his body; it was an instinctive straining for rigidity, unnormal and terrible—but it worked.

The fearsome head whipped aside, fixed in eager fascination on the ezwal, and took on a rigidity of its own.

Jamieson relaxed; his brief fear changed to brief, violent anger; he projected a scathing thought at the ezwal:

"I understood you could sense the approach of dangerous beasts by reading their minds."

No answering thought came into his brain. The giant snake flowed farther into the clearing; and before that towering, horned head rearing monstrously from the long, titanically powerful body, the ezwal backed slowly, yielding with a grim reluctance to the obvious conviction that it was no match for this vast creature.

Cool again, Jamieson directed an ironic thought at the ezwal:

"It may interest you to know that as chief scientist of the Interstellar Military Commission, I reported Eristan II unusable as a military base for our fleet; and there were two main reasons: one of the damnedest flesh-eating plants you ever saw, and this pretty little baby. There's millions of both of them. Each snake breeds hundreds in its lifetime, so they can't be stamped out. They're bisexual, attain a length of about a hundred and fifty feet and a weight of ten tons."

❖ ❖ ❖

The ezwal, now some fifty feet away from the snake, stopped and, without looking at Jamieson, sent him a tight, swift thought:

"Its appearance did surprise me, but the reason is that its mind held only a vague curiosity about some sounds it had heard, no clear, sharp thought such as an intention to murder. But that's unimportant. It's here; it's dangerous. It hasn't seen you yet, so act accordingly. It doesn't think it can get me, but it's considering the situation. In spite of its desire for me, the problem remains essentially yours; the danger is *all* yours."

The ezwal concluded almost indifferently: "I am willing to give you limited aid in any plan you might have, but please don't offer any more nonsense about our interdependence. So far there's been only one dependent. I think you know who it is."

Jamieson was grim. "Don't be too sure that you're not in danger.

That fellow looks muscle bound, but when he starts moving, he's like a steel spring for the first three or four hundred feet—and you haven't got that much space behind you."

"What do you mean? I can run four hundred feet in three seconds, Earth time."

Coldly, the scientist whipped out: "You could, *if you had four hundred feet in which to run.* But you haven't. I've just been forming a mental picture of this edge of jungle, as I saw it just before I landed.

"There's about a hundred and fifty feet of jungle, then a curving shore of mud plain, a continuation of this mud here. The curve swings back this way, and cuts you off neatly on this little outjutting of jungle. To get clear of the snake, you've got to dart past him. Roughly, your clearance is a hundred and fifty feet all around—and it isn't enough! Interdependent? You're damned right we are. Things like this will happen a thousand times a year on Eristan II."

There was startled silence; finally: "Why don't you turn your atomic gun on it—burn it?"

"And have it come out here, while I'm helpless. These big snakes are born in this mud, and live half their lives in it. It would take five minutes to burn off that tough head. By that time I'd be swallowed and digested."

The brief seconds that passed then were vibrant with reluctant desperation. But there could be no delay; swiftly the grudging request came:

"Professor Jamieson, I am open to suggestions—*and hurry!*"

The depressing realization came to Jamieson that the ezwal was once more asking for his assistance, *knowing* that it would be given; and yet it itself was giving no promise in return.

And there was no time for bargaining. Curtly, he projected:

"It's the purest case of our acting as a team. The snake has no real weakness—except possibly this:

"Before it attacks, its head will start swaying. That's almost a universal snake method of hypnotizing victims into paralysis. Actually, the motion is also partially self-hypnotizing. At the earliest possible moment after it begins to sway, I'll burn its eyes out—and you get on its back, *and hang on.* Its brain is located just behind that great horn. Claw your way there, and eat in while I burn—"

The thought scattered like a chaff, as the tremendous head began to move. With a trembling jerk, Jamieson snatched his gun—

It was not so much, then, that the snake put up a fight, as that it wouldn't die. Its smoking remains were still twisting half an hour later when Jamieson scrambled weakly from the bridge of trees and collapsed onto the ground.

When finally he climbed to his feet, the ezwal was sitting fifty feet away under a clump of trees, its middle legs also on the ground, its forelegs folded across its chest—and it was contemplating him.

It looked strangely sleek and beautiful in its blue coat and in the very massiveness of its form. And there was immeasurable comfort in the knowledge that, for the time being at least, the mighty muscles that rippled underneath that silk-smooth skin were on his side.

Jamieson returned the ezwal's stare steadily; finally he said:

"What happened to the antigravity raft?"

"I abandoned it thirty-five miles north of here."

Jamieson hesitated; then: "We'll have to go to it. I practically depowered my gun on that snake. It needs metal for recharging; and that raft is the only metal in bulk that I know of."

He was silent again; then softly: "One thing more. I want your word of honor that you won't even attempt to harm me until we are safely on the other side of the Demon Straits!"

"You'd accept my word?" The steel-gray, three-in-line eyes meditated on him curiously.

"Yes."

"Very well. I give it."

Jamieson shook his head, smiling darkly. "Oh, no, you don't, not as easily as that."

"I thought you said you'd accept my word." Peevishly.

"I will, but in the following phraseology." Jamieson stared with grim intentness at his mighty and deadly enemy. "I want you to swear by the sun that rises and by the green, fruitful earth, by the joys of the contemplative mind and the glory of immortal life—"

He paused. "Well?"

There was a gray fire in the ezwal's gaze, and its thought held a ferocious quality when finally it replied:

"You are, Professor Jamieson, even more dangerous than I thought. It is clear there can be no compromise between us."

"But you'll make the limited promise I ask for?"

The gray eyes dulled strangely; long, thin lips parted in a snarl that showed great, dark fangs.

"No!" Curtly.

"I thought," said Jamieson softly, "I ought to get that clear."

No answer. The ezwal simply sat there, its gaze fixed on him.

"Another thing," Jamieson went on, "stop pretending you can read all my thoughts. You didn't know that I knew about your religion. I'll wager you can only catch my sharpest idea-forms, and those particularly when my mind is focused on speech."

"I made no pretenses," the ezwal replied coolly. "I shall continue to keep you as much in the dark as possible."

"The doubt will, of course, harass my mind," said Jamieson, "but not too much. Once I accept a theory, I act accordingly. If I should prove wrong, there remains the final arbiter of my atomic gun against your strength. I wouldn't bet on the victor.

"But now"—he hunched his long body, and strode forward—"let's get going. The swiftest method, I believe, would be for me to ride on your back. I could tie a rope from my parachute around your body just in front of your middle legs and by hanging onto the rope keep myself from falling off. My only qualification is that you must promise to let me off before making any hostile move. Agreeable?"

The ezwal hesitated, then nodded: "For the time being."

Jamieson was smiling, his long, spare, yet strong face ironical.

"That leaves only one thing: What did you run up against that made you change your mind about killing me immediately? Could it have been something entirely beyond the isolated, static, aristocratic existence of the ezwal?"

"Get on my back!" came the snarling thought. "I desire no lectures, nor any further sounds from your rasping voice. I fear nothing on this planet. My reasons for coming back have no connection with any of your pitiful ideas; and it would not take much to make me change my mind. Take warning!"

Jamieson was silent, startled. It had not been his intention to provoke the ezwal. He'd have to be more cautious in the future, or this great animal, bigger than eight lions, deadlier than a hundred, might turn on him before it itself intended.

❖❖❖

It was an hour later that the long, fish-shaped spaceship swung out of the steamy mists that patrolled the skies of Eristan II. It coasted along less than a thousand feet up, cruel-looking as a swordfish with its finely pointed nose.

The explosive thought of the ezwal cut into Jamieson's brain: "Professor Jamieson, if you make so much as a single effort at signaling, you die—"

Jamieson was silent, his mind held stiff and blank, after one mental leap. As he watched, the great, half-mile-long ship sank visibly lower and, as it vanished beyond the rim of the jungle ahead, there was no doubt that it was going to land.

And then, the ezwal's thoughts came again, sly now, almost exultant:

"It's no use trying to hide it—because now that the actuality is here, I remember that your dead companions had awareness of another spaceship in the back of their minds."

Jamieson swallowed the hard lump in his throat. There was a sickness in him, and a vast rage at the incredibly bad luck of this ship coming here—now!

Miserably, he gave himself to the demanding rhythm of the ezwal's smooth gallop; and for a while there was only that odor-tainted wind, and the pad of six paws, a dull, flat flow of sound; and all around was the dark jungle, the occasional, queer *lap, lap* of treacherous, unseen waters. And it was all there, the strangeness, the terribleness of this wild ride of a man on the back of a blue-tinted, beastlike being that hated him—and knew about that ship.

At last, grudgingly, he yielded. He said snappishly, as if his words might yet snatch victory from defeat:

"Now I know, anyway, that your thought-reading ability is a damned sketchy thing. You didn't begin to suspect why you were able to conquer my ship so easily."

"Why should I?" The ezwal was impatient. "I remember now

there was a long period when I caught no thoughts, only an excess of energy tension, abnormally more than were customary from your engines. That must have been when you speeded up.

"Then I noticed the cage door was ajar—and forgot everything else."

The scientist nodded, gloom a sickish weight on him. "We received some awful buffeting, nothing palpable, of course, because the interstellars were full on. But, somewhere, there must have been a blow that knocked our innards out of alignment.

"Afterward, we watched for dangers from outside; and so you, on the inside, got your chance to kill a hundred men, most of them sleeping—"

He tensed his body ever so carefully, eyes vaguely as possible on the limb of the tree just ahead, concentrating with enormous casualness on the idea of ducking under it— Somehow, his real purpose leaked from his straining brain.

In a single convulsion of movement, like a bucking horse, the ezwal reared. Shattering violence of movement! Like a shot from a gun, Jamieson was flung forward *bang* against that steel-hard back. Stunned, dizzy, he fought for balance—and then it was over.

❖❖❖

The great animal plunged aside into a thick pattern of jungle, completely away from the protruding limb that had momentarily offered such sweet safety. It twisted skillfully between two giant trees, and emerged a moment later onto the beach of a long, glittering bay of ocean.

Fleet as the wind, it raced along the deserted sands, and then on into the thickening jungles beyond. No thought came from it, not a tendril of triumph, no indication of the tremendous victory it had just won.

Jamieson said sickly: "I made that attempt because I know what you're going to do. I admit we had a running fight with that Rull cruiser. But you're crazy if you think they mean advantage for you.

"Rulls are different. They come from another galaxy. They're—"

"Professor!" The interrupting thought was like metal in the sheer, vibrating force of it. "Don't dare try to draw your gun to kill yourself. One false move, and I'll show you how violently and painfully a man can be disarmed."

"You promised," Jamieson almost mumbled, "to make no hostile move—"

"And I'll keep that promise—to the letter, after man's own fashion, *in my own good time*. But now—I gathered from your mind that you think these creatures landed because they detected the minute energy discharge of the antigravity raft."

"Pure deduction." Curtly. "There must be some logical reason, and unless you shut off the power as I did on the spaceship—"

"I didn't. Therefore, that is why they landed. Their instruments probably also registered your use of the gun on the snake. Therefore they definitely know someone is here. My best bet, accordingly, is to head straight for them before they kill me accidentally. I have no doubt of the welcome I shall receive when they see my captive, and I tell them that I and my fellow ezwals are prepared to help drive man from Carson's Planet. And you will have gotten off my back unharmed—thus my promise—"

The scientist licked dry lips. "That's bestial," he said finally. "You know damned well from reading my mind that Rulls eat human beings. Earth is one of the eight planets in this galaxy whose flesh is palatable to these hell-creatures—"

The ezwal said coldly: "I have seen men on Carson's Planet eat ezwals with relish. Why shouldn't men in turn be eaten by other beings?"

Jamieson was silent, a shocked silence at the hatred that was here. The flintlike thought of the other finished:

"You may not realize how important it is that no word of ezwal intelligence get back to Earth during the next few months, but we ezwals know.

"I want you dead!"

❖❖❖

And still there was hope in him. He recognized it for what it was: that mad, senseless hope of a man still alive, refusing to acknowledge death till its gray chill lay cold on his bones.

A crash of brush roused him out of himself. Great branches of greater trees broke with wheezing unwillingness. A monstrous reptile head peered at them over a tall tree.

Jamieson had a spine-cooling glimpse of a scaly, glittering body;

eyes as red as fire blazed at him—and then that lumbering nightmare was far behind, as the ezwal raced on, contemptuous, terrible in its unheeding strength.

And after a moment, then, in spite of hideous danger, in spite of his desperate conviction that he must convince the ezwal how wrong it was—admiration flared inside him, a wild, fascinated admiration.

"By God!" he exclaimed, "I wouldn't be surprised if you really could evade the terrors of this world. In all my journeys through space, I've never seen such a perfect combination of mind and magnificent muscle."

"Save your praise," sneered the ezwal.

Jamieson hardly heard. He was frowning in genuine thoughtfulness:

"There's a saber-toothed, furred creature about your size and speed that might damage you, but I think you can outrun or outfight all the other furred animals. Then there are the malignant plants, particularly a horrible creeper affair—it's not the only intelligent plant in the galaxy, but it's the smartest. You'd need my gun if you got tangled up with one of those.

"You could evade them, of course, but that implies ability to recognize that one's in the vicinity. There are signposts of their presence but"—he held his mind as dim as possible, and smiled grimly—"I'll leave that subject before you read the details in my brain.

"That leaves the great reptiles; they can probably catch you only in the water. That's where the Demon Straits would be a mortal handicap."

"I can swim," the ezwal snapped, "fifty miles in three hours with you on my back."

"Go on!" The scientist's voice was scathing. "If you could do all these things—if you could cross oceans and a thousand miles of jungle, why did you return for me, knowing, as you must now know, that I could never reach my ship alone? Why?"

"It's dark where you're going," the ezwal said impatiently, "and knowledge is not a requirement for death. All these fears of yours are but proof that man will yield to unfriendly environment where he would be unflinching in the face of intelligent opposition.

"And that is why your people must not learn of ezwal intelligence.

Literally, we have created on Carson's Planet a dumb, beastlike atmosphere where men would eventually feel that nature was too strong for them. The fact that you have refused to face the nature-environment of this jungle planet of Eristan II and that the psycho-friction on Carson's Planet is already at the factual of point 135 is proof that—"

"Eh?" Jamieson stared at that gleaming, blue, rhythmically bobbing head, "You're crazy. Why, 135 would mean—twenty-five—thirty million. The limit is point 38."

"Exactly," glowed the ezwal, "thirty million dead."

A gulf was opening before Jamieson's brain, a black realization of where this—monstrous—creature's thoughts were leading. He said violently:

"It's a damned lie. My reports show—"

"Thirty million!" repeated the ezwal with a deadly satisfaction. "And I know exactly what that means in your terms of psycho-friction: point 135 as compared to a maximum safety tension limit of point 38. That limit, of course, obtains when nature is the opponent. If your people discovered the cause of their agony was an intelligent race, the resistance would go up to point 184—and we'd lose. You didn't know we'd studied your psychology so thoroughly."

Whitely, shakily, Jamieson replied: "In five years, we'll have a billion population on Carson's Planet, and the few ezwals that will have escaped will be a small, scattered, demoralized—"

"In five *months*," interrupted the ezwal coldly, "man will figuratively explode from our planet. Revolution, a blind mob impulse to get into the interstellar transports at any cost, mad flight from intolerable dangers. And, added to everything, the sudden arrivals of the Rull warships to assist us. It will be the greatest disaster in the long, brutal history of conquering man."

With a terrible effort, Jamieson caught himself into a tight matter-of-factness: "Assuming all this, assuming that machines yield to muscles, what will you do with the Rulls after we're gone?"

"Just let them dare remain!"

Jamieson's brief, titanic effort at casualness collapsed into a wave of fury:

"Why, you blasted fools, man beat the Rulls to Carson's Planet by less than two years. While you stupid idiots interfered with us on the ground, we fought long, delaying actions in the deeps of space, protecting you from the most murderous, ruthless, unreasonable things that the Universe ever spawned."

He stopped, fought for control, said finally with a grim effort at rational argument: "We've never been able to drive the Rull from any planet where he has established himself. And he drove us from three major bases before we realized the enormousness of the danger, and stood firm everywhere regardless of military losses."

He stopped again, conscious of the blank, obstinate, contemptuous wall that was the mind of this ezwal.

"Thirty million!" he said almost softly, half to himself. "Wives, husband, children, lovers—"

A black anger blotted out his conscious thought. With a single, lightning-swift jerk of his arm, he drew his atomic gun, pressed its muzzle hard against the great blue-ridged backbone.

"By Heaven, at least you're not going to get the Rulls in on anything that happens."

His finger closed hard on that yielding trigger; there was a white blaze of fire that—missed! Amazingly—it missed.

Instants passed before his brain grasped the startling fact that he was flying through the air, flung clear by one incredibly swift jerk of that vast, blue body.

He struck brush. Agonizing fingers of sticky jungle vine wrenched at his clothes, ripped his hands, and tore at the gun, that precious, all-valuable gun.

His clothes shredded, blood came in red, ugly streaks—everything yielded to that desperate environment but the one, all-important thing. With a bitter, enduring singleness of purpose, he clung to the gun.

He landed on his side, rolled over in a flash—and twisted up his gun, finger once more on the trigger. Three feet from that deadly muzzle, the ezwal drew up with a hideous snarl of its great, square face—jumped thirty feet to one side, and vanished, a streak of amazing blue, behind a thick bole of steel-hard jungle fungi.

Shaky, almost ill, Jamieson sat up and surveyed the extent of his defeat, the limits of his victory.

❖❖❖

All around was a curious, treeless jungle. Giant, ugly, yellow fungi towered thirty, fifty, eighty feet against a red-brown-green sky line of tangled brown vines, green lichens and bulbous, incredibly long, strong, reddish grass.

The ezwal had raged through other such dense matted wilderness with a solid, irresistible strength. For a man on foot, who dared not waste more than a fraction of the waning power of his gun, it was a pathless, a major obstacle to the simplest progress—the last place in the world he would have chosen for a last-ditch fight against anything. And yet—

In losing his temper he had hit on the only possible method of drawing his gun without giving the ezwal advance warning thoughts. At least, he was not being borne helplessly along to a great warship loaded with slimy, white Rulls and—

Rulls!

With a gasp, Jamieson leaped to his feet. There was a treacherous sagging of the ground under his feet, but he simply, instinctively stepped onto a dead patch of fungi; and the harsh, urgent tones of his voice were loud in his ears, as he said swiftly:

"We've got to act fast. The discharge of my gun must have registered on Rull instruments, and they'll be here in minutes. You've got to believe me when I tell you that your scheme of enlisting the Rulls as allies is madness.

"Listen to this: all the ships we sent into their galaxy reported that every planet of a hundred they visited was inhabited by—Rulls. Nothing else, no other races. They must have destroyed every other living, intelligent creature.

"Man has forty-eight hundred and seventy-four nonhuman allies. I admit all have civilizations that are similar to man's own; and that's the devil of the type of historyless, buildingless, ezwal culture. Ezwals cannot defend themselves against energies and machines. And, frankly, man will not leave Carson's Planet till that overwhelmingly important defense question has been satisfactorily mastered.

"You and your revolution. True, the simple people in their agony may flee in mad panic, but the military will remain, a disciplined, undefeatable organization, a hundred battleships, a thousand cruisers, ten thousand destroyers for that one base alone. The ezwal plan is clever only in its grasp of human psychology and because it may well succeed in causing destruction and death. But in that plan is no conception of the vastness of interstellar civilization, the responsibilities and the duties of its members.

"The reason I was taking you to Earth was to show you the complexities and honest problems of that civilization, to prove to you that we are not evil. I swear to you that man and his present grand civilization will solve the ezwal problem to ezwal satisfaction. What do you say?"

His last words boomed out eerily in the odd, deathly, late-afternoon hush that had settled over the jungle world of Eristan II. He could see the blur of sun, a misty blob low in the eastern sky; and the hard realization came:

Even if he escaped the Rulls, in two hours at most the great fanged hunters and the reptilian flesh-eaters that haunted the slow nights of this remote, primeval planet would emerge ravenous from their stinking hideaways, and seek their terrible surcease.

He'd have to get away from this damned fungi, find a real tree with good, strong, high-growing branches and, somehow, stay there all night. Some kind of system of intertwining vines, properly rigged up, should warn him of any beast intruder—including ezwals.

He began to work forward, clinging carefully to the densest, most concealing brush. After fifty yards, the jungle seemed as impenetrable as ever, and his legs and arms ached from his effort. He stopped, and said:

"I tell you that man would never have gone into Carson's Planet the way he did, if he had known it was inhabited by intelligent beings. There are strict laws that govern even under military necessity."

❖ ❖ ❖

Quite abruptly, answer came: "Cease these squalling, lying appeals. Man possesses no less than five thousand planets formerly occupied by intelligent races. No totality of prevarication can cover up or ever excuse five thousand cosmic crimes—"

The ezwal's thought broke off; then, almost casually: "Professor, I've just run across an animal that—"

Jamieson was saying: "Man's crimes are as black as his noble works are white and wonderful. You must understand those two facets of his character—"

"This animal," persisted the ezwal, "is floating above me now, watching me, but I am unable to catch a single vibration of its thought—"

"More than three thousand of those races now have self-government. Man does not long deny to any basically good intelligence the liberty and freedom of action which he needs so much himself—"

"*Professor!*" The thought was like a knife piercing, utterly urgent. "This creature has a repellent, worm-shaped body, and it floats without wings. It has no brain that I can detect. It—"

Very carefully, very gently, Jamieson swung himself behind a pile of brush and raised his pistol. Then softly, swiftly, he said:

"Act like a beast, snarl at it, and run like hell into the thickest underbrush if it reaches with one of those tiny, wormlike hands toward any one of the half a dozen notches on either side of its body.

"If you cannot contact its mind—we never could get in touch with it in any way—you'll have to depend on its character; as follows:

"The Rull hear only sounds between five hundred thousand and eight hundred thousand vibrations a second. That is why I can talk out loud without danger. That, also, suggests that its thought moves on a vastly different vibration level; it must hate and fear everything else, which must be why it is so remorselessly impelled on its course of destruction.

"The Rull does not kill for pleasure. It exterminates. It possibly considers the entire Universe alien which, perhaps, is why it eliminates all important creatures on any planet it intends to occupy. There can be no intention of occupying this planet because our great base on Eristan I is only five thousand light-years or twenty-five hours away by warship. Therefore it will not harm you unless it has special suspicions. Therefore be all animal."

He finished tensely: "What's it doing now?"

There was no answer.

❖❖❖

The minutes dragged; and it wasn't so much that there was silence. Queer, little noises came out of nearness and remoteness: the distant crack of wood under some heavy foot, faint snortings of creatures that were not exactly near—but too near for comfort.

A memory came that was more terrible than the gathering night, a living flame of remembrance of the one time he had seen a Rull feeding off a human being.

First, the clothes were stripped from the still-living victim, whose nervous system was then paralyzed partially by a stinger that was part of the Rull's body. And then, the big, fat, white worm crawled into the body, and lay there in that abnormal, obscene embrace while thousand of little, cuplike mouths fed—

Jamieson recoiled mentally and physically. Abrupt, desperate, panicky fear sent him burrowing deeper into the tangle of brush. It was quiet there, not a breath of air touched him. And he noticed, after a moment, that he was soaked with perspiration.

Other minutes passed; and because, in his years, courage had never been long absent from him, he stiffened with an abrupt anger at himself—and ventured into the hard, concentrated thought of attempted communication:

"If you have any questions, for Heaven's sake don't waste time."

There must have been wind above his tight shelter of brush, for a fog heavily tainted with the smell of warm, slimy water drifted over him, blocking even the narrow view that remained.

Jamieson stirred uneasily. It was not fear; his mind was a clenched unit, like a fist ready to strike. It was that—suddenly—he felt without eyes in a world of terrible enemies. More urgently, he went on:

"Your very act of asking my assistance in identifying the Rull implied your recognition of our interdependence. Accordingly, I demand—"

"Very well!" The answering thought was dim and far away. "I admit my inability to get in touch with this worm ends my plans of establishing an antihuman alliance."

There was a time, such a short time ago, Jamieson thought drearily, when such an admission would have brought genuine intellectual joy. The poor devils on Carson's Planet, at least, were not going to have to fight Rulls as well as their own madness—as well as ezwals.

He braced himself, vaguely amazed at the lowness of his morale. He said almost hopelessly:

"What about us?"

"I have already repaid your initial assistance in that, at this moment, I am leading the creature directly away from you."

"It's still following you?"

"Yes! It seems to be studying me. Have you any suggestions?"

Weariness faded; Jamieson snapped: "Only on condition that you are willing to recognize that we are a unit, and that everything else, including what man and ezwal are going to do about Carson's Planet must be discussed later. Agreed?"

The ezwal's thought was scarcely more than a snarl: "You keep harping on that!"

Momentarily, the scientist felt all the exasperation, all the strain of the past hours a pressing, hurting force in his brain. Like a flame, it burst forth, a flare of raging thought:

"You damned scoundrel, you've forced every issue so far, and all of them were rooted in that problem. You make that promise—or just forget the whole thing."

The silence was a pregnant emotion, dark with bitter, formless thought. Around Jamieson, the mists were thinning, fading into the twilight of that thick jungle. Finally:

"I promise to help you safely across the Demon Straits; and I'll be with you in minutes—if I don't lose this thing first."

Jamieson retorted grimly: "Agreement satisfactory—but don't expect to lose a Rull. They've got perfect antigravity, whereas that antigravity raft of ours was simply a superparachute. It would eventually have fallen under its own weight."

He paused tensely; then: "You've got everything clear? I'll burn the Rull that's following you, then we'll beat it as fast as your legs can carry us."

"Get ready!" The answer was a cold, deadly wave. "I'll be there in seconds."

There was no time for thought. Brush crashed. Through the mist, Jamieson caught one flashing glimpse of the ezwal with its six legs. At fifty feet, its slate-gray, three-in-line eyes were like pools of light. And then, as he pointed his gun in a desperate expectation—

"*For your life!*" came the ezwal's thought, "don't shoot, don't move. There're a dozen of them above me and—"

Queerly, shatteringly, that strong flow of thought ended in a chaotic jumble as energy flared out there, a glaring, white fire that blinked on, and then instantly off.

The mist rolled thicker, white-gray, noxious stuff that hid what *must* be happening.

And hid him.

Jamieson lay stiff and cold—and waited. For a moment, so normal had mind-reading become in these hours, that he forgot he could only catch thoughts at the will of the ezwal, and he strained to penetrate the blackout of mind vibrations.

He thought finally, a tight, personal thought: The Rulls must have worked a psychosis on the ezwal. Nothing else could explain that incoherent termination of thought in so powerful a mind. And yet—psychosis was used mainly on animals and other uncivilized and primitive life forms, unaccustomed to that sudden interplay of dazzling lights.

He frowned bleakly. Actually, in spite of its potent brain, the ezwal was very much animal, very much uncivilized, and possibly extremely allergic to mechanical hypnosis.

Definitely, it was not death from a heavy mobile projector because there would have been sound from the weapon, and because there *wouldn't* have been that instantaneous distortion of thought, that twisting—

He felt a moment's sense of intense relief. It had been curiously unsettling to think of that mighty animal struck dead.

He caught his mind into a harder band: So the ezwal was captive not corpse. So—what now?

Relief drained. It wasn't, he thought blankly, as if he could do anything against a heavily armored, heavily manned cruiser—

Ten minutes passed; and then out of the deepening twilight came the thunderous roar of a solid bank of energy projectors. There was answering thunder on a smaller scale; and then, once again, though farther away now, the deep, unmistakable roar of a broadside of hundred-inch battleship projectors.

A battleship! A capital ship from the Eristan I base, either on patrol or investigating energy discharges. The Rulls would be lucky if they got away. As for himself—nothing!

Nothing but the night and its terrors. True, there would be no trouble now from the Rulls, but that was all. This wasn't rescue, not even the hope of rescue. For days and days, the two great ships would maneuver in space; and, by the time the battleship reported again to its base, there wouldn't be very much thought given to the why of the Rull cruiser's presence on or near the ground.

Besides, the Rull would have detected its enemy before its own position would be accurately plotted. That first broadside had easily been fifty miles away.

The problem of ezwal and man, that had seemed such an intimate, soluble pattern when he and the great animal were alone, was losing its perspective. Against the immeasurably larger background of space, the design was twisting crazily.

It became a shapeless thing, utterly lost in the tangle of unseen obstacles that kept tripping him, as he plunged forward into the dimming reaches of jungle.

❖ ❖ ❖

In half an hour it was pitch dark; and he hadn't penetrated more than a few hundred yards. He would have blundered on into the black night, except that suddenly his fingers touched thick, carboniferous bark.

A tree!

Great beasts stamped below, as he clung to that precarious perch. Eyes of fire glared at him. Seven times in the first hour by his watch, monstrous things clambered up the tree, mewing and slavering in feral desire. Seven times his weakening gun flashed a thinner beam of destroying energy—and great, scale-armored carnivores whose approach shook the earth came to feed on the odorous flesh—and passed on.

One hour gone!

A hundred nights like this one, to be spent without sleep, to be defended against a new, ferocious enemy every ten minutes, and no power in his gun.

The terrible thing was that the ezwal had just agreed to work with him against the Rulls. Victory so near, then instantly snatched afar—

Something, a horrible something, slobbered at the foot of the tree. Great claws rasped on bark, and then two eyes, easily a foot apart, started with an astounding speed up toward him.

Jamieson snatched at his gun, hesitated, then began hastily to climb up into the thinner branches. Every second, as he scrambled higher, he had the awful feeling that a branch would break, and send him sliding down toward the thing; and there was the more dreadful conviction that great jaws were at his heels.

Actually, however, his determination to save his gun worked beyond his expectations. The beast was edging up into those thin branches after him when there was a hideous snarl below, and another greater creature started up the tree.

The fighting of animal against animal that started then was absolutely continuous. The tree shook, as saber-toothed beasts that mewed fought vast, grunting, roaring shapes. And every little while there would be a piercing, triumphant scream as a gigantic dinosaur-thing raged into the fight—and literally ate the struggling mass of killers.

Toward dawn, the continuous bellowing and snarling from near and far diminished notably, as if stomach after eager stomach gorged itself, and retired in enormous content to some cesspool of a bed.

At dawn he was still alive, completely weary, his body drooping with sleep desire, and in his mind only the will to live, but utterly no belief that he would survive the day.

If only, on the ship, he had not been cornered so swiftly in the control room by the ezwal, he could have taken antisleep pills, fuel capsules for his gun and—he laughed in sharp sardonicism as the futility of that line of reasoning penetrated—and a lifeboat which, of course, would by itself have enabled him to fly to safety.

At least there had been a few hundred food capsules in the control room—a month's supply.

He sucked at one that was chocolate flavored, and slowly climbed to the bloodstained ground.

❖❖❖

There was a sameness about the day, a mind-wearing sameness! Jungle and sea, different only in the designs of land shape and in the way the water lapped a curving, twisting shore. Always the substance was unchanged.

Jungle and sea—

Everything fought him—and until midafternoon he fought back. He had covered, he estimated, about three miles when he saw the tree—there was a kind of crotch high up in its towering form, where he could sleep without falling, if he tied himself with vines.

Three miles a day. Twelve hundred miles, counting what he still had to cover of this jungle ocean, counting the Demon Straits— twelve hundred miles at three miles a day.

Four hundred days!

He woke up with the beasts of the Eristan night coughing their lust at the base of his tree. He woke up with the memory of a nightmare in which he was swimming the Demon waters, pursued by millions of worms, who kept shouting something about the importance of solving the ezwal problem.

"What," they asked accusingly, "is man going to do with civilizations intellectually so advanced, but without a single building or weapon or—anything?"

Jamieson shook himself awake; and then: "To hell with ezwals!" he roared into the black, pressing, deadly night.

For a while, then, he sat shocked at the things that were happening to his mind, once so stable.

Stable! But that, of course, was long ago.

❖❖❖

The fourth day dawned, a misty, muggy replica of the day before. And of the day before that. And before that. And—

"Stop it, you idiot!" said Professor Jamieson aloud, savagely.

He was struggling stubbornly toward what seemed a clearing when a gray mass of creepers to one side stirred as in a gentle wind, and started to grow toward him. Simultaneously, a queer, hesitant thought came into his mind from—outside!

"Got them all!" it said with a madly calm ferociousness. "Get this—two-legged thing—too. Send creepers through the ground."

It was such an alien thought form, so unsettlingly different, that his brain came up from the depths to which it had sunk, and poised with startled alertness, abruptly, almost normally fascinated.

"Why, of course," he thought quite sanely, "we've always wondered how the Rytt killer plant could have evolved its high intelligence. It's like the ezwal. It communicates by mental telepathy."

Excitement came, an intense, scientific absorption in all the terrifically important knowledge that he had accumulated—about ezwals, about Rulls, and the way he had caught the Rytt plant's private vibrations. Beyond all doubt, the ezwal, in forcing its thoughts on him, had opened paths, and made it easier for him to receive all thoughts. Why, that could mean that he—

In a blaze of alertness, he cut the thought short; his gaze narrowed on the gray creepers edging toward him. He backed away, gun ready; it would be just like the Rytt to feint at him with a slow, open, apparently easily avoidable approach. Then strike like lightning from underground with its potent, needle-sharp root tendrils.

There was not the faintest intention in him to go back, or evade any crisis this creature might force. Go back where?—to what?

He skirted the visible creepers, broke through a fifty-foot wilderness of giant green ferns; and, because his control of himself was complete now, it was his military mind, the mind that accepted facts as they were, that took in the scene that spread before him.

In the near distance rested a two-hundred-foot Rull lifeboat. Near it, a dozen wanly white Rulls lay stiff and dead, each tangled in its own special bed of gray creepers. The creepers extended on into the open door of the lifeboat; and there was no doubt that it had "got them all!"

The atmosphere of lifelessness that hung over the ship, with all its promise of escape, brought a soaring joy, that was all the sweeter because of the despair of those days of hell—a joy that ended as the cool, hard thought of the ezwal struck into his brain:

"I've been expecting you, professor. The controls of this lifeboat are beyond my abilities to operate; so here I am waiting for you—"

From utter despair to utter joy to utter despair in minutes—

❖ ❖ ❖

Cold, almost desolate, Jamieson searched for his great and determined enemy. But there was nothing moving in the world of jungle, no glimpse of dark, gleaming blue, nothing but the scatter of dead, white worms and the creeper-grown lifeboat to show that there ever had been movement.

He was only dimly aware of the ezwal's thoughts continuing:

"This killer plant was here four days ago when I landed from the antigravity raft. It had moved farther up the island when these Rulls brought me back to this lifeboat. I had already thrown off the effects of the trick-mirror hypnotism they used on me; and so I heard the human battleship and the Rull cruiser start their fight. These things seemed unaware of what was wrong—I suppose because they didn't hear the sounds—and so they laid themselves out on the wet, soggy ground.

"That was when I got into mental communication with the plant, and called it back this way—and so we had an example of the kind of co-operation which you've been stressing for so long with such passionate sincerity, only—"

The funny thing was that, in spite of all he had fought through, hope was finally dead. Every word the ezwal was projecting so matter-of-factly showed that, once again, this immensely capable being had proved its enormous capacity for taking care of itself.

Co-operation with a Rytt killer plant—the one thing on this primitive world that he had really counted on as a continuous threat to the ezwal.

No more; and if the two worked together against him— He held his gun poised, but the black thought went on:

It was obvious that man would never really conquer the ezwal. Point 135 psycho-friction meant there would be a revolution on Carson's Planet, followed by a long, bloody, futile struggle and—He grew aware that the ezwal was sending thoughts again:

"—only one fault with your reasoning. I've had four days to think over the menace of the Rulls, and of how time and again I had to co-operate with you. Had to!

"And don't forget, in the Rytt-intelligence, I've had a perfect example of all the worst characteristics of ezwals. It, too, has mental telepathy. It, too, must develop a machine civilization before it can hope to hold its planet. It's in an earlier stage of development, so it's even more stubborn, more stupid—"

Jamieson was frowning in genuine stark puzzlement, scarcely daring to let his hope gather. He said violently:

"Don't try to kid me. You've won all along the line. And now, of your own free will, you're offering, in effect, to help me get back to Carson's Planet in time to prevent a revolution favorable to the ezwals. Like hell you are!"

"Not my own free will, professor," came the laconic thought. "Everything I've done since we came to this planet has been forced on me. You were right in thinking I had been compelled to return for your aid. When I landed from the raft, this creeper-thing was spread across the entire peninsula here, and it wouldn't let me pass, stubbornly refused to listen to reason.

"It's completely ungrateful for the feast of worms I helped it get; and at this moment it has me cornered in a room of this ship.

"Professor, take your gun, and teach this damned creature the importance of—co-operation!"

The Second Solution

The little thin chap with the too-sharp voice was saying:

"My point is, we didn't need Edison, Paladine, Clissler, or any particular scientist. It is the mass mind that moves inevitably in certain directions. The inventions, the ideas of individuals grow out of that mass; they would occur regardless of the birth or early death of any individual genius, so-called. There's always a second solution."

Somebody disagreed: "Inventions change the course of history. A new weapon wins a war because it was introduced when it was. A year later would have been too late."

The big man cleared his throat, drawing our attention to him. I had noticed him idle over from the club bar a few minutes earlier, and listen with that bored contempt which deep-space men have for groundlings. He had the tan of space in his hawklike countenance; and it was obvious that this was between voyages for him; and he didn't know what to do with himself.

"I hate to enter an impractical discussion," he said, "but it just happens I can illustrate your argument. You all remember the experience some years ago of Professor Jamieson with a full-grown ezwal in the ocean jungle of Eristan II—how they captured a Rull lifeship intact, and eventually escaped with its secret of perfect antigravity, and prevented a revolution and a massacre on Carson's Planet?"

We all recalled it; the big man went on: "Actually, Professor Jamieson had captured two ezwals on that visit of his to Carson's Planet. One was a male, which he took with him on his own ship, and with which he was later wrecked on Eristan II. The other was a female, which he had dispatched to Earth on an earlier ship.

"En route, this female give birth to a male about as big as a lion. The young one grew about a foot on the trip, but that wouldn't have mattered in itself. What precipitated the whole thing was the anti-gravity converters, the old, imperfect, pre-Rull type—in their fash-ion, they began to discharge torrents of free energy; and that's where the story begins."

"Does it prove my point or his?" asked the little chap with the sharp voice.

The big man grimaced at him; and silence settled over our little group.

❖ ❖ ❖

The grim, iron-hard face of Commander McLennan twisted toward the two officers. "Absolutely out of control!" he said from clenched teeth. "The Sparling free energy effect! Ship'll strike Earth in fifteen minutes somewhere in the great Toganna Forest Reserve in northern Canada.

"Carling, get the men into the lifeboats, then make contact with the superintendent of the Reserve. Tell him we've got two ezwals of Carson's Planet aboard, who'll probably live through the crash. Tell him to prepare for any eventualities; and that I'll be down to take charge of the wreck in half an hour. Brenson!"

"*Yessir!*" The white-faced younger officer sprang to rigid atten-tion as Carling whirled out of the room.

"Go down and kill those two ezwals, mother and son. We can't take a chance on those two beasts getting loose on Earth. They'll murder a thousand people before they can be killed—if they ever get free! You know what they're like. Anybody who's been to Carson's Planet—" He groaned in fury. "Damn Jamieson for having ezwals brought to Earth. I was against it from the—"

He caught himself: "And Brenson: be at the lifeboats in seven . . . no, make it six minutes for safety. Even if they're not dead! Now, *run!*"

The young man blanched whiter still. "Yessir!" he breathed again, and was gone, tugging at his gun.

For McLennan there were vital things to do, valuable papers to retrieve; and then the time was up. He plunged through the door of a lifeboat, gasped:

"Brenson here yet?"

"No, sir!"

"WHAT?"

They waited. One minute slipped by. Two. Then it was Carling who whispered:

"We've got to leave, sir. He can use that empty lifeboat, if he comes. We've *got* to leave."

McLennan looked strangely blank. "He's the son of old Rock Brenson. What'll I tell my old pal?"

Carling made no reply. And McLennan's lips twisted to the shaping of a curse, but no sound came, and no real thought of violent words was in his mind. As he slid the lifeboat smoothly into the safety of space, he heard the fierce whisper of one of the men:

"Mistake . . . send a fool like Brenson down. He's got the killer mind. That's what's holding him. He's got to kill—"

❖ ❖ ❖

From above him came the terrible snarl of his mother; and then her thoughts, as hard and sharp as crystal:

"Under me for your life! The two-legged one comes to kill!"

Like a streak, he leaped from his end of the cage, five hundred solid pounds of dark, dark-blue monstrosity. Razor-clawed hands rattled metallically on the steel floor, and then he was into blackness under her vast form, pressing into the cave of soft, yielding flesh that she made for him—taking unbreakable holds with his six hands, so that, no matter what the violence of her movements or the fury of her attacks, he would be there safe and sound, snugly deep in the folds between her great belly muscles.

Her thought came again, curt and hard as so many blows: "Remember all the things I've told you. The hope of our race is that men continue to think us beasts. If they suspect our intelligence, we are lost. And someone does suspect it. If that knowledge lives, our people die!"

Faster came her thought: "Remember, your weaknesses in this crisis are those of youth. You love life too much. Fight the resulting fear, for fear it is. Take death if the opportunity comes to serve your race by so doing."

Her brain slowed, grew cold. He watched with her then, clinging to her mind with his mind as tightly as his body clung to her body.

He saw the pole-thick steel bars of the cage; and, half hidden by their four-inch width, the figure of a man; he saw—the *thoughts* of the man!

"Damn you!" those thoughts came. "If it wasn't for you being on this ship I'd be out of danger now. I—"

The man's hand moved. There was a hard, metallic glint as he pushed the weapon between the bars. It came alive with white fire.

For the briefest moment, the mental contact with his mother blackened. It was his own ears that heard the gasping roar; his own flat nostrils that smelled the odor of burning, cooking flesh; and there was no mistaking the tangible, physical reality of her wild charge straight at the merciless flame gun projecting between the bars.

The fire clicked off. The blackness vanished from his mother's mind; and he saw that the weapon and the man had retreated from the mad, reaching threat of those mighty claws.

"Damn you!" the man flared. "Well, take it from here then!"

There must have been blinding pain, but none of it came through to his brain. His mother's thoughts remained at a mind-shaking pitch of malignance; and not for a single instant did she remain still. She ducked this way, that way; she ran with mad speed, twisting, darting, rolling, sliding, fighting with an almost inconceivable violence for life in the hopelessly narrow confines of the cage.

Like a squirrel she ran twenty feet up the bars of the cage; and then, at the ceiling, she swung along with the agility of a monkey from bar to thick bar. But always, in spite of her vaunting passion, in spite of deadly desperation, a part of her mind remained untouched, unhurried, terrible in its icy ferocity. And always that tearing fire following her, missing her, then hitting her squarely—hitting her so often that finally she could no longer hold back the knowledge that her end was near. And with that thought came another—his first awareness that she had had a purpose in keeping the weapon beyond the bars, and forcing it to follow the swift, darting frenzy of her threshing about.

By following her desperate movements the beam of the flame

gun had seared with molten effect across the hard resistance of those thick, steel bars!

"God!" came the man's thoughts. "Won't it ever die? And where is that damned young one? Another minute now, and I'll have to go. I—"

The thought stopped—stopped as sixty-five hundred pounds of the hardest organic body ever created smashed with pile-driver speed at the weakened bars of the cage. The cub strained with every ounce of tautened muscles against the thrusting compression of that wall of steel-hard tendons surrounding him—and lived because even in that moment of titanic attempt, he felt the distinct effort his mother made to prevent the smashing force of her muscles from squeezing him to jelly.

Beyond the vastness of her body, he heard the harsh grating of ripping metal as mighty bars bent and broke, where the flame had destroyed their tensile strength.

"Good Lord!" the man thought in high dismay.

Strangely, then, the preternatural sharpness of his thoughts weakened, retreated strangely into dimmer forms. The picture of him vanished; and where the mother ezwal's thoughts had been, there was no movement. The ezwal was aware of her lying above him, a great, flabby dead mass, completely covering him.

The reality of her death struck him instantly; and it explained why the man's mind and the picture of him had faded. It was his own weaker powers now that were catching the man's thoughts.

They were queerly distorted, senseless thoughts. The man mumbled: "Only got a minute, only minute . . . then I've got to go . . . get off the ship before—"

He was aware of the man crawling onto his mother's back, and tingled with dismay. It was he who was being searched for now; and if that white flame found him it would deal out equally merciless death. Frantically he pushed deeper into the yielding stomach above him.

And then—all hell broke loose. There was a piercing scream of air against the freighter's hull. The crash was world-shattering. His six hands were wrenched from their holds. He struck intolerable hardness; and the blackness that came was very real and very personal.

❖❖❖

Slowly, the darkness grew alive. Somewhere there was movement, muffled noises, and a confusing sense of many men's thoughts: incredible danger!

Alarm leaped along his nerves, faster, faster; in a spasm of movement, he pressed upward into the saving folds of his mother's flesh; and, as he lay there quiveringly still, deep into her, the world beyond and around her enveloping body began to grow clearer. Thoughts came:

"Never saw such an awful mess!" somebody's mind whispered.

"What could have ailed Brenson?" another groaned. "That fighting instinct of his got him at last, in spite of his love of life. His body's plain jam . . . what did you say, Mr. McLennan?"

"I'm talking to Kelly," came the curt, savage answer. "Kelly, I said—"

"Just a minute, boss. I was getting an important message from the patrol science headquarters. Guess what? Caleb Carson, Professor Jamieson's second in command here on Earth, is coming by air express to take charge. Carson is the grandson of old Blake Carson, who discovered Carson's Planet. He'll arrive at noon . . . that's two hours and—"

"Oh, he is, is he?" McLennan's answering thought, as it penetrated to the ezwal, was truculent, immeasurably grim. "Well, I don't think he'll be here in time for the kill."

"Kill? What kill?"

"Don't be such a fool, man!" the commander snarled. "We've got a five-hundred-pound ezwal to locate. You don't think a smash-up like this will kill one of those things."

"Lord!"

"It must be alive!" McLennan went on tersely. "And do you know what it means if an ezwal gets loose in this million square miles of wilderness? He'll murder every human being he gets hold of."

"This looks like a hunting party with a vengeance."

"You bet. That's where you come in. Phone down to the reservation superintendent's office, and tell him he's got to round up the biggest, toughest hunting dogs he can get, preferably those who've trailed grizzly bears. Make him realize that this is the most important thing that's ever happened in this forsaken land. Tell him that, on Carson's Planet, where these killers come from, settlers are being mas- sacred in droves, and that men are not even safe in fortified cities. Tell him . . . I don't care what you tell him, but get action! Parker!"

"Shoot, boss!"

"Lower your ship and let down some tackle. I've started the ball rolling for a hunting trip that may be absolutely unnecessary. But never mind that. I believe in planning. And now—I think you've got enough power in that bus to hook into this old scoundrel and turn her over. One of the tricks of this tribe is that the young ones can tan- gle themselves in their mother's skin, and—"

The ezwal let himself sink slowly through the cave of flesh. His lower, combination-feet-and-hands touched something cold and wet, and he stood there for a moment, trembling. His nose caught a draft of air, and savored the scent of cooked flesh that stank at him from his mother's body; and the memory it brought of fire and ago- nizing death sent a sick thrill along his nerves.

He forced the fear aside. With a spasmodic effort of his brain, he analyzed his chances. Wilderness, their thoughts had said; and in their minds had been pictures of brush and trees. That meant hiding places. Winter? That was harder to picture because there was only a sense of white brightness, and somehow it connected with the unfa- miliar cold wetness into which his feet were sinking. A sticky, cling- ing wetness that would slow him in the swift dash he must make through the deep, resisting softness of it.

Above him there was a sudden *brrr* of power; and the weight of his mother seemed to lift from him. Then the weight sagged again.

"Nope!" came a thought.

"Try again!" McLennan replied sharply. "You almost got it. Do a little more horizontal pulling this time—and the rest of you stand back. We may have to shoot fast."

Body taught as a drawn wire, the ezwal poked his square-shaped head out. In one swift flash his three glittering eyes verified the pic- ture he had caught from their minds.

The spaceship had broken into three massive sections. And everywhere lay an appalling litter of twisted steel girders, battered metal and a confusion of smashed cargo. For half a mile in every direction the wreckage sprawled, spotting the snow with splintered wood and miraculously unharmed boxes as well as a vast scatter of dark, chunky things impossible to identify.

And each chunk, each piece of metal, each fragment of cargo offered obstacle to the guns that would be flaming at him in just about—

"*Look!*" Somebody's mind and voice spewed forth the single word.

It was the queerest, most shattering moment in all his world; for the age-long second after that explosive yell, he was aware of the first maddening pang of pain-expectation that he had ever known. Not even when the fire was burning away his mother's life had that stark, terrible realization touched him. But now, abruptly, he knew it was a matter of—given seconds!

He quivered in every shrinking nerve. His impulse was to jerk back into the folding safety, however brief, of his mother's great, comforting mass of body. Then, even as his eyes blazed at the stiffened men, even as he caught the sudden, tremendous strain in their minds, memory came: His mother had said, in effect: Fight fear or it will destroy you!

The thought caught him in a rhythmic, irresistible sweep. His muscles galvanized frantically in enormous effort. He heaved, squeezed prodigiously, and was free of the great, crushing body above him.

Straight ahead was a run-and-hide paradise. But in that part of his brain where fear was already vanquished, the straight-ahead course was instantly dismissed as unutterably the most dangerous. To his left was a clustered group of unarmed workmen, milling in stunned panic at the appearance of an animal as big as a grown lion, and terrifying in the alien, hideous power suggested by six claw-armed limbs. And to his right—

Like a charging demon, he plunged at the little line of men with guns who were drawn up at his right. Alert guns twisted toward him; and then were fumbled in horrible dismay as the desperate thought leaped through the minds of the wielders that their fire would shear a burning path through the workmen to the left.

"You fools!" came McLennan's wail of thought from behind him. "Scatter—for your lives!"

Too late! Hissing in astounded triumph at the completeness of this opportunity to kill these murderous beings, he crashed into the group. Blood sprayed before the raking ferocity of his claws, as if he had leaped into a pool of the warm, turgid red stuff. He had a wild, desperate impulse to pause and crunch bodies with his teeth, but there was no time.

He was clear of them. The rearing bulk of tattered ship, the harsh cacophony of screaming fell away behind him; and he was running with every ounce of speed that all his six limbs could muster.

A glare of flame from McLennan's gun sizzled in the snow beside him. He dodged, twisted skillfully behind a thick section of shining, bent metal. The beam fought at the metal—and was through, reaching with incandescent violence above him as he dived into a shallow arroyo.

A dark-bluish streak, he hurtled through a spread of bush, whipped along for four hundred yards behind a shielding ledge of rock and snow that extended roughly parallel to the ship. He halted on the rock lip of a valley that curved away below him. There were trees there, and brush and a jagged, rock-strewn land, bright with glaring snow, fading away into the brilliant white haze of distance.

Incredibly, he was safe, untouched, unsinged—and to his brain reached the outer fringe of the raging storm of thoughts from the men beyond the great hind section of ship that hid them from his view:

"—Parker, yours is the fastest plane; get these men to the reservation hospital; there's death here if we don't hurry. Kelly, what about those dogs?"

"The superintendent says he can get ten. They'll have to be flown in, and that'll take about an hour."

"Good! We'll all fly to the reservation, and get started the moment this Caleb Carson arrives. With those dogs to do our hunting, a couple of hours' start won't do that thing any good."

The ezwal slid under spreading bush as the planes soared into the sky. The picture of the dogs was not clear, yet the very blur of it brought a chill. A slave animal that murdered for its killer masters.

He spat with sudden, flaring hate that only partially overcame the sudden, enormous sense of aloneness in him. He must evade those dogs before he could hope to know even the remotest sense of comfort and security—and there was only one method by which he could do it properly.

❖❖❖

Dogs followed trails; that meant they could scent things as easily as he could. That meant the reservation headquarters must be approached upwind, if he ever hoped to kill those dogs—if he could ever find the place.

The planes had certainly gone in this direction—

Planes! One diving leap and he was under cover as a great, silent plane swooped by over his head; there was the briefest blur of a man's thought—Caleb Carson's thought, the assistant of the mysterious Professor Jamieson; and then the long, shining machine settled behind some trees to his left. The village must be there.

He saw the buildings after a moment, considerably to the right of the plane. A dark machine—a car—was pushing along from the village toward the plane . . . and he was upwind . . . and if he could attack the dogs now, before that car brought the man, Carson, back to the village, before the men swarmed out to begin their hunt—

With glowing, coal-dark eyes, he stared down at the ten dogs from his vantage point on the little spread of hill. Ten . . . ten . . . ten . . . too many, many; and they were chained in a bunch, sleeping now in the snow, but they could all attack him at once.

There was a horrible, alien smell from them, but it was good, oh, so good that they were on his side of a large outhouse, that the men were inside other buildings beyond; and that it would take—minutes—before they could come out with their irresistible guns. He—

His thought scattered madly as he saw the car push over a hill a quarter of a mile away, and start along almost straight toward him. Caleb Carson would be able to see his whole attack, and even the snow that slowed the car wouldn't hold it more than two minutes—human time.

Two minutes! Time limit added to all the other things that were against him. Fury pierced him. These merciless human beings with their killer animals. At least they had had to fly the dogs in; and they'd be harder to replace. He'd have time to lose himself in these miles of forest and mountains, and—

The first dog saw him. He caught the startled thought as it lunged to its feet, heard its sharp warning yelp, and felt the blackness snap into its brain as he dealt it one crushing blow.

He whirled; and his jaws swung beautifully into the path of the dog that was charging at his neck. Teeth that could already dent metal clicked in one ferocious, stabbing bite.

Blood gushed into his mouth, stingingly, bitterly unpleasant to his taste. He spat it out with a thin snarl as eight shrieking dogs leaped at him. He met the first with a claw-armored forehand upraised.

The wolfish jaws slashed at the blue-dark, descending arm, ravenous to tear it to bits. But in an incredibly swift way, the hand avoided the reaching teeth and caught at the neck. And then, fingers like biting metal clamps gripped deep into the shoulders; and the dog was flung like a shot from a gun to the end of its chain.

The chain snapped from the frightful force, and the dog slid along in the snow and lay still, broken-necked.

❖❖❖

The ezwal reared around for an irresistible plunge at the others—and stopped. The dogs were surging away from him, fear thoughts in their minds. He saw that they had caught his unnatural scent for the first time in that one wild rush, and now—

He stood there, quivering with uncertainty. Poised there, exploring the meaning of the madly racing thought forms in the brains of the dogs. Crouched there while the engine of the motor car became a soft, *close* throb, while a veritable fury of men's thoughts approached swiftly.

Seven dogs left—and all scared to death of him. Scornfully, swiftly, he turned; and with a wild dismay saw that the car had stopped less than fifty feet distant, that there was only one man in it. The other man must have stayed behind to watch the plane.

The human being, Caleb Carson, sat in the open door of the car; and he held a long, ugly, shining gun. It pointed at him, straight and unwavering; and then—incredible fact—a thought came from the cool brain behind the weapon; a thought directed *at him!*

"See," it said, "see! I can kill you before you can get to safety. This is an express-flame rifle; and it can blow a crater where you're standing. I can kill you—but I won't.

"Think that over with your best thought. And remember this, even though you escape now, in future you live or die as I will it. Without my help you cannot get away; and my price is high. Now, before the others come—get!"

He plunged over the hill, a startled, amazed, wondering, dismayed six-legged monstrosity. Minutes later, he remembered that those dogs would not dare to pursue him. He sprawled to a sliding stop in the snow.

His brain cooled; jangled emotions straightened; and what had happened began to fit into a coherent piece. Time and again on that trip through space, his mother had told him:

"Man will only accept defeat from one source: blind, natural forces. Because we wanted them to leave our land alone we pretended to be senseless, ferocious beasts. We knew that if they ever suspected our intelligence, they would declare what they call war on us, and waste all their wealth and millions of lives to destroy us—and now, someone does suspect it. If that knowledge lives, our race dies!"

Someone does suspect! Here in this man Carson was that someone, the most dangerous man in all the world.

The ezwal shivered involuntarily. It had not been his intention to remain near this dangerous camp an instant after the dogs were neutralized. But now—

It was terribly obvious that he must act, no matter what the risk. Caleb Carson must be killed—at once!

"I can't understand those dogs not following that trail!" McLennan's thought came dimly, complainingly, from inside the house. "On Carson's Planet, they use dogs all the time."

"Only dogs that were born there!" came the unemotional reply. And it was the calmness of the mind behind the thought that sent a quiver of hatred through the ezwal, where it crouched under the little berry bush beside the house of the forest-reserve superintendent.

The superlative confidence of this man brought strange fear, unnatural rage. Carson went on curtly:

"That much I gathered for certain from Professor Jamieson's documents. The rest is merely my own deduction, based on my special studies of my grandfather's explorations. When Blake Carson first landed on the planet, the ezwals made no attempt to harm him. It was not until after the colonists began to arrive that the creatures turned so immeasurably murderous.

"Mind you, I didn't see the truth on my own. It was only when I heard yesterday that Professor Jamieson was three. . . four now. . . days overdue at the Eristan I base—"

"Eh! Jamieson missing?"

"Sounds serious, too. Some Rull warships are in the vicinity, and of course no spaceship is big enough to carry the Lixon Communicators that make the interstellar telephone possible; so he couldn't send a warning, unless he was reasonably near some point of transmission. Apparently, he wasn't; so—"

Carson paused; then: "Anyway, I thought his documents might show that he had taken a side trip. And it was in going through them that I found, no suggestion for a side trip, but my first glimpse of the truth. Everything is as vague as possible, but by putting his notes beside my own knowledge, it adds up."

It was all there, the ezwal saw, in Carson's mind. Whether the man called it conjecture, or believed it fully, here was what his mother had feared. Basically, this man knew everything. And if what they were saying about the master mind, Professor Jamieson, being missing meant what it could mean, then in this house was the only remaining person in the world with *the* knowledge.

And he was telling it. Both men therefore must—

The ezwal's thought scattered as McLennan's mind projected a surprisingly cold, unfriendly thought:

"I hope I'm wrong in what I'm beginning to suspect. Let me tell you that I've been to Carson's Planet half a dozen times. The situation there is so bad that no stay-at-home studying documentary evidence could begin to comprehend the reality. Hundreds of thousands of people have been slaughtered—"

"I won't go into that," said Carson curtly. "The very number of the dead demands an intelligent and swift solution."

"You have not," said McLennan softly, "visited Carson's Planet yourself."

"No!"

"You, the grandson of Blake Carson—" He broke off scathingly:

"It's the old story, I see, of subsequent generations sponging off the fame of the great man."

"There's no point in calling names." The younger man was calm.

McLennan's thought was harsh: "Does this truth you say you deduced include keeping this cub ezwal alive?"

"Certainly; it is my duty and your duty to deliver the young one to Professor Jamieson when and if he returns."

"I suppose you realize that it may be some time before this beast is captured, and that meanwhile it will become a killer."

"Because of the danger from the encroaching Rull enemy of man," replied Carson with abrupt chillness that matched McLennan's steel hardness, "because of the importance of finding some answer to the ezwal problem, high government policy requires that all necessary risks be taken."

"Damn government policy!" snarled McLennan. "My opinion of a government that appoints fact-finding commissions at this late date couldn't be properly put into words. A war of systematic extermination must be declared at once—that's the solution—and we'll begin with this scoundrelly little cub."

"That goes double for me!" A harsh thought from a third mind burst forth.

❖ ❖ ❖

"Carling!" McLennan exclaimed. "Man, get back into bed."

"I'm all right!" the young first officer of the smashed warship replied fiercely. "That freak accident that happened to me when we landed . . . but never mind that. I was lying on the couch in the next room and I overheard . . . I tell you, sir!" he blazed at Caleb Carson, "Commander McLennan is right. While you were talking, I was thinking of the dozens of men I've met on various trips to Carson's Planet who've simply vanished. We used to talk about it, we younger officers—"

"There's no use quibbling," said McLennan sharply. "It's an axiom of the service that the man in the field knows best. Unless he deliberately surrenders his power, or unless he receives a direct order from the commander in chief, he can retain his command regardless of the arrival meanwhile of superior officers."

"I shall have the order in an hour!" said Carson bleakly.

"In an hour," McLennan glowed triumphantly, "you won't be able to find me. By the time you do, the ezwal will be dead."

To the ezwal, the words brought an abrupt rebirth of murder purpose, the first realization of the immense opportunity that offered here. Here, under this one roof, were the three men who must be counted in both the immediate and remote sense as the most dangerous of humans to himself and his kind.

There was a door just around the corner. If he could solve its mechanism—to kill them all would be the swift, satisfying solution to his various problems.

Boldly, he glided from his hiding place.

❖❖❖

In the hallway, the first stinging sense of personal danger came. He crouched tensely at the foot of the stairs, dismayingly conscious that to go up after the men would leave his way to escape horribly unguarded. And if he were trapped up there after killing them—

A clatter of dishes from the kitchen distracted him. He suppressed the swift and burning impulse to go in and smash the woman who was there. Slowly, he started up the stairs, his purpose cold and unyielding, but his mind clinging now with fascinated intensity to the thoughts that came from the men.

"—Those things read minds!" McLennan was scoffing. He seemed quite prepared to go on talking. There was certain equipment he was waiting for, and every word spoken would delay Carson so much longer from radioing for that vital order. "Professor Jamieson must be crazy."

"I thought," Carling cut in, loyally backing his commander, "that scientists worked by evidence."

"Sometimes," said McLennan, "they get an hypothesis, and regardless of whether half the world is dying as a result of their theory, they go on trying to prove it."

There was an acrid impatience in Carson's thoughts: "I don't say that is Professor Jamieson's opinion. I merely draw that conclusion from a number of notes he made, particularly one which was in the form of a question: 'Can civilization exist without cities, farms, science, and what form of communication would be the indispensable minimum?'

"Besides"—his mind narrowed, the intention to be persuasive

strong inside him—"while the existence of intelligence in the ezwal would be wonderful, its absence would not constitute a reason for any of us to nullify Professor Jamieson's plans for keeping this young ezwal alive."

He broke off: "In any event, there's no necessity for you to go after him. He'll starve to death in three weeks on Earth food. It's practically poison, utterly indigestible to him."

Outside the door, the creature quivered with shock. Swift memory came of how bitterly unpleasant the dog's blood had tasted. He cringed; then flaring rage struck through him. At least he could kill these men who had brought such dreadful fate upon him, and there was just a chance that—

With an effort he suppressed the leaping hope that surged, memory of at least one place where food was plentiful. McLennan was saying:

"Men have eaten ezwals."

"Ah, yes, but they have to treat the meat with chemicals to render it digestible."

"I'm sick of this," McLennan snapped abruptly. "I can see it's no use arguing. So I'm just going to tell you what I've done, and what I'm going to do. A couple of dozen flivver planes will be arriving in about fifteen minutes. We'll scout every inch of the country this afternoon; and you can't tell me five hundred pounds of dark-blue ezwal can remain hidden, especially as the thing won't know— What the devil are you pointing that gun at the door for?"

Caleb Carson's frigid, steel-hard thoughts came out to the ezwal: "Because just before you came in I saw the ezwal sneaking through the brush. I was sort of expecting him, but I never thought he'd come into the house till I heard the claws rattle a few seconds ago. I wouldn't—advise—him—to—come—in. Hear that—*you!*"

One terrible instant, the ezwal froze; then, with a rasp of hatred, he launched himself at the stairs. Out the door, and then off through the brush, darting, twisting, to evade the flame that poured out the second-floor window from McLennan's pistol.

On and on he ran, harder, faster, until he was a great, leaping thing under the trees, over the snow, an incredible, galloping monster—on and on.

Of all his purposes, the only one that remained after his failure to kill, was: He must save his own life. He must have food. And there would be no food unless—

The wreck spread before him, a sprawling, skeleton structure, a vast waste of metal. No sounds, no thought-blurs of life reached out to where he lay vibrantly quiescent, probing with his mind, listening with his ears. One long, tense, straining moment; and then he was leaping forward, racing into the shelter of the deserted, shattered hulk.

Somewhere here was the food that had been brought along for his mother, enough to keep him, if he could hide it, until—

He dared not quite think of what must follow if he really hoped to save his life. There was a plane to steal, to operate, a million facts to learn about this alien civilization, and finally a spaceship—

He saw the shadow of the airplane sweep across the snow to his right—and froze to the ground in one instinctive jerk of interlocking muscles. His brain jangled so horribly it was like a discordant blare of noise. His thoughts disintegrated into one all-powerful half-thought, half-mind-wrecking emotion:

He must appear to be another piece of jetsam, one more shattered box, or chunk of metal. He—

"You needn't try to hide!" came the acrid, directed thought of Caleb Carson. "I knew you'd come up here. Even a full-grown ezwal might have taken the risk. A young one being simple and honest needed only the hint. Well, your hour of decision has come."

Snarling, he watched the plane circle, down, down, till it hovered less than a hundred feet above the ground. In abrupt despair of rage, he reared up toward it like a man on his hind legs, reached up horribly with his forearms, as if he would somehow stretch up to the plane and smash it down beside him. The cold thought came:

"That's right! Stand up and be as much of a man physically as you can. You're going to learn to be a man mentally, or die.

"Know that I have just told McLennan that you're here, and what I expect will happen. He thinks I'm a fool; and he and Carling will be here in five minutes.

"Think of that: five minutes! Five minutes to change your whole attitude toward life. I'm not going to try to pretend that this is a fair choice. Men are not angels, but I must know . . . *men* must know about ezwal intelligence. We are fighting a destroyer race called the Rulls; and we must have Carson's Planet in some form as an advance base against those damnable white worms.

"Remember this, too, it will do you no good to die a martyr. Now that the idea has come of ezwals possibly having intelligence, we'll start a propaganda campaign along those lines. Everywhere on Carson's Planet men, weary of fighting what they think is a natural force, will brace up with that curious military morale that human beings can muster in the face of intelligent enemies.

"If you yield, I'll teach you everything that man knows. You'll be the first ezwal scientist. If you can read minds, you'll know that I'm sincere in every word."

He was trapped. The knowledge beat at him, a tearing mixture of fear and—something else! It wasn't that he didn't trust this man's words; it was the sheer tremendousness of the decision.

"The proof of your choice," the cold thought penetrated to him, "will be simplicity itself. In one minute I shall land my plane. It is all-metal construction, divided into two compartments. You cannot possibly smash into my section and kill me.

"But the door of your section will be open. When you enter it will close tight and . . . good Lord, here comes McLennan!"

The big plane almost fell to the ground, so fast did Carson bring it down. It drew up in a spread of clearing a hundred feet away. A door yawned; and the scientist's urgent thought came:

"Make up your mind!"

And still he stood, taut in every nerve. He saw great cities, ships, space liners, with ezwals in command. Then he thought of what his mother had told him and that was abruptly like an immeasurable pain.

"Quick!" came Carson's thought.

Flame seared down where he had been; and there was no time to think, no time for anything but to take the initial chance. The flame missed him again, as he twisted in his swift run; this time it reached deliberately ahead across the tail of Carson's ship.

He caught the deliberateness of that act in McLennan's mind; and then he was inside the now unusable machine. The other plane landed. Two men with guns raced toward him.

He snarled hideously, as he caught their murder intention, and half turned to take his chances outside. The door clicked shut metallically in his teeth. Trapped.

Or was he? Another door opened. He roared as he leaped into the compartment where the man sat. His whole mind shook with this final, unexpected opportunity to kill this man, as his mother had charged him to do.

It was the steadiness of the other's thought that held him stiff, suppressed the deadly impulse to strike one mighty blow. Caleb Carson said huskily:

"I'm taking this terrible chance because everything you've done so far seems to show that you have intelligence, and that you've understood my thoughts. But we can't take off; McLennan's burned the tail struts. That means we've got to have finally clinching proof. I'm going to open this door that leads away from *them*. You can kill me and, with luck, escape—if you hurry.

"The alternative is to stretch yourself here between my legs, and face them when they come."

With a shuddering movement the ezwal edged forward and stiffly settled down on his long belly. He was only vaguely aware of the cursing wonder of McLennan.

He was suddenly feeling very young and very important and very humble. For there had come to him the first glimpse of the greatness that was to be his in the world of ezwals, in that world of titanic construction, the beginning of dynamic new civilization.

❖ ❖ ❖

There was silence among us, as the big man finished. Finally, somebody said critically:

"This grandson of the discoverer of Carson's Planet seems a pretty cold-blooded sort of chap."

Somebody else said: "Caleb Carson didn't know that the number of dead on Carson's Planet was actually thirty million, the morale situation proportionately more dangerous. He would never have had a real sense of urgency. His solution would have been too late."

"The point is," said the small thin chap sharply but with satisfaction, "there's always somebody else who, for various reasons, has special insight into a problem. The accumulated thought on Carson's Planet by its discoverer's grandson is what made it possible for him to read between the rather sketchy lines of Professor Jamieson's notes."

Somebody said: "Why didn't we hear about this second solution at the time?"

The sharp voice snapped: "That's obvious. It was the very next day that Professor Jamieson's own experiences and fuller solution captured all the headlines. Incidentally, I read last week that a new coordinator has been appointed for Carson's Planet. His name is Caleb Carson."

We grew aware of the big man standing up, just as a boy came over to him. The boy said:

"Commander McLennan, your ship is calling you. You can take the message in the lounge, sir."

We all stared as the giant headed briskly for the lounge-room door. A minute later the argument was waxing as hotly as ever.

MISSION TO
THE STARS

Concealment

The Earth ship came so swiftly around the planetless Gisser sun that the alarm system in the meteorite weather station had no time to react. The great machine was already visible when Watcher grew aware of it.

Alarms must have blared in the ship, too, for it slowed noticeably and, still braking, disappeared. Now it was coming back, creeping along, obviously trying to locate the small object that had affected its energy screens.

It loomed vast in the glare of the distant, yellow-white sun, bigger even at this distance than anything ever seen by the Fifty Suns, a very hell ship out of remote space, a monster from a semi-mythical world, instantly recognizable from the descriptions in the history books as a battleship of Imperial Earth. Dire had been the warnings in the histories of what would happen someday—and here it was.

He knew his duty. There was a warning, the age-long dreaded warning, to send to the Fifty Suns by the non-directional subspace radio; and he had to make sure nothing telltale remained of the station.

There was no fire. As the overloaded atomic engines dissolved, the massive building that had been a weather substation simply fell into its component elements.

Watcher made no attempt to escape. His brain, with its knowledge, must not be tapped. He felt a brief, blinding spasm of pain as the energy tore him to atoms.

❖ ❖ ❖

She didn't bother to accompany the expedition that landed on

360

the meteorite. But she watched with intent eyes through the astroplate.

From the very first moment that the spy rays had shown a human figure in a weather station—a weather station *out here*—she had known the surpassing importance of the discovery. Her mind leaped instantly to the several possibilities.

Weather stations meant interstellar travel. Human beings meant Earth origin. She visualized how it could have happened: an expedition long ago; it must have been long ago because now they had interstellar travel, and that meant large populations on many planets.

His majesty, she thought, would be pleased.

So was she. In a burst of generosity, she called the energy room.

"Your prompt action, Captain Glone," she said warmly, "in enclosing the entire meteorite in a sphere of protective energy is commendable, and will be rewarded."

The man whose image showed on the astroplate, bowed. "Thank you, noble lady." He added: "I think we saved the electronic and atomic components of the entire station. Unfortunately, because of the interference of the atomic energy of the station itself, I understand the photographic department was not so successful in obtaining clear prints."

The woman smiled grimly, said: "The man will be sufficient, and *that* is a matrix for which we need no prints."

She broke the connection, still smiling, and returned her gaze to the scene on the meteorite. As she watched the energy and matter absorbers in their glowing gluttony, she thought:

There had been several storms on the map in that weather station. She'd seen them in the spy ray; and one of the storms had been very large. Her great ship couldn't dare to go fast while the location of that storm was in doubt.

Rather a handsome young man he had seemed in the flashing glimpse she had had in the spy ray, strong-willed, brave. Should be interesting in an uncivilized sort of a fashion.

First, of course, he'd have to be conditioned, drained of relevant information. Even now a mistake might make it necessary to begin a long, laborious search. Centuries could be wasted on these short distances of a few light years, where a ship couldn't get up to speed, and where it dared not maintain velocity, once attained, without exact weather information.

She saw that the men were leaving the meteorite. Decisively, she clicked off the intership communicator, made an adjustment and stepped through a transmitter into the receiving room half a mile distant.

❖ ❖ ❖

The officer in charge came over and saluted. He was frowning:

"I have just received the prints from the photographic department. The blur of energy haze over the map is particularly distressing. I would say that we should first attempt to reconstitute the building and its contents, leaving the man to the last."

He seemed to sense her disapproval, went on quickly:

"After all, he comes under the common human matrix. His reconstruction, while basically somewhat more difficult, falls into the same category as your stepping through the transmitter in the main bridge and coming to this room. In both cases there is dissolution of elements—which must be brought back into the original solution."

The woman said: "But why leave him to the last?"

"There are technical reasons having to do with the greater complexity of inanimate objects. Organized matter, as you know, is little more than a hydro-carbon compound, easily conjured."

"Very well." She wasn't as sure as he that a man and his brain, with the knowledge that had made the map, was less important than the map itself. But if both could be had— She nodded with decision. "Proceed."

She watched the building take shape inside the large receiver. It slid out finally on wings of antigravity, and was deposited in the center of the enormous metal floor.

The technician came down from his control chamber shaking his head. He led her and the half dozen others who had arrived, through the rebuilt weather station, pointing out the defects.

"Only twenty-seven sun points showing on the map," he said. "That is ridiculously low, even assuming that these people are organized for only a small area of space. And, besides, notice how *many* storms are shown, some considerably beyond the area of the reconstituted suns and—"

He stopped, his gaze fixed on the shadowy floor behind a machine twenty feet away.

The woman's eyes followed his. A man lay there, his body twisting.

"I thought," she said frowning, "the man was to be left to the last."

The scientist was apologetic: "My assistant must have misunderstood. They—"

The woman cut him off: "Never mind. Have him sent at once to Psychology House, and tell Lieutenant Neslor I shall be there shortly."

"At once, noble lady."

"Wait! Give my compliments to the senior meteorologist and ask him to come down here, examine this map, and advise me of his findings."

She whirled on the group around her, laughing through her even, white teeth. "By space, here's action at last after ten dull years of surveying. We'll rout out these hide-and-go-seekers in short order."

Excitement blazed inside her like a living force.

The strange thing to Watcher was that he knew before he wakened why he was still alive. Not very long before.

He *felt* the approach of consciousness. Instinctively, he began his normal Dellian preawakening muscle, nerve and mind exercises. In the middle of the curious rhythmic system, his brain paused in a dreadful surmise.

Returning to consciousness? *He!*

It was at that point, as his brain threatened to burst from his head with shock, that the knowledge came of how it had been done.

He grew quiet, thoughtful. He stared at the young woman who reclined on a chaise lounge near his bed. She had a fine, oval face and a distinguished appearance for so young a person. She was studying him from sparkling gray eyes. Under that steady gaze, his mind grew very still.

He thought finally: "I've been conditioned to an easy awakening. What else did they do—find out?"

The thought grew until it seemed to swell his brainpan:

WHAT ELSE?

He saw that the woman was smiling at him, a faint, amused smile. It was like a tonic. He grew even calmer as the woman said in a silvery voice:

"Do not be alarmed. That is, not too alarmed. What is your name?"

Watcher parted his lips, then closed them again, and shook his head grimly. He had the impulse to explain then that even answering one question would break the thrall of Dellian mental inertia and result in the revelation of valuable information.

But the explanation would have constituted a different kind of defeat. He suppressed it, and once more shook his head.

The young women, he saw, was frowning. She said: "You won't answer a simple question like that? Surely, your name can do no harm."

His name, Watcher thought, then what planet he was from, where the planet was in relation to the Gisser sun, what about intervening storms. And so on down the line. There wasn't any end.

Every day that he could hold these people away from the information they craved would give the Fifty Suns so much more time to organize against the greatest machine that had ever flown into this part of space.

His thought trailed. The woman was sitting up, gazing at him with eyes that had gone steely. Her voice held a metallic resonance as she said:

"Know this, whoever you are, that you are aboard the Imperial Battleship *Star Cluster*, Grand Captain Laurr at your service. Know, too, that it is our unalterable will that you shall prepare for us an orbit that will take our ship safely to your chief planet."

She went on vibrantly: "It is my solemn belief you already know that Earth recognizes no separate governments. Space is indivisible. The universe shall not be an area of countless sovereign peoples squabbling and quarreling for power.

"That is the law. Those who set themselves against it are outlaws, subject to any punishment which may be decided upon in their special case.

"Take warning."

Without waiting for an answer, she turned her head. "Lieutenant Neslor," she said at the wall facing Watcher, "have you made any progress?"

A woman's voice answered: "Yes, noble lady. I have set up an integer based on the Muir-Grayson studies of colonial peoples who have been isolated from the main stream of galactic life. There is no historical precedent for such a long isolation as seems to have obtained here, so I have decided to assume that they have passed the static period, and have made some progress of their own.

"I think we should begin very simply, however. A few forced answers will open his brain to further pressures; and we can draw valuable conclusions meanwhile from the speed with which he adjusts his resistance to the brain machine. Shall I proceed?"

The woman on the chaise longue nodded. There was a flash of light from the wall facing Watcher. He tried to dodge, and discovered for the first time that *something* held him in the bed, not rope, or chain, nothing visible. But something as palpable as rubbery steel.

Before he could think further, the light was in his eyes, in his mind, a dazzling fury. Voices seemed to push through it, voices that danced and sang, and spoke into his brain, voices that said:

"A simple question like that—of course I'll answer . . . of course, of course, of course— My name is Gisser Watcher. I was born on the planet Kaider III, of Dellian parents. There are seventy inhabited planets, fifty suns, thirty billion people, four hundred important storms, the biggest at Latitude 473. The Central Government is on the glorious planet, Cassidor VII—"

With a blank horror of what he was doing, Watcher caught his roaring mind into a Dellian knot, and stopped that devastating burst of revelation. He knew he would never be caught like that again but—too late, he thought, too late by far.

❖❖❖

The woman wasn't quite so certain. She went out of the bedroom, and came presently to where the middle-aged Lieutenant Neslor was classifying her findings on receptor spools.

The psychologist glanced up from her work, said in an amazed voice: "Noble lady, his resistance during the stoppage moment registered an equivalent of I. Q. 800. Now, that's utterly impossible, particularly because he started talking at a pressure point equivalent to I. Q. 167, which matches with his general appearance, and which you know is average.

"There must be a system of mind training behind his resistance. And I think I found the clue in his reference to his Dellian ancestry. His graph squared in intensity when he used the word.

"This is very serious, and may cause great delay—unless we are prepared to break his mind."

The grand captain shook her head, said only: "Report further developments to me."

On the way to the transmitter, she paused to check the battle-ship's position. A bleak smile touched her lips, as she saw on the reflector the shadow of a ship circling the brighter shadow of a sun.

Marking time, she thought, and felt a chill of premonition. Was it possible that one man was going to hold up a ship strong enough to conquer an entire galaxy?

❖ ❖ ❖

The senior ship meteorologist, Lieutenant Cannons, stood up from a chair as she came toward him across the vast floor of the transmission receiving room, where the Fifty Suns weather station still stood. He had graying hair, and he was very old, she remembered, very old. Walking toward him, she thought:

There was a slow pulse of life in these men who watched the great storms of space. There must be to them a sense of futility about it all, a timelessness. Storms that took a century or more to attain their full roaring maturity, such storms and the men who catalogued them must acquire a sort of affinity of spirit.

The slow stateliness was in his voice, too, as he bowed with a measure of grace, and said:

"Grand Captain, the Right Honorable Gloria Cecily, the Lady Laurr of Noble Laurr, I am honored by your personal presence."

She acknowledged the greeting, and then unwound the spool for him. He listened, frowning, said finally:

"The latitude he gave for the storm is a meaningless quantity. These incredible people have built up a sun relation system in the Lesser Magellanic Cloud, in which the center is an arbitrary one having no recognizable connection with the magnetic center of the whole Cloud. Probably, they've picked some sun, called it center, and built their whole spatial geography around it."

The old man whirled abruptly away from her, and led the way into the weather station, to the edge of the pit above which poised the reconstructed weather map.

"The map is utterly worthless to us," he said succinctly.

"What?"

She saw that he was staring at her, his china-blue eyes thoughtful.

"Tell me, what is your idea of this map?"

The woman was silent, unwilling to commit herself in the face of so much definiteness. Then she frowned, and said:

"My impression is much as you described. They've got a system of their own here, and all we've got to do is find the key."

She finished more confidently: "Our main problem, it seems to me, would be to determine which direction we should go in the immediate vicinity of this meteorite weather station we've found. If we chose the wrong direction, there would be vexatious delay, and, throughout, our chief obstacle would be that we dare not go fast because of possible storms."

She looked at him questioningly, as she ended. And saw that he was shaking his head, gravely:

"I'm afraid," he said, "it's not so simple as that. Those bright point-replicas of suns look the size of peas due to light distortion, but when examined through a metroscope they show only a few molecules in diameter. If that is their proportion to the suns they represent—"

She had learned in genuine crises to hide her feelings from subordinates. She stood now, inwardly stunned, outwardly cool, thoughtful, calm. She said finally:

"You mean each one of those suns, their suns, is buried among about a thousand other suns?"

"Worse than that. I would say that they have only inhabited one system in ten thousand. We must never forget that the Lesser Magellanic Cloud is a universe of fifty million stars. That's a lot of sunshine."

The old man concluded quietly: "If you wish, I will prepare orbits involving maximum speeds of ten light days a minute to all the nearest stars. We may strike it lucky."

The woman shook her head savagely: "One in ten thousand. Don't be foolish. I happen to know the law of averages that relates to ten thousand. We would have to visit a minimum of twenty-five hundred suns if we were lucky, thirty-five to fifty thousand if we were not.

"No, no"—a grim smile compressed her fine lips—"we're not going to spend five hundred years looking for a needle in a haystack. I'll trust to psychology before I trust to chance. We have the man who understands the map, and while it will take time, he'll talk in the end."

She started to turn away, then stopped. "What," she asked, "about the building itself? Have you drawn any conclusions from its design?"

He nodded. "Of the type used in the galaxy about fifteen thousand years ago."

"Any improvements, changes?"

"None that I can see. One observer, who does all the work. Simple, primitive."

She stood thoughtful, shaking her head as if trying to clear away a mist.

"It seems strange. Surely after fifteen thousand years they could have added something. Colonies are usually static, but not that static."

She was examining routine reports three hours later when the astro clanged twice, softly. Two messages—

The first was from Psychology House, a single question: "Have we permission to break the prisoner's mind?"

"No!" said Grand Captain Laurr.

The second message made her glance across at the orbit board. The board was aglitter with orbit symbols. That wretched old man, disobeying her injunction NOT to prepare any orbits.

Smiling twistedly, she walked over and studied the shining things, and finally sent an order to Central Engines. She watched as her great ship plunged into night.

After all, she thought, there was such a thing as playing two games at the same time. Counterpoint was older in human relations than it was in music.

The first day she stared down at the outer planet of a blue-white sun. It floated in the darkness below the ship, an airless mass of rock and metal, drab and terrible as any meteorite, a world of primeval canyons and mountains untouched by the leavening breath of life.

Spy rays showed only rock, endless rock, not a sigh of movement or of past movement.

There were three other planets, one of them a warm, green world where winds sighed through virgin forests and animals swarmed on the plains.

Not a house showed, nor the erect form of a human being.

Grimly, the woman said into the intership communicator: "Exactly how far can our spy rays penetrate into the ground?"

"A hundred feet."

"Are there any metals which can simulate a hundred feet of earth?"

"Several, noble lady."

Dissatisfied, she broke the connection. There was no call that day from Psychology House.

The second day, a giant red sun swam into her impatient ken. Ninety-four planets swung in their great orbits around their massive parent. Two were habitable, but again there was the profusion of wilderness and of animals usually found only on planets untouched by the hand and metal of civilization.

The chief zoological officer reported the fact in his precise voice: "The percentage of animals parallels the mean for worlds not inhabited by intelligent beings."

The woman snapped: "Has it occurred to you that there may have been a deliberate policy to keep animal life abundant, and laws preventing the tilling of the soil even for pleasure?"

She did not expect, nor did she receive, an answer. And once more there was not a word from Lieutenant Neslor, the chief psychologist.

The third sun was farther away. She had the speed stepped up to twenty light days a minute—and received a shocking reminder as the ship bludgeoned into a small storm. It must have been small because the shuddering of metal had barely begun when it ended.

"There has been some talk," she said afterward to the thirty captains assembled in the captains' pool, "that we return to the galaxy and ask for an expedition that will uncover these hidden rascals.

"One of the more whining of the reports that have come to my ears suggests that, after all, we were on our way home when we made our discovery, and that our ten years in the Cloud have earned us a rest."

Her gray eyes flashed; her voice grew icy: "You may be sure that those who sponsor such defeatism are not the ones who would have to make the personal report of failure to his majesty's government. Therefore, let me assure the faint hearts and the homesick that we shall remain another ten years if it should prove necessary. Tell the officers and crew to act accordingly. That is all."

Back in the main bridge, she saw that there was still no call from Psychology House. There was a hot remnant of anger and impatience in her, as she dialed the number. But she controlled herself as the distinguished face of Lieutenant Neslor appeared on the plate. She said then:

"What is happening, lieutenant? I am anxiously waiting for further information from the prisoner."

The woman psychologist shook her head. "Nothing to report."

"Nothing!" Her amazement was harsh in her voice.

"I have asked twice," was the answer, "for permission to break his mind. You must have known that I would not lightly suggest such a drastic step."

"Oh!" She had known, but the disapproval of the people at home, the necessity for accounting for any amoral action against individuals, had made refusal an automatic action. Now— Before she could speak, the psychologist went on:

"I have made some attempts to condition him in his sleep, stressing the uselessness of resisting Earth when eventual discovery is sure. But that has only convinced him that his earlier revelations were of no benefit to us."

The leader found her voice: "Do you really mean, lieutenant, that you have no plan other than violence? Nothing?"

In the astroplate, the image head made a negative movement. The psychologist said simply:

"An 800 I. Q. resistance in a 167 I. Q. brain is something new in my experience."

The woman felt a great wonder. "I can't understand it," she complained. "I have a feeling we've missed some vital clue. Just like that we run into a weather station in a system of fifty million suns, a station in which there is a human being who, contrary to all the laws of self-preservation, immediately kills himself to prevent himself from falling into our hands.

"The weather station itself is an old model galactic affair, which shows no improvements after fifteen thousand years; and yet the vastness of the time elapsed, the caliber of the brains involved suggest that all the obvious changes should have been made.

"And the man's name, Watcher, is so typical of the ancient pre-spaceship method of calling names on Earth according to the trade. It is possible that even the sun, where he is watching, is a service heritage of his family. There's something—depressing—here— somewhere that—"

She broke off, frowning: "What is your plan?" After a minute, she nodded. "I see . . . very well, bring him to one of the bedrooms in the main bridge. And forget that part about making up one of our strong-arm girls to look like me. I'll do everything that's necessary. Tomorrow. Fine."

Coldly she sat watching the prisoner's image in the plate. The man, Watcher, lay in bed, an almost motionless figure, eyes closed, but his face curiously tense. He looked, she thought, like someone discovering that for the first time in four days, the invisible force lines that had bound him had been withdrawn.

Beside her, the woman psychologist hissed: "He's still suspicious, and will probably remain so until you partially ease his mind. His general reactions will become more and more concentrated. Every minute that passes will increase his conviction that he will have only one chance to destroy the ship, and that he must be decisively ruthless regardless of risk.

"I have been conditioning him the past ten hours to resistance to us in a very subtle fashion. You will see in a moment . . . ah-h!"

Watcher was sitting up in bed. He poked a leg from under the sheets, then slid forward, and onto his feet. It was an oddly powerful movement.

He stood for a moment, a tall figure in gray pajamas. He had evidently been planning his first actions because, after a swift look at the door, he walked over to a set of drawers built into one wall, tugged at them tentatively, and then jerked them open with an effortless strength, snapping their locks one by one.

Her own gasp was only an echo of the gasp of Lieutenant Neslor.

"Good heavens!" the psychologist said finally. "Don't ask me to explain how he's breaking those metal locks. Strength must be a byproduct of his Dellian training. Noble lady—"

Her tone was anxious; and the grand captain looked at her. "Yes?"

"Do you think, under the circumstances, you should play such a personal role in his subjection? His strength is obviously such that he can break the body of anyone aboard—"

She was cut off by an imperious gesture. "I cannot," said the Right Honorable Gloria Cecily, "risk some fool making a mistake. I'll take an antipain pill. Tell me when it is time to go in."

❖ ❖ ❖

Watcher felt cold, tense, as he entered the instrument room of the main bridge. He had found his clothes in some locked drawers. He hadn't known they were there, but the drawers aroused his curiosity. He made the preliminary Dellian extra energy movements; and the locks snapped before his super strength.

Pausing on the threshold, he flicked his gaze through the great domed room. And after a moment his terrible fear that he and his kind were lost, suffered another transfusion of hope. He was actually free.

These people couldn't have the faintest suspicion of the truth. The great genius, Joseph M. Dell, must be a forgotten man on Earth. Their release of him must have behind it some plan of course but—

"Death," he thought ferociously, "death to them all, as they had once inflicted death, and would again."

He was examining the bank on bank of control boards when, out of the corner of his eyes, he saw the woman step from the nearby wall.

He looked up; he thought with a savage joy: The leader! They'd have guns protecting her, naturally, but they wouldn't know that all these days he had been frantically wondering how he could force the use of guns.

Surely to space, they *couldn't* be prepared to gather up his component elements again. Their very act of freeing him had showed psychology intentions.

Before he could speak, the woman said, smilingly: "I really shouldn't let you examine those controls. But we have decided on a different tactic with you. Freedom of the ship, an opportunity to meet the crew. We want to convince you . . . convince you—"

Something of the bleakness and implacableness of him must have touched her. She faltered, shook herself in transparent self-annoyance, then smiled more firmly, and went on in a persuasive tone:

"We want you to realize that we're not ogres. We want to end your alarm that we mean harm to your people. You must know, now we have found you exist, that discovery is only a matter of time.

"Earth is not cruel, or dominating, at least not any more. The barest minimum of allegiance is demanded, and that only to the idea of a common unity, the indivisibility of space. It is required, too, that criminal laws be uniform, and that a high minimum wage for workers be maintained. In addition, wars of any kind are absolutely forbidden.

"Except for that, every planet or group of planets, can have its own form of government, trade with whom they please, live their own life. Surely, there is nothing terrible enough in all this to justify the curious attempt at suicide you made when we discovered the weather station."

He would, he thought, listening to her, break her head first. The best method would be to grab her by the feet, and smash her against the metal wall or floor. Bone would crush easily and the act would serve two vital purposes:

It would be a terrible and salutary warning to the other officers of the ship. And it would precipitate upon him the death fire of her guards.

He took a step toward her. And began the faintly visible muscle and nerve movements so necessary to pumping the Dellian body to a pitch of superhuman capability. The woman was saying:

"You stated before that your people have inhabited fifty suns in this space. Why only fifty? In twelve thousand or more years, a population of twelve thousand billion would not be beyond possibility."

He took another step. And another. Then knew that he must speak if he hoped to keep her unsuspicious for those vital seconds while he inched closer, closer. He said:

"About two thirds of our marriages are childless. It has been very unfortunate, but you see there are two types of us, and when inter-marriage occurs as it does without hindrance—"

Almost he was near enough; he heard her say: "You mean, a mutation has taken place; and the two don't mix?"

He didn't have to answer that. He was ten feet from her; and like a tiger he launched himself across the intervening gap.

The first energy beam ripped through his body too low to be fatal, but it brought a hot scalding nausea and a dreadful heaviness. He heard the grand captain scream:

"Lieutenant Neslor, what are you doing?"

He had her then. His fingers were grabbing hard at her fending arm, when the second blow struck him high in the ribs and brought the blood frothing into his mouth. In spite of all his will, he felt his hands slipping from the woman. Oh, space, how he would have liked to take her into the realm of death with him.

Once again, the woman screamed: "Lieutenant Neslor, are you mad? *Cease fire!*"

Just before the third beam burned at him with its indescribable violence, he thought with a final and tremendous sardonicism: "She still doesn't suspect. But somebody did; somebody who at this ulti-mate moment had guessed the truth."

"Too late," he thought, "too late, you fools! Go ahead and hunt. They've had warning, time to conceal themselves even more thoroughly. And the Fifty Suns are scattered, scattered among a million stars, among—"

Death caught his thought.

❖❖❖

The woman picked herself off the floor, and stood dizzily striving to draw her roughly handled senses back into her brain. She was vaguely aware of Lieutenant Neslor coming through a transmitter, pausing at the dead body of Gisser Watcher and rushing toward her.

"Are you all right, my dear? It was so hard firing through an astroplate that—"

"You mad woman!" The grand captain caught her breath. "Do you realize that a body can't be reconstituted once vital organs have been destroyed. Dissolution or re-solution cannot be piecemeal. We'll have to go home without—"

She stopped. She saw that the psychologist was staring at her. Lieutenant Neslor said:

"His intention to attack was unmistakable and it was too soon according to my graphs. All the way through, he's never fitted anything in human psychology.

"At the very last possible moment I remembered Joseph Dell and the massacre of the Dellian supermen fifteen thousand years ago. Fantastic to think that some of them escaped and established a civilization in this remote part of space.

"Do you see now: Dellian—Joseph M. Dell—the inventor of the Dellian perfect robot."

The Storm

Over the miles and the years, the gases drifted. Waste matter from ten thousand suns, a diffuse miasma of spent explosions, of dead hell fires and the furies of a hundred million raging sunspots—formless, purposeless.

But it was the beginning.

Into the great dark the gases crept. Calcium was in them, and sodium, and hydrogen; and the speed of the drift varied up to twenty miles a second.

There was a timeless period while gravitation performed its function. The inchoate mass became masses. Great blobs of gas took a semblance of shape in widely separate areas, and moved on and on and on.

They came finally to where a thousand flaring seetee suns had long before doggedly "crossed the street" of the main stream of terrene suns. Had crossed, and left *their* excrement of gases.

The first clash quickened the vast worlds of gas. The electron haze of terrene plunged like spurred horses and sped deeper into the equally violently reacting positron haze of contraterrene. Instantly, the lighter orbital positrons and electrons went up in a blaze of hard radiation.

The storm was on.

The stripped seetee nuclei carried now terrific and unbalanced negative charges and repelled electrons, but tended to attract terrene atom nuclei. In their turn the stripped terrene nuclei attracted contraterrene.

Violent beyond all conception were the resulting cancellations of charges.

376

The two opposing masses heaved and spun in a cataclysm of partial adjustment. They had been heading in different directions. More and more they became one tangled, seething whirlpool.

The new course, uncertain at first, steadied and became a line drive through the midnight heavens. On a front of nine light years, at a solid fraction of the velocity of light, the storm roared toward its destiny.

Suns were engulfed for half a hundred years—and left behind with only a hammering of cosmic rays to show that they had been the centers of otherwise invisible, impalpable atomic devastation.

In its four hundred and ninetieth Sidereal year, the storm intersected the orbit of a Nova at the flash moment.

It began to move!

On the three-dimensional map at weather headquarters on the planet Kaider III, the storm was colored orange. Which meant it was the biggest of the four hundred odd storms raging in the Fifty Suns region of the Lesser Magellanic Cloud.

It showed as an uneven splotch fronting at Latitude 473, Longitude 228, Center 190 parsecs, but that was a special Fifty Suns degree system which had no relation to the magnetic center of the Magellanic Cloud as a whole.

The report about the Nova had not yet been registered on the map. When that happened the storm color would be changed to an angry red.

They had stopped looking at the map. Maltby stood with the councilors at the great window staring up at the Earth ship.

The machine was scarcely more than a dark sliver in the distant sky. But the sight of it seemed to hold a deadly fascination for the older men.

Maltby felt cool, determined, but also sardonic. It was funny, these—these people of the Fifty Suns in this hour of their danger calling upon *him*.

He unfocused his eyes from the ship, fixed his steely, laconic gaze on the plump, perspiring chairman of the Kaider III government—and, tensing his mind, forced the man to look at him. The councilor, unaware of the compulsion, conscious only that he had turned, said:

"You understand your instructions, Captain Maltby?"

Maltby nodded. "I do."

The curt words must have evoked a vivid picture. The fat face rippled like palsied jelly and broke out in a new trickle of sweat.

"The worst part of it all," the man groaned, "is that the people of the ship found us by the wildest accident. They had run into one of our meteorite stations and captured its attendant. The attendant sent a general warning and then forced them to kill him before they could discover which of the fifty million suns of the Lesser Magellanic Cloud was us.

"Unfortunately, they did discover that he and the rest of us were all descendants of the robots who had escaped the massacre of the robots in the main galaxy fifteen thousand years ago.

"But they were baffled, and without a clue. They started home, stopping off at planets on the way on a chance basis. The seventh stop was us. Captain Maltby—"

The man looked almost beside himself. He shook. His face was as colorless as a white shroud. He went on hoarsely:

"Captain Maltby, you must not fail. They have asked for a meteorologist to guide them to Cassidor VII, where the central government is located. They mustn't reach there. You must drive them into the great storm at 473.

"We have commissioned you to do this for us because you have the two minds of the Mixed Men. We regret that we have not always fully appreciated your services in the past. But you must admit that, after the wars of the Mixed Men, it was natural that we should be careful about—"

Maltby cut off the lame apology. "Forget it," he said. "The Mixed Men are robots, too, and therefore as deeply involved, as I see it, as the Dellians and non-Dellians. Just what the Hidden Ones of my kind think, I don't know, nor do I care. I assure you I shall do my best to destroy this ship."

"Be careful!" the chairman urged anxiously. "This ship could destroy us, our planet, our sun in a single minute. We never dreamed that Earth could have gotten so far ahead of us and produced such a devastatingly powerful machine. After all, the non-Dellian robots and, of course, the Mixed Men among us are capable of research work; the former have been laboring feverishly for thousands of years.

"But, finally, remember that you are not being asked to commit suicide. The battleship is absolutely invincible. Just how it will survive a real storm we were not told when we were shown around. But it will. What happens, however, is that everyone aboard becomes unconscious.

"As a Mixed Man you will be the first to revive. Our combined fleets will be waiting to board the ship the moment you open the doors. Is that clear?"

It had been clear the first time it was explained, but these non-Dellians had a habit of repeating themselves, as if thoughts kept growing vague in their minds. As Maltby closed the door of the great room behind him, one of the councilors said to his neighbor:

"Has he been told that the storm has gone Nova?"

The fat man overheard. He shook his head. His eyes gleamed as he said quietly: "No. After all, he is one of the Mixed Men. We can't trust him too far no matter what his record."

❖❖❖

All morning the reports had come in. Some showed progress, some didn't. But her basic good humor was untouched by the failures.

The great reality was that her luck had held. She had found a planet of the robots. Only one planet so far, but—

Grand Captain Laurr smiled grimly. It wouldn't be long now. Being a supreme commander was a terrible business. But she had not shrunk from making the deadly threat: provide all required information, or the entire planet of Kaider III would be destroyed.

The information was coming in: Population of Kaider III two billion, one hundred million, two-fifths Dellian, three-fifths non-Dellian robots.

Dellians physically and mentally the higher type, but completely lacking in creative ability. Non-Dellians dominated in the research laboratories.

The forty-nine other suns whose planets were inhabited were called, in alphabetical order: Assora, Atmion, Bresp, Buraco, Cassidor, Corrab— They were located at (1) Assora: Latitude 931, Longitude 27, Center 201 parsecs; (2) Atmion—

It went on and on. Just before noon she noted with steely amusement that there was still nothing coming through from the meteorology room, nothing at all about storms.

She made the proper connection and flung her words: "What's the matter, Lieutenant Cannons? Your assistants have been making prints and duplicates of various Kaider maps. Aren't you getting anything?"

The old meteorologist shook his head. "You will recall, noble lady, that when we captured that robot in space, he had time to send out a warning. Immediately on every Fifty Suns planet, all maps were despoiled, civilian meteorologists were placed aboard spaceships, that were stripped of receiving radios, with orders to go to a planet on a chance basis, and stay there for ten years.

"To my mind, all this was done before it was clearly grasped that their navy hadn't a chance against us. Now they are going to provide us with a naval meteorologist, but we shall have to depend on our lie detectors as to whether or not he is telling us the truth."

"I see." The woman smiled. "Have no fear. They don't dare oppose us openly. No doubt there is a plan being built up against us, but it cannot prevail now that we can take action to enforce our unalterable will. Whoever they send must tell us the truth. Let me know when he comes."

Lunch came, but she ate at her desk, watching the flashing pictures on the astro, listening to the murmur of voices, storing the facts, the general picture, into her brain.

"There's no doubt, Captain Turgess," she commented once, savagely, "that we're being lied to on a vast scale. But let it be so. We can use psychological tests to verify all the vital details.

"For the time being it is important that you relieve the fears of everyone you find it necessary to question. We must convince these people that Earth will accept them on an equal basis without bias or prejudice of any kind because of their robot orig—"

She bit her lip. "That's an ugly word, the worst kind of propaganda. We must eliminate it from our thoughts."

"I'm afraid," the officer shrugged, "not from our thoughts."

She stared at him, narrow-eyed, then cut him off angrily. A moment later she was talking into the general transmitter: "The word robot must not be used—by any of our personnel—under pain of fine—"

Switching off, she put a busy signal on her spare receiver, and called Psychology House. Lieutenant Neslor's face appeared on the plate.

"I heard your order just now, noble lady," the woman psychologist said. "I'm afraid, however, that we're dealing with the deepest instincts of the human animal—hatred or fear of the stranger, the alien.

"Excellency, we come from a long line of ancestors who, in their time, have felt superior to others because of some slight variation in the pigmentation of the skin. It is even recorded that the color of the eyes has influenced the egoistic in historical decisions. We have sailed into very deep waters, and it will be the crowning achievement of our life if we sail out in a satisfactory fashion."

There was an eager lilt in the psychologist's voice; and the grand captain experienced a responsive thrill of joy. If there was one thing she appreciated, it was the positive outlook, the kind of people who faced all obstacles short of the recognizably impossible with a youthful zest, a will to win. She was still smiling as she broke the connection.

The high thrill sagged. She sat cold with her problem. It was a problem. Hers. All aristocratic officers had *carte blanche* powers, and were expected to solve difficulties involving anything up to whole groups of planetary systems.

After a minute she dialed the meteorology room again.

"Lieutenant Cannons, when the meteorology officer of the Fifty Suns navy arrives, please employ the following tactics—"

Maltby waved dismissal to the driver of his car. The machine pulled away from the curb and Maltby stood frowning at the flaming energy barrier that barred farther progress along the street. Finally, he took another look at the Earth ship.

It was directly above him now that he had come so many miles across the city toward it. It was tremendously high up, a long, black torpedo shape almost lost in the mist of distance.

But high as it was it was still visibly bigger than anything ever seen by the Fifty Suns, an incredible creature of metal from a world so far away that, almost, it had sunk to the status of myth.

Here was the reality. There would be tests, he thought, penetrating tests before they'd accept any orbit he planned. It wasn't that he doubted the ability of his double mind to overcome anything like that, but—

Well to remember that the frightful gap of years which separated the science of Earth from that of the Fifty Suns had already shown unpleasant surprises. Maltby shook himself grimly and gave his full attention to the street ahead.

A fan-shaped pink fire spread skyward from two machines that stood in the center of the street. The flame was a very pale pink and completely transparent. It looked electronic, deadly.

Beyond it were men in glittering uniforms. A steady trickle of them moved in and out of buildings. About three blocks down the avenue a second curtain of pink fire flared up.

There seemed to be no attempt to guard the sides. The men he could see looked at ease, confident. There was murmured conversation, low laughter and—they weren't all men.

As Maltby walked forward, two fine-looking young women in uniform came down the steps of the nearest of the requisitioned buildings. One of the guards of the flame said something to them. There was a twin tinkle of silvery laughter. Still laughing, they strode off down the street.

It was suddenly exciting. There was an air about these people of far places, of tremendous and wonderful lands beyond the farthest horizons of the staid Fifty Suns.

He felt cold, then hot, then he glanced up at the fantastically big ship; and the chill came back. One ship, he thought, but so big, so mighty that thirty billion people didn't dare send their own fleets against it. They—

He grew aware that one of the brilliantly arrayed guards was staring at him. The man spoke into a wrist radio, and after a moment a second man broke off his conversation with a third soldier and came over. He stared through the flame barrier at Maltby.

"Is there anything you desire? Or are you just looking?"

He spoke English, curiously accented—but English! His manner was mild, almost gentle, cultured. The whole effect had a naturalness, an unalienness that was pleasing. After all, Maltby thought, he had never had the fear of these people that the others had. His very plan to defeat the ship was based upon his own fundamental belief that the robots were indestructible in the sense that no one could ever wipe them out completely.

Quietly, Maltby explained his presence.

"Oh, yes," the man nodded, "we've been expecting you. I'm to take you at once to the meteorological room of the ship. Just a moment—"

The flame barrier went down and Maltby was led into one of the buildings. There was a long corridor, and the transmitter that projected him into the ship must have been focused somewhere along it.

Because abruptly he was in a very large room. Maps floated in half a dozen antigravity pits. The walls shed light from millions of tiny point sources. And everywhere were tables with curved lines of very dim but sharply etched light on their surfaces.

Maltby's guide was nowhere to be seen. Coming toward him, however, was a tall, fine-looking old man. The oldster offered his hand.

"My name is Lieutenant Cannons, senior ship meteorologist. If you will sit down here we can plan an orbit and the ship can start moving within the hour. The grand captain is very anxious that we get started."

Maltby nodded casually. But he was stiff, alert. He stood quite still, feeling around with that acute second mind of his, his Dellian mind, for energy pressures that would show secret attempts to watch or control his mind.

But there was nothing like that.

He smiled finally, grimly. It was going to be as simple as this, was it? Like hell it was.

❖ ❖ ❖

As he sat down, Maltby felt suddenly cozy and alive. The pure exhilaration of existence burned through him like a flame. He recognized the singing excitement for the battle thrill it was and felt a grim joy that for the first time in fifteen years he could do something about it.

During his long service in the Fifty Suns navy, he had faced hostility and suspicion because he was a Mixed Man. And always he had felt helpless, unable to do anything about it. Now, here was a far more basic hostility, however veiled, and a suspicion that must be like a burning fire.

And this time he could fight. He could look this skillfully voluble, friendly old man squarely in the eye and—

Friendly?

"It makes me smile sometimes," the old man was saying, "when I think of the unscientific aspects of the orbit we have to plan now. For instance, what is the time lag on storm reports out here?"

Maltby could not suppress a smile. So Lieutenant Cannons wanted to know things, did he? To give the man credit, it wasn't really a lame opening. The truth was, the only way to ask a question was— well—to ask it. Maltby said:

"Oh, three, four months. Nothing unusual. Each space meteorologist takes about that length of time to check the bounds of the particular storm in his area, and then he reports, and we adjust our maps.

"Fortunately"—he pushed his second mind to the fore as he coolly spoke the great basic lie—"there are no major storms between the Kaider and Cassidor suns."

He went on, sliding over the untruth like an eel breasting wet rock:

"However, several suns prevent a straight line movement. So if you would show me some of your orbits for twenty-five hundred light years, I'll make a selection of the best ones."

He wasn't, he realized instantly, going to slip over his main point as easily as that.

"No intervening storms?" the old man said. He pursed his lips. The fine lines in his long face seemed to deepen. He looked genuinely nonplused; and there was no doubt at all that he hadn't expected such a straightforward statement. "Hm-m-m, no storms. That does make it simple, doesn't it?"

He broke off. "You know, the important thing about two"—he hesitated over the word, then went on—"two people, who have been brought up in different cultures, under different scientific standards, is that they make sure they are discussing a subject from a common viewpoint.

"Space is so big. Even this comparatively small system of stars, the Lesser Magellanic Cloud, is so vast that it defies our reason. We on the battleship *Star Cluster* have spent ten years surveying it, and now we are able to say glibly that it comprises two hundred sixty billion cubic light years, and contains fifty millions of suns.

"We located the magnetic center of the Cloud, fixed our zero line from center to the great brightest star, S Doradus; and now, I suppose, there are people who would be fools enough to think we've got the system stowed away in our brainpans."

❖❖❖

Maltby was silent because he himself was just such a fool. This was warning. He was being told in no uncertain terms that they were in a position to check any orbit he gave them with respect to all intervening suns.

It meant much more. It showed that Earth was on the verge of extending her tremendous sway to the Lesser Magellanic Cloud. Destroying this ship now would provide the Fifty Suns with precious years during which they would have to decide what they intended to do.

But that would be all. Other ships would come; the inexorable pressure of the stupendous populations of the main galaxy would burst out even farther into space. Always under careful control, shepherded by mighty hosts of invincible battleships, the great transports would sweep into the Cloud, and every planet everywhere, robot or non-robot, would acknowledge Earth suzerainty.

Imperial Earth recognized no separate nations of any description anywhere. The robots, Dellian, non-Dellian and Mixed, would need every extra day, every hour; and it was lucky for them all that he was not basing his hope of destroying this ship on an orbit that would end inside a sun.

Their survey had magnetically placed all the suns for them. But they couldn't know about the storms. Not in ten years or in a hundred was it possible for one ship to locate possible storms in an area that involved twenty-five hundred light years of length.

Unless their psychologists could uncover the special qualities of his double brain, he had them. He grew aware that Lieutenant Cannons was manipulating the controls of the orbit table.

The lines of light on the surface flickered and shifted. Then settled like the balls in a game of chance. Maltby selected six that ran deep into the great storm. Ten minutes after that he felt the faint jar as the ship began to move. He stood up, frowning. Odd that they should act without *some* verification of his—

"This way," said the old man.

Maltby thought sharply: This couldn't be all. Any minute now they'd start on him and—

His thought ended.

He was in space. Far, far below was the receding planet of Kaider III. To one side gleamed the vast dark hull of the battleship; and on every other side, and up, and down, were stars and the distances of dark space.

In spite of all his will, the shock was inexpressibly violent.

His active mind jerked. He staggered physically; and he would have fallen like a blindfolded creature except that, in the movement of trying to keep on his feet, he recognized that he *was* still on his feet.

His whole being steadied. Instinctively, he—tilted—his second mind awake, and pushed it forward. Put its more mechanical and precise qualities, its Dellian strength, between his other self and whatever the human beings might be doing against him.

Somewhere in the mist of darkness and blazing stars, a woman's clear and resonant voice said:

"Well, Lieutenant Neslor, did the surprise yield any psychological fruits?"

The reply came from a second, an older-sounding woman's voice:

"After three seconds, noble lady, his resistance leaped to I. Q. 900. Which means they've sent us a Dellian. Your excellency, I thought you specifically asked that their representative be not a Dellian."

Maltby said swiftly into the night around him: "You're quite mistaken. I am not a Dellian. And I assure you that I will lower my resistance to zero if you desire. I reacted instinctively to surprise, naturally enough."

There was a click. The illusion of space and stars snapped out of existence. Maltby saw what he had begun to suspect, that he was, had been all the time, in the meteorology room.

Nearby stood the old man, a thin smile on his lined face. On a raised dais, partly hidden behind a long instrument board, sat a handsome young woman. It was the old man who spoke. He said in a stately voice:

"You are in the presence of Grand Captain, the Right Honorable Gloria Cecily, the Lady Laurr of Noble Laurr. Conduct yourself accordingly."

Maltby bowed but he said nothing. The grand captain frowned at him, impressed by his appearance. Tall, magnificent-looking body— strong, supremely intelligent face. In a single flash she noted all the characteristics common to the first-class human being and robot.

These people might be more dangerous than she had thought. She said with unnatural sharpness for her:

"As you know, we have to question you. We would prefer that you do not take offense. You have told us that Cassidor VII, the chief planet of the Fifty Suns, is twenty-five hundred light years from here. Normally, we would spend more than sixty years *feeling* our way across such an immense gap of uncharted, star-filled space. But you have given us a choice of orbits.

"We must make sure those orbits are honest, offered without guile or harmful purpose. To that end we have to ask you to open your mind and answer our questions under the strictest psychological surveillance."

"I have orders," said Maltby, "to cooperate with you in every way."

He had wondered how he would feel now that the hour of decision was upon him. But there was nothing unnormal. His body was a little stiffer, but his minds—

He withdrew his *self* into the background and left his Dellian mind to confront all the questions that came. His Dellian mind that he had deliberately kept apart from his thoughts. That curious mind, which had no will of its own, but which, by remote control, reacted with the full power of an I. Q. of 191.

Sometimes, he marveled himself at that second mind of his. It had no creative ability, but its memory was machinelike, and its resistance to outside pressure was, as the woman psychologist had so swiftly analyzed, over nine hundred. To be exact, the equivalent of I. Q. 917.

❖❖❖

"What is your name?"

That was the way it began: His name, distinction— He answered everything quietly, positively, without hesitation. When he had finished, when he had sworn to the truth of every word about the storms, there was a long moment of dead silence. And then a middle-aged woman stepped out of the nearby wall.

She came over and motioned him into a chair. When he was seated she tilted his head and began to examine it. She did it gently; her fingers were caressing as a lover's. But when she looked up she said sharply:

"You're not a Dellian or a non-Dellian. And the molecular structure of your brain and body is the most curious I've ever seen. All the molecules are twins. I saw a similar arrangement once in an artificial electronic structure where an attempt was being made to balance an unstable electronic structure. The parallel isn't exact, but—mm-m-m, I must try to remember what the end result was of that experiment."

She broke off: "What is your explanation? What are you?"

Maltby sighed. He had determined to tell only the one main lie. Not that it mattered so far as his double brain was concerned. But untruths effected slight variations in blood pressure, created neural spasms and disturbed muscular integration. He couldn't take the risk of even one more than was absolutely necessary.

"I'm a Mixed Man," he explained. He described briefly how the cross between the Dellian and non-Dellian, so long impossible, had finally been brought about a hundred years before. The use of cold and pressure—

"Just a moment," said the psychologist.

She disappeared. When she stepped again out of the wall transmitter, she was thoughtful.

"He seems to be telling the truth," she confessed, almost reluctantly.

"What is this?" snapped the grand captain. "Ever since we ran into that first citizen of the Fifty Suns, the psychology department has qualified every statement it issues. I thought psychology was the only perfect science. Either he is telling the truth or he isn't."

The older woman looked unhappy. She stared very hard at Maltby, seemed baffled by his cool gaze, and finally faced her superior, said:

"It's that double molecule structure of his brain. Except for that, I see no reason why you shouldn't order full acceleration."

The grand captain smiled. "I shall have Captain Maltby to dinner tonight. I'm sure he will cooperate then with any further studies you may be prepared to make at that time. Meanwhile I think—"

She spoke into a communicator: "Central engines, step up to half light year a minute on the following orbit—"

Maltby listened, estimating with his Dellian mind. Half a light year a minute; it would take a while to attain that speed, but—in eight hours they'd strike the storm.

In eight hours he'd be having dinner with the grand captain.

Eight hours!

❖ ❖ ❖

The full flood of a contraterrene Nova impinging upon terrene gases already infuriated by seetee gone insane—that was the new, greater storm.

The exploding, giant sun added weight to the diffuse, maddened thing. And it added something far more deadly.

Speed! From peak to peak of velocity the tumult of ultrafire leaped. The swifter crags of the storm danced and burned with an absolutely hellish fury.

The sequence of action was rapid almost beyond the bearance of matter. First raced the light of the Nova, blazing its warning at more than a hundred and eighty-six thousand miles a second to all who knew that it flashed from the edge of an interstellar storm.

But the advance glare of warning was nullified by the colossal speed of the storm. For weeks and months it drove through the vast night at a velocity that was only a bare measure short of that of light itself.

❖ ❖ ❖

The dinner dishes had been cleared away. Maltby was thinking: In half an hour—*half an hour!*

He was wondering shakily just what did happen to a battleship suddenly confronted by thousands of gravities of deceleration. Aloud he was saying:

"My day? I spent it in the library. Mainly, I was interested in the recent history of Earth's interstellar colonization. I'm curious as to what is done with groups like the Mixed Men. I mentioned to you that, after the war in which they were defeated largely because there was so few of them, the Mixed Men hid themselves from the Fifty Suns. I was one of the captured children who—"

There was an interruption, a cry from the wall communicator: *"Noble lady, I've solved it!"*

A moment fled before Maltby recognized the strained voice of the woman psychologist. He had almost forgotten that she was supposed to be studying him. Her next words chilled him:

"Two minds! I thought of it a little while ago and rigged up a twin watching device. Ask him, *ask* him the question about the storms. Meanwhile stop the ship. At once!"

Maltby's dark gaze clashed hard with the steely, narrowed eyes of the grand captain. Without hesitation he concentrated his two minds on her, forced her to say:

"Don't be silly, lieutenant. One person can't have two brains. Explain yourself further."

His hope was delay. They had ten minutes in which they could save themselves. He must waste every second of that time, resist all their efforts, try to control the situation. If only his special three-dimensional hypnotism worked through communicators—

It didn't. Lines of light leaped at him from the wall and crisscrossed his body, held him in his chair like so many unbreakable cables. Even as he was bound hand and foot by palpable energy, a second complex of forces built up before his face, barred his thought pressure from the grand captain, and finally coned over his head like a dunce cap.

He was caught as neatly as if a dozen men had swarmed with their strength and weight over his body. Maltby relaxed and laughed.

"Too late," he taunted. "It'll take at least an hour for this ship to reduce to a safe speed; and at this velocity you can't turn aside in time to avoid the greatest storm in this part of the Universe."

That wasn't strictly true. There was still time and room to sheer off before the advancing storm in any of the fronting directions. The impossibility was to turn toward the storm's tail or its great, bulging sides.

His thought was interrupted by the first cry from the young woman; a piercing cry: "Central engines! Reduce speed! Emergency!"

There was a jar that shook the walls and a pressure that tore at his muscles. Maltby adjusted and then stared across the table at the grand captain. She was smiling, a frozen mask of a smile; and she said from between clenched teeth:

"Lieutenant Neslor, use any means physical or otherwise, but make him talk. There must be something."

"His second mind is the key," the psychologist's voice came. "It's not Dellian. It has only normal resistance. I shall subject it to the greatest concentration of conditioning ever focused on a human brain, using the two basics: sex and logic. I shall have to use you, noble lady, as the object of his affections."

"Hurry!" said the young woman. Her voice was like a metal bar.

❖❖❖

Maltby sat in a mist, mental and physical. Deep in his mind was awareness that he was an entity, and that irresistible machines were striving to mold his thought.

He resisted. The resistance was as strong as his life, as intense as all the billions and quadrillions of impulses that had shaped his being, could make it.

But the outside thought, the pressure, grew stronger. How silly of him to resist Earth—when this lovely woman of Earth loved him, loved him, loved him. Glorious was that civilization of Earth and the main galaxy. Three hundred million billion people. The very first contact would rejuvenate the Fifty Suns. How lovely she is; I must save her. She means everything to me.

As from a great distance, he began to hear his own voice, explaining what must be done, just how the ship must be turned, in what direction, how much time there was. He tried to stop himself, but inexorably his voice went on, mouthing the words that spelled defeat for the Fifty Suns.

The mist began to fade. The terrible pressure eased from his straining mind. The damning stream of words ceased to pour from his lips. He sat up shakily, conscious that the energy cords and the energy cap had been withdrawn from his body. He heard the grand captain say into a communicator:

"By making a point 0100 turn we shall miss the storm by seven light weeks. I admit it is an appallingly sharp curve, but I feel that we should have at least that much leeway."

She turned and stared at Maltby: "Prepare yourself. At half a light year a minute even a hundredth of a degree turn makes some people black out."

"Not me," said Maltby, and tensed his Dellian muscles.

She fainted three times during the next four minutes as he sat there watching her. But each time she came to within seconds.

"We human beings," she said wanly, finally, "are a poor lot. But at least we know how to endure."

The terrible minutes dragged. And dragged. Maltby began to feel the strain of that infinitesimal turn. He thought at last: Space! How could these people ever hope to survive a direct hit on a storm?

Abruptly, it was over; a man's voice said quietly: "We have followed the prescribed course, noble lady, and are now out of dang—"

He broke off with a shout: "Captain, the light of a Nova sun has just flashed from the direction of the storm. We—"

❖ ❖ ❖

In those minutes before disaster struck, the battleship *Star Cluster* glowed like an immense and brilliant jewel. The warning glare from the Nova set off an incredible roar of emergency clamor through all of her hundred and twenty decks.

From end to end her lights flicked on. They burned row by row straight across her four thousand feet of length with the hard tinkle of cut gems. In the reflection of that light, the black mountain that was her hull looked like the fabulous planet of Cassidor, her destination, as seen at night from a far darkness, sown with diamond shining cities.

Silent as a ghost, grand and wonderful beyond all imagination, glorious in her power, the great ship slid through the blackness along the special river of time and space which was her plotted course.

Even as she rode into the storm there was nothing visible. The space ahead looked as clear as any vacuum. So tenuous were the gases that made up the storm that the ship would not even have been aware of them if it had been traveling at atomic speeds.

Violent the disintegration of matter in that storm might be, and the sole source of cosmic rays the hardest energy in the known universe. But the immense, the cataclysmic danger to the *Star Cluster* was a direct result of her own terrible velocity.

If she had had time to slow, the storm would have meant nothing.

Striking that mass of gas at half a light year a minute was like running into an unending solid wall. The great ship shuddered in every plate as the deceleration tore at her gigantic strength.

In seconds she had run the gamut of all the recoil systems her designers had planned for her as a unit.

She began to break up.

And still everything was according to the original purpose of the superb engineering firm that had built her. The limit of unit strain reached, she dissolved into her nine thousand separate sections. Streamlined needles of metal were those sections, four hundred feet long, forty feet wide; sliverlike shapes that sinuated cunningly through the gases, letting the pressure of them slide off their smooth hides.

But it wasn't enough. Metal groaned from the torture of deceleration. In the deceleration chambers, men and women lay at the bare edge of consciousness, enduring agony that seemed on the verge of being beyond endurance.

Hundreds of the sections careened into each other in spite of automatic screens, and instantaneously fused into white-hot coffins.

And still, in spite of the hideously maintained velocity, that mass of gases was not bridged; light years of thickness had still to be covered.

For those sections that remained, once more all the limits of human strength were reached. The final action is chemical, directly on the human bodies that remained of the original thirty thousand. Those bodies for whose sole benefit all the marvelous safety devices had been conceived and constructed, the poor, fragile, human beings who through all the ages had persisted in dying under normal conditions from a pressure of something less than fifteen gravities.

The prompt reaction of the automatics in rolling back every floor, and plunging every person into the deceleration chambers of each section—that saving reaction was abruptly augmented as the deceleration chamber was flooded by a special type of gas.

Wet was that gas, and clinging. It settled thickly on the clothes of the humans, soaked through to the skin and *through* the skin, into every part of the body.

Sleep came gently, and with it a wonderful relaxation. The blood grew immune to shock; muscles that, in a minute before, had been drawn with anguish—loosened; the brain impregnated with life-giving chemicals that relieved it of all shortages remained untroubled even by dreams.

Everybody grew enormously flexible to gravitation pressures—a hundred—a hundred and fifty gravities of deceleration; and still the life force clung.

The great heart of the Universe beat on. The storm roared along its inescapable artery, creating the radiance of life, purging the dark of its poisons—and at last the tiny ships in their separate courses burst its great bounds.

They began to come together, to seek each other, as if among them there was an irresistible passion that demanded intimacy of union.

Automatically, they slid into their old positions; the battleship *Star Cluster* began again to take form—but there were gaps. Segments destroyed, and segments lost.

On the third day Acting Grand Captain Rutgers called the surviving captains to the forward bridge, where he was temporarily making his headquarters. After the conference a communiqué was issued to the crew:

❖❖❖

At 0800 hours this morning a message was received from Grand Captain, the Right Honorable Gloria Cecily, the Lady Laurr of Noble Laurr, I. C., C. M., G. K. R. She has been forced down on the planet of a yellow-white sun. Her ship crashed on landing, and is unrepairable. As all communication with her has been by nondirectional sub-space radio, and as it will be utterly impossible to locate such an ordinary type sun among so many millions of other suns, the Captains in Session regret to report that our noble lady's name must now be added to that longest of all lists of naval casualties: the list of those who have been lost forever on active duty.

The admiralty lights will burn blue until further notice.

❖❖❖

Her back was to him as he approached. Maltby hesitated, then tensed his mind, and held her there beside the section of ship that had been the main bridge of the *Star Cluster*.

The long metal shape lay half buried in the marshy ground of the great valley, its lower end jutting down into the shimmering deep yellowish black waters of a sluggish river.

Maltby paused a few feet from the tall, slim woman, and, still holding her unaware of him, examined once again the environment that was to be their life.

The fine spray of dark rain that had dogged his exploration walk was retreating over the yellow rim of valley to the "west."

As he watched, a small yellow sun burst out from behind a curtain of dark ocherous clouds and glared at him brilliantly. Below it an expanse of jungle glinted strangely brown and yellow.

Everywhere was that dark-brown and intense, almost liquid yellow.

Maltby sighed—and turned his attention to the woman, willed her not to see him as he walked around in front of her.

He had given a great deal of thought to the Right Honorable Gloria Cecily during his walk. Basically, of course, the problem of a man and a woman who were destined to live the rest of their lives together, alone, on a remote planet, was very simple. Particularly in view of the fact that one of the two had been conditioned to be in love with the other.

Maltby smiled grimly. He could appreciate the artificial origin of that love. But that didn't dispose of the profound fact of it.

The conditioning machine had struck to his very core. Unfortunately, it had not touched her at all; and two days of being alone with her had brought out one reality:

The Lady Laurr of Noble Laurr was not even remotely thinking of yielding herself to the normal requirements of the situation.

It was time that she was made aware, not because an early solution was necessary or even desirable, but because she had to realize that the problem existed.

He stepped forward and took her in his arms.

She was a tall, graceful woman; she fitted into his embrace as if she belonged there; and, because his control of her made her return the kiss, its warmth had an effect beyond his intention.

He had intended to free her mind in the middle of the kiss.

He didn't.

When he finally released her, it was only a physical release. Her mind was still completely under his domination.

There was a metal chair that had been set just outside one of the doors. Maltby walked over, sank into it and stared up at the grand captain.

He felt shaken. The flame of desire that had leaped through him was a telling tribute to the conditioning he had undergone. But it was entirely beyond his previous analysis of the intensity of his own feelings.

He had thought he was in full control of himself, and he wasn't. Somehow, the sardonicism, the half detachment, the objectivity, which he had fancied was the keynote of his own reaction to this situation, didn't apply at all.

The conditioning machine had been thorough.

He loved this woman with such a violence that the mere touch of her was enough to disconnect his will from operations immediately following.

His heart grew quieter; he studied her with a semblance of detachment.

She was lovely in a handsome fashion; though almost all robot women of the Dellian race were better-looking. Her lips, while medium full, were somehow a trifle cruel; and there was a quality in her eyes that accentuated that cruelty.

There were built-up emotions in this woman that would not surrender easily to the idea of being marooned for life on an unknown planet.

It was something he would have to think over. Until then—

Maltby sighed. And released her from the three-dimensional hypnotic spell that his two minds had imposed on her.

❖❖❖

He had taken the precaution of turning her away from him. He watched her curiously as she stood, back to him, for a moment, very still. Then she walked over to a little knob of trees above the springy, soggy marsh land.

She climbed up it and gazed in the direction from which he had come a few minutes before. Evidently looking for him.

She turned finally, shaded her face against the yellow brightness of the sinking sun, came down from the hillock and saw him.

She stopped; her eyes narrowed. She walked over slowly. She said with an odd edge in her voice:

"You came very quietly. You must have circled and walked in from the west."

"No," said Maltby deliberately, "I stayed in the east."

She seemed to consider that. She was silent, her lean face creased into a frown. She pressed her lips together, finally; there was a bruise there that must have hurt, for she winced, then she said:

"What did you discover? Did you find any—"

She stopped. Consciousness of the bruise on her lip must have penetrated at that moment. Her hand jerked up, her fingers touched the tender spot. Her eyes came alive with the violence of her comprehension. Before she could speak, Maltby said:

"Yes, you're quite right."

She stood looking at him. Her stormy gaze quietened. She said finally, in a stony voice:

"If you try that again I shall feel justified in shooting you."

Maltby shook his head. He said, unsmiling:

"And spend the rest of your life here alone? You'd go mad."

He saw instantly that her basic anger was too great for that kind of logic. He went on swiftly:

"Besides, you'd have to shoot me in the back. I have no doubt you could do that in the line of duty. But not for personal reasons."

Her compressed lips—separated. To his amazement there were suddenly tears in her eyes. Angry tears, obviously. But tears!

She stepped forward with a quick movement and slapped his face.

"You robot!" she sobbed.

Maltby stared at her ruefully; then he laughed. Finally he said, a trace of mockery in his tone:

"If I remember rightly, the lady who just spoke is the same one who delivered a ringing radio address to all the planets of the Fifty Suns swearing that in fifteen thousand years Earth people had forgotten all their prejudices against robots.

"Is it possible," he finished, "that the problem on *closer* investigation is proving more difficult?"

There was no answer. The Honorable Gloria Cecily brushed past him and disappeared into the interior of the ship.

❖ ❖ ❖

She came out again a few minutes later.

Her expression was more serene; Maltby noted that she had removed all trace of the tears. She looked at him steadily, said:

"What did you discover when you were out? I've been delaying my call to the ship till you returned."

Maltby said: "I thought they asked you to call at 010 hours."

The woman shrugged; and there was an arrogant note in her voice as she replied:

"They'll take my calls when I make them. Did you find any sign of intelligent life?"

Maltby allowed himself brief pity for a human being who had as many shocks still to absorb as had Grand Captain Laurr.

One of the books he had read while aboard the battleship about colonists of remote planets had dealt very specifically with castaways.

He shook himself and began his description. "Mostly marsh land in the valley and there's jungle, very old. Even some of the trees are immense, though sections show no growth rings—some interesting beasts and a four-legged, two-armed thing that watched me from a distance. It carried a spear but it was too far away for me to use my hypnotism on it. There must be a village somewhere, perhaps on the valley rim. My idea is that during the next months I'll cut the ship into small sections and transport it to drier ground.

"I would say that we have the following information to offer the ship's scientists: We're on a planet of a G-type sun. The sun must be larger than the average yellow-white type and have a larger surface temperature.

"It must be larger and hotter because, though it's far away, it is hot enough to keep the northern hemisphere of this planet in a semi-tropical condition.

"The sun was quite a bit north at midday, but now it's swinging back to the south. I'd say offhand the planet must be tilted at about forty degrees, which means there's a cold winter coming up, though that doesn't fit with the age and type of the vegetation."

The Lady Laurr was frowning. "It doesn't seem very helpful," she said. "But, of course, I'm only an executive."

"And I'm only a meteorologist."

"Exactly. Come in. Perhaps my astrophysicist can make something of it."

"*Your* astrophysicist!" said Maltby. But he didn't say it aloud.

He followed her into the segment of ship and closed the door.

Maltby examined the interior of the main bridge with a wry smile as the young woman seated herself before the astroplate.

The very imposing glitter of the instrument board that occupied one entire wall was ironical now. All the machines it had controlled were far away in space. Once it had dominated the entire Lesser Magellanic Cloud; now his own hand gun was a more potent instrument.

He grew aware that Lady Laurr was looking up at him.

"I don't understand it," she said. "They don't answer."

"Perhaps"—Maltby could not keep the faint sardonicism out of his tone—"perhaps they may really have had a good reason for wanting you to call at 010 hours."

The woman made a faint, exasperated movement with her facial muscles but she did not answer. Maltby went on coolly:

"After all, it doesn't matter. They're only going through routine motions, the idea being to leave no loophole of rescue unlooked through. I can't even imagine the kind of miracle it would take for anybody to find us."

The woman seemed not to have heard. She said, frowning:

"How is it that we've never heard a single Fifty Suns broadcast? I intended to ask about that before. Not once during our ten years in the Lesser Cloud did we catch so much as a whisper of radio energy."

Maltby shrugged. "All radios operate on an extremely complicated variable wave length—changes every twentieth of a second. Your instruments would register a tick once every ten minutes, and—"

He was cut off by a voice from the astroplate. A man's face was there—Acting Grand Captain Rutgers.

"Oh, there you are, captain," the woman said. "What kept you?"

"We're in the process of landing our forces on Cassidor VII," was the reply. "As you know, regulations require that the grand captain—"

"Oh, yes. Are you free now?"

"No. I've taken a moment to see that everything is right with you, and then I'll switch you over to Captain Planston."

"How is the landing proceeding?"

"Perfectly. We have made contact with the government. They seem resigned. But now I must leave. Goodby, my lady."

His face flickered and was gone. The plate went blank. It was about as curt a greeting as anybody had ever received. But Maltby, sunk in his own gloom, scarcely noticed.

So it was all over. The desperate scheming of the Fifty Suns leaders, his own attempt to destroy the great battleship, proved futile against an invincible foe.

For a moment he felt very close to the defeat, with all its implications. Consciousness came finally that the fight no longer mattered in his life. But the knowledge failed to shake his dark mood.

He saw that the Right Honorable Gloria Cecily had an expression of mixed elation and annoyance on her fine, strong face; and there was no doubt that she didn't *feel*—disconnected—from the mighty events out there in space. Nor had she missed the implications of the abruptness of the interview.

The astroplate grew bright and a face appeared on it—one that Maltby hadn't seen before. It was of a heavy-jowled, oldish man with a ponderous voice that said:

"Privilege your ladyship—hope we can find something that will enable us to make a rescue. Never give up hope, I say, until the last nail's driven in your coffin."

He chuckled; and the woman said: "Captain Maltby will give you all the information he has, then no doubt you can give him some advice, Captain Planston. Neither he nor I, unfortunately, are astrophysicists."

"Can't be experts on every subject," Captain Planston puffed. "Er, Captain Maltby, what do you know?"

Maltby gave his information briefly, then waited while the other gave instructions. There wasn't much:

"Find out length of seasons. Interested in that yellow effect of the sunlight and the deep brown. Take the following photographs, using ortho-sensitive film—use three dyes, a red sensitive, a blue and a yellow. Take a spectrum reading—what I want to check on is that maybe you've got a strong blue sun there, with the ultraviolet barred by a heavy atmosphere, and all the heat and light coming in on the yellow band.

"I'm not offering much hope, mind you—the Lesser Cloud is packed with blue suns—five hundred thousand of them brighter than Sirius.

"Finally, get that season information from the natives. Make a point of it. Good-by!"

❖❖❖

The native was wary. He persisted in retreating elusively into the jungle; and his four legs gave him a speed advantage of which he seemed to be aware. For he kept coming back, tantalizingly.

The woman watched with amusement, then exasperation.

"Perhaps," she suggested, "if we separated, and I drove him toward you?"

She saw the frown on the man's face as Maltby nodded reluctantly. His voice was strong, tense.

"He's leading us into an ambush. Turn on the sensitives in your helmet and carry your gun. Don't be too hasty about firing, but don't hesitate in a crisis. A spear can make an ugly wound; and we haven't got the best facilities for handling anything like that."

His orders brought a momentary irritation. He seemed not to be aware that she was as conscious as he of the requirements of the situation.

The Right Honorable Gloria sighed. If they had to stay on this planet there would have to be some major psychologist adjustments, and not—she thought grimly—only by herself.

"*Now!*" said Maltby beside her, swiftly. "Notice the way the ravine splits in two. I came this far yesterday and they join about two hundred yards farther on. He's gone up the left fork. I'll take the right. You stop here, let him come back to see what's happened, then drive him on."

He was gone, like a shadow, along a dark path that wound under thick foliage.

Silence settled.

She waited. After a minute she felt herself alone in a yellow and black world that had been lifeless since time began.

She thought: This was what Maltby had meant yesterday when he had said she wouldn't dare shoot him—and remain alone. It hadn't penetrated then.

It did now. Alone, on a nameless planet of a mediocre sun, one woman waking up every morning on a moldering ship that rested its unliving metal shape on a dark, muggy, yellow marsh land.

She stood somber. There was no doubt that the problem of robot and human being would have to be solved here as well as out there.

A sound pulled her out of her gloom. As she watched, abruptly more alert, a catlike head peered cautiously from a line of bushes a hundred yards away across the clearing.

It was an interesting head; its ferocity not the least of its fascinating qualities. The yellowish body was invisible now in the underbrush, but she had caught enough glimpses of it earlier to recognize that it was the CC type, of the almost universal Centaur family. Its body was evenly balanced between its hind and forelegs.

It watched her, and its great glistening black eyes were round with puzzlement. Its head twisted from side to side, obviously searching for Maltby.

She waved her gun and walked forward. Instantly the creature disappeared. She could hear it with her sensitives, running into distance. Abruptly, it slowed; then there was no sound at all.

"He's got it," she thought.

She felt impressed. These two-brained Mixed Men, she thought, were bold and capable. It would really be too bad if antirobot prejudice prevented them from being absorbed into the galactic civilization of Imperial Earth.

She watched him a few minutes later, using the block system of communication with the creature. Maltby looked up, saw her. He shook his head as if puzzled.

"He says it's always been warm like this, and that he's been alive for thirteen hundred moons. And that a moon is forty suns—forty days. He wants us to come up a little farther along this valley, but that's too transparent for comfort. Our move is to make a cautious, friendly gesture, and—"

He stopped short. Before she could even realize anything was wrong, her mind was caught, her muscles galvanized. She was thrown sideways and downward so fast that the blow of striking the ground was pure agony.

She lay there stunned, and out of the corner of her eye she saw the spear plunge through the air where she had been.

She twisted, rolled over—her own free will now—and jerked her gun in the direction from which the spear had come. There was a second centaur there, racing away along a bare slope. Her finger pressed on the control; and then—

"Don't!" It was Maltby, his voice low. "It was a scout the others sent ahead to see what was happening. He's done his work. It's all over."

She lowered her gun and saw with annoyance that her hand was shaking, her whole body trembling. She parted her lips to say: "Thanks for saving my life!" Then she closed them again. Because the words would have quavered. And because—

Saved her life! Her mind poised on the edge of blankness with the shock of the thought. Incredibly—she had never before been in personal danger from an individual creature.

There had been the time when her battleship had run into the outer fringes of a sun; and there was the cataclysm of the storm, just past.

But those had been impersonal menaces to be met with technical virtuosities and the hard training of the service.

This was different.

All the way back to the segment of ship she tried to fathom what the difference meant.

It seemed to her finally that she had it.

❖❖❖

"Spectrum featureless." Maltby gave his findings over the astro. "No dark lines at all; two of the yellow bands so immensely intense that they hurt my eyes. As you suggested, apparently what we have here is a blue sun whose strong violet radiation is cut off by the atmosphere.

"However," he finished, "the uniqueness of that effect is confined to our planet here, a derivation of the thick atmosphere. Any questions?"

"No-o!" The astrophysicist looked thoughtful. "And I can give you no further instructions. I'll have to examine this material. Will you ask Lady Laurr to come in? Like to speak to her privately, if you please."

"Of course."

When she had come, Maltby went outside and watched the moon come up. Darkness—he had noticed it the previous night—brought a vague, overall violet haze. Explained now!

An eighty-degree temperature on a planet that, the angular diameter of the sun being what it was, would have been minus one hundred eighty degrees, if the sun's apparent color had been real.

A blue sun, one of five hundred thousand— Interesting, but— Maltby smiled savagely—Captain Planston's "No further instructions!" had a finality about it that—

He shivered involuntarily. And after a moment tried to picture himself sitting, like this, a year hence, staring up at an unchanged moon. Ten years, twenty—

He grew aware that the woman had come to the doorway and was gazing at him where he sat on the chair.

Maltby looked up. The stream of white light from inside the ship caught the queer expression on her face, gave her a strange, bleached look after the yellowness that had seemed a part of her complexion all day.

"We shall receive no more astro-radio calls," she said and, turning, went inside.

Maltby nodded to himself, almost idly. It was hard and brutal, this abrupt cutting off of communication. But the regulations governing such situations were precise.

The marooned ones must realize with utter clarity, without false hopes and without the curious illusions produced by radio communication, that they were cut off forever. Forever on their own.

Well, so be it. A fact was a fact, to be faced with resolution. There had been a chapter on castaways in one of the books he had read on the battleship. It had stated that nine hundred million human beings had, during recorded history, been marooned on then undiscovered planets. Most of these planets had eventually been found; and on no less than ten thousand of them great populations had sprung from the original nucleus of castaways.

The law prescribed that a castaway could not withhold himself or herself from participating in such population increases—regardless of previous rank. Castaways must forget considerations of sensitivity and individualism, and think of themselves as instruments of race expansion.

There were penalties; naturally inapplicable if no rescue was effected, but ruthlessly applied whenever recalcitrants were found.

Conceivably the courts might determine that a human being and a robot constituted a special case.

Half an hour must have passed while he sat there. He stood up finally, conscious of hunger. He had forgotten all about supper.

He felt a qualm of self-annoyance. Damn it, this was not the night to appear to be putting pressure on her. Sooner or later she would have to be convinced that she ought to do her share of the cooking.

But not tonight.

He hurried inside, toward the compact kitchen that was part of every segment of ship. In the corridor, he paused.

A blaze of light streamed from the kitchen door. Somebody was whistling softly and tunelessly but cheerfully; and there was an odor of cooking vegetables, and hot *lak* meat.

They almost bumped in the doorway. "I was just going to call you," she said.

The supper was a meal of silences, quickly over. They put the dishes into the automatic and went and sat in the great lounge; Maltby saw finally that the woman was studying him with amused eyes.

"Is there any possibility," she said abruptly, "that a Mixed Man and a human woman can have children?"

"Frankly," Maltby confessed, "I doubt it."

He launched into a detailed description of the cold and pressure process that had molded the protoplasm to make the original Mixed Men. When he finished he saw that her eyes were still regarding him with a faint amusement. She said in an odd tone:

"A very curious thing happened to me today, after that native threw his spear. I realized"—she seemed for a moment to have difficulty in speaking—"I realized that I had, so far as I personally was concerned, solved the robot problem.

"Naturally," she finished quietly, "I would not have withheld myself in any event. But it is pleasant to know that I like you without"—she smiled—"qualifications."

Blue sun that looked yellow. Maltby sat in the chair the following morning puzzling over it. He half expected a visit from the natives, and so he was determined to stay near the ship that day.

He kept his eyes aware of the clearing edges, the valley rims, the jungle trails, but—

There was a law, he remembered, that governed the shifting of light to other wave bands, to yellow for instance. Rather complicated, but in view of the fact that all the instruments of the main bridge were controls of instruments, not the machines themselves, he'd have to depend on mathematics if he ever hoped to visualize the kind of sun that was out there.

Most of the heat probably came through the ultraviolet range. But that was uncheckable. So leave it alone and stick to the yellow.

He went into the ship. Gloria was nowhere in sight, but her bedroom door was closed. Maltby found a notebook, returned to his chair and began to figure.

An hour later he stared at the answer: One million three hundred thousand million miles. About a fifth of a light year.

He laughed curtly. That was that. He'd have to get better data than he had or—

Or would he?

His mind poised. In a single flash of understanding, the stupendous truth burst upon him.

With a cry he leaped to his feet, whirled to race through the door as a long, black shadow slid across him.

The shadow was so vast, instantly darkening the whole valley, that, involuntarily, Maltby halted and looked up.

The battleship *Star Cluster* hung low over the yellow-brown jungle planet, already disgorging a lifeboat that glinted a yellowish silver as it circled out into the sunlight, and started down.

Maltby had only a moment with the woman before the lifeboat landed. "To think," he said, "that I just now figured out the truth."

She was, he saw, not looking at him. Her gaze seemed far away. He went on:

"As for the rest, the best method, I imagine, is to put me in the conditioning chamber, and—"

Still without looking at him, she cut him off:

"Don't be ridiculous. You must not imagine that I feel embarrassed because you have kissed me. I shall receive you later in my chambers."

A bath, new clothes—at last Maltby stepped through the transmitter into the astrophysics department. His own first realization of the tremendous truth, while generally accurate, had lacked detailed facts.

"Ah, Maltby!" The chief of the department came forward, shook hands. "Some sun you picked there—we suspected from your first description of the yellowness and the black. But naturally we couldn't rouse your hopes—Forbidden, you know.

"The axial tilt, the apparent length of a summer in which jungle trees of great size showed no growth rings—very suggestive. The featureless spectrum with its complete lack of dark lines—almost conclusive. Final proof was that the orthosensitive film was overexposed, while the blue and red sensitives were badly underexposed.

"This star type is so immensely hot that practically all of its energy radiation is far in the ultravisible. A secondary radiation—a sort of fluorescence in the star's own atmosphere—produces the visible yellow when a minute fraction of the appalling ultraviolet radiation is transformed into longer wave lengths by helium atoms. A fluorescent lamp, in a fashion—but on a scale that is more than ordinarily cosmic in its violence. The total radiation reaching the planet was naturally tremendous; the surface radiation, after passing through miles of absorbing ozone, water vapor, carbon dioxide and other gases, was very different.

"No wonder the native said it had always been hot. The summer lasts four thousand years. The normal radiation of that special appalling star type—the æon-in-æon-out radiation rate—is about equal to a full-fledged Nova at its catastrophic maximum of violence. It has a period of a few hours, and is equivalent to approximately a hundred million ordinary suns. Nova O, we call that brightest of all stars; and there's only one in the Lesser Magellanic Cloud, the great and glorious S-Doradus.

"When I asked you to call Grand Captain Laurr, and I told her that out of thirty million suns she had picked—"

It was at that point that Maltby cut him off. "Just a minute," he said, "did you say you told Lady Laurr *last night?*"

"Was it night down there?" Captain Planston said, interested. "Well, well—By the way, I almost forgot—this marrying and giving in marriage is not so important to me now that I am an old man. But congratulations."

The conversation was too swift for Maltby. His minds were still examining the first statement. That she had known all the time. He came up, groping, before the new words.

"Congratulations?" he echoed.

"Definitely time she had a husband," boomed the captain. "She's been a career woman, you know. Besides, it'll have a revivifying effect on the other robots . . . pardon me. Assure you, the name means nothing to me.

"Anyway, Lady Laurr herself made the announcement a few minutes ago, so come down and see me again."

He turned away with a wave of a thick hand.

Maltby headed for the nearest transmitter. She would probably be expecting him by now.

She would not be disappointed.

The Mixed Men

The globe was palely luminous, and about three feet in diameter. It hung in the air at approximately the center of the room, and its lowest arc was at the level of Maltby's chin.

Frowning, his double mind tensed, he climbed farther out of the bed, put on his slippers, and walked slowly around the light-shape.

As he stepped past it, it vanished.

He twisted hastily back—and there it was again.

Maltby allowed himself a grim smile. It was as he had thought, a projection pointing out of sub-space at his bed, and having no material existence in the room. Therefore, it couldn't be seen from the rear.

His frown deepened with gathering puzzlement. If he didn't know that *they* did not possess such a communicator, he'd guess that he was about to be advised that the time had come for action.

He hoped not, fervently. He was as far as ever from a decision. Yet who else would be trying to reach him?

The impulse came to touch the button that would connect the control center of the big spaceship with what was going on in his room. It wouldn't do to have Gloria think that he was in secret communication with outsiders.

Maltby smiled grimly. If she ever got suspicious, even the fact that he was married to her wouldn't save his two minds from being investigated by the ship's psychologist, Lieutenant Neslor. Still—

He had other commitments than marriage. He sat down on the bed, scowled at the thing, and said:

"I'm going to make an assumption as to your identity. What do you want?"

A voice, a very strong, confident voice spoke *through* the globe:

"You think you know who is calling, in spite of the unusual means?"

Maltby recognized the voice. His eyes narrowed, he swallowed hard; then he had control of himself. Memory came that there might be other listeners, who would draw accurate conclusions from his instant recognition of a voice. It was for them that he said:

"The logic of it is comparatively simple. I am a Mixed Man aboard the Earth battleship *Star Cluster*, which is cruising in the Fifty suns region of the Lesser Magellanic Cloud. Who would be trying to get in touch with me but the Hidden Ones of my own race?"

"Knowing this," said the voice pointedly, "you have nevertheless made no attempt to betray us?"

Maltby was silent. He wasn't sure he liked that remark. Like his own words, he recognized that these were aimed at possible listeners. But it was not a friendly act to call the attention of those listeners to the fact that he *was* keeping this conversation to himself.

More sharply than before it struck him that he had better remember his political situation both here on the ship, and out there. And weigh every word as he uttered it.

❖❖❖

Born a Mixed Man, Maltby had been captured as a child by the Dellian and non-Dellian robots of the Fifty Suns, and educated to a point where he felt a semiloyalty to his captors. Years of a life in which he was never quite trusted had culminated in his being assigned to destroy the Earth battleship.

In this he had only been partially successful, the end result having been a forcible re-shaping of his minds to be sympathetic to Earth. And this, in its turn, had ended in marriage to the youthful and dynamic Lady Laurr, commander of the mightiest war machine that had ever entered the Lesser Magellanic Cloud.

As a result of his varied experience, he now had three sympathies. That was the trouble. *Three* sympathies. He understood the motivations and beliefs, not only of the Dellian and non-Dellian robots, but also of the hidden race of Mixed Men and of the human beings from the main galaxy.

Literally, he couldn't take sides *against* any of them. His only hope, long held now, was that somewhere amid the welter of conflicting fears and desires was a solution that would be satisfactory to all three groups.

He knew better than to expect that such a hope would occur to any of the three. It was time he spoke again, and it would be advisable to bring the identity of the man beyond the light-thing into the open. He stared at it, and said curtly:

"Who are you?"

"Hunston!"

"Oh!" said Maltby.

His surprise was not altogether simulated. There was a difference between an inward recognition of a voice, and having that recognition verbally verified. The implications of the identity somehow sank in deeper:

Hunston, his enemy among the Mixed Men, and for many years now the acting leader.

Softly, Maltby repeated an earlier question: "What do you want?"

"Your diplomatic support."

Maltby said: "My what?"

The voice grew resonant and proud:

"In accordance with our belief, which you must surely share, that the Mixed Men are entitled to an equal part in the government of the Fifty Suns, regardless of the smallness of their numbers, I have today ordered that control be seized of every planet in the System. At this moment the armies of the Mixed Men, backed by the greatest assembly of super-weapons known in any galaxy, are carrying out landing operations, and will shortly attain control. You—"

The voice paused; then quietly: "You are following me, Captain Maltby?"

The question was like the silence after a clap of thunder.

❖❖❖

Slowly, Maltby emerged from the hard shock of the news. He climbed to his feet, then sank back again. Consciousness came finally that, though the world had changed, the room was still there. The room and the light-globe and himself.

Anger came then like a leaping fire. Savagely, he snapped:

"*You* gave this order—"

He caught himself. His brain geared to lightning comprehension, he examined the implications of the information. At last, with a bleak realization that in his position he could not argue the matter, he said:

"You're depending on acceptance of a *fait accompli*. What I know of the unalterable policies of Imperial Earth, convinces me your hope is vain."

"On the contrary," came the quick reply. "Only Grand Captain, the Lady Laurr must be persuaded. She has full authority to act as she sees fit. And she is your wife."

Cooler now, Maltby hesitated. It was interesting that Hunston, having acted on his own, was now seeking his support. Not too interesting though. What really held Maltby silent was the sudden realization that he had *known* something like this would happen—had known it from the very instant the news had been flashed that an Earth battleship had discovered the robot civilization of the Fifty Suns many months ago now.

Ten years, five years, even one year hence, the seal of Earth's approval would be set forever on the Fifty Suns democratic system *as it was*.

And the laws of that government expressly excluded the Mixed Men from any participation whatsoever. At this moment, this month, a change was still theoretically possible. After that—

It was clear that he personally had been too slow in making up his mind. The passions of other men had surged to thoughts of action, and finally to action itself. He would have to leave the ship somehow, and find out what was going on. For the moment, however, caution was the word. Maltby said:

"I am not averse to presenting your arguments to my wife. But some of your statements do not impress me in the slightest. You have said 'the greatest assembly of super-weapons in any galaxy.' I admit this method of using sub-space radio is new to me, but your statement as a whole must be nonsense.

"You cannot possibly know the weapons possessed by even this one battleship because, in spite of all my opportunity, I don't know. It is a safe assumption, furthermore, that no one ship can carry some of the larger weapons that Earth could muster at short notice anywhere in the charted universe.

"You cannot, isolated as we have all been, so much as guess what those weapons are, let alone declare with certainty that yours are better. Therefore, my question in that connection is this: why did you even mention such an implied threat? Of all your arguments, it is the least likely to rouse any enthusiasm for your cause. Well?"

❖ ❖ ❖

On the main bridge of the big ship, the Right Honorable Gloria Cecily turned from the viewing plate, which showed Maltby's room. Her fine face was crinkled with thought. She said slowly to the other woman:

"What do you make of it, Lieutenant Neslor?"

The ship's psychologist said steadily: "I think, noble lady, this is the moment we discussed when you first asked me what would be the psychological effects of your marriage to Peter Maltby."

The grand captain stared at her subordinate in astonishment. "Are you mad? His reaction has been correct in every detail. He has told me at great length his opinions of the situation in the Fifty Suns; and every word he has spoken fits. He—"

There was a soft buzz from the intership radio. A man's head and shoulders came onto the plate. He said:

"Draydon, Commander of Communications speaking. In reference to your question about the ultrawave radio now focused in your husband's bedroom, a similar device was invented in the main galaxy about a hundred and ninety years ago. The intention was to install it into all the new warships, and into all the older ships above cruiser size, but we were on our way before mass production began.

"In this field at least, therefore, the Mixed Men have equaled the greatest inventions of human creative genius, though it is difficult to know how so few could accomplish so much. The very smallness of their numbers makes it highly probable that they are not aware that our finders would instantly report the presence of their energy manifestation. They cannot possibly have discovered all the by-products of their invention. Any questions, noble lady?"

"Yes, how does it work?"

"Power. Sheer, unadulterated power. The ultra rays are directed in a great cone towards a wide sector of space in which the receiver ship is believed to be. Every engine in the sending ship is geared to the ray. I believe that experimentally contact was established over distances as great as thirty-five hundred light-years."

"Yes, but what is the principle?" Impatiently. "How, for instance, would they pick out the *Star Cluster* from a hundred other battle-ships?"

"As you know," came the reply, "our battleship constantly emits identification rays, on a special wave length. The ultra rays are tuned to that wave length, and when they contact, react literally instanta-neously. Immediately, all the rays focus on the center of the source of the identification waves, and remain focused regardless of speed or change of direction.

"Naturally, once the carrier wave is focused, sending picture and voice beams over it is simplicity itself."

"I see." She looked thoughtful. "Thank you."

❖❖❖

The grand captain clicked off the connection, and turned again to the image of the scene in Maltby's room. She heard her husband say:

"Very well, I shall present your arguments to my wife."

The answer of the light-globe was: it vanished. She sat cold. The whole interview had been registered on a beam; and so the part she had missed didn't matter. She'd run it off again later. She turned slowly to Lieutenant Neslor, and expressed the thought that hadn't left her mind for an instant:

"What are your reasons for what you said just before we were interrupted?"

The older woman said coolly: "What has happened here is basic to the entire robot problem. It is too important to allow any interfer-ence. Your husband must be removed from the ship, and you must allow yourself to be conditioned out of love with him until this affair is finally settled. You see that, don't you?"

"No!" Stubbornly. "I do not. On what do you base your opinion?"

"There are several notable points," said the psychologist. "One of them is the fact that *you* married him. Madam, you would never have married an ordinary person."

"Naturally." The grand captain spoke proudly. "You yourself have stated that his I.Q.'s, both of them, are greater than mine."

Lieutenant Neslor laughed scathingly. "Since when has I.Q. mattered to you? If that was a reason for recognizing equality, then the royal and noble families of the galaxy would long ago have become saturated with professors and scholars. No, no, my captain, there is in a person born to high estate an instinctive sense of greatness which has nothing to do with intelligence or ability. We less fortunate mortals may feel that that is unfair, but there is nothing we can do about it. When his lordship walks into the room, we may dislike him, hate him, ignore him or kowtow to him. But we are never indifferent to him.

"Captain Maltby has that air. You may not have been consciously aware of it when you married him, but you were, subconsciously."

The young woman protested: "But he's only a captain in the Fifty Suns navy, and he was an orphan raised by the state."

Lieutenant Neslor was cool. "He knows who he is, make no mistake. My only regret is that you married him so swiftly, thus barring me from making a detailed examination of his two minds. I am very curious about his history."

"He has told me everything."

"Noble lady," said the psychologist sharply. "Examine what you are saying. We are dealing with a man whose lowest I.Q. is more than 170. Every word you have spoken about him shows the bias of a woman for her lover.

"I am not," Lieutenant Neslor finished, "questioning your basic faith in him. As far as I have been able to determine he is an able and honest man. But your final decisions about the Fifty Suns must be made without reference to your emotional life. Do you see now?"

There was a long pause, and then an almost imperceptible nod. And then:

"Put him off," she said in a drab voice, "at Atmion. We must turn back to Cassidor."

❖ ❖ ❖

Maltby stood on the ground, and watched the *Star Cluster* fade into the blue mist of the upper sky. Then he turned, and caught a ground car to the nearest hotel. From there he made his first call. In an hour a young woman arrived. She saluted stiffly as she came into his presence. But as he stood watching her some of the hostility went out of her. She came forward, knelt gingerly, and kissed his hand.

"You may rise," Maltby said.

She stood up, and retreated, watching him with alert, faintly amused, faintly defiant gaze.

Maltby felt sardonic about it himself. Earlier generations of Mixed Men had decided that the only solution to leadership among so many immensely able men was an hereditary rulership. That decision had backfired somewhat when Peter Maltby, the only son of the last active hereditary leader, had been captured by the Dellians in the same battle that had killed his father. After long consideration, the lesser leaders had decided to reaffirm his rights.

They had even begun to believe that it would be of benefit to the Mixed Men to have their leader grow up among the people of the Fifty Suns. Particularly since good behavior on his part and by the other captured, now grown-up children, might be a way of winning back the good opinion of the Fifty Suns' people.

Some of the older leaders actually considered that the only hope of the race.

It was interesting to know that, in spite of Hunston's action, one woman partially recognized his status. Maltby said:

"My situation is this: I am wearing a suit which, I am convinced, is tuned to a finder on the *Star Cluster*. I want someone to wear it while I go to *the* hidden city."

The young woman inclined her head. "I am sure that can be arranged. The ship will come at midnight tomorrow to the rendezvous. Can you make it?"

"I'll be there."

The young woman hesitated. "Is there anything else?"

"Yes," said Maltby, "who's backing Hunston?"

"The young men." She spoke without hesitation.

"What about the young women?"

She smiled at that. "I'm here, am I not?"

"Yes, but only with half your heart."

"The other half," she said, unsmiling now, "is with a young man who is fighting in one of Hunston's armies."

"Why isn't your whole heart there?"

"Because I don't believe in deserting a system of government at the first crisis. We chose hereditary leadership for a definite period. We women do not altogether approve of these impulsive adventures, led by adventurers like Hunston, though we recognize that this is a crisis."

Maltby said gravely: "There will be many dead men before this is over. I hope your young man is not among them."

"Thank you," said the young woman. And went out.

❖❖❖

There were nine nameless planets, nine hidden cities where the Mixed Men lived. Like the planets, the cities had no names. They were referred to with a very subtle accent on the article in the phrase "*the* city." *The!* In every case the cities were located underground, three of them beneath great, restless seas, two under mountain ranges, the other four—no one knew.

Actually, no one knew. The outlets were far from the cities, the tunnels that led to them wound so tortuously that the biggest spaceships had to proceed at very low speeds around the curves.

The ship that came for Maltby was only ten minutes late. It was operated mostly by women, but there were some older men along, including three of his long-dead father's chief advisers, fine-looking old men named Johnson, Saunders and Collings. Collings acted as spokesman:

"I'm not sure, sir, that you should come to *the* city. There is a certain hostility, even among the women. They are afraid for their sons, husbands and sweethearts, but loyal to them.

"All the actions of Hunston and the others have been secret. For months we have had no idea what is going on. There is positively no information to be had at *the* hidden city."

Maltby said: "I didn't expect there would be. I want to give a speech, outlining the general picture as I see it."

There was no clapping. The audience—there were about twenty thousand in the massive auditorium—heard his words in a silence that seemed to grow more intense as he described some of the weapons on board the *Star Cluster*, and the policies of Imperial Earth with respect to lost colonies like the Fifty Suns.

He knew the verbal picture he was drawing was not pleasing them, but he finished grimly:

"My conclusion is this: Unless the Mixed Men can arrive at some agreement with Earth, or discover some means of nullifying the power of Earth, then all the preliminary victories are futile, meaningless and certain to end in disaster. There is no power in the Fifty Suns strong enough to defeat the battleship *Star Cluster* let alone all the other ships that Earth could send here in an emergency. Therefore—"

He was cut off. All over the great hall, mechanical speakers shouted in unison:

"He's a spy for his Earth wife. He never was one of us."

Maltby smiled darkly. So Hunston's friends had decided his sobering arguments might get him somewhere, and this was their answer.

He waited for the mechanized interruptions to end. In vain! The minutes flew by, and the bedlam grew rather than lessened. The audience was not the kind that approved of noise as a logical form of argument. As Maltby watched, several angry young women tore down reachable loud-speakers. Since many were in the ceiling, it was not a general solution. The confusion increased.

Tensely, Maltby thought: They must know, Hunston and his men, that they were irritating their followers here. How did they dare take the risk?

The answer came like a flash: They were playing for time. They had something big up their collective sleeve, something that would overwhelm all irritation and all opposition.

A hand was tugging at his arm. Maltby turned. And saw that it was Collings. The old man looked anxious.

"I don't like this," he said urgently above the uproar. "If they'll go this far, then they might even dare to assassinate you. Perhaps you had better return at once to Atmion, or Cassidor, wherever you wish to go."

Maltby stood thoughtful. "It has to be Atmion," he said finally. "I don't want the people aboard the *Star Cluster* to suspect that I have been wandering. In one sense I no longer have any commitments there, but I think the contact might still be valuable."

He smiled wryly, because that was an understatement if there ever was one. It was true that Gloria had been conditioned out of love with him, but he had been left conditioned *in* love with her. No matter how hard he tried he couldn't dismiss the reality of that.

He spoke again: "You know how to get in touch with me if anything turns up."

That, too, was to laugh. He had a pretty shrewd idea that Hunston would make particularly certain that no information came to *the* hidden city on *the* nameless planet.

Just how he was going to obtain information was another matter.

Quite suddenly, he felt completely cast out. Like a pariah, he left the stage. The noise faded behind him.

❖❖❖

He wandered out the days; and the puzzling thing to Maltby was that he heard nothing about the *Star Cluster*. For a month of hours, he went aimlessly from city to city; and the only news that came through was of the success of the Mixed Men.

Highly colored news it was. Everywhere, the conquerors must have seized radio control; and glowing accounts came of how the inhabitants of the Fifty Suns were wildly acclaiming their new rulers as leaders in the fight against the battleship from Imperial Earth. Against the human beings whose ancestors fifteen thousand years before had massacred all robots they could find, forcing the survivors to flee to this remote cloud of stars.

Over and over the theme repeated. No robot could ever trust a human being after what had happened in the past. The Mixed Men would save the robot world from the untrustworthy human beings and their battleship.

A very unsettling and chilling note of triumph entered the account every time the battleship was mentioned.

Maltby frowned over that, not for the first time, as he ate his lunch in an open-air restaurant on the thirty-first day. Soft, though vibrant music, poured over his head from a public announcer system. It was almost literally *over* his head, because he was too intent to be more than dimly aware of outside sound. One question dominated his thought:

What had happened to the battleship *Star Cluster*? Where *could* it be?

Gloria had said: "We shall take immediate action. Earth recognizes no governments by minorities. The Mixed Men will be given democratic privileges and equality, not dominance. That is final."

It was also, Maltby realized, reasonable IF human beings had really gotten over their prejudice against robots. It was a big if; and their prompt unloading of him from the ship proved that it wasn't a settled problem by any means.

The thought ended, as, above him, the music faded out on a high-pitched note. The brief silence was broken by the unmistakable voice of Hunston:

"To all the people of the Fifty Suns, I make this important announcement: The Earth battleship is a danger no more. It has been captured by a skillful trick of the Mixed Men and it is at Cassidor, where it is even now yielding its many secrets to the technical experts of the Mixed Men.

"People of the Fifty Suns, the days of strain and uncertainty are over. Your affairs will in future be administered by your kin and protectors, the Mixed Men. As their and your leader, I herewith dedicate the thirty billion inhabitants of our seventy planets to the task of preparing for future visitations from the main galaxy, and of insuring that no warship will ever again venture far into the Lesser Magellanic Cloud, which we now solemnly proclaim to be our living space, sacred and inviolable forever.

"But that is for the future. For the moment, we the people of the Fifty Suns have successfully circumvented the most hideous danger of our history. A three-day celebration is accordingly declared. I decree music, feasting and laughter—"

❖ ❖ ❖

At first there seemed nothing to think. Maltby walked along a boulevard of trees and flowers and fine homes; and, after a while, his mind tried to form a picture of an invincible battleship captured with all on board—if they were still alive.

How had it been done. By all the blackness in space, *how?*

Mixed Men, with their hypnotically powerful double minds, if allowed aboard in sufficient numbers to seize mental control of all high officers, could have done it.

But who would be mad enough to let that first group get into the ship?

Until a month ago, the *Star Cluster* had had two protections at least against such a disastrous finale to its long voyage. The first was the ship's able psychologist, Lieutenant Neslor, who would unhesitatingly pry into the brain of every person who entered the machine.

The second safeguard was Captain Peter Maltby, whose double brain would instantly recognize the presence of another Mixed Man.

Only Maltby was not on the ship, but walking along this quiet, magnificent street, consuming himself with amazement and dismay. He was here because—

Maltby sighed with sudden immense understanding. So that was why the light-globe had appeared to him, and why Hunston had been so plausible. The man's words had had nothing to do with his intentions. The whole act had been designed to force off of the ship the one man who would instantly sense the presence of Mixed Men.

scovered them. To betray one's kin to death for the love of an alien woman, was almost unthinkable.

Yet he couldn't have allowed *her* ship to be captured.

Perhaps, his course would have been to warn the would-be conquerors to keep away.

The choice, forced upon him at the flash moment of attack, would have taxed the logic capacity of his brain.

It didn't matter now. The events had fallen their chance ways without reference to him. He couldn't change the larger aspect of them: The political seizure of the Fifty Suns government, the capture of a mighty battleship, all these were beyond the influence of a man who had been proved wrong by events, and who could now be killed without anybody, even his former supporters, worrying too much about him.

It wouldn't do to contact *the* hidden city in this hour of Hunston's triumph.

There remained a fact that he had to do something about. The fact that if the *Star Cluster* had been captured, then so had the Right Honorable Gloria Cecily. And the Lady Laurr of Noble Laurr was in addition to all her great titles Mrs. Peter Maltby.

That was the reality. Out of it grew the first purely personal purpose of his lonely life.

❖❖❖

The naval yard spread before him. Maltby paused on the side-walk a hundred feet from the main officers' entrance, and casually lighted a cigarette.

Smoking was primarily a non-Dellian habit; and he had never contracted it. But a man who wanted to get from planet IV of the Atmion sun to Cassidor VII without going by regular ship needed a flexible pattern of small actions to cover such moments as this.

He lit the cigarette, the while his gaze took in the gate and the officer in charge of the guard. He walked forward finally with the easy stride of a person of clear conscience.

He stood, puffing, while the man, a Dellian, examined his per-fectly honest credentials. The casualness was a mask. He was think-ing, in a mental sweat: It *would* be a Dellian. With such a man hyp-notism, except under certain conditions of surprise, was almost impossible.

The officer broke the silence. "Step over to the postern, captain," he said. "I want to talk to you."

Maltby's primary mind sagged, but his secondary brain grew as alert as steel suddenly subjected to strain.

Was this discovery?

On the verge of slashing forth with his minds, he hesitated. Wait! he warned himself. Time enough to act if an attempt was made to sound an alarm. He must test to the limit his theory that Hunston wouldn't have had time to close all the gates against him.

He glanced sharply at the other's face. But the typically handsome countenance of a Dellian robot was typically impassive. If this was dis-covery, it was already too late for his special brand of hypnotism.

The robot began in a low voice, without preamble:

"We have orders to pick you up, captain."

He paused; he stared curiously at Maltby, who probed cautious-ly with his minds, met an invincible barrier, and withdrew, defeated but nonplussed. So far there was nothing menacing.

Maltby studied the fellow narrowly. "Yes?" he said cautiously.

"If I let you in," the Dellian said, "and something happened, say, a ship disappeared, I'd be held responsible. But if I don't let you in, and you just walk away, no one will guess that you've been here."

He shrugged, smiled. "Simple, eh?"

Maltby stared at the man gloomily. "Thanks," he said. "But what's the idea?"

"We're undecided."

"About what?"

"About the Mixed Men. This business of their taking over the government is all very well. But the Fifty Suns navy does not forswear, or swear, allegiance in ten minutes. Besides, we're not sure that Earth's offer was not an honest one."

"Why are you telling me this? After all, I am physically a Mixed Man."

The robot smiled. "You've been thoroughly discussed in the mess halls, captain. We haven't forgotten that you were one of us for fifteen years. Though you may not have noticed it, we put you through many tests during that period."

"I noticed," said Maltby, his face dark with memory. "I had the impression that I must have failed the tests."

"You didn't."

❖❖❖

There was silence. But Maltby felt a stirring of excitement. He had been so intent on his own troubles that the reaction of the people of the Fifty Suns to cataclysmic political change had scarcely touched him.

Come to think of it, he had noticed among civilians the same uncertainty as this officer was expressing.

There was no doubt at all, the Mixed Men had seized control at a beautifully timed psychological moment. But their victory wasn't final. There was still opportunity here for the purposes of others.

Maltby said simply: "I want to get to Cassidor to find out what has happened to my wife. How can I manage it?"

"The grand captain of the *Star Cluster* is really your wife! That wasn't propaganda?"

Maltby nodded. "She's really my wife."

"And she married you knowing you were a robot?"

Maltby said: "I spent weeks in the battleship's library looking up Earth's version of the massacre of the robots, which took place fifteen thousand years ago. Their explanation was that it was a brief revival in the mass of the people of old-time race prejudices which, as you know, were rooted in fear of the alien and, of course, in pure elemental antipathy.

"The Dellian robot was such a superbly handsome being, and with his curious physical and mental powers *seemed* to be superior to naturally born men that, in one jump, the fear became a panicky hate, and the lynchings began."

"What about the non-Dellian robots, who made possible the escape, and yet about whom so little is known?"

Maltby laughed grimly. "That is the cream of the jest. Listen—"

When he had finished his explanation, the officer said blankly:

"And do the people of the *Star Cluster* know this?"

"I told them," Maltby said. "They were intending to make the announcement just before the battleship went back to Earth."

There was silence. Finally the Dellian said: "What do you think of this business of Mixed Men seizing our government and organizing for war?"

"I'm undecided."

"Like the rest of us."

"What troubles me," said Maltby, "is that there are bound to be other Earth battleships arriving, and some of them at least will not be captured by trickery."

"Yes," said the robot, "we've thought of that."

The silence settled, and lasted longer this time before Maltby brought out his request:

"Is there any way that I can get to Cassidor?"

The Dellian stood with closed eyes, hesitating. At last he sighed:

"There's a ship leaving in two hours. I doubt if Captain Terda Laird will object to your presence aboard. If you will follow me, captain."

Maltby went through the gate, and into the shadows of the great hangars beyond. There was an odd relaxedness inside him; and he was in space before he realized what it meant.

His taut sense of being alone in a universe of aliens was gone.

❖ ❖ ❖

The darkness beyond the portholes was soothing to his creative brain. He sat staring into the black ink with its glinting brightness that were stars; and felt a oneness.

Nostalgic memory came of all the hours he had spent like this when he was a meteorologist in the Fifty Suns navy. Then he had thought himself friendless, cut off from these Dellian and non-Dellian robots by an unbridgeable suspicion.

The truth, perhaps, was that he had grown so aloof that no one had dared to try to close the gap.

Now, he knew the suspicion had long dimmed almost to vanishing. Somehow that made the whole Fifty Suns problem his again. He thought: a different approach to the rescue of Gloria was in order. A few hours before the landing, he sent his card to Captain Laird, and asked for an interview.

The commanding officer was a non-Dellian, lean and gray and dignified. And he agreed to every word, every detail of Maltby's plan.

"This whole matter," he said, "was threshed out three weeks ago, shortly after the Mixed Men seized power. In estimating the total number of warcraft available to Imperial Earth, we arrived at a figure that was almost meaningless, it was so large.

"It wouldn't be surprising," the officer continued earnestly, "if Earth could detach a warship for every man, woman and child in the Fifty Suns, and not perceptibly weaken the defenses of the main galaxy.

"We of the navy have been waiting anxiously for Hunston to make a statement either privately or publicly about that. His failure to do so is alarming, particularly as there is some logic in the argument that the first penetration of a new star system like our Lesser Magellanic Cloud, would be undertaken on the orders of the central executive."

"It's an Imperial mission," said Maltby, "working on a directive from the Emperor's council."

"Madness!" Captain Laird muttered. "Our new rulers are madmen."

He straightened, shaking his head, as if to clear it of darkness and confusion. He said in a resonant voice:

"Captain Maltby, I think I can guarantee you the full support of the navy in your effort to rescue your wife if . . . if she is still alive."

As he fell through the darkness an hour later, down and down and down, Maltby forced the warming effects of that promise to dim the grim import of the final words.

Once, his old sardonicism surged like a stirred fire; and he thought ironically: almost incredible that only a few months had passed since circumstances had made it necessary for Lieutenant Neslor, the *Star Cluster*'s psychologist, to force on him an intense emotional attachment for Gloria; that attachment which, ever since, had been the ruling passion of his life.

She on the other hand had fallen for him naturally. Which was one of the reasons why their relationship was so precious.

The planet below was brighter, larger, a crescent sitting comfortably in space, its dark side sparkling with the silver flashing lights of tens of thousands of towns and cities.

That was where he headed, towards the twinkling dark side. He landed in a grove of trees; and he was burying his spacesuit beside a carefully marked tree, when the total blackness struck him.

Maltby felt himself falling over. He hit the ground with a sharp impact, distinctly aware of his consciousness fading out of his mind.

❖ ❖ ❖

He woke up, amazed. And looked around him. It was still dark. Two of the three moons of Cassidor were well above the horizon; and they hadn't even been in sight when he landed. Their light shed vaguely over the small glade.

It was the same grove of trees.

Maltby moved his hands—and they moved; they were not tied. He sat up, then stood up.

He was alone.

There was not a sound, except the faint whispering of wind through the trees. He stood, eyes narrowed, suspicious; then, slowly, he relaxed. He had heard, he remembered suddenly, of unconsciousness like this overwhelming non-Dellians after a long fall through space. Dellians were not affected; and until this instant he had thought Mixed Men were also immune.

They weren't. There was no doubt about that.

He shrugged, and forgot about it. It took about ten minutes to walk to the nearest air stop. Ten minutes later he was at an air center.

He knew his way now. He paused in one of the forty entrances and, probing briefly with his two minds, satisfied himself that there were no Mixed Men among the masses of people surging towards the various escalators.

It was a tiny satisfaction at best. Tiny because he had known Hunston couldn't possibly spare the men for complicated patrol duty. The leader of the Mixed Men could talk as glibly as he pleased about his armies. But—Maltby smiled darkly—there was no such force.

The *coup d'etat* that had won Hunston control of the Fifty Suns was a far bolder, more risky accomplishment that was readily apparent. It must have been undertaken with less than a hundred thousand men—and the danger to Peter Maltby would be the point of disembarkation at the mighty city Della, capital of the Fifty Suns.

He had just bought his ticket, and was striding towards a fourth level escalator when the woman touched his arm.

In a single flash, Maltby had her mind, then as swiftly he relaxed.

He found himself staring at Lieutenant Neslor, chief psychologist of the *Star Cluster*.

❖ ❖ ❖

Maltby set down his cup, and stared unsmilingly across the table at the woman psychologist.

"Frankly," he said, "I am not interested in any plan you may have for recapturing the ship. I am in a position where I cannot conscientiously take sides on the larger issues."

He paused. He studied her curiously, but without any real thought. The emotional life of the middle-aged woman had puzzled him at times. In the past, he had wondered if she had used the machines in her laboratories to condition herself against all human feeling. The memory of that thought touched his brain as he sat there.

The memory faded. It was information he wanted, not addenda on her character.

He said, more coldly: "To my mind, you are responsible for the ignominious capture of the *Star Cluster*, first because it was you, in your scientific wisdom, who had me, a protective force, put off the ship; second because it was your duty to explore the minds of those who were permitted aboard. I still can't understand how you could have failed."

The woman was silent. Thin and graying at the temples, handsome in a mature fashion, she sat sipping her drink. She met his gaze finally, steadily. She said:

"I'm not going to offer any explanations. Defeat speaks for itself."

She broke off, flashed: "You think our noble lady will fall into your arms with gratitude when you rescue her. You forget that she has been conditioned out of love with you, and that only her ship matters to her."

"I'll take my chances on that, and I'll take it alone. And if we are ever again subject to Earth laws, I shall exercise my legal rights."

Lieutenant Neslor's eyes narrowed. "Oh," she said, "you know about that. You did spend a great deal of time in the library, didn't you?"

Maltby said quietly: "I probably know more about Earth laws than any other individual on the *Star Cluster*."

"And you won't even listen to my plan, to use the thousand survivors to help in the rescue."

"I've told you, I cannot participate in the larger issues."

The woman stood up. "But you *are* going to try to rescue Lady Gloria?"

"Yes."

She turned without another word, and walked off. Maltby watched her until she disappeared through a distant door. After a moment there seemed nothing at all to think about the interview.

❖ ❖ ❖

Grand Captain, the Right Honorable Gloria Cecily, the Lady Laurr of Noble Laurr, sat in the throne chair of her reception dais, and listened unsmilingly to the psychologist's report. It was not until the older woman had finished that the bleakness of the listener showed abatement.

Her voice, however, was sharp as she said:

"Then he definitely didn't suspect the truth? He didn't discover that the *Star Cluster* has never been captured. He didn't realize that it was you who made him unconscious when he landed in the grove of trees?"

Lieutenant Neslor said: "Oh, he was suspicious. But how could he so much as guess the larger truth? In view of our silence, how could he suspect that Hunston's triumphant announcement was only a part of the ever deadlier game he and we are playing, in our attempts to destroy each other? The very fact that Hunston *has* got an Earth battleship makes it particularly impossible for anybody to realize the truth."

The young noblewoman nodded, smiling now. She sat for a moment, proud eyes narrowed with thought, lips parted, gleaming white teeth showing.

That had not been the expression on her face when first she had learned that the Mixed Men also had an Earth battleship, and a marvelously new model at that, a ship whose type had been in the design stage for nearly eight hundred years.

Sitting there, all the knowledge she had on the subject of that new thundership, as it was called in the naval yards, was flashingly reviewed in her mind. How its nine hundred billion separate parts had gone into mass production seventy-five years before, with the expectation that the first ship would be completed at the end of seventy years, and additional ones every minute thereafter for five years.

The five years were up. Very few of the vessels would actually be in service as yet, but somewhere along the line one of them had been stolen.

Her feelings concerning the possession by the Mixed Men of such a battleship had been an imbalance of relief and alarm. Relief that the super-inventions of the Mixed Men were after all only stolen from the main galaxy. And alarm at the implications of such a capture.

What were Hunston's intentions? How *did* he intend to get around the fact that Imperial Earth had more warships than there were men, women and children in the Fifty Suns?

She said slowly: "Undoubtedly, the Mixed Men sent a ship to the main galaxy the moment they heard about us; and, of course, if enough of them ever got aboard one of our warships there would be no stopping them."

She broke off, more cheerfully: "I am glad that Captain Maltby did not question your account of how you and a thousand other crew members escaped when Hunston made his so-called seizure of the *Star Cluster.* I am not surprised that he refused to have anything to do with your hare-brained scheme for recapturing the battleship.

"The important thing is that, under cover of this pretty little story, you learned what we wanted to know: His love fixation for me is driving him to an attempt to board Hunston's battleship. When the indicator we have had pointing at him since he left us at Atmion indicates that he is inside the ship, then we shall act."

She laughed. "He's going to be a very surprised young man when he discovers what kind of clothes he is wearing."

Lieutenant Neslor said: "He may be killed."

There was silence. But the faint smile remained on the finely molded, handsome face of Lady Laurr. Lieutenant Neslor said quickly:

"Do not forget that your present antagonism towards him is influenced by your present comprehension of how deeply you had previously committed yourself to an emotional attachment."

"It is possible," admitted the grand captain steadily, "that your conditioning was over enthusiastic. Whatever the reason, I have no desire to feel other than I do now. You may therefore consider this a command: Under no circumstances am I to be reconditioned into my former state.

"The divorce between Captain Maltby and myself, now that it has taken place, is final. Is that clear?"

"Yes, noble lady."

❖❖❖

Here were ships. Ships, ships, ships, more than Maltby had ever seen in the Cassidor yards. The Fifty Suns navy was undoubtedly being demobilized as fast as the Mixed Men could manage it.

The ships stretched in ranks to the north, to the east, to the south, as far as the eye could see. They lay in their cradles in long, geometric rows. Here and there surface hangars and repair shops broke that measured rhythm of straight line. But for the most part the buildings were underground, or rather, under sheeted plains of metal, hidden by a finely corrugated sea of translucent steel alloy.

The Earth battleship lay about four miles from the western entrance. The distance seemed to have no diminishing effect on its size.

It loomed colossal on the horizon, overshadowing the smaller ships, dominating the sky and the planet and the sections of city that spread beyond it. Nothing on Cassidor, nothing in the Fifty

Suns system could begin to approach that mighty ship for size, for complication, for sheer appearance of power.

Even now, it seemed incredible to Maltby that so great a weapon, a machine that could destroy whole planets, had fallen intact into the hands of the Mixed Men, captured by a trick.

With an effort, Maltby drew his mind from that futile contemplation, and walked forward. He felt cold and steady and determined. The officer at the gate was a pleasant faced non-Dellian, who took him through, saying:

"There is an electronic matter transmitter focused from the ship's hold into the doorway of that building."

He motioned a hundred yards ahead and to one side, and went on:

"That will get you inside the battleship. Now, put this alarm device in your pocket."

Maltby accepted the tiny instrument curiously. It was an ordinary combination sending and receiving tube with a lock button to activate the signal.

"What's this for?" he asked.

"You're heading for the Grand Captain's bridge, are you not?"

Maltby nodded, but there was a thought beginning in his mind; and he did not trust himself to speak. He waited. The young man continued:

"As soon as you can, make every effort to go over to the control board and nullify energy flows, force connections, automatic screens and so on. Then press the signal."

The thought inside Maltby was an emptiness. He had a sudden sense of walking along the edge of an abyss.

"But what's the idea?" he asked blankly.

The answer was quiet, almost cool. "It has been decided," said the young officer, "to try to take the battleship. We got hold of some spare transmitters, and we are ready to put a hundred thousand men aboard in one hour from the various concentration centers. Whatever the result, in the confusion of the attack your chances of escaping with your wife will be augmented."

He broke off crisply: "You understand your instructions?"

Instructions! So that was it. He was a member of the Fifty Suns navy, and they took it for granted that he was subject to orders without question.

He wasn't of course. As hereditary leader of the Mixed Men, who had sworn allegiance to the Fifty Suns, and married the representative of Imperial Earth, his loyalty was a problem in basic ethics.

The wry thought came to Maltby that only an attack by the survivors of the *Star Cluster* was needed now. Led by Lieutenant Neslor, their arrival would just about make a perfect situation for a man whose mind was running around in circles, faster and faster every minute.

He needed time to think, to decide. And, fortunately, the time was going to be available. *This* decision didn't have to be made here and now. He would take the alarm device—and sound it or not according to his determination at the moment.

Relieved, he slipped the instrument into his pocket. He said quietly: "Yes, I understand my instructions."

Two minutes later he was inside the battleship.

❖❖❖

The storeroom, in which Maltby found himself, was deserted. That shocked him. It was too good to be true.

His gaze flashed over the room. He couldn't remember ever having been in it when he was aboard the *Star Cluster*. But then he had never had any reason to wander all over the mighty ship. Nor, for that matter, had he had time.

The room was a storehouse, ordinary, without interest for him.

Maltby walked swiftly over to the inter-room transmitter, reached up to press the toucher that would enable him to step from the hold into the grand captain's bridge. But at the last instant, his fingers actually on the toucher, he hesitated.

It had been wise, of course, to do everything boldly. The whole history of warfare taught that planned boldness, tempered with alertness, weighed heavily in the balance of victory.

Only he hadn't really planned.

Consciously, he let his secondary, his Dellian mind tilt forward. He stood very still, mentally examining his actions from the moment that Hunston had projected the globe of force into his bedroom, through the trip to Cassidor, the talk he had had with Lieutenant Neslor, and the suddenly announced plan of the Fifty Suns navy.

Thinking about it, it struck him sharply that the over-all,

outstanding effect was of complication. The Dellian part of his brain, with its incisive logic, usually had little difficulty organizing seemingly unrelated facts into whatever unity was innate in them.

Yet now, it was slow in resolving the details. It took a moment to realize why: Each fact was a compound of many smaller facts, some of them partially resolvable by deduction, others though undoubtedly there, refused to come out of the mist.

There was no time to think about it. He had decided to enter the grand captain's cabin—and there was only one way to do it.

With an abrupt movement, he pressed the toucher. He stepped through into a brightly lighted room. A tall man was standing about a dozen feet from the transmitter, staring at it. In his fingers he held an In-no gun.

It was not until the man spoke that Maltby recognized Hunston. The Leader of the Mixed Men said in a ringing voice:

"Welcome, Captain Maltby, I've been waiting for you."

For once, boldness had failed.

❖❖❖

Maltby thought of snatching his own In-no gun from its holster. He thought of it, but that was all. Because, first, he glanced over at the control board, to the section that governed the automatic defenses of the interior of the ship.

A single light glowed there. He moved his hand slowly. The light flickered, showing awareness of him. He decided not to draw his weapon.

The possibility that that light would be on had made it highly inadvisable to enter the main bridge, weapon in hand.

Maltby sighed and gave his full attention to the other. It was seven years since he had seen Hunston. The man's physical development since then was worthy of attention. Like all men with Dellian blood in them, like Maltby himself, Hunston was a superbly well-proportioned being.

His mother must have been a blonde and his father a very dark brunette, because his hair had come out the curious mixture of gold and black that always resulted from such a union. His eyes were gray-blue.

Seven years before Hunston had been slenderer, and somehow

immature in spite of his confidence and personality. That was all gone now. He looked strong and proud, and every inch a leader of men. He said without preamble:

"Basically, the facts are these: This is not the *Star Cluster*. My statement about that was political maneuvering. We captured this battleship from a naval yard in the main galaxy. A second battleship, now in process of being captured, will soon be here. When it arrives, we shall engage the *Star Cluster* in a surprise attack."

The change of Maltby's status from rescuer to dupe was as swift as that. One instant he was a man tensed with determination, geared to withstand any danger; the next a fool, his purpose made ludicrous.

He said: "B-but—"

It was a sound, not a reaction. A word expressing blankness, a thoughtless state, which preceded the mind storm, out of which grew understanding. Before Maltby could speak, Hunston said:

"Someone advised us that you were coming. We assume it was your wife. We assume furthermore that there is hostile purpose behind every move she is making. Accordingly, we prepared for any emergency. There are ten thousand Mixed Men inside this ship. If your arrival here is to be the signal for an attack, it will have to be well-organized indeed to surprise us."

Once more, there were too many facts. But after a moment, Maltby thought of the Fifty Suns navy men, waiting to enter the battleship, and flinched. He parted his lips to speak, and closed them again as his Dellian mind projected into his primary the memory of his meeting with Lieutenant Neslor.

The logic capacity of that secondary mind was on a plane that had no human parallel. There was a flashing connection made between the meeting with the psychologist and the blackness that had struck him down at the moment of his landing on Cassidor.

Instantly, that marvelous secondary brain examined a thousand possibilities, and, since it had enough clues at last, came forth with the answer.

The suit he was wearing!!! He must have been made unconscious, in order to substitute it for the one he *had* been wearing. Any minute, any *second*, it would be activated.

Sweating, Maltby pictured the resulting clash of titans: Ten thousand

Mixed Men versus a major portion of the crew of the *Star Cluster* versus one hundred thousand men of the Fifty Suns navy.

If only that last group would wait for his signal, then he could save them by not sounding it. Sharp consciousness came that he ought to speak, but first—

He must find out if the suit had been energized.

He put his arm behind his back, and pushed his hand cautiously *into* his back. It went in four inches, six inches; and still there was only emptiness. Slowly, Maltby withdrew his arm.

The suit was activated all right.

Hunston said: "Our plan is to destroy the *Star Cluster*, then Earth itself."

"W-what?" said Maltby.

He stared. He had a sudden feeling that he had not heard correctly. He echoed, his voice loud in his own ears:

"Destroy Earth!"

Hunston nodded coolly. "It's the only logical course. If the one planet is destroyed, on which men know of the *Star Cluster*'s expedition to the Lesser Magellanic Cloud, then we shall have time to expand, to develop our civilization; and eventually, after a few hundred years of intensive breeding of Mixed Men, we will have enough population to take over the control of the main galaxy itself."

"But," Maltby protested, "Earth is the center of the main galaxy. All the government is there, the Imperial symbol. It's the *head* of the planets of 3000 million suns. It—"

He stopped. The fear that came was all the greater because it was not personal.

"Why, you madman!" he cried angrily. "You can't do a thing like that. It would disorganize the entire galaxy."

"Exactly." Hunston nodded with satisfaction. "We would definitely have the time we need. Even if others knew of the *Star Cluster* expedition, no one would connect it with the catastrophe, and no other expedition would be sent."

He paused. Then went on:

"As you see, I have been very frank with you. And you will not have failed to note that our entire plan depends on whether or not we can first destroy the *Star Cluster*. In this," he finished quietly, "we naturally expect the assistance of the hereditary leader of the Mixed Men."

❖❖❖

There was silence in the great room. The bank on bank of control board remained impassive, except for the solitary anti-light that glowed like a faint beacon from its deep-inset tube.

Standing there, Maltby grew aware of a thought. It had only an indirect relation to the request Hunston had just made, and it wasn't new. He tried to fight it, but it remained strong, and grew stronger, a developing force in his mind. It was the conviction that he would yet have to take sides in this struggle of three powerful groups.

He couldn't allow Earth to be destroyed!

With a terrible effort, he finally forced the thought aside, and looked at Hunston. The man was staring at him with a narrow-eyed anxiety that abruptly startled Maltby.

He parted his lips to make a sardonic comment about a usurper who had the gall to ask help from the man he was striving to displace. But Hunston spoke first:

"Maltby—what is the danger? What is their plan in having you come here? You must know by this time."

Almost, Maltby had forgotten about that. Once more he was about to speak. But this time he stopped himself.

There was another thought forming in the back of his mind. It had been there for many months, and in its more detailed conception it was actually his solution to the whole Fifty Suns problem. In the past, the knowledge that the solution required one man to convince three groups, actually to control the three hostile groups at a given hour, and to force them to yield to his will, had made the whole idea ridiculous and impractical.

Now, in one mental jump, he saw how it could be done. But hurry, hurry! Any instant the suit he was wearing would be used. He said violently:

"It's this room! If you value your life, get out of it at once."

Hunston stared at him, bright-eyed. He seemed unafraid. He asked in an interested tone:

"This room is the danger point because you're in it?"

"Yes," said Maltby—and held his arms out slightly, and his head up, so that the energy of Hunston's In-no gun would not hit them. His body tensed for the run forward.

Instead of shooting, Hunston frowned.

"There's something wrong. Naturally, I wouldn't leave you in charge of the control room of this battleship. Accordingly, you're practically asking me to kill you. It's obvious that if you're the danger, then you must die. Too obvious."

He added sharply: "That anti-light watching you—the moment I fire, its automatic defenses are nullified; and you can use a gun too. Is that what you're waiting for?"

It was.

All Maltby said was: "Get out of this room. Get out, you fool!"

Hunston did not move, but some of the color had faded from his cheeks. He said:

"The only danger we've been able to imagine is if somehow they managed to get a *Star Cluster* transmitter aboard."

He stared at Maltby. "We haven't been able as yet to figure out how those transmitters work, but we do know this: There is no liaison between the transmitters of one ship and another. They're tuned differently, and set. No amount of manipulation can change them, once completed. But YOU must have had opportunity to learn the secret of their operation. Tell me."

Tell me! It was clear now that he would have to attack in spite of the anti-light. That meant muscles only, which needed a fractional surprise. Starting to tell might do the trick.

But what an odd irony that Hunston and his technical experts had correctly reasoned out the exact nature of the danger. And yet now Hunston, standing in front of a man who was wearing a suit of clothes, both the back and front of which were transmitters, did not begin to suspect.

Maltby said: "Transmitters work in much the same way that the first Dellian robots were made, only they use the original components. The robot constructors took an electronic image of a human being, and constructed an exact duplicate from organic matter. Something was wrong of course because the Dellians never were mental duplicates of the original human beings, and there were even physical differences. Out of the difference grew the hatred that eventually resulted in the robot massacres of fifteen thousand years ago.

"But never mind that. These matter transmitters reduce the body to an electronic flow, transmit without loss, and then rebuild the body. The process has become as simple as turning on a light and—"

It was at that point that Maltby launched his attack.

The awful fear that Hunston would aim at his feet, arms or head, ended. Because in that ultimate moment, the man hesitated and like a thousand million men before him was lost.

The In-no gun did flash, as Maltby grabbed at the wrist of the hand that held it. But the fire sprayed harmlessly against the impregnable floor. And then the gun clattered out of the fight.

"You scoundrel!" Hunston gasped. "You knew I wouldn't fire on the hereditary leader of the Mixed Men. You traitor—"

Maltby had known nothing of the kind. And he did not waste time in consideration of it. Hunston's voice stopped because Maltby had his head in a vicelike grip, and was pulling it towards and *into* his chest. The surprise of that must have been staggering. For a vital moment Hunston ceased his struggling.

During that moment, Maltby stuffed him through the transmitter seemingly right into his own body.

Even as the last squirming foot was shoved out of sight, Maltby was tearing at the fasteners of the suit. He rolled the suit down, so that the transmitter surfaces faced one against the other.

Frantically, he climbed all the way out of the suit and, racing over to the control board, adjusted the anti-light to work *for* him, and made a dozen other adjustments that he knew about. A minute later, the ship was his.

There remained the necessity of telling the three groups *his* decision. And there remained—Gloria!

The Dellians and non-Dellians of the Fifty Suns accepted the decision the moment they realized the *Star Cluster* had not been captured by the Mixed Men, and that Earth guaranteed them protection.

The information that the non-Dellians were NOT robots at all but descendants of human beings who had helped the original robots to escape from the massacres did not have the sensational effect anticipated by Maltby. It merely made everything easier, to realize that human beings had pretended to be robots for the sake of subsequent generations; and that it had worked out all right.

The Mixed Men, their volatile leader Hunston a prisoner aboard the *Star Cluster*, agreed because Maltby was after all their hereditary chieftain, because their chances of ever capturing another battleship were zero, now that all ships in the main galaxy would be warned of their methods. And because their new status was that of complete equality within the government of the Fifty Suns, INCLUDING a guarantee that when a Dellian married a non-Dellian, the couple would no longer be forbidden to have children by the cold-pressure system.

Since the child resulting from such a union would invariably be a Mixed Man, it assured that ultimately and by legal and natural development there would only be Mixed Men in the Fifty Suns—and eventually in the main galaxy, too.

On the tenth day, the captains in session aboard the *Star Cluster* sat on an entirely different case. The case of Grand Captain, the Right Honorable Gloria Cecily, the Lady Laurr of Noble Laurr, estranged from her husband, Peter Maltby, by psychological means because of an emergency.

The judgment handed down made intergalactic legal history. The judges held:

(1) That the law relating to the reintegration of artificially imposed psychological pressures did not apply to Captain Maltby, a non-citizen of Imperial Earth at the time he was conditioned, but does apply to the Lady Gloria, a citizen born.

(2) That since Captain Maltby has been made permanent agent to Earth for the Fifty Suns, and since this is the Lady Gloria's last trip into space on a warship, no geographical barriers exist to a continuation of the marriage.

(3) It is accordingly ordered that the Lady Gloria be given the necessary treatment to return her to her former condition of loving affection for her husband.